I thoroughly enjoyed reading Levi falling in love with his Luna and Cal's confidence grow • Another great book by a fabulous author! • This is such an amazing book! I absolutely love your work • Amazing story, I thoroughly enjoyed the journey • So yeah, you left me teary-eyed. It was beautiful • I freaking loved this book! • I'm so sad it's over but I'm happy how it ended. Great book! Bravo!

The readers of Taming My Alpha all agree - it is 100% worth the emotional rollercoaster ride!

Such a good book! I would love more books on these characters • Thank you again for a GREAT READ! I look forward to reading more of your books • This has been a very unique and pleasant read! • It was so good! I loved all the character growth and seeing Cal and Levi becoming the great couple they were supposed to be • I love an empowering woman story! • This is honestly a book where I want more

TAMING *my Alpha*

LOUISE CLEMENT

The characters and events portrayed in this book are fictitious. Any similarity to real persons, living or dead, is coincidental and not intended by the author.

ISBN: 9798355675417

Cover design by: Louise Clement
Printed in the United States of America

In memory of my beloved Yorkshire Terrier, Crystal,
who passed away on January 19, 2022.

May your spirit live forever in the pages of this book.

CHAPTER ONE

Calliope

"Shit!" the deep-brown-haired boy yelled, quickly dodging the liquor that fell to his feet.

Today is Kai's eighteenth birthday, as well as his Alpha Ceremony party. Naturally, he had spent the last couple hours drinking with his Beta, Gamma, and other high-ranking members of neighboring packs, while I had been assigned the task of keeping an eye on them. In his drunken state, he accidentally hit one of the many glass bottles off the table. As it crashed on the ground, it shattered into a million pieces, the remainder of alcohol pooling over the marble floor.

I watched cautiously as Kai's mossy-green eyes turned to me, and I instantly knew what was coming next.

"Calliope, get someone to clean this mess, will you?" He didn't even bother addressing me by my title. Why would he? I was just a useless Delta.

"Yes, Alpha." I nod at him. But as I was about to turn around and leave, I heard his annoying voice again.

"Actually, since it seems you've got nothing else to do, why don't you clean it up yourself?"

His smirk caused my anger to bubble up. As I blinked at him, I imagined what would happen if I punched his silly face. Just a quick jab. But I couldn't bring myself to do it. After all, I was just a Delta - *his* Delta.

"Calliope? You deaf?" he mocked after my long silence, making all of his friends burst with laughter beside him.

"I'll go get the mop, Alpha," I told him, turning to leave again, but he surely wouldn't let me off that easily.

"We don't have time for that!" he barked, eyeing me from head to toe. His sinister smile evinced that he had just gotten a wicked idea. "Why don't you use your shirt to clean it."

"My...shirt?" I raised an eyebrow at him. He couldn't be serious.

"Yeah," he replied shortly.

I blinked a few times as we stared at each other in silence. Behind my innocent mask, I felt my blood boil as a faint voice inside my head screamed *fight back!* But, as always, I didn't. Kai gave me that crooked look, letting me know he was getting impatient. All I could do was sigh, acknowledging defeat.

I kept a straight face as I hesitantly took off my shirt in front of the boys, determined not to let them see my embarrassment. My plain black bra was soon the only piece of cloth preventing my well-endowed breasts from getting exposed. The men in front of me howled and whistled like wild animals as I crouched next to the ground, overcome with humiliation. Thankfully, they didn't dare touch me, so I just ignored them like I always did whenever they messed with me.

After my shirt was soaking wet - the floor was mostly clean - I rose back up. I noticed our Beta, Elliot, had his attention focused on me as he licked his lips hungrily. He didn't even bother hiding the fact that he was checking me out; he knew I wouldn't do anything about it. Again, I turn around to leave, but it seemed like my torture would never be over.

"Damn, Cal! If my mate doesn't show up in a few weeks, you could really become my Beta Female," Elliot chanted.

"What're you talking about, man? She's just a Delta." Kai scoffed. Once again, his disgusted gaze fell upon me. "A weak one, at that."

I left the room without uttering a word. I knew I could get into trouble for not excusing myself in the presence of the Alpha, but I just couldn't bring myself to speak after the way he humiliated me. Luckily for me, it seemed he was already too drunk to care. As soon as I was out of their sight, I put my shirt back on. Although it was drenched in the stench of alcohol, I'd rather not walk down the corridors of the packhouse half-naked.

This was a normal day for me in the Moonstone Pack. Ever since my parents, the former Deltas, died, I was deemed as their weak litter. They had perished in battle, giving their lives to protect their Alpha. It happened shortly after I turned sixteen. To me, they were heroes; they took down more than twenty enemies before they bled out, fighting together until their dying breath.

However, instead of recognizing their sacrifice, everyone attributed their deaths to the fact that they were weak. Not even Kai's father, our now former Alpha, stood by their side. Less than a month after they were gone, he forced me to take the Delta role earlier than normal. Since then, I've pretty much become the pack's pet.

"That's not true, Cal," my wolf, Nava, whispered inside my head. She had been my only friend for the past two weeks since our connection was established upon me turning eighteen. *"A Delta is one of the most important pillars of a pack. They would be*

lost without us."

"Yeah, but no one seems to recognize that fact. Not even the Omegas respect me despite them being the lowest rank." I sighed, and this time, she couldn't argue with me.

Absorbed in my conversation with my wolf, I almost didn't hear when a familiar voice called my name; it was Berthold, our former Alpha and Kai's father. He seemed distracted, probably busy tending to the guests while his son got wasted.

"Calliope, where's the..." As soon as his gaze fell on me, he couldn't bring himself to finish his sentence. He crinkled his nose in revulsion, clearly judging my appearance. "What the hell happened to you?"

At first, his expression was one of pure anger. However, it didn't take long before it turned into one of pity and disappointment. I stayed silent as I tried to think of a way to explain the situation. Thankfully, I didn't need to, as the older man just sighed, pinching the bridge of his nose.

"Just...go get changed. I can't have the guests see my Delta like this." His tone was filled with disgust as he massaged his eyes, waving me off right after.

"Yes, Alpha." I bowed curtly before leaving.

Thankfully, I didn't run across anybody else before I reached my cottage. After I went inside, locking the door behind me, I was finally able to breathe. The house where I'd been living alone since my parents' passing wasn't as luxurious as the other ranked members' rooms in the main building, but it was still bigger than those of warriors, hunters, and sentinels. And most importantly, it was my safe haven, far away from the madness of the packhouse.

I rushed into the bathroom, lazily tossing my dirty shirt into the laundry basket before grabbing a wet towel to clean my upper half. I didn't have enough time to shower, so this would have to do. I threw on a simple black party dress, taking a moment to examine my reflection in the mirror to make sure I looked presentable.

I was taller than the average she-wolf, standing at 5'9" and slightly more muscular too. Due to the many hours I spent under the sun, tending to the pack and training among the other warriors, my skin was nicely tanned. My long, wavy light brown hair fell just below my shoulders. Although quite common, my honey-colored eyes were my favorite feature; despite all the mistreatment I suffered here, they still shone brightly and full of life.

"There's nothing common about you, Calliope. You're beautiful," my white wolf chanted, making me feel a little bit better. As I watched my reflection in the mirror, I found myself agreeing with her, even if just for a brief moment. She always at least tried to make me feel good about myself despite everyone else constantly reminding me why I shouldn't.

"Thank you, Nava," I replied with a smile, heading towards my room to take a few more quiet breaths before I had to dive into the hellish party once again.

"We're together in this," she emphasized. *"You just have to endure the teasing and the harassment a little longer. I'm working on finding our mate, and once I do, we'll be free."*

I just nodded at her. She was right; now that I had come of age, I'd finally be able to recognize my mate if we crossed paths. I put on my best smile and walked out of my cottage with enough confidence to make it through the night. As I made my way towards the Event Hall, where everyone was celebrating the rise of a new Alpha, I couldn't help but think about what my wolf had told me.

Ever since I turned eighteen, I considered leaving Moonstone. However, joining other packs was hard, especially given my background, and without a proper place to go, I'd end up becoming a rogue. Despite no one recognizing my importance here, and everyone constantly underestimating me, they still gave me a home, a roof to live under. It was better than being on my own, defenseless against the dangers of the world. Yet, I still dreamt of the day I could run away from here.

My only hope was to find my mate soon so he could save me from this nightmare and allow me a new start in life. I held tight onto that lovely thought, easily forgetting one crucial factor.

What would happen if they didn't want me either?

CHAPTER TWO

Calliope

Through my wolf's eyes, I saw the pearly-white teeth of the ebony wolf coming for us. With a swift jump, Nava managed to escape her opponent's jaws by just a few inches.

At Moonstone, we trained three times a week, two hours each day. For the first sixty minutes, the warriors sparred in human form, then repeated the process in wolf form during the second hour of the training session.

Delta is the only rank that can be occupied by either men or women - all other positions were reserved for males only, following the rules of our patriarchal society. In Moonstone, females weren't allowed to become warriors either, so I was always the only girl in training. Also because of my rank, I was required to be just as strong as any of the men.

As much as I hated to admit it, fighting males when you're a female isn't a walk in the park. We are naturally smaller and possess less physical strength - a difference that became even more noticeable in wolf form. Being the Delta, I had to train two times harder than the other warriors to match their attributes. However, after three years of training, I had learned to turn my weaknesses into strengths.

My snowy-white wolf had her shiny golden eyes locked on our opponent - Jax, our Gamma Gregor's wolf. She studied him carefully, trying to read his next move. Since males were usually guided by their anger, staying calm and collected offered us an advantage.

The two wolves circled each other in a slow, cautious dance, but as expected, it didn't take long for Jax to lunge in our direction. Attentive, Nava easily ducked, watching as the adversary flew over her. For us, every second mattered, and without wasting time, she jumped on top of the fallen wolf, pinning him to the ground.

The dark-furred beast struggled for a while, but with Nava's open mouth around his jugular, he had little chance to escape. He let out an annoyed growl before he gave up, shifting back into his human form. Nava stepped back, allowing Gregor to stand up. He flashed her a look of pure fury - I knew it too well; it was the death-stare every male gave us whenever we managed to beat them.

"That's not fair! You're fighting dirty!" There it was - the same excuse they always used.

Before I could shift back to defend myself, something hit my wolf on the side, unexpectedly throwing her to the ground. I quickly noticed it was our Beta's counterpart, Murphy. When Nava tried to stand back up, the male wolf pressed his paw against her muzzle, preventing her from moving. He flashed us a wolfish grin before Elliot took his place.

"You know you're not allowed to just dodge, Cal." What? I fought the urge to roll my eyes; he had just made that up. "In the event of an actual attack, are you gonna keep running while the others do all the work for you?" He snickered, lowering himself to stare into my wolf's intense eyes. "The only place you can get dirty is in bed. With me. Now that's something I'd like to see."

Filled with disgust, Nava struggled to be released, taking a few steps back. Both boys laughed at my wolf's reaction. She wanted to growl at them, but being a good Delta, she couldn't disrespect her superiors. I hoped they'd let me go, but I was obviously wrong.

"Come on, training is over." Elliot clapped his hands, and soon everyone started to leave the gym.

The Beta was also in charge of conducting training, so all of the warriors respected him. Soon enough, everyone was gone, and only the three of us remained at the training grounds. Once again, Elliot approached me. Nava backed away, trying to stay clear of his dirty hands.

"Why don't you shift back like everyone else, Cal?" My eyes widened in horror at his insinuation.

In order to avoid being seen by these horny unmated males, I'd hide before assuming my human form. As the Gamma and Beta stood there in front of me, completely naked, I prayed it was just a joke.

"Your Beta gave you an order. What are you waiting for?" Gregor smiled menacingly.

I looked around me, desperately searching for a way out, but there was none. Closing my eyes hesitantly, I realized I'd have to endure the humiliation one more time. Nervously, I took a deep breath. At least, I'd go through it with my head held high.

Nava allowed me back control, and little by little, our bones began to shrink and break. Shifting was a painful process, but after doing it so many times over the past couple weeks, I had gotten used to it. As soon as I was back to my human form, I felt the men's gazes on me. My heart was beating fast, but I tried to remain calm as I stared at the wall, not wanting to give them the satisfaction of my attention.

It didn't take long for them to start circling me like sharks.

"You're hot, Cal," Elliot cooed. I closed my eyes when he inched closer, praying to the Goddess he wouldn't touch me. "Your place is not here, damaging that pretty body of yours. It'd suit you a lot more being in a strong man's bed, producing heirs."

Once again, I felt my blood boil with rage. The voice in the back of my head screamed *fight back!* louder than ever. As I felt the Beta's hot breath on my neck, I closed my eyes, concealing my rage. An animalistic growl threatened to escape my throat, my wolf blinded with fury at the rude comment. But before I could do anything, I heard a voice inside my head.

"Where the fuck are you, Cal? I need you in my office!" Kai roared impatiently, closing our connection before I could even reply.

For the first time in my life, I was actually grateful for him; he had just offered me an escape.

"The Alpha wishes to see me." My voice was barely a whisper as I tried to control my ragged breathing. "I'm sorry, I need to go."

I rushed out of the gym with warm tears streaming down my face. It was too much for me to take.

My clothes were in a backpack under the shade of a tree. I always left them there, so I could change without being seen. I was shaking as I dressed. Afterward, I slid my back down the trunk until I was sitting in the dirt. Kai would be mad at me for taking so long, but I needed a few seconds to breathe. My heart was beating too fast and the tears didn't seem to stop coming.

"It's okay, Cal. You were brave," my wolf kindly reassured me. Her sweet voice, soft like cotton, helped calm me. *"You didn't let them see you cry. You held your head up high, and you got through it. You're strong."*

"I'm weak!" I snapped. *"That's why they're always messing with me! Because I'm weak."*

"The sole fact that you got through this hell alone day after day before I came along proves you're tough. Not many are capable of that."

Nava's presence always made me feel better during my breakdowns. She was my best friend - my *only* friend - and I have no idea how I managed to survive so long without her. Even if I didn't completely trust her words, they helped ease my tension away. It didn't take long before I was back up to my feet, wiping the sweat and tears off my face as I made my way towards the packhouse.

When I reached the Alpha's office, I knocked on the door. Kai angrily told me to come in. As soon as I did, my eyes fell on the she-wolf sitting on his desk - Chloe, his sister. Her Alpha genetics helped her grow into a beautiful girl. At the peak of her nineteen years, she had a tall, curvy build, chocolate brown eyes, and shiny ebony hair. She was probably the prettiest she-wolf in the pack. Not that great of a personality, but definitely better than her brother's.

"Finally! What took you so long?" Kai grumbled.

"I..." I started, but he instantly facepalmed.

"It was a rhetorical question. I really couldn't care less." He was definitely in a worse mood than usual today. "Listen up,

Cal. As you know, Alpha Levi of Blood Eclipse will be visiting us tonight. He's searching for a Luna, and we were one of the lucky packs chosen to show him our best females. I believe you already have the list of the seven she-wolves that must get ready to meet him today."

"Yes, Alpha."

"Great. But here's the deal..." He smirked, giving a quick glance to his sister. "You must make sure Chloe is the one he picks. Get her the best dress, find her the best hair stylist, the best make-up artist. Everything. Levi's a picky man; he has turned down every she-wolf he's met so far, but none of them had Alpha blood. If we can get him to marry my sister, we'll be able to establish an alliance with his pack."

Blood Eclipse Pack was one of the most gruesome packs to ever exist. It had grown a lot ever since their Alpha, Levi Griffon, took over. He went on a rampage for the first two years of his rule, taking down other leaders and absorbing other packs. He was also a ruthless Alpha, known to have killed every member who dared disrespect him. It was a long list of names, and no one knew exactly how many wolves he had murdered.

"Make sure to get those bath salts, too. They make my skin healthy and shiny," Chloe added, pulling me from my thoughts. She was too smiley for someone who was basically a peace offering to a serial killer.

"Yes, Chloe. Alpha." I bowed at them before excusing myself.

It was a lot of work to do. The Delta was responsible for taking care of every background detail and ensuring the pack would always run smoothly. During big events, I was the one in charge of all the preparations, a hard task to do alone.

As always, I managed to get everything done at the cost of my exhaustion. By the evening, the seven chosen she-wolves were all dressed in beautiful gowns, though the most outstanding one belonged to Chloe. She was pretty as a picture, while I was a wreck. But it didn't matter. I wasn't supposed to be the center of attention, she was.

The young females were all standing in line in the lounge, gossiping as they waited for the Alpha of Blood Eclipse to arrive. While Kai and his father drank some fancy wine with the Beta and Gamma, I ran around the place taking care of the final details. Before long, our special guest finally walked through the door.

And as soon as he did, my eyes locked on him. I had never paid much attention to boys, but this man looked incredibly attractive. He was very tall - probably around 6'3" - and his muscular body could be seen through his white button-up shirt. His dark blonde hair, almost a metallic gray, was wildly spiked up. When his icy blue eyes fell over me, I froze.

"Mate!" My wolf howled in delight.

CHAPTER THREE

Levi

The muffled sounds coming from outside of my soundproof office were quite easy to ignore. After finishing reading the pack's weekly reports, I started tossing one of my thousands of stress balls against the wall, paying no mind at all to the noise outside. At least until one sentence, louder than the other mumbles, caught my attention.

"You're already 26, and this pack needs a Luna!" my beta screamed, banging his fists on the door. "If you don't get your ass off that chair, we'll be late!"

I rolled my eyes, already annoyed. I stopped bouncing the ball, squeezing it in my fists. It popped like a balloon in less than a second; I told the pack doctor they were useless, but he kept saying it'd help *control my rage*.

Bullshit.

Just like the pressure everyone was putting on me to find a fucking Luna. After all these years, I've remained undefeated, leading and defending my pack just fine. In fact, Blood Eclipse has grown more during my reign than it ever had under my father's rule. I didn't need a mate to be strong - in fact, that's what made me stand out among other lovesick Alphas.

"You know I couldn't care less about finding our mate," my wolf, Odin, agreed. *"But our pack will never be at its best without*

a Luna. The members know our strength; they respect and fear us. However, they still need a heart, someone who will make them feel safe and heard. As displeased as I am with the situation, we must do it for our pack."

I let out a frustrated grunt before standing up. Most of the time I enjoyed being Alpha, but this was one of those days when I'd rather be rogue. I buttoned up my white shirt, grabbed my black jacket, and headed towards the mirror. My light stubble beard was quickly growing in, but I looked presentable enough for a meeting with a smaller pack, so I just went with it. Once I was ready to leave, I realized my Beta still hadn't stopped slamming his fists against the door. He only stopped when I pulled it open.

"Finally!" he yelled, scowling at me. "Come on, the driver's already waiting for us."

Darrell Crawford was my best friend, and the one person I loved to piss off. At twenty-four years old, he was the best warrior of our pack, which made sense since he was a born Beta. The dark-skinned man had a well-built body, black circle beard, ebony hair styled in curls and a temple fade, and two enchanted crocodile tooth piercings on his left ear - they were capable of adapting to his wolf form when he shifted.

Having grown up together, we usually got along well, but for the past few days, he was really annoying me. He was the one who came up with the idea of getting neighboring packs to show me their best she-wolves, in hopes I'd take a liking to any of them. So far, the candidates had been nothing but futile weaklings, desperate to have a taste of my power.

"Please, Levi, bring our Luna home today," he begged as soon as we got into the limousine.

"Sure. If any of them are fit to stand by my side."

"Moonstone is the last pack that agreed to offer us one of their best females." He sighed, massaging his temples. "If you come back empty-handed, everyone will be disappointed. Just try to make an effort."

"I'll try." I showed him my most sarcastic smile, making him roll his eyes at me. This was his idea in the first place, so if I was unhappy, I'd make sure he would be too.

After an hour-long drive, we crossed the borders of Moonstone Pack. The territory wasn't as large as mine, and the buildings were pretty simple. I doubted my perfect Luna would be in such a place, but I'd just have to go along with it.

The Alpha and Beta of the pack received us at the entrance. Kai had just stepped in as the new leader. He was young, and from the amount of rubbish he was talking, I could tell he was also foolish. As we made our way towards the lounge where the girls were waiting, he tried to impress me with some of his irrelevant conquests. Pathetic.

"Well, here we are," the boy said as he opened the door. "These are our finest she-wolves. I'm sure you'll find a worthy chosen mate among them."

As soon as I took my first step in, a peculiar scent hit me. It was intense, like dark coffee being brewed in the morning, spiced up with cinnamon. Although strong, it also had a faint hint of the purest blooming lily - so innocent and green. I closed my eyes for a second, dwelling on the fragrance until it dawned on me.

As I turned my head in the direction of the smell, my gaze instantly fell on a poorly dressed she-wolf with a worn-out expression. Her beautiful honey eyes were so full of hope, it disgusted me. She knew who I was, and it obviously meant trouble. I growled in anger, trying to resist my urge to pin her on the floor and make her mine while everyone watched. Were those my thoughts?

"Odin, control yourself!" I told my wolf furiously. *"You know we can't have a mate! It'll make us weak! I should reject her right now and put an end to this."*

"Wait! Don't!" His tone was a little more desperate than I would like, but I decided to hear what he had to say. *"This is actually perfect. Having our real mate will be better than taking a chosen one."*

"Enlighten me."

"Her soul is tied to ours, which will make it easier for her to obey us. Also, if the Moon Goddess paired her with us, it means she was born to be a Luna. She will be the best for our pack."

As much as I wanted to disagree with him, I knew there was truth in his words. This wasn't the outcome I was expecting, but it would put an end to my problems, and that was enough for me. Unaware of what was happening, everyone eyed me with expectation, waiting for me to pick one of the girls on display.

"I have found my mate," I announced at last.

The girl's eyes shone brighter than ever as she flashed me a sweet smile, but I didn't bother returning the gesture. I tried to approach her so we could go home and finally be over with this, but the sorry excuse of an Alpha got in my way.

"This is wonderful news, Alpha Levi! I am sure my sister Chloe will serve you well." He waved his hand in the direction of a girl in the center wearing the most extravagant dress. Pretty, but too much of an attention-seeker.

"This is not the woman I chose," I growled, finding it hard to remain calm. Then, I pointed at my mate with my head. "This is the one I'll be taking home with me."

Both the Alpha and his sister widened their eyes in horror. I ignored them, trying to make my way towards the poorly-dressed girl. Kai dared interrupt me again, and this time, I showed him my canines. He shivered, but didn't move. This guy was getting on my nerves.

"Alpha Levi, I advise you to reconsider. This girl is just a Delta of weak blood," he spat, and a part of me wanted to twist his neck for speaking ill of my mate. "My sister is a born Alpha. No one will make a better Luna for you than her."

"Really?" I barked, almost giving in to my anger. "I believe the Goddess doesn't think so. This woman is my true mate."

Once again, they gasped in shock, but didn't try to stop me again. Wise choice. As I crossed the distance between me and the girl, I looked at Kai over my shoulder.

"There is nothing left for me to do here. I'll take my mate and leave," I declared, but the Alpha was still too speechless to respond.

When I finally reached the mysterious girl, I took a second to quickly analyze her. She was tall, but I still towered over her. Despite her dirty clothes and tired look, I had to admit she was beautiful. And when her golden eyes locked on mine, my lips parted as I suspired in delight. But I abruptly shook my head, remembering to stay focused.

"What's your name?" I asked her calmly.

"Calliope, Alpha Levi," she replied promptly, bowing respectfully at me.

"Calliope..." I repeated, and Odin purred in my head when

her name left our lips. "Come with me."

I turned around to leave, knowing the longer I stared at her, the harder it would be to control myself. But when I noticed she still wasn't following me, clearly confused by my attitude, it annoyed me.

"I said *come*," I repeated firmly, almost growling.

Like a good Delta, she didn't utter a word as we walked to the car. Both her and my Beta remained quiet as I thought about the situation. I hoped she wouldn't give me a hard time, but if she did, I'd waste no time disciplining her.

CHAPTER FOUR

Calliope

As we made our way towards the limousine waiting outside, Nava was howling excitedly inside my head. Somewhere inside me, beneath my wolf's joyful sounds, I couldn't help but feel worried about my situation.

The Beta opened the door for us, showing me a warm smile before taking his place beside the driver. I watched through the window as I left my pack behind, as well as all my painful memories. There was a chill to my bones when it occurred to me - would my new home be any better?

"I'll send someone to get your things later," the Blood Alpha uttered, not bothering to look at me. Those were his first and last words to me during the ride.

I didn't know how far away Blood Eclipse Pack was from my old home. Alone with my thoughts, the minutes soon seemed to turn into hours. As anxiety filled me, my eyes roamed toward my mate. It was impolite to stare at an Alpha, but I had to study him closer, and since he wasn't paying any attention to me, I figured it couldn't hurt. This gorgeous man was my mate? On the seat right next to mine, he was so close, yet he felt so distant...

Wasn't my mate supposed to be the one who would love me beyond limits? I only had the chance to look into his eyes for a brief second. They were so beautiful, but exhibited a coldness that chilled me to the bone. There was no sign of love in them, or in his words, or his attitude.

Maybe the rumors were true. Maybe he was a ruthless, emotionless Alpha. If so, was I in danger? He didn't seem the least bit pleased by my presence, but did he actually want to hurt me? The idea of leaving a land where I was constantly abused just to move to another place where I would find myself in the same situation made my heart stop.

"Don't be such a dummy, Cal!" Nava scolded me. Her tone and words stunned me; she was always so polite. *"Levi is our mate, he would never hurt us. He came to rescue us from this hell. We just have to get to know him better. You'll see."*

Lacking any evidence to the contrary, I decided to stop tormenting myself with negative questions and trust my wolf. It was still painful to ride in such silence with someone whose touch I already yearned for, so I distracted myself by watching the landscape roll past my window.

Eventually, we stopped briefly in front of a majestic stone gate. It was very tall and seemed to go on forever, probably securing the borders of the territory. A man on top of a small tower nodded at the car before opening the metal gateway to let us through. Not too long after, I heard loud howls as two beautiful long-furred wolves, one light blond and the other black, jumped out of nowhere to escort us.

As my attention fell on the land before me, I was immediately awestruck by Blood Eclipse's grandiosity. It was very large with tons of colossal pine trees. Slowly, the forest became less dense until it turned into peaceful plains. White wooden houses were scattered around, wolves in both animal and human form sharing the space peacefully. There was even a crystal-clear lake in the distance. This didn't look one bit like the haunted home of a bloodthirsty Alpha.

"I told you, Cal! You worry too much," Nava chuckled. *"Our new home is so lovely!"*

Before I noticed it, the car came to an abrupt stop. We parked in front of a majestic building that looked like some kind of mansion with tall white walls, large glass windows, and scarlet details. There was also a beautiful rose garden in the front.

Once again, the Beta opened up the door for me, offering me his hand to help me up.

"Welcome home, Luna!" he said with a bright smile.

I was stunned for a second. Did he just call me Luna?

"Of course, he did! You're the Alpha's mate, silly!" My she-wolf's happiness was so contagious, I even let a small smile light up my face.

"Thank you, Beta..." I stopped, realizing I still didn't know his name.

"Please, call me Darrell." He bowed curtly.

Levi scoffed, making both of our heads turn in his direction. "I'll introduce you to everyone, then we can talk. Come."

He turned his back to me, just like he'd done back at Moonstone. It made my heart shatter, but I couldn't go against an Alpha's orders. Darrell flashed me an apologetic look before he accompanied us.

The inside of the packhouse was impeccable, even more dazzling than the outside. The white marble floor glistened, the tall walls were perfectly decorated with a silver wallpaper that had a glamorous royal pattern. Sofas, rugs, chairs, paintings - every single one of the decorations was of the same crimson color. Chandeliers that seemed to be made of real diamonds hung from the ceiling, adding to the grandiosity of the place.

"Is this her?!" An excited female voice echoed through the large halls, catching my attention.

The woman was as tall as me. She had gleaming, long blonde hair, and intense blue eyes. Her porcelain skin had a few bags, evincing her age - she seemed to be around her fifties. She looked like a queen dressed in a red velvet dress.

Then, my gaze fell on the two people behind her. The first one, a young man, had a blue headband to prevent his messy wild blonde hair from falling over his caramel brown eyes. Judging by his fairly white skin, I guessed he was someone who spent a lot of time indoors. Beside him was an intimidatingly beautiful woman. She had voluminous, wavy ebony hair and vivid yellowish-green eyes. Unlike the other guy, her shiny skin was very tan. They both looked very similar to the wolves I spotted earlier when we entered the territory.

"Yes. This is my true mate..." He turned to me with a quizzical look, and I had to blink a few times to understand what he wanted. Did he really forget my name?

I masked my hurt and showed everyone a small smile. "Calliope Gaumond. It's a pleasure to meet you all."

"You're so beautiful, my dear!" The older woman approached me, offering me a hug. I stiffened at the gesture; I couldn't remember ever being hugged since my parents died. "Oh, I'm so sorry about my manners! I was so excited to finally meet you," she explained herself quickly, backing away to allow me some space. "I'm Calanthe, Levi's mother."

"It's a pleasure to meet you, Luna Calanthe." I bowed respectfully at her.

She just waved me off. "No need for formalities! You are our Luna now."

"I'm honored to meet you, Luna." The young man approached me, lowering his eyes. "I'm Ivar Leonhardt, Gamma of this pack." I nodded at him.

"Name's Bellatrix, but you can call me Trix," the other woman chimed in, eyeing me from head to toe. She didn't seem as welcoming as the other ones, which made me swallow dry.

After we were formally introduced, they started showering me with questions. Even Beta Darrell joined them. As nice as everyone was to me, it still felt a little overwhelming. The place, the people, they were all so... majestic. Powerful. And I was just a weak Delta.

"I can show you around if you'd like, Luna Calliope," Ivar suggested, offering me his hand.

"Please, just call me Cal," I insisted. I figured it would be easier to adapt to my new life without the titles. "And that would be lovely."

"You can do that later," Levi snapped, slightly growling. The Gamma immediately stepped away from me, bowing at his Alpha. "There are some things we need to discuss first. We'll be back soon," he informed the others before leaving them behind. By now, I already knew that meant I had to follow him again.

As I walked past Levi's mother, I swear I saw concern in her eyes. Was she afraid for me? My heart raced faster, and my attention fell on my mate. I wanted to feel safe around him, like Nava did, but it bothered me not knowing where he would take me. I was probably overreacting; like my wolf said, our mate would never hurt us. Right?

Long minutes went by as we walked through the hallways, taking four flights of stairs towards the top floor. He stopped in front of a white door, opening it for me. I hesitantly walked in, stiffening when I heard it shut behind me. It looked like an office. There was a white shiny wooden desk, a very regal black chair, shelves with thousands of books and folders.

Levi didn't bother taking his seat. He just rested his weight against the desk before his penetrating icy-blue eyes fell on me. Part of me wanted to look away, but I simply couldn't, whether it was because of the mate bond or because I was paralyzed with fear.

"Listen up. I don't like repeating myself," he started. His tone was just as cold as his gaze. "I have no interest in having a mate. Your only purpose here is to be the Luna of this pack."

And just like that, my heart broke.

CHAPTER FIVE

Calliope

I couldn't believe his words. Even Nava, who had been howling and jumping around cheerfully inside my head all day, had suddenly gone completely silent. It seemed like I was right all along - just like everyone else, our mate didn't want us. I shouldn't have been surprised, yet the sadness I felt was unbearable.

Tears threatened to fall, but I held them back as best as I could. My lips parted, ready to scream in agony, but no words came out. It was as if my voice had been stolen. For the past two years I had been rejected; why did it feel so bad when he did the same? I thought I'd be used to it.

"We don't have to be enemies, you know," he continued. My eyes instinctively lifted up to meet his. Could he see the hurt in them? "We can get along just fine, as long as you follow the rules."

"Rules?" I managed to breath out in a barely audible tone.

"Yes." He crossed his arms, his stern look intensifying. "First, we will share the same bedroom, like the Alpha couple is supposed to, but we won't touch. I don't want you to develop any feelings for me. Our relationship is merely political, as I previously stated." His gaze never left me. With every word, he made it harder for me to succeed in masking my pain. "Second, you can't be with other men. Cheating would make both of our wolves weak, which is the opposite of what I want. To be fair, I won't have other women either." Did he seriously think there was anything fair about the absurdities he was telling me? "If we both feel like we need a release, we can have sex. But no cuddling afterwards."

Levi went on about the rules for what seemed like an eternity, my heart aching during his entire speech. He gave me instructions on how to act around him during events, how much time we were allowed to spend together daily, what we could and couldn't do with each other. There weren't too many, but my sensitive state made it hard for me to remember everything.

Like me, Nava was quietly listening to his demands, but she was even more shocked than I was. I could understand her feelings. She was confident our mate would be the one to save us - our knight in shining armor. In the end, it turned out he was just another one of the villains. Maybe this is what I deserved for being born weak. I should've just run away when I had the chance.

"It's not that hard," he finally concluded. "Follow my rules, and you will live happily as the Luna of the most successful pack in the country." He shrugged, as if it was that simple. Maybe to him it was. "Fail to obey me, and...well, let's hope it doesn't come to that."

He stood back up, turning around to leave. I had lost count of how many times he had done that in the short couple of hours we had known each other. The same familiar voice echoed in my head - *fight back!* But as usual, all I could do was watch him head for the door, completely speechless. As he opened it, I heard his cruel voice again.

"Are we clear?"

The voice inside my head became louder. Ignoring it, I just nodded, afraid no sound would come out of my mouth if I tried to speak.

"Good. My Gamma will show you to our room. I have other things to do," he informed me before leaving the office. "I'll see you later."

"Why is mate walking away?" Nava whimpered. She was wise most of the time, yet she couldn't seem to understand our current situation. Actually, she could understand it, she just didn't want to believe it.

The Beta and Gamma were already waiting outside. Confused, they watched Levi leave before their eyes turned to me, immediately widening with concern. Only when I noticed the look on their faces, I realized warm tears were streaming down my face. Apparently, I wasn't able to hold them back any longer. The two men rushed to my side like personal bodyguards, wasting no time to console me.

"Why are you crying, Luna?" Ivar's voice was filled with worry.

"Stay with her. I'm gonna go talk to him," Darrell said before storming out of the office.

At that moment, I started sobbing. Though I tried my best to control my ragged breathing, it seemed to be impossible. I brought my hands up to cover my face, in hopes it'd make me look less pathetic.

All this time waiting for my mate, eager to know love again...and he turned out to be just as cruel as everyone else. I don't even know why I expected it to be any different. My naive thoughts and innocent hopes had dragged me into a new place, where I didn't know anyone or anything. To top it off, I was now stuck here, bound by my duty to this pack. How was I even supposed to be a Luna when my own Alpha didn't want me?

"Please don't cry, Luna," the Gamma begged me. His hands were fidgeting; he was clearly unsure of how to handle the situation. "I know the Alpha can be a little rough sometimes, but you're his mate. If anyone can tame the beast inside of him, it's you."

I allowed myself to look at him, immediately finding his warm smile. It somehow comforted me, even if just a little bit. He became slightly less uncomfortable when he noticed I had stopped crying.

"Anyway, let's not think about this now." He reached out for my hand, helping me take a few steps. "Come on, Lun- I mean, Cal. I'll show you to your room."

Not knowing what else I could do, or where I could go, I decided to follow the Gamma - *my* Gamma. It felt so weird to be above other people in rank. I had gotten used to being the lowest ranked member in a pack. It suited me; I was allowed to do everything on my own, enjoying my peace and quiet. At least, my new Beta and Gamma seemed very sweet, unlike the douchebags in my previous pack.

"So, what was it like in Moonstone?" Ivar asked me in a clear attempt to break the ice as we crossed the large hallways.

Terrible. Awful. A living nightmare. "It was...great," was all I could mutter. Damn Delta loyalty! Even after leaving that hell, I still couldn't bring myself to speak about the many monsters who dwelled there.

"Really? Doesn't seem like it." Ivar scoffed. "I've done quite a lot of research on them. Because I'm the Gamma, you know. Head strategist and all..." He got off track for a moment. He seemed like the type who loved talking, and it actually made me feel more comfortable. "Anyway, from what I gathered, that guy... Kai? He sounds like a jerk. And if titles weren't inherited, I doubt his Beta and Gamma would ever make it to the top. They seem completely incompetent." He paused for a second, turning to look at me. "You used to be the Delta, right? How did you manage to cope with those idiots?"

This time, I couldn't hold back my small chuckle. "I was loyal to my pack. There's really nothing else to say about it." I shrugged.

"I see. Oh, we're here already!" the Gamma chanted, waving his hand towards a big double door with golden door knobs.

He held out a key, promptly using it to open the entrance. As soon as he did, my jaw dropped. The room was ginormous! The color scheme followed the same one as the rest of the packhouse, with the addition of some golden detailing. There was a huge king-sized bed placed against one of the walls over a large fluffy white rug. Glass sliding doors led to a balcony with an amazing view of the territory. A very comfortable-looking sofa was placed in front of a gigantic television, right next to a desk with a computer. There was even a jacuzzi in one of the corners!

"How do you like the Alpha suite?" Ivar's voice was filled with expectation.

"It's...amazing," I whispered in awe.

"Well, come on in! This is your room now. And the Alpha's, of course."

I walked around for a little bit, taking everything in. I couldn't believe this is where I would be living. My heart even felt lighter for a while, before I remembered I'd be staying here with the mate who didn't want me. This could be my fairytale, but I had a feeling it would just be another nightmare.

"Look, Cal!" Ivar called me, turning my attention towards an empty closet. "This is where your clothes will go."

"I don't even have enough clothes to fill this," I stated blankly. The size of this closet was ridiculous; I'd go as far as to say it was bigger than my entire old home.

"Don't worry about that. I'm sure someone will take you shopping sometime soon, so you can fill it all up!"

"Delta salary isn't that great, you know. I can't afford to buy so much."

He laughed. "You won't be needing your salary anymore. Hey, why don't we watch something until the Alpha is back?" He jumped over the sofa, quickly grabbing the remote.

Ivar was a wonderful person to be around. It was easy to see that he was probably the jokester of the bunch, always eager to make others smile. As the hours went by, he helped me distract myself as we chatted over some silly TV show.

Before I noticed it, the sun had already set. I had almost completely forgotten about my complicated situation when the door suddenly burst open. In came the Alpha, and his cold eyes fell straight on me. I instantly felt a chill to my bones as he walked towards me.

CHAPTER SIX

Levi

After I explained the rules to the future Luna, I walked out of my office, mentally preparing myself for all the business I had to take care of by the end of the day. As the Alpha of the largest pack in the country, I naturally had a lot on my plate; my mate's arrival only added more tasks to my list.

I had neither the time nor the interest to help her get acclimated to her new life here. At least, I didn't expect her to cause me any problems until I was done. Like my wolf suggested, she seemed quite innocent and obedient - traits I could confirm just by the look on her face as I left.

"Maybe you went too far by threatening to punish her..." I heard my wolf's quiet voice inside my head, almost like a loud thought.

"She needed to know there will be consequences if she breaks the rules. It was only fair to let her know now rather than when I have to punish her," I argued.

"She won't break them," Odin stated rather assuredly.

"We'll have no problems then."

Before I was even able to make a turn at the end of the hallway, I heard loud footsteps behind me. My brows scrunched in annoyance as I realized I couldn't have a second of peace. I stopped dead in my tracks, not bothering to turn around to face my pursuer - I already knew who it was.

"I finally found a Luna for this pack. What else do you want?" It was hard to mask my irritation, but to be fair, I wasn't really trying.

"She's not just some girl, Levi." Darrell tried to remain calm, but his judgemental tone didn't help me do the same. "She's your *mate*!"

"I never wanted a mate, and I've always been honest about that," I said plainly. "She's not my problem."

Realizing this discussion was headed nowhere, I continued on my way. There were a thousand things I still had to do today, and arguing with my Beta was not on my list. But of course, he wouldn't let me off easily. Using his werewolf speed, Darrell jumped in front of me, blocking my way.

"For fuck's sake, Levi! Has your heart been replaced with a block of ice?" The disapproval in his eyes only added to my anger. I am the Alpha; I don't need anyone's approval. He heard me growling, but completely ignored my warning. "She's been here for less than an hour and she's already crying! What do you think it's like for her? Being in a new place, with no friends or family. And her mate, the one person who should look after her, only makes her feel worse!"

Silence filled the air, and I contemplated whether I should answer him or not. My fists were clenched as rage threatened to take over my whole being. Taking deep breaths, I uselessly tried to keep my control. Odin was fuming at our Beta's attitude.

"Again, she's not my problem," I said through gritted teeth.

I was ready to push him aside so I could carry on with my

day, but Darrell was adamant. He was as solid as a rock when our shoulders slammed against each other, his determination further annoying me. My Beta was only a few inches smaller than me, so he barely had to look up to face me. Both of us were glaring at each other.

"I won't let you do this, man. You know I can't." For a second, I saw hurt in his eyes. It disgusted me. Pain and love made even the most powerful werewolves weak.

"Stop living in the past, Beta. We're done here." My words were both a warning and an order; he couldn't disrespect me. I finally pushed him aside, looking at him over my shoulder. "Find my mother and tell her to start preparing Calliope to take up the Luna role. The marking ceremony will happen in three days."

"No...you can't do this to her!" he pleaded, eyes wide with horror. So pathetic.

Darrell took a few steps closer, ready to try and convince me to change my mind, but stopped dead in his tracks when I growled louder. I was sure my pale blue eyes had become even more intense as Odin neared the surface.

"It's not up for you to decide!" He finally lowered his head in defeat. "Now if you're done wasting my time, follow my orders, Beta."

I turned away angrily, not waiting for an answer; I was tired of his whines. Thankfully, he finally stopped following me. It was time to get to work.

I'd usually take care of most matters in my office, occasionally mindlinking specific people when needed. But from the moment Calliope stepped into the room, her strong, innocent scent permeated the whole space - just like poison, it made my mind hazy. It was best if I stayed far away from the top floor until I was finished.

In desperate need of some fresh air to clear my head and forget the alluring feminine fragrance, I rushed out of the packhouse. Although it was more time-consuming, I had a nice opportunity to talk to some people personally. It was necessary for any leader to show himself and check on their subordinates' work.

Once I was done requesting the organization of the traditional welcome events for a Luna, I headed towards the library to go through some documents to formalize everything. It was almost sundown when I decided to head back to my room - the room I now shared with my mate. Work helped me distract myself, and I was ready to deal with her again.

Even before I walked through the doors of the Alpha suite, I stiffened when my nose picked up a strange aroma. The scent I had involuntarily memorized was now mixed with another - a more earthly, manly one. I could feel my frustration building up, the hairs on my neck bristling as a roar threatened to escape my throat.

I entered the room without hesitation. My eyes immediately landed on my Gamma, who was sharing the couch with *my* mate. I tried to mask the irrational anger that coursed through me when they both turned to look at me.

"Good evening, Alpha!" Ivar's voice has never sounded so irritating to me before. It was almost as unbearable as his silly smile. "Cal and I were-"

"Leave, Gamma." His face fell. "I'll take it from here."

"Very well, Alpha. Luna." He lifted up from his seat,

bowing his head at the both of us before disappearing through the double doors.

The girl stood to her feet moments after, just a few feet away from me. She lowered her head before me - a clear tendency from her years serving as a Delta. I noticed a small smile play on her lips before they parted.

"Good evening, Alpha Levi. How was your day?" Her shy voice was so calming.

"Busy," I replied shortly, and it probably hit her like a slap to the face. *We don't have to be enemies*, I reminded myself as I looked away from her. "Your belongings have arrived. They only managed to fill two boxes, was that all?"

"Yes, Alpha. I don't have a lot."

"I see." I paused briefly to gaze at her over my shoulder. "That reminds me, my Beta will take you shopping early tomorrow. As the Luna, you must start dressing accordingly." She just nodded at me, so I went on. "I'll be ordering room service for us tonight. I'd like to avoid unnecessary rumors until you're officially introduced to the pack tomorrow at dinner. Is that fine?" My last question slipped out of my mouth involuntarily. Why would I ask her that? Of course, it was fine! She had to do as I said, regardless of what she thought.

"Yes, Alpha. Thank you," she answered ever so sweetly.

"Just call me Levi. It would be weird if pack members noticed the Luna addressing me by my title."

Once again, she nodded. Those were the last words we exchanged, as we also ate in silence - welcomed silence. The way she behaved made me inexplicably mad, but the room was thankfully spacious enough to allow me my privacy, even in her presence.

After sharing our meal, I took a shower to calm my nerves down. While she was in the bathroom, I gathered her stuff in my office and left it by the door for her to get dressed. Then, I headed to the balcony, the only place that hadn't been poisoned by her scent.

In my short moment of peace, I tried to figure out my situation. This obedient Delta intrigued me in a way no one else had before. When I was in her presence, my emotions spoke louder than ever. I was a mix of anger, frustration, and... excitement? There was something about her I couldn't quite figure out, and for my own good, I didn't really want to.

The low noise of the glass doors sliding open broke my concentration. I turned around to find the young girl wearing a white silk nightdress, slightly flowing with the wind. The full moon glistened over her tan skin, making it shine like porcelain, her arms exposed by the short sleeves. Her mesmerizing honey-colored eyes met mine, causing the air to leave my lungs in a moment. She looked like an angel.

What was this girl doing to me? I shook my head, breaking her spell the second I looked away from her.

"If you're ready, we can go to sleep," I told her, turning my back to her as we walked back inside. "Please, make yourself comfortable." I gestured towards the spacious king-sized bed.

She hesitated a bit before she laid over the clean white sheets. I glanced at her one last time before I walked towards the couch, resting my head on one of the many pillows.

"You're not sleeping in the bed?" she asked in a whisper. There was fear and confusion mixed in her voice.

"I may be your mate, but as I told you before, I will not be your boyfriend," I spat, almost missing the way she gasped.

"We will be sleeping separately."

I wasn't expecting a response after my harsh words, but she surprised me. "I understand, Levi. Goodnight." She showed me a sad smile before she shifted in the mattress, turning away from me.

For the first time, my heart sank.

CHAPTER SEVEN

Calliope

Only in my sweet dreams was I able to escape the harsh reality. Unfortunately, it was just momentary - an imaginary shelter that I had to leave too soon. Even through my closed eyes, I could sense the bright sun rays shining through small slits between the curtains, illuminating the spacious room.

The first scent I smelled in the morning made my nose crinkle as a soft smile played on my lips. At first, it seemed cold and minty like pine needles on a snowy night; a single sniff was capable of chilling me from the inside out. It also slightly resembled wood smoke, like a warning for a devastating fire raging somewhere close by. Strangely, if I dwelled in it for too long, I could also feel the welcomed warmth of the flames, the faint scent of melting snow, and the fresh grass that grew under it. It was so comforting and hopeful.

My eyes finally fluttered open as I shifted in bed, searching for the source of the fragrance I had so quickly fallen in love with. However, my smile faded as soon as I noticed Levi was nowhere to be seen. His lingering scent tricked me into feeling his presence, even after he was already gone. Where could he be?

Nava purred in delight inside my head, urging me to inhale a deep breath of the marvelous scent. It made her wag her tail and sprint like a cheerful bunny inside my head. My sadness was suddenly replaced by content when I felt my wolf's joy. She had been quietly laying with her ears down after her mate's coldness the day before.

A question popped up in my mind. Nava heard it loud and clear. *"Could Levi be anything like his scent? Can we melt the ice and reach for his heart?"*

My wolf seemed a little less radiant as she remembered the way our mate treated us. But she was even more hopeful than me.

"He's our mate, Cal. I'm sure he'll warm up to us," she encouraged. I noticed her voice wasn't as confident as it had once been. *"We just have to give him some time."*

Before I could think about what she said, there were gentle knocks on the door. Startled, I briskly sat up on the bed, pulling the sheets up to hide beneath them. A few more taps followed, and I wondered who it could be.

"Good morning, Luna Calliope!" I heard a male voice chant from the other side, almost as if he was answering my question. Though I wasn't too familiar with it, I recognized it to be Darrell. "We're going shopping, right? I'm ready whenever you are!"

I expected him to be the least annoyed by the fact he'd have to accompany me on an annoying trip to the mall, as I'm sure he had much better things to do. Not even I was too thrilled about it. I didn't need to give my mate any more reasons to be mad at me. But the Beta actually seemed excited to go out with me. I wondered why; no one usually enjoyed my company.

"I'm sorry, I'm late," I barely whispered, but I'm sure his

werewolf hearing allowed him to catch it. "I'll be ready in a minute."

"No rush!" he promptly replied. "I'll be waiting for you outside. Take your time."

For the past couple years of my life, I had always felt like a burden, and I hated it, so I would always try my best to do things quickly. I jumped out of bed and crouched down beside the two boxes containing my belongings, fishing for something appropriate. After a few seconds of searching, I found one of my favorite dresses. It was light green with a floral pattern, and I loved the way it contrasted my tan skin and deep brown hair. I matched it with golden sandals and hopped towards the door.

"I'm here!" I chanted as I walked out, being immediately greeted by Darrell's radiant smile. "I'm sorry to keep you waiting."

"It's no problem at all, Luna," he replied, frowning soon after. "Actually, you asked me to address you as Cal, right? Sorry, I'm just so used to formalities."

"Please, if you could. I don't wanna cause you any trouble. I just feel more comfortable this way."

"You're my Luna. If you want me to call you Cal, I'll call you Cal," he said simply, shrugging. "Come on, let's get to work!"

Darrell led me towards the underground floor, which seemed to be a garage. My eyes immediately widened as I realized there had to be at least a dozen high-end luxury cars. The Beta pulled out some keys and one of the vehicles lit up - a wine red Mercedes Maybach. I didn't know a lot about cars, but I was sure it was very expensive. Back at my old pack, none of the ranked members could afford something like this. Beta salary here must pay really well.

The drive to the nearest mall didn't take too long. We chatted a little along the way, and Darrell tried his best to make me feel comfortable. He wasn't as much of a jokester as Ivar, but it was still nice having his company. I wondered how Blood Eclipse's Beta and Gamma could be so cheerful when their Alpha was always gloomy.

"Alright, here we are." He waved his hands towards the multiple shop windows, grabbing something in his pocket soon after. "Levi gave me a list of shops for you to choose from. Where would you like to start?" He handed me the piece of paper.

As I read each one of the options, a small gasp escaped my lips. When I felt Darrell's gaze on me, I noticed I must have been making a pretty weird face.

"What's wrong, Luna? Do you not like any of them?" His voice was full of concern.

I shook my head. "No, these are great, but...they're too expensive." I sighed, putting the paper down to take a look at the few hundreds in my purse. "I didn't think we'd be spending this much money..."

"It's fine." He waved me off.

I took out a few notes, counting them. "I have my Delta salary, but-"

"Keep it," he cut me off and pushed my hands back. "The Alpha gave me strict orders to use his credit card."

After debating for a few seconds I finally nodded and got out of the car. Again, the last thing I wanted was to make Levi mad, so I'd just have to roll with it.

I was a little lost at first, since most of my clothes were casual. I had a few working clothes, but mostly Deltas weren't required to dress extravagantly. Never in my life had I gone shopping for ball gowns and fine clothing. Nothing about these shops was even the slightest familiar to me. My experience could be summed up as contacting the most famous dressmakers to create the best outfits for the Luna and her daughter. Thankfully, Darrell stepped in to offer me some guidance.

I was impressed by how much he knew about formal dresses. Being the Beta and a male, I had no idea how he was so familiar with the topic. Of course, he also consulted the sales woman to give us a hand, but for the most part, he was the one to suggest dresses that would fit me and my (now elevated) style. Surprisingly enough, I loved each one of his choices.

Once we were done shopping, Darrell insisted on carrying the dozens of bags with my new outfits, high heels, and even some new casual clothes. In the couple of hours we spent together, I felt as if we had grown a little bit closer and I was confident enough to ask him the question that was lingering on my mind.

"Darrell, how do you know so much about dresses?"

"I'm not an expert or anything..." He shrugged. "But I helped my sister prepare for her wedding."

"You have a sister?" I smiled brightly. "I'd love to meet her!"

He instantly went silent, and I immediately knew I had said something wrong. "I'm afraid that won't be possible, Cal... Marisol passed away a couple of years ago."

"I'm so sorry, Darrell... I shouldn't have asked," I said

quieter, drowning in guilt. Me and my stupid big mouth.

"It's alright, Luna. What's past is past." He showed me a sad smile before we headed towards the car.

The ride back home was a little more silent, as my last question seemed to have evoked some hurtful memories. I was afraid I had ruined my first opportunity of making a new friend, but soon enough the Beta was back to his usual cheerful self. He helped me take the bags to my room as I discreetly scoured through the hallways for any signs of my Alpha. Unfortunately, I had no such luck.

As I was placing my new items inside the gigantic wardrobe, I heard footsteps coming in, only then realizing I had left the door open. I turned around to find a majestic woman - Levi's mother. She showed me a fond smile before approaching me.

"Calliope, my dear!" Her voice was as sweet as it was the day before. "How was shopping?"

"It was good," I replied, returning her smile.

"Are you busy right now?"

"No, I actually just finished hanging all of these." I gestured towards the dozens of dresses.

"They're wonderful. I'm sure you'll look stunning in every single one of them," she complimented, briefly analyzing the pieces of delicate fabric. She then turned to me, her intense blue eyes piercing through me. "Well, I think it's time for your first Luna lesson. We need to prepare you for your marking ceremony in two nights!"

Her tone was cheerful, but her words caught me by surprise. The thought of being marked so soon by a man who'd never wanted me in the first place made my heart stop as I froze with fear. How was I supposed to do this?

CHAPTER EIGHT

Calliope

High-ranking wolves are able to perceive and hide emotions quite well. I only have Delta blood, but I managed to perfectly conceal my fears while training with Luna Calanthe. Luckily, following orders was the one thing I actually excelled at, so I pushed my thoughts aside to focus on my lessons.

After she mentioned the marking ceremony would happen in less than forty-eight hours, I was a whirlwind of thoughts and emotions. Nava went crazy inside my head, happy to hear our mate would finally claim us. She insisted he wouldn't be able to resist us after that.

As much as I wanted to believe her, I wasn't so sure. Levi was a strong Alpha, probably the strongest in the country. He had shown no signs of attraction towards me ever since we met. There was no kindness in his eyes, no passion in his words, no love in his gestures. Was I to expect he would just change suddenly after the ceremony? All I could do was hope the marking process would make him give in to our bond.

Nevertheless, Luna training allowed me a distraction. It also helped that Calanthe was very patient and a total sweetheart. The way she acted was so different from her son. At times, I couldn't even believe she was the mother of the ruthless Alpha. I wonder where he got his gruff attitude from.

Maybe his father? Levi never mentioned him, nor did the former Luna.

After we were done, Calanthe released me. There was nowhere else to go, so I went back to my room...back to the loneliness I knew so well. Darrell was very busy since he missed morning duty to take me shopping, and Ivar apparently had his hands full with some issue at the borders. I had no idea where Levi was, but being the Alpha, I assumed he'd be doing something important too.

It was just me and Nava for a few hours, but I enjoyed her company. We sat on the balcony, admiring our beautiful new pack lands that turned a breathtaking shade of orangey-gold as the sun hid behind the tall trees. Just then, Levi walked in, quickly ordering us a private meal so we could dine together.

When the food arrived, we sat in front of each other at the glass table. My wolf sang the sweetest melodies inside my head; just his presence was enough reason for her to be ecstatic. To me, it was torture. My mind raced, there were butterflies in my stomach, and I had to fight the urge to touch him. The mate bond pulled us together, but he seemed unbothered by it.

At least, he appeared to be in a good mood. He hadn't uttered a word aside from *good evening* since he'd entered the room, but his aura was...lighter. Even if we hadn't marked each other yet, mates could feel each other's energy, so I knew he would at least be amiable. I, on the other hand, was a complete mess on the inside. Being alone for a while allowed my thousands of questions to come rushing back, and having no answers made me anxious.

"What's wrong?" Levi's powerful voice echoed through

the room, breaking the silence.

My eyes widened as I shifted my focus from the plate to his handsome face. I immediately looked away from his eyes; tonight, they were just slightly less cold, and I couldn't afford to get lost in them. How did he know there was something wrong, and why did he care?

"We're mates. I can tell something's troubling you," he explained, not bothering to look at me as he spoke. "This is your home now. Regardless of our political relationship, you should feel comfortable here."

I hesitated, but the words left my mouth involuntarily. "It's…the marking ceremony."

"What about it?"

"It concerns me not to know what it'll be like," I said cautiously.

"I see." He dropped the cutlery and propped his elbows on the table, lacing his fingers. He finally looked at me. Just his gaze sent pleasant shivers down my spine. "It's tradition here at Blood Eclipse for the Alpha to mark his Luna in front of the whole pack. We have to rush it because the pack has been waiting years for their Luna, but as long as you don't have stage fright, you'll be fine."

"I used to be a Delta. I'm used to being surrounded by the pack members." I shrugged.

"Nothing to worry about then." I swear I could see the faint shadow of a smile on his face, and just that slight show of emotion made my cheeks turn red. "You'll spend the day being spoiled by maids. Then, you'll put on your best dress and we'll gather in front of the lake. We will both shift, Odin will mark Nava, and that's it."

Nava howled with joy, both at the mention of her wolf mate's name, and the way her name came out of Levi's mouth. It was hard to conceal my emotions when hers were so strong that they mixed with my own. Somehow, I managed to just show our mate a fond smile.

"Thank you. I feel a lot better now," I replied at last.

He nodded at me, and that was the end of our conversation. Until we went to bed - or better yet, until *I* went to bed and he laid on the couch. There were no more exchanges between us, but I was inexplicably happy as I drifted off to sleep.

* * *

When I woke up in the morning, Levi had disappeared again. I sighed, unable to contain my sadness, but just the memory of how he treated me last night made me hopeful. Maybe Nava was right in the end.

"I told you he would warm up to us! Just wait until we're fully marked and mated..." she cooed dreamily.

Before I got lost in thought, I hopped out of bed with a new found energy. There was breakfast on the table, which the Alpha probably ordered before he left for training. I grabbed a bite before I left the room, since I had lessons to attend to as well.

The only problem was, Luna Calanthe never told me where I should meet her for the next lesson. She had taught me in my room the previous day, but seeing as she hadn't stopped by, I figured I'd have to find her myself. It shouldn't be too hard;

she was famous around here. Someone had to know where she was.

The large, tall hallways of the silver and crimson packhouse were quite intimidating. I hadn't been on more than a couple of strolls outside the room, mostly because my mate and new friends were usually busy. Everything about Blood Eclipse was so glorious and big, I couldn't help but feel small amidst such grandiosity.

As I walked adrift through the hallways, I ended up at a marble gateway that led to a beautiful garden outside. I had never been here, but I assumed I was in the back part of the mansion. Moved by my curiosity, I postponed my search momentarily to explore the secret garden. Following the stone path, I eventually ended up at a large dirt field, which looked a lot like the training grounds. My suspicions were confirmed when I spotted the pack's Delta practicing some moves on her own.

"Maybe we could ask her where Calanthe is," Nava suggested. *"She's the Delta. If anyone knows about the former Luna's whereabouts, it's her!"*

"I don't know, Nava..." I weighed my options for a moment. *"She wasn't too friendly the first few times we met."*

"She's probably just not as outgoing as the Beta and Gamma. You should be fine," she insisted.

I sighed, finally deciding to trust my she-wolf's instincts. I walked up to Bellatrix slowly, still unsure about what I was doing. With her heightened senses, she noticed me when I was just a few feet away from her. The two of us just looked at each other for long seconds until her stare became a frown.

"What are you doing here?" she asked coldly.

"Good morning, Trix." I showed her a small smile in hopes it would help ease the tension between us. "I was wondering if-"

"The training grounds are meant for warriors only," she cut me off, making me shut up immediately as my smile faded. "You're a Luna, not a fighter. Why don't you go see if someone else wants to pamper you?"

I stood there blinking for some time, trying to process her words. How could she say I wasn't a warrior? I might be weak, but I had been a Delta - all my life I had worked hard to be just as strong as the ranked males. To hold my own. Behind my calm expression, my anger was bubbling up. This time, the voice inside my head screamed louder than ever.

Fight back!

But of course, I didn't.

"I see. I'm sorry to bother you." I smiled politely before turning away from the Delta, neither of us uttering another word. She seemed content with my decision to leave her alone.

As I walked back towards the packhouse, I tried to calm myself down. I don't know why I felt so offended by her comment. I was used to being talked down to, and I'd normally just carry on with my day. But for some reason, the way she talked to me made me mad.

Lost in thought, I accidentally bumped into someone when I was just outside the garden. I lifted up my eyes to look at the person in front of me, already mumbling an apology. But as soon as I recognized the powerful woman, I gasped in shock.

CHAPTER NINE

Calliope

"Luna Calanthe!" I immediately bowed before her. "I'm so sorry, I should've paid more attention to where I was going!"

With closed eyes, I kept my head down until I felt a warm hand softly resting over my shoulder. Calanthe was the former Luna of the strongest pack in the country; it was very disrespectful of me to bump into her, even by accident. I expected to see rage or disgust in her eyes, the same emotions the Luna of my previous pack showed me whenever I ran into her. Instead, I was surprised to notice her kind smile.

"I told you before, I'm not Luna anymore. You are," she observed, holding me at arms length. "It's no trouble, my dear. I was looking for you. Shall we continue our training?"

"Of course, Lu- Calanthe," I quickly corrected myself, and off we went to the Luna's office.

Though I had only begun training yesterday, I was handling it pretty well. On top of being a proud grade-A student, I was a quick learner. Memorizing every single one of the etiquette rules and procedures was a walk in the park for me. I hardly had any questions; I was good at listening and obeying. It also helped that Calanthe was a sweet, patient teacher. I loved being around her.

Our four-hour training went by in the blink of an eye. By

the end of the lesson, Calanthe assigned me a few books to read before she ordered us lunch. While we waited for the food to arrive, we sat across one another at the table and chatted a little bit. Nava was begging me to ask her about her son, but the last time I tried, she didn't seem too comfortable with it. A sad smile crossed her face whenever I mentioned Levi's name, so I eventually convinced my wolf to drop it. We were building a good relationship with our mate's mom. I wasn't about to ruin it.

After we finished our meal, Calanthe accompanied me to the door so we both could go on with our days. Since she hadn't been Luna for a few years, she was usually free all day long. However, after I came along, she had been spending most of her time organizing my various Luna ceremonies. Today, she had her hands full with the final details for the official dinner presentation, so I didn't want to bother her anymore.

"Thank you for your time and attention, Calanthe. I'm sorry to cause you so much trouble." I smiled apologetically, halfway through the door.

"Nonsense, my dear! It was killing me having nothing to do all day. I'm glad to be of service to our long-awaited Luna." She embraced me in a quick hug before staring deeply into my eyes. "You're doing really well in training, Cal. But I'm afraid there are things you'll have to learn on your own."

I cocked my head to the side, concerned. "What do you mean, Luna?"

"You have a big heart, my dear. I can tell you used to be a wonderful Delta," she complimented me. "However, in order to become a powerful Luna, you must stop belittling yourself so much. Humbleness is a noble trait, but it takes strength to rule over fierce wolves. There's a hidden strength within you, I can tell." She analyzed me carefully, almost as if she could see the depths of my soul. "Unfortunately, I can't make you see it. You'll have to find it by yourself."

What was she talking about? All my life, I had been nothing but a weak Delta. I was flattered she thought there was more to me than a frail little girl, but it pained me to fool her. I knew I would disappoint her when she realized this is all I am.

Unaware of what to say, I swallowed my guilt and thanked her before I headed towards the Alpha suite. When I opened the door, I was surprised to find Levi inside; he'd usually be out for most of the day, only returning at night. My amazement didn't stop Nava from making her usual happy noises as she lost herself in our mate's scent, begging me to approach him. For once, I actually listened to her, stopping when only two feet separated us.

"How was Luna training?" he asked, concentrating on reading a few papers. He didn't seem the least interested in my answer, but as pathetic as it was, I allowed myself to be happy for the sole fact that he decided to interact with me.

"It was great. Your mother is very sweet."

"I'm glad the two of you are getting along well," he said before putting the papers aside. His icy blue eyes then fell on me, and I froze. "As you know, your presentation dinner will happen tonight. Before I formally introduce you to my pack, there's a few things I'd like to brief you on."

My mate's strong, powerful voice was like music to my ears. With Nava's loud howling, it was hard to concentrate on his instructions, but I somehow managed to do it. He explained what the event would be like, what I should wear, and how I should behave in front of the rest of the pack. Everything was pretty standard, so I was confident I wouldn't blow this. After he was done, he excused himself to take care of some business before the night began, leaving me to prepare by myself.

Not too long after, some Omegas brought me special bath products, as well as the books Calanthe assigned to me. I decided to start reading them to pass time while I prepped my hair and skin. When I walked out of the bathroom, it was already sundown.

After putting on the dress Levi had personally picked out for me, I checked my reflection in the mirror, and I almost didn't recognize myself. My tan amber skin was gleaming, as was my slightly wavy deep brown hair. The pine-green dress with a shiny rounded skirt was long, just barely exposing my glistening rose gold high heels. I looked like a straight-up princess.

"*You are very beautiful, Calliope. I always tell you,*" Nava cooed, making me smile. She was such a confidence-booster. "*You look like the loveliest Luna. I'm sure our pack will love us once they see how stunning you are.*"

"*Do you think Levi will like it too?*" I silently asked.

And with the most perfect timing, our mate walked through the door. Our eyes instantly met, golden sun rays diving into the blue ocean like sunrise at the beach. He was dressed in a forest-green suit, a silver tie complementing the look. In that moment, he was the most handsome man I'd ever laid eyes on.

I swear I could catch the sound of his heart skipping a beat as his lips slightly parted to let out a small sigh. The longer he stared at me, the more intense his pale blue eyes became, as if his wolf was nearing the surface. Before I had time to analyze his reaction, he looked away. When his eyes fell on me again, they were back to their usual coldness. In fact, they probably never changed; I must have been fantasizing about it.

"You're ready," he stated, clearing his throat. "Great. It's time to go."

He reached out for my hand, and for the first time, we touched. It was impossible to ignore the sparks that ran through my body upon our contact, lighting up a fire inside of my heart. It immediately made me blush, but when I looked up at him... Nothing. Unphased. Could he really not have felt *anything*? The thought saddened me for a brief second before he pulled me closer, leading me towards the dining hall.

As soon as we walked through the tall double doors, I was stunned. Chandeliers hung from the ceiling, red balloons decorated the gray walls, golden tableware had been placed over every single one of the hundreds of tables, all dressed in crimson tablecloths. The place was gigantic - as it should be in order to accommodate most of the one thousand pack members. All of their eyes turned to me, but I wasn't the least nervous. Though I had never been the center of attention, I was used to dealing with pack members.

Before we even made it to the ranked members table, the Beta and Gamma walked up to us, both dressed in black suits. Two details caught my attention about Ivar: first, he wasn't wearing his characteristic blue headband; second, there was a girl holding hands with him. She had beautiful wavy blonde hair, and piercing green eyes. Her peaches-and-cream complexion suited her sweet appearance.

"Calliope, you look beautiful," Darrell complimented, and I felt Levi's grip on my arm tighten. As I thanked him, I couldn't take my eyes off the mysterious girl, wondering who she was.

My unspoken question was soon answered by the Gamma. "Cal, this is my mate Hailey. I'm sure the two of you will be great friends."

"I've been anxiously waiting to meet you, Luna!" she said excitedly, flashing me a sincere smile. "Ivar has told me a lot about you already."

"I hope I'll meet your expectations, then," I replied shyly.

"Why don't you hang out with Hailey for a minute while I talk to the Beta and Gamma?" Levi suggested, but it was more like an order. I quickly nodded, hearing Nava sigh as he walked away from us.

Thankfully, Ivar's mate was just as kind and easygoing as he was. She was very nice, and insisted on introducing me to a few more people. So far, everyone was being surprisingly nice to me; they probably couldn't disrespect me, since I was their future Luna. Or so I thought, until I heard two girls whispering next to us.

"Can you believe Levi is actually mated to *this* girl?" One of them scoffed, making me stop dead in my tracks.

"I know, right?! She's not fit to be Luna. She's too... average," the other one agreed. They knew I could hear them; it was clear by the way they looked at me.

Hailey seemed too entertained in a conversation to notice, but my heart instantly fell. I had only been here for half an hour, but I had already disappointed Calanthe. There was no inner strength within me, and these girls could definitely see it.

But then, I heard that same voice inside my head. It was usually just a whisper, a faint shadow of my desire to prove everyone wrong. To show them I was more powerful than they could see. But here, I was so pathetic.

"*You're not pathetic, Cal!*" My she-wolf growled inside my head. She was usually sweet and peaceful; I had never seen her so angry before. *"Fight back!"* she demanded, but before I could even react, she took control over me.

"Good evening, members of Blood Eclipse." The words came out of my mouth loud and clear, but it wasn't me - it was Nava. She somehow got everyone's attention, making the room go silent. "My name is Calliope Gaumand. I am the soon-to-be Luna of this pack. I hope we can all get along well."

As sweet as my voice - Nava's voice - was, her last sentence sounded a lot like a threat. I heard some surprised gasps before everyone slowly, one by one bowed their heads at me. I watched the two girls as they reluctantly did the same. Only four people stood tall against my aura - Hailey, Ivar, Darrell, and Levi. When my mate's eyes fell on me, I immediately froze.

What. Just. Happened?!

CHAPTER TEN

Calliope

At first, I was angry at Nava for hijacking my body, even if to defend us in a way I'd never have the courage to do by myself. I knew some wolves were harder to contain, but I usually let my guard down with my wolf because she was always sweet and kind. Maybe I should start keeping an eye on her from now on.

I thought she might have made our scary mate angry by embarrassing us in front of everyone, but thankfully, no one seemed to mind my sudden introduction - not even him. In fact, he barely said a word to me all night, unless he was introducing me to the most notorious members of our pack.

After dinner, Levi led me back to our room, wishing me a good night before lying down on the couch as usual. I couldn't believe I actually got away with my little stunt...well, Nava's little stunt. Her voice was quite similar to mine, which should explain why no one paid much attention to what happened. They probably thought their Luna just wanted to have a friendly start with the pack, but I'm sure the two girls still got the message Nava tried to send them.

There was a lot going on inside my head. Of course, I blocked Nava out for the first time in my life after her stunt. It pained me to keep her from explaining herself, but I needed some time alone with my thoughts. It took me some time, but I eventually managed to calm down and fall asleep.

When I woke up in the morning, I noticed Levi wasn't in his makeshift bed anymore. However, his scent was still strong, which led me to believe he was somewhere near - probably the bathroom. His tranquilizing fragrance allowed me to think clearly, and I decided to finally let Nava talk while we were still alone.

"I'm so sorry, Cal!" she cried out the second I restored our connection. She had given me a small headache trying to reach me all night. *"I don't know what came over me, I should've never taken over without your permission! Please don't block me again,"* she pleaded.

"It's alright, Nava. As long as you promise to never do such a thing again," I scolded her, and she immediately whimpered.

"I won't," she stated firmly. *"But when those random girls started talking crap about you, I just lost it. You need to start standing up for yourself, Cal!"*

"Why? We're lucky most people like us here, unlike how it was back in our old pack. You should've just let them talk."

"You should've shut them all up back then!"

Those words made something click inside my head.

All this time, Nava was the one faintly screaming for me to fight back - she was projecting those thoughts to me.

"Do you remember what Calanthe said? You're the Luna now; you need to ensure pack members will respect you. If you can't trust yourself, then trust me, *Cal,"* she begged, actually getting my attention. *"The wolves in your old pack wanted you to believe you were weak because* they *were weak, too. They were afraid of what you'd do if you realized how strong you actually are. They*

managed to break you, and I'm sorry I wasn't here earlier to stop it."

"*Nava...*" I whispered, unable to comprehend the words she was feeding me.

"You're strong, Calliope. You need to believe that."

"You're up." Levi's voice broke my concentration, interrupting my conversation with Nava. I lifted my head up to look at him, instantly noticing he was shirtless. My cheeks warmed as I shamelessly stared at his muscular body. I knew I was blushing, but he didn't seem to mind it at all. "So, today's the big day. Here's how it's gonna be."

My mate sat down at the edge of the bed beside me. Though he was still a couple feet away from me, his proximity made my heart skip a beat. He explained he wasn't allowed to spend the day with me, following tradition - the distance would supposedly make our wolves more excited for the marking process. Maids would be sent to help me prepare, and meals would be served in the room so I could eat during breaks. Honestly, I didn't like the idea of sitting through the day while people waited on me; it wasn't part of my nature as a Delta. But I obviously didn't complain.

"Well, that's it. If you need anything, ask one of the Omegas to get Calanthe," Levi instructed me, already getting up. I thought he would turn around and leave, but he approached me instead. Confused, I got up as well, my heart racing faster than ever. "Before I go, I'd like to talk to you about what happened yesterday."

Oh no! He was going to punish me for my outburst. I knew he was.

"What was that about?"

I hesitated, looking away from him. "I heard two girls bad-mouthing me. I'm really sorry for the way I handled the situation. It was improper."

"I see," he replied thoughtfully. "Seems like a valid reason. Just...don't do that again."

I looked up at him, my eyes wide with confusion. That was it? A warning?

"See you tonight, Calliope," he said, allowing his hand to rest on my shoulder.

The instant he touched me, we both stiffened. The electricity caused by the mate bond made my chest light up with fireworks as my breathing became ragged. I instinctively lifted my gaze up, expecting him to remain neutral as usual, but what I found made me gasp in surprise. Much like yesterday, his blue eyes had lost their coldness, turning a more intense shade of blue like ice melting into water. He stared at me for a few seconds before he abruptly turned around to leave, not uttering another word.

I remained silent, perplexed as I watched him roughly close the door. It took me some time to recompose myself and understand what had just happened. Was that...love I saw in his eyes, even if for a brief moment?

"He's falling for you, Cal!" Nava chanted excitedly. *"After the marking ceremony tonight, he won't be able to resist the mate bond anymore. I just know it!"*

A shy knock on the door prevented me from processing the situation any further. I opened it up, surprised that the four maids had already arrived. And just like that, my pampering princess day began. The last day before I officially became a Luna, bound to this pack by their Alpha - *my* Alpha.

The maids were very nice to me. They patiently took care of my hair and body, making sure I'd be as stunning as possible. However, as time went by, my spa day was slowly becoming lonely and boring. As kind as the maids were, they clearly didn't want to risk bothering their Luna, so they were mostly quiet. After lunch, I was sure my day would keep dragging on.

Until two unexpected visitors came in.

When the door burst open, I instinctively turned in its direction to identify who walked in, which caused one of the maids to blur my makeup. I apologized before turning back to Darrell and Ivar, who both had bright smiles on their faces.

"Boys?" I arched my eyebrows in confusion. "What are you doing here?"

"We thought you might want some company," the Gamma cheerfully explained.

"We can leave if you want us to, though," the Beta said softly.

"No. I'm really glad you're here!" They just saved the rest of my day.

"Just don't tell Levi about this, okay? He'd probably snap our necks if he knew we saw his Luna before she was ready," Darrell joked, but his tone made me feel like he was serious.

"Anyway..." Ivar dismissed him, approaching me with a huge grin. "What was that yesterday? You showed the whole damn pack you're not to be messed with! And you did it in a very poised and elegant way. Such a Luna move!"

"Yeah," the Beta agreed. "That was quite a show you put on back there!"

I felt my cheeks flushing again, and I uselessly tried to hide it by facing forward, but the mirror in front of me caused the opposite effect. I cleared my throat, realizing there was no way out.

"While I was going around with Hailey, two girls were talking crap about me. When I heard them, I… I don't know. I just lost it." I sighed, expecting them to disapprove of my actions.

"They definitely got the message. I'm sure they won't be messing with you anymore," Darrell assured me, patting me on the shoulder.

"Right! But don't worry about it, Cal. In such a big pack, it's impossible to be loved by everybody. Even we hear nasty comments sometimes." Ivar shrugged before a playful smile crossed his face. "And by we, I mean Levi and Darrell. I mean, who could dislike me? I'm awesome!"

"Woah… Slow down there, buddy." Darrell frowned. "Let's not forget you annoy quite a few people with your damn jokes."

"Only Trix ever complains about them!" The Gamma pouted. "Have you seen that girl? It's impossible to make her laugh! I bet she only does when puppies are crying or something."

I laughed. For the first time since I'd arrived at the most ruthless pack in the country, I actually laughed. The boys seemed satisfied with my lighter mood, and just like that, all of my worries were gone. They stayed for a couple of hours until it was time for me to get dressed. Once I was done, the maids surrounded me with mirrors to allow me a 360-degree view of myself.

After a long day of being pampered, I looked even more breathtaking than the day before. My hair had been decorated with a white rose crown, and my nails had been painted with magical bright red nail polish, which was supposed to stick to Nava's claws when I shifted. Darrell helped me pick my dress when we went shopping - a ruby, sleeveless gown with a rounded skirt. It was decorated with a slightly darker flower pattern.

"You look beautiful, Luna!" one of the maids complimented as she bowed her head at me. The other three soon followed her lead.

"Thank you," I replied with a fond smile. "And thank you for helping me prepare today."

"It was an honor, Luna," another one added before they all excused themselves.

Luna Calanthe arrived shortly after to walk me towards the lake, where the ceremony was held. She kept trying to calm me down when she noticed how nervous I was, saying it had been a wonderful experience when her mate marked her the same way decades ago. Little did she know, it wasn't the event that worried me.

I was anxious to know how Levi would react. I could only hope Nava was right, and he would fully accept us after tonight.

When we arrived, I was immediately stunned by the decorations. There were warm yellow lights hanging from the tall pine trees, rose petals scattered around the fresh green grass, candles floating on top of water lilies over the calm waters of the huge lake. A thousand pack members surrounded the clearing, but they all disappeared when my eyes landed on my mate. He was a long distance away from me, but I knew he looked gorgeous.

Calanthe left me there in the center, and soon after, an

Elder began reciting some kind of ceremonial speech - I was too lost in thought to listen. I only heard him when he instructed me to shift, and I gladly gave Nava control. Her pearly white fur looked beautiful under the moonlight, her intense honey-colored eyes shining brighter than any star. She fought to remain still in her spot as we watched our mate shift for the first time.

Odin was a gigantic wolf, easily standing taller than eight feet. Just his strong, imposing posture made it easy to see he was truly an Alpha. His fur was a beautiful shade of metallic gray, except for his chin and neck, which were cream-colored. He was as handsome as Levi.

But when he bolted in our direction, my heart stopped. The closer he got, the easier it was to notice his icy blue eyes. They were even colder than usual, almost as if he had become a true beast. Whatever hint of love I saw in my mate's eyes earlier was completely gone. And when he jumped onto Nava, knocking her to the ground, all I could feel was fear.

CHAPTER ELEVEN

Levi

The moment I closed the door to the room I now shared with Calliope, I threw my fists against the wall. I knew the mate bond was strong; it could completely blind even the most powerful wolves and make them weak. However, I thought I was stronger than the pull, until I touched my mate a minute ago. The sparks I felt lit up a fire inside me, a crazy fever that pushed me to take her then and there. She was mine, yet I couldn't have her - I *didn't want* to have her.

As I rushed towards the guest room, where I would be preparing for the marking ceremony, I felt an aching pain in my chest. I struggled to breathe, like the oxygen was heavier. Only when I dove under the cold shower, letting the water douse the fever, I drew in a long, desperate breath that finally filled my lungs. Panting, I lifted my hand up to stare intently at it. If I closed my eyes, I could still feel the tantalizing sensation of touching Calliope.

What the hell was wrong with me?!

"*You know very well the answer to that question,*" my wolf's voice echoed inside my head. "*The longer we resist the matebond, the harder it becomes to fight it. This is the price for dismissing the Moon Goddess' wishes.*"

Deep down, I knew he was right. Still, there had to be

some way around it. Turning off the water, I let my back rest against the cold tile wall, revisiting my memories of the recent event. From a young age, I had been taught to control my emotions, which was why I could easily repel the strong passion I should feel whenever I was around my mate. But there were times when her scent drove me insane. When my eyes became lighter, and I could see her in a different light. Almost as if I were a completely different person.

Wait...

"*It's you!*" I yelled at Odin. "*You're the one giving in to the matebond! You're the one letting your feelings get the best of you, and you're projecting them onto me!*"

"*I want to be with my mate, Levi!*" he snarled, finally confessing. If it wasn't for my rage taking over me, I would've felt surprised. We had a pretty similar mindset, so we never argued before.

"*Love is a luxury, Odin! Possibly the only one we cannot afford to have,*" I growled. "*We're Alphas. There's people counting on us, people we swore to protect. How can you be so selfish as to put your stupid wishes above our own pack?*"

"*We deserve to be loved, too!*" he cried out in despair.

"*At what price?*" My question finally seemed to catch his attention. "*Have you forgotten what happens when powerful wolves get too caught up in love? Have you forgotten how my father was killed?*"

There was silence for a while, but in the end, my wolf sighed. "*I haven't forgotten. I'm sorry,*" he whispered. "*It was a moment of weakness.*"

"*Exactly! You're already becoming weak, and we haven't even marked Calliope yet!*"

My words seemed to make something click for him because the next second he regained his Alpha posture.

"You're right. We must continue fighting the pull, for the sake of our people," he said assertively. *"I will mark our mate tonight, but it shall not have any impact on our agreement. She will never be anything other than the Luna of our pack."*

"I'm glad you remember now," I snorted before closing our connection.

After the issue was settled, I walked out of the bathroom and put on some clothes to make a few calls. Even though today was an important day, I had so much work on my hands I couldn't take the day off. In the end, it didn't really bother me, since working helped keep my mind off my confusing feelings. Besides, I didn't need a lot of time to prepare.

An hour before the beginning of the ceremony, I went back to the guest suite to get dressed in the ceremonial clothes that were brought in earlier by one of the Omegas. The outfit was crimson red, following tradition, and I complemented it with a golden tie. Once I was ready, I headed towards the lake to wait. Not too long after, Calliope showed up, leading to the beginning of the event.

I didn't dare look at her too long, even from a distance - I was afraid her beauty would bring back the emotions I was trying so hard to fight off. When she shifted into the purest white wolf, I almost lost it again. This was my first time seeing her animal form, and she was just as magnificent. I shook my head when I heard the Elder's request for me to shift.

"You know what you have to do," I told Odin as I allowed him control.

"Yes. You don't need to remind me," he barked.

Being of Alpha blood, my transformation only lasted a few seconds. I could see through Odin's pale blue eyes as they locked on our mate, as if she was his next prey. Proving his determination, he bolted off in her direction. For a brief second, my heart ached as I noticed the fear in her eyes, but I quickly shook it off. It needed to be done; the marking had to be completed.

Shocked gasps filled the cold nightly air when my gray wolf roughly knocked his mate to the ground. Scared, she tried to stand back up, but Odin was quicker. He climbed on top of her, his massive weight preventing her from moving as he forced her to submit. Her innocent honey-colored eyes searched for her mate, but my wolf dismissed her pleading gaze. He had truly become a beast - the beast we needed to be.

Without a second thought, Odin abruptly lowered his head, sinking his canines deep into the spot that connected Nava's neck and shoulder. She howled in pain as the blood began to drip out of the newly opened wound, painting her white fur red. We held onto her flesh for a few seconds to make sure the mark would stay.

And that's when I felt it.

Odin closed his eyes hastily, pulling away as a pounding headache hit us. The magical soul link that bound us to our mate had been established. Now, we could sense her every feeling as if it was our own.

Her striking pain was harder to ignore than anything else.

"*It's done,*" Odin stated sadly before allowing me back control.

Back to my human form, I watched as Nava silently laid on the floor, shaking. The marking process was quite painful, even for high-ranking wolves, but she handled it extremely well. There were no whimpers, no heavy breathing. But what stunned me the most was when our mate's intense yellow eyes turned to me with nothing but hurt. It destroyed me in an inexplicable way, making my legs tremble as I struggled to stay on my feet.

Before I could make sense of my emotions, Calliope shifted back. I offered her my hand to help her up, but she completely dismissed it, fighting back her tears as she rose with the elegance of a queen. She looked into my eyes for a brief second before the Elder offered us red robes to cover our naked bodies. No one noticed our exchange; to everyone else, the ceremony had gone as expected.

Once again, I reached out for Calliope's hand, and she reluctantly placed it over mine. Cheers and howls erupted from the crowd as we walked past them. I was astonished when I noticed Cal smile through her tears - a sign of true strength. Every pack member congratulated us on the solidification of our bond, praising their Luna and saluting their Alpha. I was on autopilot as I walked my mate back to our room, a thousand thoughts crossing my mind.

Calliope immediately went to the bathroom to clean herself as I headed to the couch and pretended to fall asleep. I noticed the moment she laid on the bed alone with her back turned to me. After a while, I stopped watching her, staring at the ceiling instead in an attempt to minimize the effect she had on me.

Her emotions were so loud now - betrayal, hurt, even anger. But the absolute worst was her pain. It wasn't physical pain, the kind our rapid healing bodies were able to handle quite well; it was emotional pain. Her mind had been broken by my actions, and I doubt she would be able to fall asleep as long as she felt that way. I sure knew I wouldn't.

Multiple times during the night as I laid awake on the couch, I felt the urge to get up and soothe her. The uncanny feeling only added to my stress. Why did I feel sorry for her? I didn't do anything wrong... Did I?

"*What's done is done!*" Odin barked, clearly annoyed at me. After all, I had been the one to convince him we should act the way we did, even though we had both agreed it was the only way in the end. Still, I couldn't help the pinch of regret that grew bigger by the second.

CHAPTER TWELVE

Calliope

I couldn't sleep that night, the pain too great.

Not the physical pain; the bite only hurt for a few minutes until it healed. The emotional pain, which started when I realized how cruel Levi was capable of being, is what truly shattered me.

I knew the marking could be quite painful, since a mate's teeth had to reach very deep to prevent the wound from healing immediately. Most wolf couples do it while mating, when pleasure usually numbs the pain. It made sense for a strong, ruthless pack like Blood Eclipse to hold such a brutal ceremony, where the future Lunas had to publicly show their strength by enduring the entire process with no sort of relief or distraction.

But it was still supposed to be a beautiful moment - the event in which soulmates' lives become tied as one. The way Levi did it... It was just plain evil. He didn't try to be the least gentle, and he made sure to let me know the mark wouldn't change anything. Our relationship would remain political, as he wished.

For too long, I dreamt my destined partner would be the one to treat me fairly, and save me from the hell I used to live in. Ever since I came here, the thrill of having met my mate had completely prevented me from realizing the dangerous truth about him: Levi wasn't my knight in shining armor; he was the big bad wolf who could eat me alive at any moment. At least, I could finally see him for the cold, ruthless Alpha everyone said he was.

"I'm sorry I made you believe he would become a better man after the marking ceremony, Cal." Nava whimpered inside my head. She too was surprised by our mate's actions. It was impossible not to notice how betrayed she felt last night. But now, all I could sense was her regret. *"I should've protected you."*

"It's not your fault, Nava," I reassured her. *"You didn't choose Levi to be our mate."*

"But the Goddess did, and she always knows best." Her words confused me. Did she mean my destiny was to be trapped with this cruel man forever? If so, I was definitely the Goddess' least favorite child. *"We may not always understand her reasons, but she makes no mistakes. Time will come for us to figure out why we're mated to Levi and Odin. Until then, I'll stop pushing you to give in to him. You must save yourself, Cal. I should've never convinced you someone else would do it for you."*

She retreated to the back of my mind as I heard my mate getting up from the couch, probably to get ready for training. I could somehow feel his eyes on me for what seemed like minutes, but I pretended to be asleep until he left the room. I didn't have the energy for his coldness and his rude comments today.

Once he was gone, I got up and headed to the bathroom to brush my teeth. I was met by my reflection in the mirror, the mark on my shoulder immediately catching my attention. I inched closer to have a better look at it, my hand instinctively moving up to touch the spot. My fingers carefully traced the bite stamped on my skin - the mark of an Alpha. It wasn't red anymore, but as I assessed it, something occurred to me; Levi and I were now tied to each other, yet I still couldn't feel his emotions.

"Because I'm blocking them out," Nava quickly answered my unspoken question. *"I don't want us to suffer anymore. I'm afraid his feelings could have a negative impact on us."*

"Thank you," I replied, unsure if it was truly the best thing to do. At least I wouldn't feel his anger, his disgust, or his lack of love, even if it hurt me.

Calanthe was too busy arranging the details for the Luna Ceremony - which should happen in a week or so - so we wouldn't have our usual lessons today. Since I had a free morning, I decided to return to the secret garden I found the day before. Something about the colorful flowers and their intense fragrance made me feel safe. My mother would dedicate some of her time to gardening as a hobby, and she would constantly take me to the personal garden she grew. She was the only one who cared for it. Needless to say, the flowers died not too long after she did.

The memory of her brought feelings to the surface I had kept bottled up for a long time. My life started going downhill after my parents' death. Since then, I was always looked down upon; no one cared about the weak offspring they had left behind. Not even my mate.

Silent tears streamed down my face as I sat on the marble bench, alone. Always alone. No one wanted me, yet I kept craving for their love. Even after what Levi did, I still wanted him to be with me. I was destined to be a pathetic little she-wolf, an average girl who couldn't do anything right.

"Hey...Calliope, right?" I was so absorbed in my own wallowing I didn't even notice someone approaching me. The female voice was slightly familiar, but I only realized it was Trix when I stopped hiding my face in my palms. For a second, my emotions got the best of me.

"Go ahead, say how pathetic your future Luna looks crying alone, hiding away," I spat, not bothering to look at her. "I know you don't like me anyway. It's okay, you're not the only one."

She stayed silent for a second, expressionless. It was impossible to read her. "Can I sit with you?" she asked, taking me by surprise. I hesitated for a while, and she sighed. "Screw it, I'm sitting here," she decided before taking her place beside me. What did she want with me now? "Look, I know I haven't been the most welcoming Delta. I'm sorry."

I lifted my face up, scrunching my eyebrows together. "What?"

"I won't say it again." She crossed her arms, frowning. But then, her stubborn expression turned into a sad one. "I misjudged you, Cal. I thought you were just some stuck-up, power-hungry she-wolf. After last night, though... I noticed how wrong I was about you." She offered me a sympathetic smile. "Levi was a jerk to you yesterday."

The way she talked about her Alpha stunned me, but it somehow comforted me to know she was on my side. "Yeah. Has he always been this..."

"Much of an asshole?" Trix finished. My eyes widened. "Actually, no. Things...happened. He changed." She looked down. "Maybe you're the one who can bring him back. But in order to achieve that, you must show him he can't treat you like this. You must tame him, Cal."

"How? He's the Alpha, and I'm a weak Delta." I sighed.

"You're his *Luna*. You have as much power around here as he does," she stated. "Besides, I'm a Delta by blood too, and I don't take crap from anyone. Not even the Alpha."

"I don't know if I can do that," I confessed.

We both stayed silent for a second before Bellatrix abruptly got up. I immediately turned my head in her direction, and she offered me her hand to help me up.

"Get up, Cal. Let's spar," she said decisively.

This woman surprised me in many ways. She was the only one who didn't address me by my new title, and she seemed to not submit to anyone, regardless of rank. Her aura was strong, even though she was just a Delta. Could I ever be strong like her?

"You can be even stronger, Cal. Accept her offer," Nava insisted.

It couldn't hurt to try. I obliged, finally taking Trix's hand. We exchanged smiles before she led me to the training grounds, just past the small garden. She instructed me to let Nava out so we could train in wolf form, and just a few seconds later, she shifted as well. I had only seen her wolf, Nyx, once, on the day I arrived here. However, this was the first time I was able to properly look at her. She had a long snout, elegant pointy ears, and piercing red eyes. Her shiny long fur was as black as a starless night sky. Nyx was intimidatingly beautiful.

At first, I was unsure of what to do, but the Delta gladly took the lead. Our wolves engaged in friendly combat, black and white resembling yin and yang as they surrounded each other in a cautious dance. We managed to put up a fight in the beginning, but Nyx was quick to learn our moves and predict them. In the end, she pinned Nava to the ground four times before I finally gave up. Trix flashed me an apologetic look as we both shifted back, getting dressed again.

"It's useless." I sighed in defeat, too ashamed to look at her. "I'm not strong like you are."

"I'm older than you. I have a lot more battle experience, especially because our pack is not as peaceful as your old one," she observed. In a way, I knew she was right, but it didn't change the fact that I felt weak. "How often did you use to train?"

"Three times a week."

"Yeah, I train everyday here," she countered, gently touching my shoulder. "But, just from our short session, I can already tell you have a lot of potential. You just need to practice some more."

I was beginning to lose hope when a bold idea crossed my mind. It was a long shot, but for once, I grasped onto the words my wolf would always tell me - I was finally ready to fight back.

"Can you teach me, Trix?" I asked with determination.

Her eyes widened with surprise, but a proud smile soon crossed her face. "Sure. Are you free now?"

CHAPTER THIRTEEN

Darrell

The way Levi treated Calliope was really bothering me.

As Beta, it was my duty to protect the Luna. Make her feel safe. It wouldn't take long for her to officially take the position - she was already carrying the Alpha's mark. The way he decided to place it on her pissed me off. The marking ceremony was traditionally rough in our pack, but even the strongest leaders would try to be as gentle as possible to ease the pain for their mates. When I noticed the fear in Cal's eyes, I saw red.

The need I felt to protect her was instinctive, but not only because she was my Luna. At only eighteen years old, she reminded me so much of my younger sister. The smile that lit up Cal's face the first time she saw her mate was exactly the same as Marisol's. Everyday I watched it become a little less bright, and I couldn't bear the thought of letting such a tragedy happen again.

"Levi's our Alpha, and he's always done what's best for our pack," my wolf, Banyan, chimed in. *"His past experiences may have...changed him, but he would never hurt our Luna. He's not a monster."*

"He sure looked like one last night," I pointed out.

Odin was a powerful wolf. It was rare to see him without his usual stern look. However, what I saw last night weren't the eyes of a formidable leader, they were the cold eyes of a wild beast. I don't think anyone else noticed the change, since they were all thrilled about finally having a Luna after so many years. Had I known this is how Levi would treat her, I wouldn't have encouraged him to go looking for her.

"You know very well Blood Eclipse needed their Luna," Banyan observed. *"A pack without a heart can never reach its full potential."*

"Our Alpha clearly doesn't have one, and he's ready to rip out hers, too."

The moment I said those words, I stopped dead in my tracks. I was coming back from training, walking down the hallway, when my eyes landed on Calliope. She was sitting on one of the marble benches in the small backdoor garden, her face hidden behind her hands. When my werewolf ears caught the sound of her faint sobs, even my wolf let out a low growl. He was strict about our position as the Alpha's right hand, but deep down, I know he worried for our Luna too.

As I watched her crying from a distance, the memories flooded my mind. Memories I usually tried to keep out. But it was impossible not to think about one of the last times I saw Marisol, only three days before she was killed. When I asked why she was crying, she told me not to worry about it, that she and her mate would work things out. He was an Alpha, so he had no trouble getting away with the murder of his unofficial Luna. I should have known better; I should have saved her before it was too late.

I definitely wouldn't make the same mistake again.

Moved by my anger, I ran through the hallways towards the library, where I knew Levi would be. I found him in the back, reading over some documents we would need for today's meeting. It was hard to control my urge to just punch him in the face, but I managed to stop short a few feet away from him. He lifted his head up to look at me, and for a brief moment, I noticed he seemed...tired.

"What was that about yesterday?" I spat.

"What?"

"The marking ceremony!"

"I don't follow," he said, deadpan. It only fueled my anger.

"She doesn't deserve to pay for your grieving problems!" I barked at once. "Do you even know how she felt after what you did?!"

"As a matter of fact, I do," he growled, his eyes never leaving mine as he stood up. "She bears my mark now, so I can feel her emotions. Why do they concern you so much?"

"Because she's my Luna!"

"She's *my* Luna!" he roared, grabbing me by the hem of my shirt. Through his rage, I managed to see a hint of fear in his eyes. "Back away from her," he was using his Alpha tone, giving me a command I could not disobey, "and focus on your own problems. There's a meeting we need to attend."

I narrowed my eyes at him before replying, "I'm ready whenever you are." We both remained silent as we stared at each other for a few more seconds before he finally released me from his grip.

"Good. Tell Trix to have the car ready for us in ten. I'll meet you out front," he told me before walking out of the room.

It took me a few minutes to process our conversation. I imagined he would be angry, but I definitely didn't expect him to be desperate and possessive over a mate he didn't want. He probably saw her as a toy he didn't want to share. After I contacted Trix like he asked, I decided to link Ivar to have him keep an eye on Cal while we were out.

We were visiting Solar Hunt Pack today. We currently have a neutral relationship with them, but Levi has been trying hard to convince them to establish an alliance with us. Though they weren't as big as us, they were still a pretty wealthy pack, and we could definitely benefit from having a treaty with them.

After an hour-long drive, we reached the borders of the pack. Alpha Julius received us at the entrance of the packhouse alongside his Beta. He courteously led us towards his office, where he poured us some whiskey. A few minutes of formalities later, Levi cut straight to the point; he always had a short temper, but he seemed even less patient today.

"Have you had the time to read our alliance proposal yet?" Levi asked, carefully studying the other Alpha's reaction.

Julius scratched his thin beard, clearing his throat. "I have, Alpha Levi. And I must say the terms are quite appealing. However..." He hesitated, shrinking in his seat. "I'm afraid I'll have to refuse it. You see, another pack offered us an even better deal, which was impossible to dismiss."

"Which pack?" My friend was already clenching his teeth as he tensed up in his chair.

The other leader took a deep breath before finally answering, "The Silver Waters Pack."

* * *

Levi

The second I heard his response, I stood up from my seat. Out of all the packs Julius could have allied with, he chose the very pack whose late leader took my father's life. Silver Waters had gone downhill after the battle against Blood Eclipse a decade ago, but they had been growing at a steady pace for the past few years, and it seemed their new goal was to seek everything my pack might have an interest in.

"I'm sorry, Alpha Julius, but you should know, any ally to Silver Waters is an automatic enemy to Blood Eclipse," I declared, my eyes locked on his.

"I see." He sighed. "Well, I hope you don't regret your decision."

Did he just dare to threaten me? "I should say the same."

Not bothering to speak another word, I turned around to leave. Darrell got up right after without questioning me; he agreed we shouldn't keep a neutral relationship with any pack allied with our greatest enemy. As we made our way back home, it was hard to control my rage. What a waste of my time. I was one of the strongest Alphas of the country. I was used to winning. However, lately I only seemed to be losing.

Once we arrived home, I dismissed my Beta and locked myself in the library for the rest of the day. Taking care of pack matters usually helped keep my mind off my troubles, but this time, it was useless. I tried to focus on a single emotion - anger - in an attempt to feel less overwhelmed by everything else, but that made it even worse. No matter how hard I tried to deny it, what angered me most was myself.

Nothing I did could get the image of my mate's fearful expression out of my head. The way her intense honey eyes widened, reflecting the image of the ravenous beast inside of me, truly tore me apart. Why? Why did I care so much about what she thought of me? I looked at my hands, instantly realizing they were shaking. What was happening to me?

As I tried to concentrate, one single thought crossed my mind. Suddenly, everything went clear. The reason why I felt so stressed… I needed a release.

Odin snorted. "*You can't be serious.*"

"*Stop invading my thoughts, mutt!*" My wolf and I rarely fought, but after last night, he barely listened to me. "*You know as well as I do that our feelings get more intense after the marking. We must complete the mating process.*"

"*You must be delusional if you think our mate will want to be anywhere near us after what we did last night!*" he barked. "*I can't even show Nava how sorry I am. She blocked me out!*"

"*You should have blocked Calliope's feelings out too, then. This way we could have gotten some sleep!*"

"*No! We deserve to be in as much pain as we put her through,*" he replied adamantly.

For some reason, his words struck me like lightning. Odin eventually retreated to the depths of my mind, leaving me alone with my thoughts again. For a while, I pondered over what I should do, but I came to the conclusion he had to be wrong. Calliope should be just as willing to mate with us, especially if she needed emotional release. This was the best for both of us…and it might fix the terrible impression I caused on her the night before.

Taking a deep breath, I went back to the Alpha suite. My

mate wasn't inside, which was weird; she barely left since she didn't know her new home well enough yet. I felt somewhat anxious, but I shrugged it off and decided to take a shower while I waited for her. Just as I walked out of the shower, her strong innocent scent filled my nostrils - she was here. Not bothering to put on any clothes, I wrapped a towel around my waist and walked out.

My eyes immediately fell on the mark stamped on her shoulder - *my* mark - as I leaned against the bathroom door frame.

"You're back," I stated blankly. She turned to look at me, but I didn't see her usual smile. "How was your day?"

"It was great, actually." She shrugged, and it stunned me. For the first time, I noticed I couldn't feel her pain anymore. Was she okay already? And why did I feel relieved?

"Oh. Good." I hesitated for a second, not knowing where to start. "So, uh...Cal, do you remember the rules?"

"Yes. I've been following them, haven't I?" I swear I could see a small frown on her face.

"Let me cut to the chase. I said we could have sex if we felt like we needed it. And today was a...rough day." Odin snorted inside my head, probably realizing how pathetic I sounded. But it was too late to turn around. "No feelings attached. Just sex. What do you say?"

Because of her mark, I could feel everything she felt. I couldn't help but notice her disgust, and it cut through my heart like a knife. She didn't say the words out loud, but I could already feel the pain of her silent rejection. Of course, she was going to deny my suggestion! Why did I even think she would want to have an intimate moment with me after last night?

"Okay," she finally replied, leaving me perplexed.

"Okay?" I had to confirm.

"Okay," she repeated.

I blinked a few times, still unable to believe it. "Alright then. How would you like to do this?"

She immediately went silent, turning away from me. At first, I thought she was shy, and the thought of how many males she slept with before me made anger rise up to my throat again. *Why did I even care?* I shook my head, pushing my feelings back down.

"It's okay, I won't judge you for what you've done with other males," I encouraged her, even though the thought actually made my stomach turn. "Just tell me what you didn't enjoy from your last experiences."

"I...I've never had sex before," she whispered, and just like that, my mind went blank.

CHAPTER FOURTEEN

Calliope

My nose twisted in disgust at his proposal. I know he is an Alpha - a very powerful and feared one - but did he *seriously* expect me to be head over heels for him after the cruel way he marked me, less than 24 hours ago? To be honest, had Trix not reminded me I had the right to stop him if he suggested anything that made me uncomfortable, I would probably have continued being his doormat. Thankfully, her reminder helped me feel confident enough to deny my inconsiderate, horny mate.

"*Wait, Cal! That's not it,*" Nava chimed in, making me stop right as my lips parted. "*Don't you see how nervous he is? He isn't demanding you to do anything. He truly just wants you.*" I was about to roll my eyes, thinking she was giving in to the mate bond again, when she continued, "*The mark is making him anxious, and he doesn't know how to deal with it. This is our body, and you still have the final say; I won't tell you what to do. But if I continue blocking our mate's emotions out, it's more likely he'll be attached after mating rather than the other way around. If you accept it, you'll turn the situation around. He'll be wrapped around your finger.*" She finally caught my attention. "*Sex isn't only about love. In fact, it's mostly about power. At least right now it is.*"

I remained silent for a minute, digesting my wolf's thoughts. As a Delta, I was in charge of controlling various details regarding the pack, but at the same time, I was never the one in control of anything. All I did my whole life was follow orders, yet destiny threw me into a leadership position by forcing me to become Luna. The idea of taking control for once suddenly appealed a lot to me.

In a blaze of courage, I looked into Levi's eyes. "Okay."

"Okay?" There was a mix of confusion, disbelief, and excitement in his voice.

"Okay," I repeated, loud and clear.

"Alright then. How would you like to do this?"

My mind went blank as it immediately occured to me that I didn't know the answer to his question. I couldn't possibly know; I was still a virgin! Aside from being busy all the time, I was too repulsed by the males from my old pack, even those who showed any interest in me. Even if I did reciprocate their feelings, I'm sure they were only doing it to tease me. How could I find a way out of this situation?

"It's okay, I won't judge you for what you've done with other males," Levi said after my long silence. Oh, if he only knew. "Just tell me what you didn't enjoy from your last experiences."

Uncertain of how he would react, I looked away from him before confessing, "I... I've never had sex before."

I noticed he stopped breathing as his eyes widened. He blinked at me a few times, processing the information, before he pushed off the door frame and started anxiously pacing around the room. The way he desperately ran his hands through his metallic blonde hair evinced his distress. Was he mad at me?

"I can't just take your virginity as if it meant nothing," he whispered, more like a loud thought to himself. What, was he suddenly capable of being compassionate now? I froze when he turned to look at me. He walked quickly in my direction, crouching in front of me. "Okay. Just this one time, I'll make love to you. But this will be the first and last time you'll see this side of me. Understand?"

As stupid as it was, my heart skipped a beat. Part of me despised him and his entitlement, but another wanted him close. It was hard to fight the mate bond, especially when Levi's pale blue eyes, slightly twinkling with expectation, were locked on mine. One last time, I decided to trust Nava's advice.

"Alright," I agreed, holding my head up.

The Alpha stared at me for a while longer before he jolted up, crashing his lips against mine. I squeaked out a yelp in surprise, but closed my eyes in delight nonetheless. We had never been so close to each other. Before this moment, our physical contact was limited to accidental touching or, in public settings, holding hands. Feeling his tongue invade my mouth as he ran his hand down my arm made me completely forget how to breathe. My entire body warmed up, and it was extremely hard to prevent moans from escaping my lips. Could I really get to the end of this without losing myself to him?

"He's our mate. Despite who he is or what he's done, he'll always have this effect on us," Nava purred. *"We can enjoy this moment, but it doesn't mean we have to be submissive to him. We can tame him, Cal."*

She was right; I deserved to feel good after so much abuse. I opened my eyes just in time to watch Levi lifting my dress above my thighs. His fingers delicately traced my skin as he reached between my legs, caressing me through my panties. The cold air hit my lower area when he skilfully removed the thin piece of cloth, but soon his warm hand made me heat up again. He started rubbing on my clit while one of his fingers teased my already wet entrance.

"I'll have to get you used to it first, okay?" Levi breathed out, his eyes never leaving mine.

The second I nodded, he slipped his finger inside me. It was impossible to keep holding in my moans. I had never gotten so intimate with anyone before, and the thrill of the experience made my body melt. He started moving slowly, thoroughly caressing my walls. My breathing became more ragged the faster his movements got.

"Shit, you're so tight!" My mate grunted. "I'm gonna try two now."

Before I could process his words, I felt another one of his fingers slide inside me. The surprise made my head fall back as his hand continued thrusting in and out, picking up the pace.

"How does it feel, Cal?" he asked, never ceasing his movement. I heard him, but I couldn't concentrate on forming a verbal response. "Answer me," he demanded.

"Good," I replied breathlessly . "It feels so good."

I could feel his grin upon me. "Don't hold back."

I didn't understand what he meant at first, but when his free hand cupped one of my breasts through my clothes, my core pooled with heat. He pinched my nipple while his thumb circled my clit, and before long, I felt pleasure building up inside of me. Before I could realize what was happening, my legs started shaking. My fists clenched the sheets tighter. The next thing I knew, waves of ecstasy rolled over me, making me see stars.

"That's a good mate," Levi breathed out close to my ear, and the hairs on the back of my neck bristled.

I was still coming down from my high, trying to catch my breath, when I felt him remove his fingers. I groggily opened my eyes to watch him slowly get rid of his thin towel, allowing his member to spring free.

"*Goddess,*" I muttered subconsciously. *That* couldn't possibly fit inside of me!

"Don't worry. We'll go slow," Levi reassured me, laying on top of me.

When his lips brushed against mine yet again, the electricity made me feel lighter. But as I felt his tip press against my entrance, I instantly tensed up again. To my surprise, Levi didn't thrust in immediately. Instead, his hands moved up to my shoulders, massaging them, while he placed soft kisses on my chin and neck. He made me relax in no time. How could this monster be so gentle?

"I'll go in now, okay?" he whispered. "It'll hurt. You need to tell me if it gets too much."

I drew in a long breath before nodding. He went back to kissing my skin, slowly pushing himself inside of me. Despite how wet I was from that first orgasm, I still held my breath when his dick stretched my insides. The sparks from our contact combined with his tenderness eased the pain, but it still hurt like hell. I was on the verge of crying, but I held back my tears by forcing my eyes shut.

"Just breathe, Calliope." Hearing him say my name was like the sweetest melody. I immediately obliged, parting my lips to suck in some air. "Good. How bad is it?"

"It hurts," I said honestly.

"You want me to pull out and stop?"

"No!" I quickly replied. As painful as it was, part of me still loved the way he filled me. "Just...wait a little bit, please."

"As long as you need."

Levi remained completely still inside of me, patiently waiting for my body to adjust to his presence. His kisses soothed me, his caress warmed me. After a few minutes, the pain subsided and I nodded for him to go on. He hesitated before he finally started moving, eyeing me cautiously as if he was looking for any sign of discomfort on my expression. His first thrusts still hurt a little, but it didn't take long for fire to consume me. Soon enough, I instinctively started moving with him.

Noticing my pleasure, he felt comfortable enough to pick up the pace. Inch by inch, I took in his entire length; it was even better than feeling his fingers. My moans became louder and so did his groans each time he thrusted deeper, faster. His rhythmic movements were getting sloppier, slightly rougher, making my walls clench around his member in response.

"Fuck!" he grunted out before turning to me. "I'm not going to last long if you keep doing that to me."

"Faster!" I pleaded, completely ignoring his warning. His eyes widened at my unexpected request, but in the end, he snickered.

"As you wish, my Luna."

Suddenly, his tenderness was gone, but I actually...liked it. He pummeled my core repeatedly, making my eyes roll back in my head. Again, and again, and again. Each time was better than before. I felt the fire building up inside of me again, and with a final moan, I gave in to him. He spurted his seed inside of me as he too reached his climax, groaning loudly.

For a while, he remained on top of me, regaining his composure. When he finally removed himself from me, he unexpectedly pulled me into his arms. As we laid together in bed, we were a mess of sweaty bodies, but it didn't bother me one bit. In fact, for the first time in a long while, it made me feel safe. Tired, I relaxed against his chest, peacefully closing my eyes. But his next words caused me to abruptly reopen them.

"You're mine, Calliope. No one will ever take you away from me."

As possessive as he may have sounded, his tone was soft - loving, even. I lifted my head up to examine his expression, to make sure I wasn't delusional, but he had already drifted off. Afraid he would turn back into a beast when he woke up, I decided to shrug it off. Eventually, I fell asleep in his arms. For the first time, we were sleeping together in the same bed.

* * *

When I opened my eyes in the morning, I immediately noticed Levi was already gone. Thankfully, I didn't get my hopes up that anything would change after we mated. However, as I sat up in bed groggily brushing my eyes, they landed on something I wasn't expecting to find. Over the messy sheets, there was a fancy golden food tray with croissants, jelly, and various exotic fruits.

I wondered if I was still dreaming when I noticed a piece of paper next to the plate. I picked it up, quickly realizing it was a note with the words: *Left for training - enjoy your breakfast.* Did Levi leave this behind? It wasn't extremely romantic, but for the cold, ruthless Alpha he had proven himself to be, it was a start.

"I told you, Cal!" Nava celebrated. *"Now, you're the one in control,"* she said, a hint of mischief in her tone.

Me? Controlling the Alpha? It couldn't possibly be true. Not after just one night. I shook my head; the gesture probably meant nothing to him. Unwilling to waste my time figuring this man out, I got up to head for training myself. First, Luna training, then warrior training with Trix.

Calanthe was even more cheerful than usual today. She complimented me on how fast I was learning, telling me how much I reminded her of herself when she stepped in as Luna. After we were done with our lessons for the day, we chatted for a while. Time flew by, and before I noticed it, I was late to meet the Delta.

When I reached the training grounds, she was already waiting for me.

"Sorry, I'm late!" I said, still trying to catch my breath after running down the stairs.

"Don't stress yourself, Cal." She smiled reassuringly at me. Then, she furrowed her brows, pointing her nose up as she sniffed the air. Her confused demeanor suddenly turned into a grin. "Seems you've already started taming the mighty Alpha. Well done," she teased.

It took me a few seconds to understand what she meant, but when I did, my eyes widened. My scent! I was in such a rush in the morning I didn't even have time to shower. Trix could probably smell my scent mixing with Levi's. I blushed in embarrassment, looking away from her.

"I'm just messing with you!" She laughed. "Come on, let's get to training. We've gotta get you in shape again."

Training was split into two different sections, like at Moonstone - first in human form, then in wolf form. Trix's teaching method was rough, but at the same time, she was very patient. She took off her shirt when we started, staying only in her sports bra, and I noticed a faint mark on her shoulder. It got me curious, but I didn't want to interrupt our training with such an unimportant question.

After almost two hours of sparring, we took a small break, and she invited me to relax in the secret garden with her. Again, my eyes fell on her mark, questions floating through my mind. I hesitated for a while before eventually deciding to ask her about it.

"You're marked, but I've never seen your mate." I noticed her stiffen, and for a moment, I was afraid I had crossed a line. "Sorry. I don't mean to be intrusive-"

"You're not. I hear this question a lot." She showed me a sad smile before looking up at the sky. "My mate was a warrior. He...he gave his life to save mine in a battle against another pack, a few years ago."

A pinch of pain struck me. Me and my dumb mouth again.

"I'm sorry."

"Don't be. He lives in me; his sacrifice made me strong. Now, every time I'm in a battle, I fight for him." After a brief pause, she turned to me. "What do *you* fight for, Cal?"

CHAPTER FIFTEEN

Calliope

Nava was right.

A week had gone by since Levi and I mated. In such a short period of time, his behavior had already changed a lot. He would still avoid being too close to me, but I noticed he was trying hard to fit me into his busy schedule. He came to see me after morning training every day, and we always had our meals together. Though he refrained from touching me, I could sense him opening up to me during our talks, when he momentarily let his walls down.

On top of that, he started breaking his own rules. Since our first night together, he never went back to sleeping on the couch. The king-sized bed was large enough for us to sleep while keeping a safe distance from each other, but I could still feel his hands slightly brush my arms every now and then. He also spent more time with me outside the room, showing me around so I would become more familiar with the territory. However, I had the feeling he only took me on walks to have an excuse to hold my hand.

Regardless of his change in attitude, I wasn't ready to completely let my guard down yet. When I first came here, I let my hopes and dreams of being loved control my actions; I was guided by my feelings, and it only led to disappointment.

Of course, after learning how good he could make me feel, I often caught myself fantasizing about doing it a second time. But with Trix and Nava's help, I was finally realizing it was better to take care of myself first. Like the Luna I was training to become, I should think with my brain before listening to my heart.

"Focus, Cal!" The Delta's voice brought me back to reality just in time to dodge one of her punches, when her fists were inches away from my face. She took a few steps back, frowning at me, and I instantly knew she was going to scold me. "A single moment of distraction can cost you your life in a fight. Don't zone out, even when you're sparring with someone."

I shook my head, sighing. "I'm sorry. My mind drifted off for a second."

"Alright. Let Nava come out, I wanna see how she's doing." Trix backed off, allowing me some space to shift as she too gave her black wolf control.

"*You ready for this?*" I asked my wolf.

"*Are you starting to doubt me now?*" She snorted in response. Just like me, she too had grown a bit braver. She had always been strong, but she used to be a lot quieter. "*Of course, I am.*"

"*Just checking.*" I laughed.

I took a deep breath before giving her control. Despite not having my wolf for long, I could already complete my transformation almost as fast as Trix, and it wasn't as painful anymore. The second Nava was out, she stretched her legs and shook her beautiful white fur before her intense honey-colored eyes focused on Nyx.

During our first days of secretly training with the Delta,

we would mostly take a beating with little chance to defend ourselves. Trix never took it easy on us, always pointing out our mistakes and pushing us to become better warriors. Today, after almost an hour of sparring in wolf form, Nava was capable of pinning her opponent on the ground for the first time. Nyx's vivid red eyes widened in surprise when she turned to look at us from underneath our paws. We let her go, and she flashed us a wolfish grin before shifting back.

"That was impressive, Cal," Trix complimented me for the first time. "You're a quick learner. It's a shame your old pack didn't take advantage of your potential. Don't worry though, we'll get you up to speed in no time." She smiled fondly at me, patting my shoulder as she walked past me. "Let's wrap it up for today. Get some rest, we'll pick up where we left off tomorrow."

"Thank you, Trix," I said shyly. Not turning to look at me, she raised her hand, making a peace sign with her fingers.

Taking a few seconds to fix my hair and recompose myself, I headed back to the Alpha suite. With Luna lessons and warrior training, I had a pretty busy morning schedule, but I always tried to get back before Levi did. I didn't know how he would react to the fact that I was having secret training sessions with Trix, so I didn't want to risk him finding out. It was almost lunch time when I walked through the doors of my room, but to my surprise, my mate was already there.

Levi was standing on the balcony, looking over the land. The second he heard me come in, he abruptly turned his head to look at me. His icy blue eyes locked on mine as he approached me, and I immediately froze.

"Good morning," I whispered, trying to hide the

shakiness in my voice in hopes he wouldn't figure out where I had been.

"Good morning," he replied. I noticed a sudden change in his tone. I thought he was warming up to me, but today he seemed...colder than expected. "Lunch will be here in an hour, but I won't be able to stay and eat with you today. There's... something I need to do."

"Oh?" I blinked at him, eager to get more information, but he had already turned to walk away, forcing me to look over my shoulder.

He stopped in front of the door. "I'll be out for the entire day. You're not to come looking for me."

"What will you be doing?"

"You don't need to know."

I was taken aback by his words. For an entire week, he had been a lot kinder towards me. He hadn't turned into a perfect gentleman of course, but he had stopped being rude for no reason. I could even notice a new spark in his pale eyes. It was subtle, but I was slowly starting to believe I was actually capable of changing him. What happened?

"His guard is up again. Something is troubling his mind. Though I'm still blocking out Odin's emotions, I can sense they're stronger now. Heavier..." Nava carefully analyzed. *"Talk to him, Cal. Let him know you're not satisfied."*

"What if I *want* to know?" I said out loud, following my wolf's advice. He turned to me with surprise.

My heart started racing as I slowly approached him, unable to believe what came over me. Was Nava lending me her strength? Was my confidence finally coming back after Trix's training? For every step I took in his direction, Levi backed away, until he hit his back against the door. I continued walking towards him, my eyes locked on his, until our bodies were mere inches away. He stopped breathing when I lifted my hand up to touch his face.

"W-what?" he stuttered.

"I said, what if I *want* to know?" I repeated firmly. He was slightly shaking under my touch - the mighty Alpha was putty in my hands. "I think I have the right to know what my *mate* will be doing without me for an entire day."

For a brief moment, time seemed to stop. His lips parted in shock as I could feel him letting go of his control. I could hear his heart beating faster, threatening to jump out of his chest. Towering over me, he started lowering his head slowly. But before our lips touched, he gently pushed me away, swiftly opening the door and running away without saying another word.

After he left, I was shaking from the adrenaline. Did that really almost happen?

* * *

Levi

After I got out of the room, I needed a few seconds to stabilize my heart rate and breathe in some fresh air. I started holding my breath as Calliope approached me - I knew if I took in her scent while she was so close, I wouldn't be able to control myself. What was this girl doing to me? Every day it was becoming harder and harder to stay away from her.

But I couldn't let her get to me. I needed to keep my goals in mind, learn from my father's mistakes. Even the most powerful Alphas could be blinded by the mate bond if they weren't careful. No matter how hard it was to resist her, I had to take the reins of the situation. I hated how weak my future Luna made me feel, but...part of me also wanted to take her in my arms and protect her.

It got even harder after we mated. It came to a point where I couldn't think clearly when she wasn't around, so I instinctively tried to spend more time with her. The more we talked, the harder I fell for her. Calliope wasn't just a pretty face or an obedient Delta I could boss around. She was intelligent, assertive. And on top of it all, she was kind. It pained me to see how her kindness wasn't directed towards me much after I marked her. I could understand why - she resented me.

As I made my way down the stairs towards my private wine cellar, I shook my head. I couldn't think about her. Not today. It was the anniversary of my father's death - the day that reminded me of why I couldn't distract myself with a mate. I locked the door behind me and poured the first of many glasses I would be drinking.

Exactly ten years ago, my father perished in battle, a victim of the mate bond. We were under attack by the Silver Waters Pack, our biggest rival at the time. My mother, the former Luna, wasn't supposed to join the warriors, but she felt the need to when she noticed our Betas had been ambushed by the enemies. She was able to save them, but she caught the rival Alpha's attention at that moment. He captured her, using her as ransom to convince my father to surrender.

When he saw his beloved mate under the claws of his

enemy, he gave in. He completely forgot about his pack and his own son. He put our lives at risk to save his destined partner; he was too blind to notice it was a trap. The rival Alpha took advantage of my father's moment of weakness and ordered his soldiers to murder him, while I watched from my window. Ezekiel, the opposing leader, would have killed my mother too, and the whole pack afterwards if I didn't get to him in time. I was only sixteen back then, but I was forced to shift earlier than most wolves in order to finish what my father couldn't.

At his funeral, I swore I would never give in to the mate bond. His death would be an eternal reminder of how Alphas couldn't surrender themselves to love. Since then, my mother and I grew apart. I changed because I thought it was necessary. Even at such a young age, I became a feared Alpha, defeating and absorbing packs across the country. On this day every year, I isolated myself from anyone as I drank away the pain, and recalled why I couldn't allow myself to fall in love.

However, for the first time since my father's death, the lesson I'd ingrained in my mind all these years didn't seem to make sense anymore.

As the hours went by, the number of empty bottles surrounding me increased. The drunker I got, the harder it was to get Calliope's image out of my head. My feelings became louder, harder to control. For the past ten years, I believed a mate was a curse. How come it felt so right when I was near her?

"Because she was made for us. The Goddess paired her with us for a reason..." I heard Odin's faint voice inside my head. It was harder for him to reach me when I was drunk. *"Now that we found our mate, I can finally see. Your father made a mistake,*

but not the one you think. He only got as far as he did because your mother helped him along the way. She wasn't his weakness, she was his strength."

"That can't be right, Odin." I started pacing around nervously.

"What if it is?"

For a brief second, my buzz was completely gone as my mind cleared. Had I been wrong all of these years? Fear struck me. My Luna, my mate, my Calliope... I had treated her so poorly all this time. Even if I decided to accept her now, would *she* be willing to accept *me*?

In a blaze of madness, I rushed out of the cellar. Despite how faint her scent was, I instinctively followed it as I stumbled through the many hallways, searching for her. When I walked out of the packhouse, I realized the sun had already set, but I paid no attention to it as I continued to track down my mate. I needed to see her. I needed to be with her.

But when I found her near the lake, I froze. She was sitting on the grass, happily laughing, with my Beta by her side. I gave him clear orders to stay away from her, yet he dared defy me! The alcohol heightened my emotions, and I saw red. A guttural growl echoed in my throat, immediately catching their attention. When Darrell's eyes found me, I didn't think twice before charging in his direction.

I will teach him to not touch what's mine!

CHAPTER SIXTEEN

Calliope

After Levi ran away, leaving me alone in our room, my heart was beating fast. I had to take a few breaths to calm myself down and process what had just happened. The mate bond made butterflies swarm in my stomach whenever I was near him, but what really stunned me was the way I handled the situation. I felt him melt under my touch as he almost gave in to me. I couldn't believe I actually had so much control over him, even if just for a brief second. Maybe I really was capable of taming him...

As the minutes went by in the silent room, my nervousness died down. It gave me space to think of what my mate told me before leaving, and it slowly started to make me feel uneasy. He was usually busy with his Alpha duties throughout the day, and it never bothered me. But for some reason, his determination to not tell me what he'd be doing today really annoyed me. He gave me strict orders not to go looking for him though, and despite my bravery earlier, I think it would be best not to anger him.

In an attempt to distract myself, I decided to go for a walk around the packhouse once I was done with lunch. It didn't take long for me to come across Luna Calanthe, who was wearing one of her many beautiful long dresses. A smile lit up her face the second she noticed me, and she immediately held me in her arms.

"Calliope, my dear, I have been looking for you!" she cooed, making me arch an eyebrow at her. We had our lessons earlier - why else would she need me? "I thought maybe we could spend some time together, since my son won't be around today."

"That would be lovely, Luna Calanthe, but...has he told you what he'll be doing?" I asked, unable to contain my curiosity. However, when her smile faded, I was afraid I had crossed a line.

"He doesn't need to tell me," she replied vaguely. I decided not to push her. "Why don't we go to my room? We can have some tea, and talk."

When I nodded in response, Calanthe led me towards her suite. She was silent for the entire time, until we were behind closed doors. She showed me an apologetic smile, pointing at a chair placed next to a small table in the corner of the room, offering me a seat. She quickly prepared us some tea before joining me.

"Levi has been through a lot, Cal." She poured me some of the hot drink. I don't know if she wanted to explain to me what her son couldn't, or if she just needed to vent. "He lost his father at a very young age, and the event took a toll on him. It changed his view of the mate bond."

A twinge of pain struck me when I noticed her beautiful blue eyes mist. She was telling me her son's story, but her reaction told me it was a very delicate matter for her as well.

"Please, Luna, you don't need to explain anything to me," I reassured her, placing my hand over hers to comfort her.

"You deserve to know, my dear. He's your mate, after all." She took my hand in both of hers, squeezing it tightly. "I made a mistake on the night his father died. I shouldn't have been outside, and my decision cost my mate his life. I'll never forgive myself for it." Her voice cracked a little when she sobbed. "Levi blames me too. How could he not? It truly was my fault. But I don't think he's right about the mate bond," she confessed, staring deeply into my eyes. "Oh, Cal, maybe you're the one who can bring him back to me. He used to be such a radiant little boy…"

"I'll see what I can do. I promise." I smiled sympathetically at her. She looked away, standing up from her seat.

"I'm sorry. I shouldn't be asking you to do such a thing," she said immediately, cleaning up her tears with a cloth tissue. "I know he's been doing you wrong. I'm sorry I didn't have the strength to talk to him about it. You're a sweet girl, my dear, and you deserve better."

"It's okay, Luna Calanthe. None of this is your fault. And about your son, well… He's been a bit nicer these last few days," I said, trying to be as positive as I could.

The tears stopped streaming down her face as she smiled back at me. "Thank you, Calliope. You have been so patient with him." She hugged me before guiding me towards the door. "I'll stop filling your head with sad stories and absurd requests. Why don't you go find the Gamma Female? The two of you seem to get along quite well."

"Thank you for the suggestion, Luna. I'll see if I can find her." I nodded at her before walking out the door.

I hadn't talked to Hailey much after the presentation dinner, except when Trix invited me to hang out with them while Levi was busy. Where could she be right now? It would be much easier if I could link her, but I wouldn't be able to communicate with any other members until the Luna Ceremony, when I would be bound to the pack by blood. My best option was to wander about in hopes of finding her; instead, I stumbled upon Darrell. Maybe he could help.

"Hey, Cal!" He smiled brightly when I approached him. "What are you up to?"

"Nothing, really." I shrugged. "I was looking for Hailey. Do you happen to know where she is?"

"Oh, I think the Gamma couple is out on a date today. But if you want some company, we can hang out. I'm free for the rest of the day."

"That'd be awesome, Darrell."

The Beta had been extremely nice to me since the first day I arrived. Unlike Ivar, he was reserved, but he treated me with respect and kindness - something my mate wasn't good at showing me yet. He took me to the lake, which had easily become one of my favorite spots, and we started chatting.

I watched the sky fade to a beautiful shade of orangey-purple as we talked away. I was comfortable with sharing details about my horrible life back at my old pack, and Darrell was shocked to hear it. He too had some rough years after his sister passed. The more he talked about her, the more I wished I'd gotten to know her. She seemed like an amazing person.

"You remind me of her. A lot," the Beta said honestly. "Like you, she was kind, and had an inner strength she wasn't always capable of seeing. She was going to be Luna, too."

"I bet she would've made an amazing Luna."

"Yeah." His dreamy semblance soon turned into a playful

one. “She’d have to work on her organization skills, though. You should’ve seen the state of her room. It was always a mess!”

“Really? I thought Beta’s were supposed to be tidy and all.”

“We are. But she definitely wasn’t born with those genes,” he chuckled. “She once lost a slice of pizza in there. I was convinced she ate it and forgot about it, until I found it six weeks later when she asked me to pick up some clothes for her.”

“Ew! No way!” I laughed, and he soon joined me.

Our joking, however, was about to end.

I stopped abruptly when I smelled the tantalizing scent I had come to crave. When I turned in its direction, I was surprised to see Levi. His aura was so heavy it scared me. What was he doing here? He told me he’d be out all day. I flashed Darrell a confused look, but he was too tense to notice it. He had his hands on the grass, ready to get up, and his eyes were locked on Levi. I couldn’t understand his tension until a menacing growl came out of my mate’s throat.

The next second, there were shreds of clothes floating in the air as Odin lunged in our direction. Before I could even react, the Beta pushed me behind him, turning into a black and brown wolf in a matter of seconds. The two beasts engaged in a ferocious battle, and I was left to watch in horror.

There was something wrong about Levi. I knew he had anger issues, but why would he attack his own Beta out of the blue? His scent was slightly different too... It was sour and sickly. That’s what he had been doing all day? Drinking? The loud growls and whimpers pulled me from my thoughts, making my eyes lock on the two wolves in front of me again. I was pretty sure they were ready to kill each other.

"*We have to stop Odin, Cal!*" Nava called out to me in despair. "*They'll both get hurt if we don't do anything!*"

"*What can I do? We're not strong enough to physically beat either of them!*"

"*We don't need to!*" She insisted. "*Despite being a jerk, Levi is still our mate! He'll stop when he sees us!*"

I don't know whether it was her courage or the way she blatantly called our mate a jerk, but I was stunned. Either way, she was right - as Luna, I needed to stop the Alpha and Beta from killing each other. Taking a deep breath, I got up with clenched fists and waited for an opportunity. Darrell's wolf, Banyan, managed to push Odin off him for a second, and that's when I decided to act.

But I should have thought my plan through before I jumped in the middle of two ravenous beasts. The second he noticed me, Banyan stopped growling, widening his eyes in both confusion and fear. Odin, however, didn't have the reaction we expected. The alcohol and the rage didn't blend well together. He jumped in my direction, sinking his canines into the delicate flesh on my shoulder.

As soon as Odin realized it was me, he backed away, lowering his ears. It all happened too fast for me to assimilate anything. I didn't even feel pain until I brought my hand up to the spot where my mate's huge canines had previously been. My bloody palm was the last thing I saw before everything went black.

CHAPTER SEVENTEEN

Calliope

It was strange to be locked inside my own head. I could hear a buzzing noise, but the sounds were too muffled for me to comprehend. It was also dark...and cold, like I was at the bottom of the ocean, floating in the vast silence. It was peaceful and quiet, but also tedious and empty. Little by little, I started levitating towards the surface, where it was brighter. Two intense golden rays beamed at me, like beacons guiding me out.

"*Wake up, Cal!*" Nava called out to me, her radiant honey-colored eyes focused on me. "*Your body is healed. You're fine now.*"

"*What happened, Nava?*" I asked, but she had already closed her eyes, and I slowly opened mine.

It was normal for wolves to hibernate for a couple of hours after their human counterpart was injured; healing our body from deeper wounds drained a lot of their energy. While Nava rested, I was left to assess the situation on my own. My mind was blurry, and the light headache didn't help me think clearly. It took me a couple of minutes, but I soon recalled the last chain of events before I blacked out. I was talking to Darrell near the lake, when Levi showed up and tried to attack him. Then, I had the *brilliant* idea to throw myself in the middle of two fighting beasts. Why was the Alpha so angry?

"You think Levi hurt her on purpose?" A familiar voice pulled me from my thoughts. Ivar.

"I don't think so. He was drunk, and he seemed quite desperate when he brought her here," Trix replied. Were they talking about me? Where were we? "But he definitely tried to hurt Darell."

A low grunt escaped my lips as I shifted in the small bed, trying to recognize my surroundings. The all-white color scheme of the room reminded me of a pack hospital. My eyes eventually fell on the Gamma and Delta, blinking at me a few times before getting up from their seats.

"You're up!" Ivar showed me a bright smile, but his surprise soon turned into concern. "I'll get the doctor!" he said as he bolted out the door.

"How are you feeling?" Trix asked, helping me sit up in the hospital bed.

"I'm okay." Other than a mild headache, I wasn't in any pain. I brought my hand up to touch my shoulder, where Odin had bitten me earlier. I expected to see a nasty scar, but only found a large bandage covering it.

"Don't worry. The doctor said the teeth didn't reach deep enough to leave a scar. Now, you can say you survived the bite of an Alpha twice," the Delta joked, trying to ease my tension. "It must have hurt a lot."

"Honestly, I don't even recall being in any pain. It all happened too fast," I said sincerely.

"Oh, Luna! I'm glad you're up." A different voice echoed through the small room, interrupting our conversation

I turned around to find a man in his mid fifties smiling

warmly at me. He was dressed in a white coat, and was holding a metal clipboard close to his chest. Ivar, who was right behind him, was quick to wave at me. His goofiness made me chuckle.

"I bet the situation must have been scary, but thankfully, you didn't have any grave injuries," the doctor explained, carefully approaching me. "I applied an antibiotic cream to help your wolf heal you. She did most of the work, so it's normal for her to feel tired for a little bit. May I check on your wound?"

"Of course. Thank you." I smiled shyly at him, remaining still as he gently pulled off the bandage.

"As expected, you have healed just fine!" he announced cheerfully, taking a few steps back. "You're free to go, Luna." He bowed respectfully at me.

Before I could stand up, the Delta blocked the doctor from leaving. "Keep her medical reports private. We don't want rumors about this accident spreading around."

Her tone was firm, but judging by her facial expression, I noticed she wasn't comfortable with her request. However, as a Delta, I understood her actions too well - it was her duty to clean up the Alpha's mess. The doctor froze when her yellowish-green eyes locked on him, but he eventually nodded before excusing himself, and Trix moved out of his way

"Well, we should probably go to sleep now. We have training tomorrow." Trix winked at me. Ivar seemed oblivious to the fact she was referring to our secret sparring lessons.

"I'm sorry you had to stay here and look after me," I said quietly, rubbing my arm apologetically.

"Nonsense! We stayed because we wanted to make sure you were alright." The Delta waved me off. "Also, I had to make sure your asshole of a mate wouldn't disturb you. He wanted to stay with you until you woke up, but considering how bad he fucked up this time, I convinced him to leave. Thought you would need some space."

I widened my eyes, shocked at the way she disrespected her own Alpha. Ivar had the same reaction as me, probably still not used to her...honesty. He was the youngest of the ranked members. Trix, on the other hand, was the same age as Levi, which would explain why she seemed to know him so well.

I blinked a few times before shaking my head. "Thank you, I really appreciate it. Do you know where he is now?" My question was directed to the woman, but the Gamma was faster.

"He should be right outside. He and Darell were...working things out," he replied hesitantly.

The image that came to my mind wasn't the least pleasant; it made my heart stop. I had just witnessed the two men almost kill each other. After what happened, Levi could be even angrier. I wouldn't doubt it if he blamed his Beta for the accident, and if that was the case... Oh, Goddess! Without uttering a word, I rushed out of the pack hospital, leaving the Gamma and the Delta behind. They must have been confused, but I didn't have time to voice my concerns.

Since I had never been to the pack hospital before, its white corridors felt like a maze, but I managed to find my way out after a while. The moon was shining bright in the navy blue sky, and I wondered how long I had been out; probably a couple of hours. My eyes scoured through the green area outside until they landed on the two men sitting at a picnic table. To my surprise, there was no blood, or teeth, or claws. In fact, they looked so civilized I couldn't even believe they had been brutally fighting not long ago. I sighed loudly in relief, immediately catching their attention.

Levi's gaze locked on me, but he didn't move. Darrell was the first one to approach me. "Cal! I'm so glad you're okay." He gave me a quick hug, smiling at me. "I'm sorry you got caught in the crossfire. I should've protected you-"

"It's not your fault," I quickly reassured him, yet my eyes were still focused on my mate.

When the Alpha finally stood up, his Beta took a few steps back. Levi towered over me, but something about his aura made him seem so small. He was hesitant, uncertain. For long seconds, he just stared at me as our eyes engaged in a silent conversation; so much was being said, yet no words were being used. When he was ready, he drew in a long breath.

"Calliope..." Just the sound of my name coming from his lips made my heart flutter. Even after what he had just done, the pull still urged me to be near him. The mate bond was indeed dangerous. "I apologize for my behavior. I wasn't thinking clearly." He switched his gaze to Darrell, then back to me. "Can we talk...in private?"

"I think we should," I replied assertively. He began lifting his hand to ask for mine, but stopped abruptly, clenching his fist. Instead, he simply stretched his arm towards the packhouse, gesturing for me to take the lead.

As I walked in front of him, I didn't know what to think. Nava wasn't here to help me this time. Whatever happened next, I would have to take care of it on my own.

* * *

Levi

My eyes never left my mate as we made our way towards the Alpha suite. I noticed how she avoided looking at me, how her breathing was slightly labored, how her heart was beating faster than usual. Was she scared of me?

"She should be! I just attacked her! For the second time!" Odin howled in shame. My head was already pounding because of the hangover, and his self-pity tantrum wasn't helping.

But he was right.

After I hurt Calliope in my blaze of rage, a switch flipped in my head. I finally realized how much of a jerk I had been to her. She was so pure, so kind. Innocent even. She didn't deserve such a problematic mate. All this time, I thought I was in control, when I was actually being guided by my insecurities. I wasn't worthy of my beautiful Luna, but I was too selfish to let her go.

Ever since I'd met her, I denied my attraction towards her. I didn't want a relationship; I was responsible for my pack, and I didn't want the mate bond to make me reckless. But she was *never* supposed to get hurt. When I went looking for her earlier, I was ready to confess my feelings and fix the damage I had caused. Instead, I ended up causing her to suffer more. At least, the pain I felt made me realize I was ready to change.

I knew it would be hard to convince her, but I was ready to try. As soon as I closed the door behind us, I took a deep breath and prayed the mate bond would be enough for her to forgive me.

"I'm sorry, Calliope! For everything! Everything I've done

to you, every time I hurt you," I started, looking up into her eyes. "I was wrong. I thought I knew better than everyone else, but I don't. I have a lot to learn, and I see that now. I know you hate me, and you have every right to, but please, forgive me. I promise to be the mate you deserve." Once words started coming out of my mouth, they didn't stop. I had been silent for so long, bottling up my feelings. I used to think I was strong; now I knew I had just been a fool.

I waited eagerly for a response. A reaction. Anything, really. However, for long minutes, all I heard was...nothing. It was hard to even decipher her feelings, since her emotions were all mixed up. Studying them only made me feel more anxious. When her eyes finally turned to me, I hoped to see them shining with kindness like usual. Instead, they were filled with doubt.

"No one changes overnight," was all she said, making my heart shatter.

The pain I felt at her rejection... Was this how I had been making her feel all along?

"Please, Calliope." For the first time in my life, I begged. I took a step closer to her, ready to take her in my arms. All she did was back away, her eyes watching me with caution. Again, my chest ached. "I know I don't deserve your forgiveness, but please, believe me. I promise you I will never hurt you again. If Nava can stop blocking Odin, you will see our intentions are true!" I argued, raising my voice as my despair grew.

"Prove it," she demanded, making me stop in confusion. I was anxious, but she remained calm and poised. "If you really want me to believe you, prove it. Prove to me that you are ready and willing to change."

I blinked a few times, my heart fluttering with hope. "How can I do that?"

"By fixing the relationships you ruined before I came along."

"What do you mean?" Again, I was utterly confused and desperate.

"Your mother. Your Beta," she clarified, though I still couldn't quite understand. "You owe them an apology as much as you owe me."

"They have nothing to do with us!" I argued, frowning.

"Actually, they do," she stated firmly. "If you can't even respect your closest friends and family, how can I expect you to respect *your mate*?"

I opened my mouth to counter, but closed it almost immediately, realizing it wasn't worth it. After all, she did have a point. Still, I hesitated. I was ready to do whatever it took to repair our relationship. But was I ready to reconcile with my second-in-command? He'd done nothing but stress me out over the past month. Even worse, was I ready to forgive my mother after resenting her for a decade?

"Swallow your pride, Levi!" Odin growled. *"We are lucky she is even offering us an opportunity to show her how sorry we are. Don't fuck this up as well."*

As hard as it was to admit it, I knew he was right.

"Okay," I finally replied. At first, my voice was barely a whisper, but as I looked into her eyes, it became louder. Bolder. "If that's what it takes to win you back, I'll do it."

CHAPTER EIGHTEEN

Levi

For the entire week after my mate moved in with me, I couldn't sleep well. I blamed it on her presence, convincing myself that it made me uneasy. Also, as comfortable as the couch was, it wasn't meant to be used as a bed. However, deep down I knew none of the excuses I tried to come up with were true. The reason why I was restless was because it took all of my strength to fight the mate bond.

Once we mated, I finally started sharing the bed with her. After the stressful evening, tonight was no different. There was enough space on the large mattress for us to sleep comfortably without touching each other, but for the first time, I actually wanted to be near her. However, seeing how wary she was of me (rightfully so) I decided to keep my distance. Thankfully, she seemed to have had a good rest despite my presence.

I was used to my routine; I didn't need an alarm clock to wake up for morning training. Yet, I couldn't get out of bed immediately today. My eyes landed on Calliope sleeping so peacefully beside me, her delicate face resting against the white pillow. How could I have been so blind as to hurt her repeatedly? I instinctively lifted my fingers, ready to brush her slightly rosy cheeks, but stopped midway, sighing heavily. It was too soon; I couldn't risk scaring her by touching her in her sleep.

However, she seemed to be a light sleeper, because she suddenly woke up. I froze, afraid my gaze would frighten her. To my surprise, when her big honey-colored eyes landed on me, she showed me a gentle smile. It made my heart melt and my body heat up. Was I blushing? Hopefully, the darkness would cover my stupid reaction. Realizing we were just staring at each other, I cleared my throat, looking away.

"Good morning," I managed to utter.

"Good morning." Her angelic voice echoed through the room, so sweet and calming. It almost made me lose focus, but looking into her eyes once again I was pulled back to reality.

"So…I, um, have training…soon," I stated the obvious, silently cursing myself right after.

Why was it so hard to find the right words with her? What were the right moves? I am known as the most ruthless Alpha of the entire country. I don't think twice, I don't stutter. I'm assertive, known for snapping necks in the blink of an eye without hesitation. And yet with her, I felt so lost.

"I know," she spoke after my long silence.

I slowly placed my hands over hers, careful not to scare her. To my joy, she didn't fight me. For once, I allowed the electricity to course through my body. I had been fighting this feeling for so long.

"I can come back for breakfast, if you'd like," I finally said.

She pulled back for a moment, but her eyes never left mine. Her gaze was hypnotizing. "I thought you were going to talk to Darrell after training."

"Why do you care so much about him anyway?" I snapped

without thinking. In the blink of an eye, my calm was gone, and all I could feel was anger as my Beta's name left my mate's mouth.

I thought she would be afraid, or angry; I had given her many reasons to feel both ways towards me. However, she gently put her hand over mine again, squeezing it lightly. Just like that, my fury was gone. My muscles relaxed as I welcomed the sparks. The effect she had on me... It was insane.

"First of all, because I'm soon going to be Luna, and he will also be my Beta. Second, you agreed to show me that you are willing to change," she stated firmly. "If you can't even apologize to your childhood friend, how can I believe you're willing to change for a woman you just met?"

"You're my mate," I corrected her, immediately widening my eyes. A short time ago, I was convinced I would never let the mate bond guide my actions.

"You'll do it for me, then." Calliope's tone was different. It was strong, demanding even. She wasn't the obedient Delta anymore. Maybe I hadn't known her at all. No, that wasn't it; she was changing, blossoming into the Luna she was born to become. The only girl capable of taming the ruthless Alpha.

I sighed at last. "Fine. I'll talk to him."

She smiled triumphantly. "Good. I'll be waiting for you for lunch, eager to know how it went."

Since I was already running late, I just nodded at her before getting up to quickly change into my gray athletic shorts and a loose black tank top. I had to run a little, but managed to get to the training grounds on time. Darrell was waiting for me there; since he was the only warrior who could match my strength, we always sparred together.

Despite the events of last night, training with him wasn't weird or awkward. As Calliope said, we had known each other since we were pups. He was used to my mood swings and anger issues. In fact, he would often be the one to keep me sane, as a Beta should. But for different reasons, we both changed over the years. We both lost family members who were very dear to us, and it had an impact on our personalities. While I became colder, he turned into a careful man. We weren't playful pups anymore; we were grown wolves with our own scars.

The two-hour training session went by in the blink of an eye as I thought out my next steps. Only a few superficial bruises covered my skin, and I barely even sweat. What truly made me nervous was the conversation I would soon have with Darrell. I noticed the way he eyed me with caution all the time, trying to figure out my emotions, but he didn't dare say a word. He was ready to turn around and leave when I approached him from behind, grasping his shoulder. When our eyes locked, he stiffened.

"Are you busy now?" I asked him, unsure of how to begin.

"I have to take care of a few things, but I can start after breakfast. Why?" he asked, slightly cocking his head to the side in confusion.

"Can we talk?"

My Beta hesitated for a second. "Sure. Is this about a pack matter?"

"No," I confessed, looking away. "Well, kind of. How about we stop by the cafeteria to grab something to eat and head outside?"

"Fine by me." He shrugged.

There was only silence as we walked side by side. When

did it become so hard to talk to him? We were best friends; we used to hang out all the time. It felt like ages since we last had some down time together. Was it all my fault? The harder I tried to fix the damage I had caused, the more I realized how badly I had screwed everything up. Calliope was just the tip of the iceberg… I had hurt so many more people. *How could I have not seen it all earlier?* I shook my head, clearing my throat as soon as we stepped into the front garden. I couldn't delay this any longer.

"I'm sorry for attacking you yesterday." I cut to it, not bothering to measure my words. "You could've gotten seriously injured, and well…Calliope did." There was a pinch of pain in my heart as I confessed all this. "I was jealous, even though I had no right to be. I had been pushing her away since the day she got here, and I…I did the same to you." Shit, this was hard. I wasn't used to apologizing. I wasn't used to being vocal about my feelings. It made me feel so pathetic. But at the same time…I could feel a heavy weight being lifted off my shoulders. "You're my Beta, I should have listened to you from the start."

Darrell stopped walking abruptly, probably shocked. Honestly, I was too; in my twenty six years, I don't think I ever admitted my mistakes to anyone. I expected him to either get angry or shrug it off, since those had been the results of every single one of our conversations lately. But when I turned around to face him, I was surprised to notice a hint of sadness in his expression.

He sighed. "I guess it's kind of my fault, too." It was my turn to be confused. "I shouldn't have pushed you when I knew you weren't ready to find your mate."

"You were just doing your job. The pack couldn't wait for their Luna any longer."

"Yeah, but it was not up for them to decide. Nor me," he acknowledged as we continued on our way. "But after she got here, I noticed how sad she was, and I just..." He trailed off and heaved a sigh before continuing, "I just wanted to offer her some comfort. Be her friend. She reminds me so much of Marisol, man." His voice cracked at the mention of his sister's name. He drew in a long breath, regaining his composure before continuing, "And the way you treated Calliope reminded me of the Alpha who killed her. I just couldn't watch history repeat itself."

I furrowed my brows, disgust flashing in my eyes. Did my best friend take me for a monster? How could he compare me to such a cruel male? I shook my head, realizing I couldn't really blame him. All this time, I didn't notice how many lines I had been crossing. If it weren't for Calliope, I could've become a heartless beast.

"I might have been convinced I wouldn't fall for her, but I would've never gone *that* far." *Or at least I hoped so.* "Anyway, you acted right. Thank you for protecting my Luna when I couldn't do so myself. You went against my orders to ensure her safety. I couldn't be prouder of the fine Beta you've become."

By now, we had already arrived at one of the many picnic tables outside, where we would be having breakfast. For a moment, we exchanged looks, enjoying the unusual peace between us. My best friend smiled, and I found myself doing the same. I couldn't remember the last time my customary frown left my face. It actually felt...nice.

"You've been a great leader to Blood Eclipse as well. I'm sure Cal will help you turn into an even greater Alpha." He nodded at me, stretching his hand out in my direction.

Hesitantly, I took it. As simple as the gesture was, it meant a lot to us. It was our reconciliation, proof that we were both ready to learn from our past mistakes. This sincere handshake marked the rebirth of our friendship, as well as the death of our old, troubled selves. It was refreshing, but also scary to leave the past behind. After everything I had done, could I really change?

"*Our mate is changing, and she is encouraging us to do the same.*" I heard Odin's strong voice inside my head. He was a lot calmer now that I was ready to accept our Luna.

"*She carries the mark of an Alpha now. It's pushing her to be stronger,*" I observed. Ranked members had the ability to alter a normal wolf's genes by biting them, enhancing their abilities. It was the Goddess' gift to ensure all fated couples would have similar strength despite their ranks.

"*Yes, but it takes longer for the power we shared with her during the marking process to be completely absorbed,*" he retorted. "*There must be something else pushing her to change.*"

"*She used to be a Delta, but she has the heart of a Luna,*" I replied with a small smile. "*She's fierce.*"

"*There's no denying that,*" he chuckled.

CHAPTER NINETEEN

Calliope

After training with Trix, I went back to the Alpha suite to wait for Levi so we could have lunch together. I was quite anxious to know how his talk with Darrell had gone; even Nava was a little skeptical about how our mate handled it. It was sad to see how she had her hope taken away from her so fast, but it was somewhat relieving to watch her grow into a more careful, independent wolf. Together, we were learning to rely on each other rather than on other people, and I was slowly realizing how it made us stronger.

Also, the question Trix asked me a few days ago still rang inside my head, forcing me to search for purpose. To find myself. What *did* I fight for? All my life, I let others push me around. I always preferred to adapt myself to the world around me, squeeze into the shape people expected me to fit in. But for once, I was consumed by this drive to let my voice be heard and put myself first. Was I finally fighting for my freedom? Or was I fighting for the love of my mate, and the attention I longed for?

My train of thought was interrupted by the sound of the door. Standing on the porch, I turned around to find Levi. A polite smile crossed my face, and I watched as he nodded in response before walking in. I wanted to ask him if he had managed to reconcile with his friend, but he was mostly silent.

Seeing as he was in a much lighter mood than usual, I didn't want to ruin it by pushing him too far. If I really wanted to tame him, I had to be careful in order to make him bend instead of break, which is why I decided it would be smarter to wait until he was ready to talk.

A few Omegas came in at the same time as usual to set the table for us. I noticed how Levi made an effort to learn a little more about me during lunch, though he was still visibly nervous. It was the first time we'd actually had a meaningful conversation since I'd moved here, and it restored a tiny bit of hope inside me. I wasn't ready to fully commit to it yet, but for once, I felt like we were taking a step in the right direction.

As soon as we were done, he excused himself to go back to work. Before he left, he carefully took my hand, placing a gentle kiss on it. Looking into his melting icy blue eyes, I knew he wanted more, but he was respecting my wishes and giving me space. It made my heart flutter as I momentarily allowed myself to dream of what we could become one day. But I had to keep focused. I shook my head. It was too soon; I wouldn't foolishly fall for the mate bond again.

Once he was gone, I started thinking of what I could do in the afternoon. I usually had a busy morning, however, I mostly spent the rest of the day reading in the library or wandering through the lovely territory.

I didn't need to think much though, since the answer to my question came knocking on my door - quite literally.

"Cal! Are you busy?" Hailey chanted as soon as I opened the door for her. The way she matched her mate's energy level made me chuckle. They had clearly been made for each other.

"Not really. I was actually just thinking of something to

do," I replied honestly.

"Great!" She was already pulling me out of my room, dragging me down the hall. "Calanthe wanted you to choose the dress for your Luna Ceremony, as well as some of the final decorations. I thought it would be a great opportunity for us to have some girl time!"

I hesitated for a moment when she mentioned the event. After the turmoil of the previous night, I had completely forgotten about it. At first, I was uneasy due to my rocky relationship with my mate. But soon enough, I remembered that this wasn't about us. Blood Eclipse needed me, and I had to act like the Luna I was destined to be.

"Sounds nice." I forced a smile, hoping the Gamma Female didn't notice my insecurities.

When we were almost at the former Luna's door, she came to an abrupt stop. By the way her face was shining, I knew she had just gotten a crazy idea.

"Oh! We should invite Trix, too!" she suggested.

I immediately raised an eyebrow at her. "Is she even into this kind of stuff?"

"What do you mean?" Hailey cocked her head to the side.

"Well, you know… She doesn't seem to be much into party decor."

"Nonsense!" She waved me off. "Let me link her." Her eyes clouded over, and three seconds later, she frowned. "She told me to fuck off."

I couldn't hold my laughter. That was the most *Trix* response she could have gotten. But Hailey didn't seem the least shaken by it; she insisted the Delta would be the one missing out on all the fun. We took a few more steps until we reached Calanthe's room. She was quick to open the door for us, receiving us with a big smile.

The idea of how our afternoon would go seemed quite peaceful in my mind; we would sit down, drink some tea, and calmly look over beautiful options for the party. In reality, it was a lot more overwhelming. Both the Luna and Gamma kept throwing magazines at me, fighting over what design would fit me best, and I barely had a say in any of it. Most of the time, I just shrunk in my chair and prayed they wouldn't kill each other.

Surprisingly enough, I couldn't help but smile at the situation. I've never had people worry so much about me. To think they were working so hard to make sure I would have the best ceremony... It warmed my heart.

"I'm telling you, gold will match her beautiful eyes!" Hailey barked.

"Red will highlight her hair and skin tone! Besides, it's Blood Eclipse's traditional colors!" Calanthe frowned. I gasped when both enraged women glared at me. "What do you think, Cal?"

"I, uh..." I stuttered for a moment, afraid they would dismiss my idea. I flipped through the pages, pointing at a dress which had really caught my attention. "I was actually thinking about going with green," I revealed shyly.

The two of them exchanged looks, blinking a few times as they processed the information. For a second, I regretted saying anything at all. They would definitely come at me for not choosing any of their options. But then, they both smile excitedly.

"Green! How did we not think about that before?" Hailey

scoffed, as if it was obvious.

"Right? It's the perfect color for you, dear." The Luna brushed my arm gently before she leaned closer to scour through the options with me. "How about teal green?"

"Or forest green?" Once again, the two of them locked eyes. I expected them to start fighting again, but to my surprise, they just grinned at each other. As if they were communicating telepathically, they soon excitedly yelled in unison, "Emerald green!"

* * *

After a few hours, we finally finished organizing everything for the party happening in three days. I was a little nervous, but the more I talked to the girls about it, the more my anxiety turned into excitement. When I got back to the room, the table was already set and Levi was waiting for me. Although Nava wasn't ready to unblock Odin, she still purred whenever our mate's earthly scent hit our nostrils.

"Good evening," Levi greeted me, ready to stand up to pull out a seat for me.

But I was faster. "Don't worry. I got it." Once I was comfortably seated, he gestured for me to fill my plate. I obliged before I casually tried to start a conversation with him. "How was your day?"

He hesitated for a moment. It was interesting to see how the big bad Alpha was trying hard to let his walls crumble for me. "I...I talked to Darrell."

"Did you guys work things out?" I asked calmly, trying not

to pressure him.

"Yes," my mate's response was quicker this time. "It was... good, actually. I hadn't realized how much the two of us had grown apart. We decided to set our differences aside." He paused for a brief moment, thoughtful. "Thank you, Calliope. I really missed my best friend."

His sincerity made my heart flutter. "I'm glad the two of you are getting along again." I slowly lifted my gaze to look at him. When our eyes locked, he stopped breathing. "You should really reconcile with your mother too."

"Can we take this one step at a time, please?" He frowned, looking away, and I instantly knew I had crossed a line. This man was a hard nut to crack. I nodded at last, offering him a comforting smile. "What about you? How was your day?"

"It was great," I replied honestly. "I spent most of it looking over some options for the Luna Ceremony. I really love the dress we chose."

"About that..." He sighed longingly, slowly lifting his hand to brush mine. "With everything that's happened lately, I understand if you're not ready for your Luna Ceremony. We can postpone it until you're more comfortable with the idea."

"It's fine." I shrugged. "It would be rude to change it all after the effort everyone put into organizing it. And I'm actually kind of looking forward to it," I confessed.

I swear I saw Levi smile. Just for a quick second...but still. "It's settled then." He took the first bite of his meal, turning to me again after a while. "Listen, I know I haven't been the most reliable mate yet... I mean, I haven't been reliable at all." He frowned at himself. When his clear blue eyes landed on me, they were filled with regret. "But I'm a man of my word. I promise you can count on me for your party. I'll be with you the whole time. If it gets too much, just let me know and we can leave."

The way he looked at me, his concerned tone... I wasn't expecting it at all. A genuinely happy smile crossed my face as a fire started in my heart. He was showing me signs that he was really trying to change. Despite everything he did, I think I needed to give him credit for his effort. Of course, I couldn't bring myself to forgive him or blindly trust him again, but I liked the way we were slowly advancing down the right path. When we first met, we took it too fast while walking in opposite directions - I was fully giving into the mate bond, and he was denying it completely. Even after such a short time, I could feel we were both changing, slowly learning from our past mistakes.

After we were done eating, Levi sat on the balcony while he waited for me to take a quick shower. We stayed outside for a few more minutes, just quietly enjoying each other's presence, before we decided to head back inside and call it a day. He laid in bed beside me, and I didn't protest when he slowly inched closer to me. Once I closed my eyes, it only took me a few seconds to start drifting off - an effect of the mate bond; I felt extremely calm when I was near him.

However, before I finally left for the land of the dreaming, I was surprised to feel his hand reach out for mine. He stopped when I stiffened, but as soon as I relaxed again, he intertwined our fingers. My skin burned under his warm touch as butterflies danced in my stomach, and I smiled as I noticed him taking initiative. It wasn't much, but it was a start.

And it meant a lot to me.

CHAPTER TWENTY

Levi

Waiting for Calliope to get ready was torture. Following the pack's tradition, the Alpha wasn't supposed to see his Luna until it was time for the ceremony. After I repeatedly failed her, not being by her side during such an important moment was tearing me apart. I tried to convince myself that she was in great company with my mother, the Gamma Female, and the Delta, but the way Odin couldn't simmer down was driving me insane. Since Nava was still blocking him out, he was even more nervous.

I watched the golden skies fade into a dark shade of blue through the huge floor-to-ceiling windows as I impatiently paced around the Alpha suite. My mate's absence bothered me immensely, but the fact that I couldn't remain calm annoyed me even more. Raised to be the most powerful Alpha, I learned to control my emotions from a young age - well, except for my anger. *Control.* That word seemed to easily slip my mind whenever I was near Cal, or even just thinking about her. How could an innocent Delta have so much influence over me?

I finally heard the doorknob turn with a light click, preventing my thoughts from torturing me any longer. My head instinctively turned to the entrance of the room, and when my gaze landed on the most beautiful angel I had ever seen, I was at a loss for words. Honestly, I think I even forgot how to breathe as my eyes roamed over her with all of my concentration.

Calliope looked like a princess - a queen, in fact. Her long wavy brown hair was even shinier than usual, styled in angelic curly ends. A delicate silver tiara with a single emerald in the middle adorned her head like a halo. Her tan skin was already flawless, but it looked even more beautiful with a touch of natural makeup and dark green eyeshadow. Her perfect lips had been decorated with reddish-brown lipstick, making it stand out; I couldn't help but imagine what it would feel like to taste them now.

What caught my attention the most, however, was her emerald green dress. It was elegantly tight around her upper-half, accentuating her curves, while the long skirt was a little looser. It had off the shoulder sleeves with a lacy flowery pattern, showing just enough skin. The design suited her perfectly, enhancing her grace and natural beauty. Staring at her, I felt tranquil as if I was taking a stroll in the forest. And I wanted so badly to get deeply lost in her...

"Do you not like it?" she asked, worried after my long silence. Shit! I can't get one thing right with her.

"I love it." My voice was barely a whisper. "Pardon my loss for words, mate. You look stunning."

The smile she showed me was so bright it could light up the whole territory. Goddess, how I wanted to make her smile like that every day. Odin was howling like a hungry beast inside my head, begging me to tear off her dress and ditch the ceremony. I honestly considered doing it, but I didn't want to disappoint her. This was her special day.

"Thank you. You look great as well. Green suits you," she chuckled. Subconsciously, I straightened my silver bowtie and my white shirt underneath the green suit.

It took me a minute to understand that this beautiful woman in front of me was mine. Only mine. The mark on her exposed shoulder would let everyone know that. With a few more breaths, I regained my composure and strode over to her, offering my arm. I waited for her to take it and nod at me, signaling she was ready, before I led her out of the room.

I could feel my heart beating faster as we walked downstairs, arm in arm. It was hard to take my eyes off her, but I didn't want to creep her out, so I did my best to hold my head high and look forward. As soon as we entered the Event Hall, all heads turned to us. A lot of people had come to meet my Luna, but my ranked members were the first to approach us.

"You look beautiful, Cal!" Ivar chanted, bowing his head respectfully at my mate. Then, he turned to Hailey, who was holding hands with him. "You did a wonderful job, babe." The way he looked at her... Did I have hearts in my eyes when I was staring at Cal? Goddess, I hope not.

"She's a natural beauty. It wasn't hard to work on her!" the Gamma Female complimented, causing Cal to blush. It made it so much harder to fight my desire to kiss her. "Besides, I only did her hair and helped her pick the dress. The makeup was on Trix."

"What?" Ivar had a look of disbelief on his face. He shrunk with fear when the Delta glared at him.

"Just because I can kick your ass in a fight, doesn't mean I don't know how to dress up." She rolled her eyes.

"Is there anything the wonderful Bellatrix can't do?" my

Beta teased, making her frown. He laughed before turning to me, almost as if he was asking for permission. Reluctantly, I let go of Cal's hand, watching as the two shared a short hug. "You look amazing, like the Luna you will soon be." He smiled fondly, then turned to the others. "Come on, we should let them have some fun."

Darrel winked at me before he started dragging everyone away. My mate offered her hand back to me, and I didn't hesitate to take it.

"What do we do now?" she whispered, her eyes scanning the crowded place.

"The Elder will call us to the stage soon. Then, we'll go around to greet some important people, mostly other Alphas of prestigious packs," I explained. "I invited Alpha Kai, too."

"You what?!" Her eyes widened, and I immediately realized I had made a mistake. "Why would you do that?!"

"I thought you would like your old pack to be present," I replied, my heart beating faster in fear.

"Not at all!" She was panicking, but she didn't seem mad... thankfully.

"I'm sorry. I should've asked you," I sighed, my heart sinking as I realized I barely knew her even after spending so many days with her. "Don't worry. There are more than fifteen hundred people here tonight. We probably won't even come across them." I squeezed her hand reassuringly.

"I hope not..." She seemed to calm down, so I did too.

We walked around a little more, tasting some of the fine entrées and champagne. It didn't take long for the Elder to link me, informing it was time for the ceremony to officially start. I had previously briefed Cal on how it would go, making sure she was ready before I guided her towards the stage. The ancient man received us with nods before he turned to the rest of the wolves.

"Good evening, everyone," he started. Elders were at the top of the werewolf hierarchy, even above Alphas. He didn't have to speak too loud for everyone to go silent. "We are gathered here today to celebrate the new Luna of Blood Eclipse Pack. For almost a decade, we have anxiously awaited her arrival. Tonight, she will finally take her place as our rightful Luna!"

The second the Elder raised his hand in Calliope's direction, the crowd erupted in claps and cheers. She smiled shyly at the hundreds of wolves, holding her head up high. Becoming Luna of the strongest pack of the country was a heavy weight, but she didn't shake. Every second I spent by her side, I was more and more in awe of all of her majesty.

Once the Elder positioned himself in front of a marble pedestal, the guests went silent again. He gestured for us to come forward, and together, we raised our hands over the chalice.

"Calliope Gaumond, do you swear to protect and care for the members of Blood Eclipse Pack?" the man asked, loud and clear.

"I do," my mate answered at once.

"Do you promise to serve them with your life, rising and falling by their side?"

"I do."

With a silver dagger, the man sliced both of our palms open, our blood mixing and dripping into the glass. The metal made our skins burn, but only for a short time until our wounds started healing. By the time our hands were completely healed, the blood in the chalice had magically turned a light shade of blue. The Elder then raised the glass, showing it to the crowd.

"Blood Eclipse, welcome your new Luna, Calliope Gaumond!" At the man's command, the crowd cheered once again.

Offering my mate a reassuring nod, I gently took her hand to step down with her. She seemed a little dizzy, so I took the opportunity to slip my arm around her waist to help support her. Having her closer made flames dance inside my body while Odin howled with joy. I needed to draw in a long breath to remain under control. It seemed to have an effect on her too, as she soon turned to me.

"The first minutes after the connection to the pack is established can be a bit overwhelming," I whispered in her ear, not wanting anyone to notice how she momentarily lost her composure. I didn't mind it, but I'd hate to have to tear another high-ranking wolf's throat out for speaking ill of my mate.

"It's just... There's a lot of voices in my head." She held my hand tighter.

"I know the feeling." The moment she looked into my eyes, she showed me a sympathetic smile. Oh, how I wanted to dive inside those pools of warm honey.

Before I gave into my wild thoughts, I sat down at one of the tables with her to wait until she was feeling better. One of the Omegas working at the event brought us plates so we could fill our stomachs. Once we were done, Calliope let me know she was ready for the following part of the event.

For the next hour or so, I introduced her to the most

prevalent guests - Alphas and Betas of ally packs. I got along well with some of them, but I merely tolerated a few; it was part of the diplomatic work of a leader. Everything was going exceptionally well...until it wasn't. I sensed my mate tense up before my eyes landed on the two young wolves.

"It's a pleasure to see you again, Cal. And as a Luna! Who would've thought?" Kai's voice was extremely irritating, and the fake smile he showed my mate made Odin growl inside my head. When he looked into my eyes, I held my head up higher - I was easily five inches taller than him. "Thank you for the invitation, Alpha Levi." He held his hand out for me to shake it, and I reluctantly did.

"Alpha Levi! You look breathtaking. Green is definitely your color!" The black-haired girl had an even more annoying voice. She had so much makeup on her face I could barely see her real skin tone. If it wasn't evident enough, her bridal dress showed how desperate she was to steal the spotlight.

My Luna squeezed my hand tighter, still not uttering a word. I could feel how uncomfortable she was, and it took all of my restraint not to rip off the heads of these two stuck up siblings.

"Where is your Beta, Alpha Kai?" I asked, trying to hide the slow-rising anger in my tone.

"Oh, he was sick, so I brought my sister Chloe instead. Hope that's not a problem." He shrugged.

"Lies!" my wolf roared. *"Not only is this foolish man stressing out our mate, he also dared lie to us!"* He was one step away from hijacking my body. I'd learned to keep him at bay even before I met him - a very useful skill at the moment. I closed my eyes and pushed him away, not wanting to ruin my

mate's ceremony.

"Alpha Levi, your pack is so beautiful!" The moment I let my guard down, Chloe took my hand, pulling me closer to her. "As your guest, I'd love it if you could show me around!" She chuckled without a care in the world.

A loud growl made her freeze immediately. And this time, it didn't come from Odin.

* * *

Calliope

Surprisingly, I wasn't nervous at all about ruling over such a big pack. As a Delta, I was used to dealing with a lot of members at the same time, but I had never been the center of attention. I imagined I would feel at least slightly overwhelmed by the idea, yet somehow it seemed almost... fitting. Nava always told me we would find our place in this world, but I never expected it would happen by becoming a Luna.

Everything felt so right. The moment I started hearing the voices of my new pack members, all welcoming me wholeheartedly, I was sure I had found my family. Of course, the amount of people simultaneously reaching out to me made my head hurt a little, but once I learned to block their thoughts out, I was completely content.

That is, until I saw Kai and his sister walking towards us.

The grin on his face brought back the terrible memories of the days I used to serve him. I was never physically abused at Moonstone, but the way they treated me was inhumane. Despite being a Delta by blood, they made me believe I was weaker than any other wolf. That I wasn't worthy of anyone's respect. I was always cleaning up their messes, yet I had never heard a single 'thank you' for it. Not only did I lose my parents to this pack, but they also took away my confidence. Seeing them again made all of my conviction melt away, until I was back to being the weak and obedient Cal.

I wanted to scream at them for everything they put me through. To look down at them as I showed them the powerful Luna I had become. I parted my lips, but no words came out. I was petrified. Maybe this was all a façade; maybe I never grew stronger, and I was just surrounded by people who didn't make me feel weak. Part of me wanted to run away and hide. But then, I saw the way Chloe threw herself at my mate, and it made me stiffen.

The day I met Levi, Kai wanted him to pick Chloe as his chosen mate. Neither of them cared that the Alpha of Blood Eclipse was my true mate. Why would they? I was just their weak Delta. Not even Levi wanted me at first. Yet, I had somehow been capable of making the ruthless man beg for me. Want to change *for me*. Slowly, this new Luna was taming the powerful Alpha.

"Fight back, Cal!" I heard Nava roar louder than ever. *"Fight for what is ours!"*

I didn't know if she was talking about my mate, my pride, or my position. Maybe she meant all of them. I hadn't yet figured out what I needed to fight for; a little time ago, I barely had anything *to* fight for. Still, my heart started beating faster as a loud growl echoed inside my chest. My canines were showing, as were my claws.

"Take your filthy paws off my mate," I said through gritted teeth.

Chloe's eyes widened in fear, but she never learned when to shut up. "What did you say, Delta?"

"I'm not your Delta anymore! Thank Goddess!" I spat. By now, I couldn't tell whether it was me or Nava choosing the words. "I'm the Luna of Blood Eclipse pack now, and you will not disrespect me in my own home!"

She sneered, ignoring me as she turned to my mate. "Alpha Levi, I can't believe you have such a disrespectful she-wolf as your Luna! If I was by your side..."

I could feel my anger rising. For a moment, all I could picture was me slashing her neck open, her blood staining her pathetic white dress. It scared me for a second; I wasn't a violent person. I was a warrior, yes, but I despised meaningless killing. But as my wolf fought to take control, I almost wanted to let her do it.

"Enough!" Levi yelled, making the entire room shake. All eyes turned to us, and for a second, my mate seemed annoyed. I was afraid he would scold me for causing a scene. Instead, he protectively pushed me behind him before he grabbed Kai by his throat. "I want you and your sister off our territory, now! For an Alpha, you seem quite stupid." He scoffed, making Kai shiver in fear. "Don't worry, I'll teach you a valuable lesson before you go. Because of your disrespect, effective immediately, I declare Moonstone an enemy to Blood Eclipse. You have ten minutes to leave before I change my mind and behead you!"

My mate let go of Kai's neck, and the boy fell onto the

floor. His scared eyes locked on me, and I smirked at how our roles had been switched - I was now the one looking down at him. Another growl from Levi made the siblings remember his promise, and without wasting anymore time, they both rushed out.

A single glare from their Alpha was enough to make everyone stop staring. That was how powerful he was.

And I was now his equally powerful Luna.

When he turned to me, there was only regret in his eyes. "I'm so sorry I invited them. If I knew this was how the night would turn out-"

"It's okay." I smiled, his calm voice helping ease away my tension. "Sorry for drawing so much attention."

For the first time, I saw him smile triumphantly. "You just showed everyone present why you're my rightful mate." I was too surprised to say anything else, so Levi just took my hand, intertwining our fingers before he gently pulled me into his arms. "Come on, Cal. This is your night."

CHAPTER TWENTY-ONE

Calliope

The rest of the night was peaceful, thankfully. After Levi finished introducing me to every single one of his allies, we joined the other ranked members at our reserved table. We talked and drank for a few hours before the guests started to leave. My mate wanted to get me out of there much sooner, concerned that the whole situation with my former Alpha might have stressed me, but I reassured him I was fine. In fact, I had quite a lot of fun with our friends before we finally went back to our room to sleep.

It still felt a little strange to fall asleep beside Levi. While I was still guarded, afraid he could go back to being the monster I first met at any time, part of me felt comfortable in his presence. I wasn't ready to cuddle with him just yet, but I loved the way my skin would burn with pleasant tingles every time we accidentally touched. The furthest we had gone was holding hands in our sleep. As simple as it was, I really appreciated it; it was a small step I was comfortable taking, and it made me feel safe.

I woke up the next morning to my mate gently brushing the back of my hand with his thumb. As soon as I opened my eyes, I found his eyes locked on me, probably watching me sleep. This time, however, he didn't turn away when I looked at him.

"Good morning, Cal. Did you sleep well?" His hoarse voice was a little softer than usual; melodic, even.

I stretched a little before replying, "Like a pup." I smiled.

"Good." He sighed in relief, breaking eye contact as he sat up. "I'm really sorry for inviting those brainless mutts to your ceremony. I didn't know just how stupid they could be."

"It's not your fault, and it's been already dealt with," I reassured him, rising up as well.

Levi's gaze fell on me yet again as he carefully studied my expression. He lifted his hand up to my face slowly, asking for permission. When I remained still, he placed his index finger under my chin while his thumb tenderly massaged my lower lip. His attention focused on my mouth for a second, and I noticed his icy blue eyes become slightly more vivid before they abruptly locked on mine.

"I didn't expect you to publicly stake your claim on me last night," he whispered, leaning closer. "You can mark me too, if you want." I widened my eyes at his proposal. "It will let everybody know I'm taken, which might prevent the situation from repeating itself."

I studied his expression for a second, realizing he was dead serious. Honestly, with everything going on, the possibility of marking him didn't even cross my mind. In an attempt to think clearer, I pulled away, noticing how his face immediately fell. He respected my distance though, which I highly appreciated.

Did I want to mark him? The mate bond compelled me to say yes, but I listened to it from the moment I met my mate and it only made me vulnerable. He had started treating me better, and I could recognize his efforts to change for me. Still, I thought it was a little too soon. I didn't know if I could fully trust him. Nava still had her reservations about Odin, and she didn't let him reach out to us yet. Maybe it would be best to wait. Our relationship was finally starting to work out; I didn't want to ruin it by moving faster than I should.

"I...I don't think I'm ready for that yet," I replied honestly. I could feel his subtle change of mood, a hint of sadness in his pale blue eyes, but he didn't push me.

"I see," he uttered, standing up at last. He walked around the bed towards me, gently bringing my hand up to his lips. His sweet kiss made my cheeks turn red as my heart beat faster. "I have to leave now to take care of a few things. I'll come back as soon as possible."

I nodded in response, watching as my mate quickly got dressed and left the room. It was Sunday, which meant there was no training today. I wondered what he needed to do at such an early hour, but didn't want to pry into his business - or better yet, I didn't want to chase him by asking him when he clearly didn't want to tell me. Fortunately, I had my own routine to prevent my own curiosity from consuming me.

As soon as I was done with my Luna lessons for the morning, I headed out to meet Trix at our usual training spot. As tiring as it was, she insisted I would get stronger faster if I took no days off. I could definitely see my improvement, so I never argued about it. It was usually a little harder to sneak out from Levi on Sundays though.

We started our training session sparring in human form, as usual. However, we couldn't fight for long before an unexpected voice echoed inside my head.

"Meet me at the stables as soon as you can." I was stunned to hear Levi. His tone sounded a little more playful.

Ever since he marked me weeks ago, we never tried mindlinking each other. I couldn't quite understand his peculiar request, but before I could ask him any questions, he cut off our connection. I could reach him again if I wanted to, but I had the feeling it wouldn't be of much use - if he had the intention of giving me more information, he would have done so.

I got scolded by Trix when I cut our training session short, but she let me go when I told her Levi wished to see me. On my way towards the stables, I stopped by one of the many mirrors in the hallway to check my condition. The Delta usually avoided hitting me in exposed areas to prevent my bruises from being noticed before Nava could heal them, since we still didn't want anyone to find out about our secret sessions. As expected, I was in perfect shape; I just fixed my hair a little before continuing on my way.

The stables were located just outside the farthest left exit of the gigantic packhouse. It was a big wooden building, which I had only seen from a distance before. Horses were very sensitive creatures, and they rarely got along well with wolves. They got stressed as soon as they picked up on our scents, making it impossible for any shifter to ride them - unless someone raised them from a very young age, earning their trust over time. For that reason, I couldn't comprehend why Levi would want to meet me there.

I was hesitant as I pushed open the large wooden doors to enter the structure. It was quite spacious on the inside, though there weren't many horses. If I remember correctly, there were only four of them, three of which belonged to Levi, and a mare that was his mother's. I was afraid they would all freak out as soon as they noticed my presence, but to my surprise, they didn't seem to mind. Upon further investigation, I noticed each individual stall was protected by a magical barrier. I didn't understand a lot about spells, but I figured these ones probably prevented the animals from sensing anyone unless they entered their stalls.

"Over here, Cal!" My mate's clear voice pulled me from my thoughts.

He was standing at the back, waving at me from the furthest stall, which seemed to be empty. I slowly made my way over to him, both hesitant due to not knowing his intentions, and careful not to scare the other horses. A million questions crossed my mind as I shortened the distance that separated us. Though I was a little wary, I was mostly curious. Nava seemed just as confused as I was, yet she kept encouraging me to find out what our mate wanted to tell us.

Nothing could have prepared me for what was waiting for me.

When I entered the stall where Levi was, I was awestruck. I couldn't believe my eyes as they landed on the small creature lying over the hay on the floor. It was the size of an adult dog, and it was entirely white - an even brighter white than Nava, like it had been created from a fragment of the moon. Its fur was longer on its hooves, and also near the tip of its long, majestic tail. Its deep eyes were like shiny black pearls, contrasting with its purity. The most outstanding detail, however, was the big horn shaped like a crescent moon at the top of its head.

"What... How..." I was at a loss for words.

"It's a unicorn," Levi declared with glee, confirming my suspicions. "Come on, don't be shy." He waved his hand towards the magnificent creature. A little hesitant, I lowered myself to the ground, kneeling in front of the foal. Its curious eyes studied me carefully as I gave it some time to adjust to my presence.

Soon, my wide eyes were back on my mate. "How did you find one of those?"

"It wasn't easy, but I have my contacts." He shrugged.

"Levi, he must have cost you a fortune," I stated blankly, still unable to believe what was happening.

"It's a she, actually." He crouched beside me, his eyes full of sincerity once again. "And no money can pay for my mistakes. I'm really sorry about the way I treated you, Calliope. I don't expect you to ever forgive me, but I'll keep trying to show you how serious I am about this, " he confessed, gently brushing my hair with one of his hands. "Go ahead, pet her. She's all yours."

My gaze shifted between Levi and the little foal before I finally found the confidence to stretch my hand in her direction. She tried to back away at first, but once she realized I meant no harm, she slowly allowed me to rest my hand on her forehead, right under her beautiful horn. The next second, an intense light took over the room, and when I retreated my hand, I noticed a glowing crescent on my palm. It went away after a few seconds.

"Unbelievable," Levi uttered.

"What? What was that?" I asked in confusion.

"They say unicorns only accept riders who have a pure

heart," he explained. "I mean, I was sure you had one, but I didn't expect her to accept you so soon."

I couldn't help but smile at the little foal, who neighed in response. "I think she knows she doesn't have to fear Nava."

"I'm sure of that. I was hoping she could keep you company whenever I'm busy with the pack."

"I love her. Thank you," I told him sincerely, never taking my eyes off the unicorn. Her hair was so soft, it felt as if I was touching a cloud.

"Do you have a name for her yet?"

I was thoughtful for a second, before a bright smile lit up my face. "I will call her Crystal."

CHAPTER TWENTY-TWO

Calliope

The days following the unicorn foal's arrival were a lot less lonely. Most days, Levi was working during the afternoon, so were his ranked members. Sometimes Hailey would stop by my room to chat, or Calanthe would invite me to have some tea with her. However, I was usually alone with nothing to keep me entertained, except for the books I would eventually get from the library.

Taking care of Crystal was a nice change in my boring routine. I never had a pet before; in fact, the idea never even crossed my mind. Werewolves don't get along well with a lot of animals, and horses were mostly owned by Alphas as a symbol of status. There was a lot I still had to learn about how to raise a unicorn, but aside from doing my own research, the pack's witch had been helping me figure out the basics.

Not only did my new pet keep me busy, but she also kept me company. She was extremely loving, and once she accepted me, she always wanted to be by my side. I would spend as much time as I could with her, brushing her hair, feeding her, playing with her and taking her on short strolls outside the stables. As the days went by, I noticed our connection becoming stronger.

The only time I wasn't with Crystal was during the morning. As soon as I was done training with the Delta,

I headed straight to Calanthe's room to continue my Luna lessons. Today was my last day of training; according to her, I had excelled in the classes and 'graduated' much sooner than she expected. To celebrate, she invited me to drink a very expensive tea she had imported from China, called Original Da Hong Pao.

"What do you think, Calliope?" the former Luna asked me, delicately taking a sip from her own teacup.

"It's amazing!" I was honestly surprised. It seemed like an explosion of flavors in my mouth. "It's a little earthy and spicy, but also smooth."

"You have an expert palate!" She smiled amusedly. "It has hints of sandalwood, stone fruit, and molasses, which gives it an earthy feel. The tobacco notes are what make it spicy," she explained. I was impressed by her tea knowledge - I wish to someday be this passionate about something. "Now that you're a Luna, my dear, you are allowed to have a refined taste. The perks of being at the top, huh?" she joked.

"I don't think I'll ever get used to this lifestyle. I'm happy with what I have here," I replied sincerely.

"Which is why I'm sure you'll be a fine Luna." The woman offered me a reassuring smile. "But after the unicorn you got, I'm sure my son will spare no expense to give you a luxurious life." I noticed her eyes getting watery as she looked straight at me. "I'm so happy he's started to treat you right. After everything he did to you upon your arrival, I thought it wouldn't be long before you rejected him. I'm afraid if you did, he would be beyond saving." Her expression darkened for a moment before she smiled again. "Thank you so much for giving him a second chance. As a mother, I couldn't be more grateful to you."

I smiled in return, but I felt as if I weren't being completely honest with her. "I haven't really forgiven him yet," I confessed in a low voice. "He is the one who decided to change, I'm merely offering him an opportunity to prove it. Then, I'll decide if I can truly forgive him."

"Either way, it's more than he deserves. You are very mature, my dear, and your decision proves you have a truly pure heart."She rested her hand over mine, brushing it affectionately as she stared into my eyes. "It's all because of you, Cal. You're bringing my cheerful little boy back... I can see it." She sighed dreamingly, shifting her gaze to a family portrait on her desk. There were hints of sadness in her expression. "I wish he could find it in his heart to give me a second chance, too."

"I'm sure he will." I couldn't help but be empathetic toward her.

Calanthe smiled before standing up. "Let me stop before I start getting emotional again. I don't want to keep you; it's almost lunchtime, after all. Thank you for the company, my dear."

"I should be the one thanking you."

"Nonsense!" She waved me off, opening the door for me. "From the day you arrived here, I knew you would make all of our lives better. We're lucky to have you."

My heart fluttered at the woman's faith in me. She had always treated me kindly; she received me with open arms when not even her son wanted me. Like Trix, she played a big part in helping me find my confidence, and now, I really wanted to do the same for her. As I walked out to head towards my room, there were only two questions in my mind. First, was Levi ready to make amends with his mother, like he promised me he would?

And more importantly: Would I be willing to forgive him after he did?

* * *

Levi

It was a beautiful day. The sun was shining in the clear blue sky, illuminating every acre of my land. It was warm, but the light breeze made the temperature enjoyable outside. Taking advantage of the opportunity, I requested that the Omegas set the table outside so Calliope and I could have lunch on the balcony. Most times, she would come back before me, but today I sat and waited for her arrival.

As I basked in the sun, I thanked the Goddess for the wonderful mate she had sent me. I still couldn't believe she was even considering offering me a second chance after the cruel way I treated her. I used to think I was the most powerful Alpha, yet I couldn't even notice how my teenage trauma had still blinded me. My anger and thirst for revenge helped me get to where I was now, but if I hadn't met Calliope, I doubt I would be able to become the great leader I aspired to be. Of course, I still had a long way to go if I wanted to fix what I broke in the first place, and it wouldn't be easy. But I could feel her acceptance of me grow a little bit every day, and it was more than I deserved.

"You disrespect and deny our mate, and I'm the one who has to pay for it!" Odin's voice disrupted my peaceful lounging. We still couldn't see eye to eye after the whole situation. *"You convinced me to fight our feelings for her, and while Calliope seems to at least tolerate you, Nava wants nothing to do with me!"*

"I didn't convince you to do anything." I frowned at his accusation. *"You agreed with me from the start. I gave you control during the marking ceremony; you did what you thought was right then."*

"But I wouldn't have done it if you weren't so adamant about the bond making us weaker!" He snarled. *"I was ready to accept our mate that night, but* you *had to fight me."*

"What's done is done!" I barked back, repeating the words he said to me on that fateful night. *"Just believe me when I say I want Nava to accept us as much as you do. She is part of Calliope, and neither of them will truly forgive us unless they both agree on it."*

Before he could further annoy me, my beautiful Luna walked into the room. She was wearing one of the many flowery sun dresses she had bought during her first week here. A single one of her radiant smiles was enough to wash away all of my troubles. Once we sat at the table, she started to inform me about her last Luna lesson, and I couldn't help but admire the way her wavy brown hair shone under the sun. The way she drew me in was pure madness.

"You're officially Blood Eclipse's Luna now," I pointed out proudly. "You've had your ceremony, and today you just finished your lessons. I think it's time for you to fully take on your Luna duties now..." I made a brief pause, studying her reaction. I didn't want to pressure her. "If you want to."

"Of course, I do," she replied at once, and I let out a breath I didn't even know I was holding. "It's just...it's a little scary to lead such a big pack. My decisions can deeply affect so many people."

"It's natural to be hesitant," I reassured her, subtly reaching out for her hand. "But we'll do it together. This pack has waited a long time for you, and I know you'll serve them well."

She took a deep breath, smiling soon after. "Okay. Where do I start?"

* * *

I led Calliope towards my office; it was the first time she's been here since the day she arrived, the day I told her about my stupid rules. I couldn't believe how much of a jerk I had been to her, but looking into her honey-colored eyes, I had hope. She gave me strength to prove I could be a better mate, no matter how hard it was for me to change. She accommodated herself in the chair I'd recently bought specifically for her before I started briefing her on basic pack politics.

First, I gave her more information about the ally Alphas she had met during her Luna Ceremony. It was important for us to know who our friends were, and what they had to offer. Alliances are a two-way street, and it was important to keep track of how much one pack was able to help each other. Our contracts were updated annually, and when that time came, we should know which alliances were worth keeping, and which didn't yield fruits.

Then, I told her about Blood Eclipse's biggest enemy - Silver Waters Pack. I explained in detail about how their former Alpha was an ambitious man who didn't play by the rules. He didn't mind stepping on others to get ahead, and he didn't care how much blood he had to spill. The day he attacked our pack and killed my father was a big example of that. Honorable Alphas would confront each other fairly, but he knew he couldn't take my father down on his own, so he used my mother as leverage.

"None of this would have happened if she had just followed a simple order," I thought out loud as my resentment surfaced. It was hard to keep my emotions under control whenever I discussed this delicate topic. Knowing my mother was the reason I lost my father, resulting in trauma which almost cost me my mate as well, made me furious.

"She made a mistake, but her intentions were good," Calliope reasoned, grabbing my attention. "From what I heard, Darrell's parents were surrounded. If she hadn't helped them-"

"A Beta's job is to protect their Luna, not the other way around!" I snapped, but immediately regretted it when I noticed Cal wince. In an attempt to control my anger, I looked straight into her eyes and placed my hand over hers. Touching her always helped keep me sane. "A Luna is the heart of a pack. You won't win a battle if you leave your heart exposed. My mother knew that, and she still went against my father's orders. She was the one who killed him in the end."

"And how do you think that affects her? She has been suffering alone for all these years. Don't you think she regrets it?"

"Her regret won't change anything."

"Really?" My eyes widened as realization hit me like a truck. For the past few days I had been trying to right my wrongs, earn back Calliope's trust by proving to her I had learned from my mistakes. Yet, I wasn't willing to do the same for my mother. "Don't you think she deserves a second chance as well?"

I looked away. "I don't know."

"You said you would talk to her, Levi." She leaned closer, grabbing my hand in hers again. The sparks from our contact made me want to say yes just so I could get lost in her eyes for a while longer.

"Do it!" Odin begged. *"If this will get her to trust us more, then screw your pride! I want Nava to forgive me, too."* It pained me to see how miserable my strong wolf was.

After a long silence, I sighed. "Fine. I'll talk to her." I wanted to furrow my brows in annoyance, but Calliope's warm smile prevented me from feeling anything but love.

"Thank you," she uttered sincerely. "It's getting quite late. I think I'll check on Crystal before I go back to our room. See you there?"

I knew it was her sneaky way of getting me to meet with my mother now, but I nodded anyway. Part of me was proud of how adamant she was to get her way. She was already acting like a Luna, and I loved it. Even more than I loved the shy Delta she once was. With a long sigh, I left my office and walked towards my mother's room. I hesitated for a while, but eventually knocked on her door. As soon as she opened up, her eyes widened in surprise.

"Good evening, mother. Can I come in for a second?"

CHAPTER TWENTY-THREE

Levi

I was tense as I sat in my mother's room, face-to-face with her. It was unusual for me to be nervous, since I would usually just destroy or ignore anything that bothered me before it could even have an effect on me. She was one of the problems I chose to avoid; just looking at her would bring back memories of the fateful attack - the day I was forced to kill the boy I was and become a man, much sooner than I should have needed to. Once I decided to remove her from my life, I had no regrets. No fear. No feelings.

Yet right now, my palms were sweating and I couldn't stop repeatedly tapping my foot on the floor.

"Is everything alright, darling?" My mother's delicate voice cut through the silence. For some reason, the compassion in her eyes annoyed me deeply. "Do you need my assistance?"

"When did I ever need you for the past eight years?" I snapped, angry at her for assuming I had come to her for help. All this time, I had been working hard to fix her mistakes on my own. I noticed the way her face fell, and for a brief second, I felt something different - hurt.

"*You came here to fix things, not to make them worse.*" my wolf reminded me. "*It's understandable for you to blame her, but think about what our mate said. We let the past control us for too long, Levi. It's time to leave it behind."*

I sighed, agreeing with Odin for the first time in a while. "I just wanted to talk to you. It's been a long time since we last did that," I finally said. Her eyes shone with hope again.

This was impossible. No matter how much I tried, I couldn't find the right words. Making amends with her was harder than making up with Darrell. Being in the same room as her brought back my worst memories, the ones I had been trying my hardest to avoid. Looking into her eyes, I didn't see the mighty Alpha - I only saw the scared young boy who had just witnessed his father's murder.

"This isn't bad, you know." Once again, Odin chimed in. *"Your trauma has kept you in the past. In order to forgive her, you have to go back there. Face your fears. You have to be that boy again, even if just for a few minutes."*

"I don't think I can do that." My answer startled me. I used to think there was nothing I couldn't do. The Alpha of Blood Eclipse has always been unbeatable, invincible, even unstoppable.

"I know what you've been through, Levi. I felt everything you felt, and I know how hard you've battled with it all, both against your enemies and against yourself. I was with you then, and I am with you now." His words had a huge impact on me. First, Calliope decided I was worthy of a second chance. Now my wolf, with whom I had been constantly fighting lately, was offering me his full support. If they could forgive me, the least I could do was give my mother the same opportunity.

"I know you resent me, son," the woman continued. There was true regret in her semblance. "I made a terrible mistake.

Not a single day goes by when I don't think about it. After I realized the high price I had to pay..." She covered her mouth as she started sobbing, looking away from me. "I can't help but wish it would have been me instead of him. I pray to the Goddess every night, begging her to switch our souls. You had such a strong connection with your father. If he was here instead of me, you would be smiling right now. You would be smiling, and that...that would bring me peace. If I could-"

I couldn't listen to her anymore. Her misery, her regret, her fear; she reminded me of myself. All this time, I had been blaming her without realizing she had been doing the same to herself. After my father passed, she was in the hospital for almost a month. Not once did I go visit her. I thought *I* had lost everything while completely ignoring the fact *she* had not only lost her mate in the attack, but also her son. I shut her out when she needed me the most.

In a rush of pain, I hugged my mother. For the first time in eight years, I felt her warmth and breathed in her scent as she sobbed into my chest. And it made me feel...whole. I could feel my hate and anger melting away, and when she hugged me back, I felt her love again.

I don't know how long we stayed there in silence as I waited for her to calm down. I never had a way with words, but my gesture seemed to be enough for her. When she finally pulled away, her tears were dry and a small smile lit up her face.

"I'm sorry for blaming you, mother. I wish I could have seen what you were going through sooner," I uttered, pouring my heart out.

"You had every right to blame me. But if you can allow me

just the chance to fix my mistakes... I miss you so much, my baby boy."

"I miss you too, mom."

It was hard, but once we both cleared up everything, I felt lighter. As if a heavy weight I didn't even know I was carrying had just been lifted off my shoulders. At that moment, I was finally able to free the young boy inside of me, letting go of the past I had so tightly been holding on to. And of course, I was grateful to Calliope - if it weren't for her, I probably wouldn't have realized my mistake until it was too late.

As my mother continued talking to me, her sadness slowly turned into joy. We had a lot to catch up on, but we didn't focus on the past for long - we had an entire future ahead of us. At some point, she brought up my mate's name, and Calliope became our next topic. All of a sudden, I was telling her everything about the way I regretted treating my Luna poorly, and how I was doing my best to prove to her I wanted to change.

"This young girl has the purest heart I have ever seen. I'm sure she'll learn to forgive you." My mother's sincerity filled me with hope. "Can I just offer you some advice?" she asked shyly, careful not to cross any lines.

"Of course."

"Women don't just want gifts. Especially not Calliope. Instead of showering her with expensive things, you should take her on a date and be real with her. Tell her how you feel."

I was thoughtful for a moment. My mother's idea made sense, and she definitely had a lot more experience than me on the matter. Still, I didn't consider myself a romantic man. It was Odin's idea to give Calliope a pet unicorn. He was sure she would recognize our efforts if we gifted her something rare and meaningful. And as hard as it was to find a unicorn foal, I found one and all I had to do was pay for it. I had no idea how to plan a date...but deep inside of me, I felt brave enough to attempt it.

"I will try that. In fact, I think I'll find my Luna now," I informed my mother, already standing up. However, before I left the room, I looked at her over my shoulder. "Can we, uh... maybe talk again sometime?"

Her eyes widened in surprise, but soon the cheerful smile was back to her face. "I would love that. My door is always open for you, my boy."

* * *

I didn't have a lot of time to plan an extravagant date, but I figured something was better than nothing. It was around dinner time, but instead of eating with Calliope in our room as usual, I decided to stop by the kitchen and order a few special snacks for a nighttime picnic. I found my mate in the stables with her new pet, and the smile on her face was priceless. The magical creature had been worth every penny, and I wouldn't hesitate to spend it all again if it would make her smile like that. We walked together towards the lake, where we set everything up.

"You seem calm. I take it your talk with your mother went well?" my Luna guessed. The way her tan skin gleamed under the moonlight was incredibly distracting, but I held on to my focus.

"It was enlightening. Thank you for encouraging me to

see her," I told her before I looked away, searching for my next words. "It feels nice to have her back in my life, but it also helped me realize something else. After the attack, I changed. A lot. I thought I was pursuing my goals, when in actuality, I had just been running from the past."

To my surprise, she smiled. "Maybe we are not as different as it seems." She shrugged, making me arch an eyebrow in confusion. "I lost both of my parents when I was two years younger than you were when you lost your father."

"You're an orphan?" I concluded in shock as she nodded. I didn't even know it was possible to feel any worse about the cruel way I treated her, but I did. "I didn't know. I'm sorry."

"It's okay. It's in the past, and they loved me beyond limits for as long as they were alive," she replied sadly. "Their deaths changed me as well, but in a different way. I became insecure. I felt like I had to try and please everyone so I wouldn't end up alone. At the same time, nothing I did seemed good enough." It was rather interesting to hear how we had gone through pretty much the same experience, yet our trauma affected us in opposite ways. "But when I came here, I met people who showed me I was worth something. They gave me a reason to change... In a way, *you* gave me a reason to change."

"Me?" I was in disbelief. "After the way I treated you..."

"It was an awful experience, yes. However, it helped me realize I needed to start standing up for myself."

It hurt me to know I had broken her when she had hoped I would be the one to save her - when I *should* have been the one to save her. But deep down, I also felt...proud. I couldn't believe how mature my Luna was. She was only eighteen, yet she seemed to know so much more about life than me. Even being eight years younger than me, she was always teaching me something new. That was what attracted me to her so much. More than her beauty, her wits drove me insane.

Under the light of the moon, I couldn't look away from her dazzling honey colored eyes. They drew me in. In fact, every fiber of my body urged me to bring her closer. And for the first time, I didn't want to fight it anymore. Instead, I got so lost in the feeling I forgot to ask her for permission before I placed my lips on hers. I could feel her emotions, and I thought she wanted it as much as I did.

However, overwhelmed by her passion, I missed the hint of uncertainty mixed with it.

Our lips merely brushed before she hesitantly turned away from me. Her silent rejection made my chest ache, my heart being pierced by a thousand needles. As she breathed heavily, unwilling to look into my eyes, I froze with fear.

I had done what she asked. I had fixed the relationships I had messed up. Was it not enough? And if so, what could I even do to win her back at this point?

I could feel my hope fading away when I heard Odin's voice inside my head. "*We can still give her what we value the most.*"

CHAPTER TWENTY-FOUR

Levi

After Calliope rejected my kiss, I felt...broken. Lost. Up until then, I thought I had been doing good towards my path to redemption. Despite how hard it was to put the past behind me, I did it. I managed to earn my best friend's trust again, and more impressively, fix my relationship with my mother. They both believed me when I showed them I wanted to change. I was hoping it would be enough to convince my Luna of the same, but she hadn't known me for as long as they had. She had never seen a different side to me.

All she knew was the monster.

At that moment, my mate took away all of my hope, much like I had done to her not long ago. I knew very well I was merely paying the price for the shit I had done, but I thought I would be able to quit my debts at the end of the day. It hurt more than any battle would to realize that wouldn't be possible. At least I thought it wouldn't, until Odin's suggestion ignited my dream of redeeming myself again. I was ready to give up everything, to do whatever it took to get Calliope back.

But I knew I couldn't risk doing it just yet. I had already pushed her too far in one night. She needed more time, and regardless of how much it hurt me, I decided to give it to her. In order to fix the awkwardness between us, I simply put my hand over hers. She stiffened at first, but I could feel her slowly relaxing under my touch. We stared at the stars in silence for a few more minutes before I took her back to our room.

Even after my disastrous move, sleeping next to her helped me calm down. Odin, however, was still restless. He had been devastated for the past couple of days, as the fragile bond between us and our mate consumed his vitality. I was truly hoping I could convince Nava to let my wolf speak to her today, in hopes it would help her and Calliope become more accepting of us.

With that in mind, I decided to work harder the next morning to get out of training a little earlier than usual. Following my mother's advice, I intended to spend some time with my Luna before lunch to get to know her better and plan our next date. But as soon as I made it back to our room, I was surprised to not find her there. My first instinct was to link my Beta and Gamma to figure out if they were with her, but I quickly remembered they were probably still sparring. Then, I tried linking Calliope, only to be met by a block.

"Check the stables. She might be there with the foal," Odin suggested.

My heart was beating faster. It made me uneasy not to know where my mate was, and why she was blocking me out. Ever since I marked her, I only linked her once; I thought it was invasive to reach inside her mind when she hadn't fully accepted me yet. Still, I couldn't see why she would purposely block our connection. Instead of wasting time thinking about it, I closed my eyes and took a deep breath, deciding to do as my wolf said.

However, when I couldn't find her in the stables either,

I started to panic. Where else could she be? What was she doing that she felt the need to block me out? As I weighed my options, I remembered I still had one card to play before I sent the trackers out to look for my Luna. A mate's scent was stronger than any other wolf's for their destined partner. Still, our sense of smell had a limit, which made it impossible for a normal wolf to track their mate if they were more than half a mile away. Thankfully, being an Alpha, my senses were stronger than a regular werewolf's. If I concentrated hard enough, blocking out every other scent around me, I could easily distinguish hers. And once I picked up on it, I ran as fast as I could.

When I realized it led towards the packhouse, I was a little more relaxed. If she was inside the most secure building in the pack, she couldn't be in any danger, and she definitely wasn't avoiding me. Yet, I couldn't quite figure out what she would be doing alone outside of our room. I reached the secret garden at the back, and my eyes immediately locked on her. At first, I didn't understand what she was doing here with my Delta, but as I watched Bellatrix land a punch in my mate's stomach, I lost it.

My angry growl echoed through the place, immediately catching their attention.

* * *

Calliope

My heart stopped when I saw Levi standing in front of us,

fuming with rage.

What was he doing here? He was never free after training, which is why Trix and I had decided on this time to have our secret sparring sessions. So why was he looking for me today? My eyes widened as I realized he must have tried to link me for some reason, but couldn't reach me because of the block. We usually didn't communicate through mindlink, but after he interrupted one of our training sessions, Trix advised me to put up a block to prevent me from losing focus. Now, I knew we were both screwed.

"What is the meaning of this?" my mate roared, stomping on the ground as he approached the Delta.

"The Luna has requested me to train her, Alpha." Trix immediately lowered her head at him. I had never seen her in such a submissive posture, but she probably knew it was no use fighting fire with fire.

Levi's eyes switched to me for a brief second before they locked on her again. "And why did this request not go through me? You answer to me, and only me, Bellatrix!"

"She was only following my orders." I stepped between them to defend her, earning a confused look from the Delta.

When Levi's gaze fell on me, I noticed his eyes flick between their usual pale hue to a more intense, fiery blue as he tried to fight the beast inside of him. I hadn't seen him this furious since the day he attacked his Beta.

"Calliope, go to our room, now. Please," he ordered through gritted teeth. I didn't like his tone, and part of me wanted to stand my ground. However, I also knew it would be best for us to discuss the matter privately. As soon as I walked past him, I heard him tell Trix, "I'll deal with you later."

I kept my head high all the way towards the Alpha suite with Levi following close behind me. Old Cal would be trembling with fear for upsetting her ruthless mate, but she had been slowly learning how to deal with him. However, I couldn't help but feel a little nervous. Yesterday, it seemed like we were really starting to connect with each other. He was opening up to me, and though I didn't feel ready to kiss him then, I thought he was truly starting to change. Maybe I was right to hold my reservations about him.

As soon as the door closed, Levi began pacing from side to side, clearly distressed. In an attempt to ease his tension, I remained calm as I sat in one of the many chairs scattered across the room. A mate's touch usually helped their other half relax, but I knew it was best not to approach him when he was in such a volatile state. Instead, I just waited until he was ready to voice his concerns. He was hard to deal with, and I couldn't begin to understand what would have gotten him so angry, but I was patient.

After a few minutes, he finally looked at me. "Is this true, or were you trying to protect her? Did you really ask her to train with you?"

"It's true." My answer seemed to have two opposing effects on him. On one hand, he seemed pleased with my honesty, but if anything, it only made him angrier. "After the marking ceremony, I was...shattered." I chose my words carefully, both because I didn't feel comfortable sharing all of my feelings with him, and because I didn't want to further upset him. "Bellatrix found me the following morning, and we talked. She kindly agreed to train me so I could become stronger, as a Luna should be."

"A Luna has no place in the battlefield! You don't need to learn how to fight!" he barked. After what he shared with me last night, I finally started to understand where his rage was coming from, but I still didn't approve of his reaction. "You will never be anywhere near a battle! Besides, I'll always be here to protect you."

"I was a Delta before a Luna. It is my instinct to fight for my pack." He was ready to retort, but I was faster. I was adamant about getting this through to him. "It doesn't matter whether you will allow me to join you in the battlefield or not. This is not why I asked for her help in the first place," I revealed, and he seemed to calm down. "I started sparring with her so I could learn to take care of myself, because it makes *me* feel better. It helped *me* find my inner strength."

Levi's anger began to die down as he crouched in front of my chair. "If that's the case, I could have trained you myself. Why didn't you talk to me first?"

"You weren't the most approachable person at the time." The words slipped my mouth, and a hint of pain flashed in his eyes. I took a deep breath, regaining my composure. "And honestly, would you have let me start training if I simply asked you?"

He looked away. "Probably not. But the fact that you went against my wishes doesn't make me feel any less angry. I'm still the Alpha."

"And now you have a Luna." His eyes widened. "You have led this pack on your own for a long time, but we're supposed to do it together now. If you really want to make this work, you need to understand something, Levi. I'm not someone you can boss around, a princess you can keep locked away in a tower. I have my own wishes too, and I should have as much power as you around here."

The Alpha stood back up with a heavy sigh, letting his head fall backwards as he covered his face with his palms. He turned away, pinching the bridge of his nose as he processed the information. I was afraid of how he would take it; until now, no one dared to defy him. His desires were absolute, as were his orders. I expected him to be at least a little reluctant to share his power, but when he looked at me again, I was surprised to find understanding in his eyes. He offered me his hand to help me up, not wasting a second before snaking his arms around me.

"Fine. You are my Luna, and you shall get what you want." His words definitely shocked me, but when his fingers delicately brushed against my cheek, I couldn't hold back a small smile. "But I have two conditions."

"And what would they be, my Alpha?" I whispered. My heart was beating faster because of his proximity, but for once, I actually enjoyed it.

A small grunt left his lips as he pulled me closer, our lips almost touching. "First, I'll let you continue your training, as long as you do it where I can keep an eye on you, make sure you are safe. You can join warrior training in the morning with me."

"Seems fair. And?"

"And...I don't want you to hide anything from me for now on. If we're supposed to rule together, I should have the right to be aware of your decisions." He leaned closer, brushing his lips against my ear. "I want no more secrets between us."

CHAPTER TWENTY-FIVE

Calliope

The following days after my talk with Levi, I really felt our bond strengthen. Not because he was trying to make me swoon - he hadn't tried to make another move on me, which I appreciated - but because he was finally treating me as his equal.

After he fixed things with his mother and Beta, I allowed myself to hope that he could become the man he said he wanted to be - the man I deserved. Even if I weren't ready to have a physical connection with him yet, I had the feeling we were taking small steps in the right direction. His outburst made me fear we would lose the small progress we had done, but his understanding surprised me. For once, I could envision a healthy relationship between us.

He had truly been making an effort to include me in most pack matters lately, patiently teaching me a lot about politics, and even asking for my opinion on topics I had a better grasp of. There were certain subjects I was even more familiar with than him, and he was starting to realize that having a former Delta as his Luna could be quite helpful. After all, I already had a pretty good notion of how to deal with pack members - something the ruthless Alpha hadn't bothered learning until now.

Following his request, I joined warrior training with him in the morning. I was still sparring with Trix, only now we didn't do it in secret anymore. At first, the other pack members seemed confused about my presence in the gym, but of course, no one dared to question the Alpha's decision. I was also improving a lot with Darrell's assistance. The Delta was a good teacher, but having an actual coach to correct my mistakes made me progress much faster.

Once we started working side by side, we got to spend a lot more time together, which helped us understand each other better. Little by little, we were both starting to leave the past behind, and I started to consider building a future with him. I didn't forget the poor way Levi treated me when I arrived, or the many times he had hurt me; however, I was slowly learning to move past it.

I knew how hard it was to change, and I recognized his constant attempts at becoming a better mate. It made me believe in a possible new beginning for our relationship. Even Nava seemed to be warming up to him, surprisingly. Since our minds were connected, I didn't need to talk to her to find out that she was considering unblocking her wolf mate.

The only time I wasn't with Levi was in the evening, when I would go to the stables to care for Crystal while he stayed in his office to finish some paperwork. Calanthe would usually come with me to check on her mare, Edelweiss, which was almost as white as my unicorn. The former Luna seemed a lot more radiant after her reconciliation with her son, and I couldn't be happier for them. She was also good company for me. I really treasured our moments together.

"Crystal is growing quite fast," Calanthe observed as she

brushed her mare's blonde mane.

"Definitely," I chuckled. According to the seller Levi got her from, she was only two years old, yet she had pretty much doubled in size since she arrived. "From what I read, a unicorn's growth depends on how much love they're given, so they might grow slower or faster than horses."

"They truly are magical creatures, aren't they?" she said in amusement. "It's not surprising that she's getting so big, then. Anyone can see how affectionate she is towards you." Almost as if Crystal could understand her words, she pushed her long nose against my hand, asking me to pet her. "At this rate, you'll be able to ride her in no time."

"I'm really looking forward to it," I confessed, smiling at my pet. "I've been planning on introducing her to other werewolves, so she won't be afraid to leave the stables."

"That's a wonderful idea," she chanted.

The next second, I sensed Crystal's agitation as a delicious smell hit my nostrils. I instinctively lifted my head up to find Levi standing at the entrance of the stables. He had his usual neutral semblance, but I could hear his heart beating faster, evincing his happiness to see me. It immediately made my own heart flutter.

"Good evening, mother." He nodded at the older woman before turning to me. "I'm done for the day."

"Oh, okay." I caressed the filly's cheek one last time before whispering to her, "I'll be back tomorrow, Crystal." She neighed in response, making me laugh slightly.

As I walked out, I said my goodbyes to Calanthe before I finally met Levi outside. It was a beautiful night; the houses already had their lights off, making it easier to spot the many stars in the navy blue sky. The green grass danced in the mild breeze, adding movement to the calm landscape. My attention turned to my mate when he grabbed my hand, intertwining our fingers. Along with the usual sparks, I could instantly feel his passion, as well as a hint of nervousness. He wasn't a man of many words, but his gestures spoke loudly.

"It's such a lovely night," I observed in an attempt to break the tension.

"Indeed," he replied, staring into my eyes for a while. He cleared his throat when he turned away. "Would you like to take a stroll? Or are you tired?"

"I'd love to. It's refreshing to spend some time outside, especially when the weather is so nice."

He stayed silent for a second, searching for the right words. "I was wondering if...If there was any chance Nava would be willing to...talk to Odin?" His request stunned me for a moment, but the idea of seeing his beast again didn't scare me as much anymore. He seemed to have sensed my hesitation as he soon went on, "I know he hurt you - we hurt you. But we're changing."

"I can see that," I reassured him.

"But you don't fully believe it yet," he pointed out, catching me by surprise. "Maybe...maybe if you can feel what we're feeling, you will understand that we mean it. Please, at least allow him a chance to apologize. It's killing him not being able to communicate with either of you in any way." His despair made me feel slightly bad.

"I'm not sure, Cal," my wolf replied immediately. *"Part of me wants to talk to him. I know I'll never see a different side to him if I keep blocking him out, but...I still can't get that image out of*

my head. His cold eyes..."

"I know," I sighed. *"I don't want to pressure you. I'll just tell him we need more time."*

As soon as we reached an agreement, I cut our connection to turn my attention back to Levi. My heart ached as I found his clear blue eyes filled with expectation. They drew me in, and for a moment, I almost wanted to say yes just so his pain would go away, but I knew it wouldn't be fair to my counterpart. I looked away and into the deep forest, readying myself to turn him down a second time.

"Nava said-" I started, but before I could finish my sentence, an unexpected thud distracted me.

I turned around to find the ruthless Alpha of the Blood Eclipse Pack with his knees on the grass in front of me. I gasped in disbelief. The gesture might not mean much to humans, but to wolves, it meant a lot. It was a sign of submission. Looking down at Levi for the first time felt uncanny, but...I couldn't deny that it satisfied the Luna side of me. I didn't quite understand what he was doing at first, but it soon became clear as day.

He was offering me what he valued most - his power.

Wolves of Alpha blood were extremely dominant. They bowed to no one. Showing submission went against their nature. It was evident in the way my mate's muscles contracted as he fought his own instincts. I watched in horror as he gritted his teeth and held his breath. He seemed to be in actual pain.

"Levi, stand up!" I demanded, but he didn't budge.

"No. Not until I get this through to you, Calliope," he insisted. When his eyes locked on me again, it was like I could see through his soul. Although Nava was still blocking his emotions, I could understand them perfectly. "I am yours, whether you want to claim me or not. I'm begging you, my Luna. Allow me to show you how sorry I am."

I was at a loss for words, my heart beating faster. What should I do?

"I'll talk to him!" Nava screeched inside my head, confusing me. *"I...I'll talk to Odin,"* she repeated in a calmer voice.

"Are you sure? Nava, if you're not ready-"

"I'm sure. I can't stand seeing him like this. It just...It doesn't feel right," she whined.

With a deep breath, I nodded at her before stepping closer to Levi. He was still struggling to remain in his spot in front of me, but as soon as I rested my hand on his shoulder, he seemed to relax a little bit.

"Stand up, Levi," I repeated. "Nava said she will talk to Odin, but you have to stand up first." His eyes widened with hope, and he finally obliged. The moment he did, I sighed in relief.

"Thank you, Calliope." He inched closer, ready to pull me into his arms, but I gently stopped him by placing my palm on his chest.

"On one condition." I heard his heart stop beating before I went on. "Let me talk to him first."

"Of course. Anything you want."

As we stood near the tall stone walls that enclosed the territory, both Levi and I hesitated for a second. The outcome of this conversation could have a great impact on our relationship. Our bond would never be complete until the four of us accepted each other, and considering mine and Nava's trauma, Odin would have to put on quite a show to get our trust back.

"Alright." The Alpha sighed at last. "I'll let him take control now. If you start feeling uncomfortable at any moment, just call my name and I'll force him to retreat."

"Okay. I'm ready."

Drawing in a long breath, Levi closed his eyes. When they reopened, they had become much more intense - a vivid blue, beautiful, but dangerous.

"Mate." Odin's voice was slightly deeper than his counterpart's. He rushed over to me, his firm hands gripping my waist with the roughness of a beast. However, he didn't seem fearsome, he seemed lost. "Thank you for allowing me a chance to talk to you. You deserve my apology as much as Nava does, Calliope. I broke you both."

I couldn't help but feel slightly sad for him. In one of Levi's many attempts to convince me of how serious he was, he mentioned his wolf was getting quieter and weaker because Nava was blocking him out, but I had no idea how serious he was until now.

"I am listening. We both are."

His eyes glistened with hope. "At first, I blamed my human for everything that happened. I failed to recognize my mistakes." He pulled me closer, inhaling my scent as if it was his oxygen. "It's true that he was reluctant about falling for you, but so was I. For the most part, I agreed with him. We were both wrong. Still, I was the one who physically hurt you. The marking is a special moment, and I didn't have to be so cruel. I shouldn't have been so cruel. Once our connection was established and I felt your pain, it destroyed me." As he traced the mark on my neck with his fingertips, he winced, regret flashing in his expression. "All I was thinking about then was to not let the mate bond control me. I had no intention of hurting you, mate. I will never do such a thing again. Please, mate, forgive me," he begged.

My heart sank, and a low whimper from Nava let me know she felt his pain too. "*Tell him to shift. I need to see him again.*"

"Will you show us your true form, Odin?" I asked him, following her request.

"Whatever you want, mate."

After taking a few steps back, the man's body began to change. In less than a second, the tall beast with metallic gray fur and vivid blue eyes was standing a few inches away, towering over us. He lowered his head to stay at my eye-level, showing me he meant no harm. I couldn't help but stretch my hand out in his direction, caressing his muzzle. Nava and I had only seen Odin twice - in both cases, he was a ferocious beast ready to draw blood. Today, he was more like a lost puppy. Seeing him so weak and vulnerable seemed to flip a switch inside of us.

"*Can I come out, Cal?*"

I nodded at her before closing my eyes."*Sure.*"

Once our transformation was complete, my white wolf stood tall in front of her mate. We were still a lot smaller than him, but with his head low, he wasn't as intimidating. The way Odin's tail wagged shyly evinced his joy to see our animal form, but he didn't move; he stayed still, afraid he would scare us if he came closer.

I definitely wasn't expecting what he did next. Nava's honey-colored eyes widened as she watched our mate drop to the floor, exposing his neck to her. Despite being an Alpha, he was so desperate for our affection that he didn't mind submitting to us, much like his human had done a moment ago. It took us a moment to fully understand what he wanted, but his insistent cries quickly made it clear.

"*He wants me to mark him...*" my wolf revealed in disbelief. "*The same way he marked me.*"

"*Please, mate,*" Odin's voice echoed inside our heads. For a second, Nava let her guard down and he managed to break through her barrier. "*Please, let me in. Give me your mark. Make me yours.*"

There was a fire burning in our chest as my wolf approached her mate still lying on the floor. For a few seconds, she just stared at him thoughtfully. Then, a low growl echoed through her throat and she bared her fangs at him, sinking her canines deep into his neck. I couldn't tell if Odin was howling in pain or in joy - possibly a combination of both - but there was pure happiness in his eyes when Nava pulled away. Although the taste of his blood was still in our mouth, his wound had already healed. And it was incredibly satisfying to see our mark on him, our bond finally complete.

Odin rose from the ground slowly, asking for permission before he dove his muzzle into the fur around Nava's neck. It didn't take him long to find our mark, and the moment his tongue flicked over it, the electricity set my heart on fire. Nava followed his lead, licking the mark she had just placed on him, which caused the beast to purr in delight.

Before they could go any further, Levi took back control,

and so did I. Back to our human forms, we remained in silence as the sound of our rapidly beating hearts echoed through the forest. There was a strong force pulling me towards him; we had finally completed the marking process, and our bodies craved each other. I was still hesitant, but Levi seemed to have no more doubts as he rushed over to me, his lips roughly capturing mine. As his hands traveled down my curves, I felt something hard press against my stomach, reminding me we were both still naked. In the middle of the forest. In any other circumstance, it would have felt wrong, but now, it seemed extremely right.

In a quick movement, Levi laid me on the floor under him, my back resting against the grass. Everything was happening so fast. My emotions were overwhelming. I had been dismissing them for so long, I hadn't realized how dire my desire had become. In a mess of hot breaths and wet tongues, I instinctively parted my legs, feeling his tip press against my entrance.

"Can I have you, Calliope?" he breathed out desperately.

"You already had me once," I recalled.

"No, I used you. And you used me." He was right - the first time we mated, we were both playing each other. Back then, I wanted control, and he wanted release. "I wanna worship your body like it's the first time. It *will* be our first time. Can I do that?"

"Yes, Alpha," I replied hungrily. I have used those two words many times as a sign of submission. But now, repeating them made me feel powerful. He was my Alpha, and I was his Luna.

A loud roar escaped his lips as he plunged inside of me,

soon mixing with the sound of my first moan. I thought I would be used to the sensation of having him inside of me, but it was completely different. I could feel his emotions, his hunger, his fire - it made the experience so much more overwhelming, in an amazingly good way. He started moving slowly, my walls tightening every time he pulled out, only to expand again when he pushed back in. While his length stroked my insides thoroughly, his mouth was still on mine, allowing me to taste him. He knew exactly how to please me, and it drove me insane.

Every single one of his thrusts was slightly faster, reaching deeper than the last. The fullness I felt was bewildering, causing my moans to grow louder. I gasped when his lips left my mouth to curl around my nipple, gently biting and sucking on it. The pressure of his body moving against mine made me want to wrap my legs around his waist, to pull him closer to me. The heat inside of me was unbearable as I felt my core getting wetter.

"Levi!" I cried out his name, lost in lust.

"What is it, my Luna?" he muttered in between kisses, his lips traveling down my neck. "Everything you want, you shall have."

"I'm so close!"

A smirk crossed his face before he switched our positions, sitting up so I straddled his lap without removing himself from me. I let my head fall backwards as he kept pounding me. My nails instinctively dug onto his back, ripping a groan from his throat, which only encouraged him to go harder. I could feel the pleasure building up inside of me. I was inches away from my release.

"Mark me, Calliope!" he pleaded, my eyes snapping open to look at him. There was only love in his eyes. "Make me yours, too!"

Another thrust made it unable to think - I just obliged. My canines elongated and I mercilessly sunk them into Levi's neck, on the exact spot Nava had marked him moments ago. The second I did, a roar of pure pleasure left my mate, at the same time his dick started throbbing inside of me. As he exploded inside of me, he too bit down on my shoulder, forcing me to reach my climax. He held my trembling body to prevent me from falling while I enjoyed the long wave of ecstasy.

As I started to come back down, Levi pulled me closer to his chest and lied back down on the grass, trying to catch his own breath. I laid on top of him in the middle of the forest, feeling whole. For once, I was safe in his company, and I didn't feel bad for wanting him near. Since Nava stopped blocking Odin out, I knew he wanted me too.

"You're finally mine," I whispered in disbelief.

"I've always been yours," he replied quickly, brushing his nose against mine. "I was just too foolish to admit it before."

CHAPTER TWENTY-SIX

Levi

I had been sleeping in the bed with Calliope for weeks now, yet today, it felt like the first time. In a sense, it was; for the first time, there were no barriers between us. No walls, neither mine, nor hers. No secrets. No hidden past. She never voiced her forgiveness to me, but I could feel it in the way she rested peacefully in my arms. I could literally *feel* it, because her wolf stopped blocking us out. And how magical it was to sense her tranquility, her passion, her kindness.

Finally, we were one, as it was always supposed to be. If it weren't for the twisted lessons I learned as a scared, cowardly boy, I wouldn't have had to wait so long to have her. Either way, it was in the past - at least, for me. I had no intentions of going back to being the cruel beast who denied the mate bond, but I knew it would still take a while for my Luna to get the image of the old me out of her mind. Until then, I would keep showering her with the love and attention she deserved in hopes that the bad memories would eventually be replaced by good ones. I knew some mistakes were impossible to fix, but it wouldn't stop me from trying. Now that she had fully accepted me, we had all of the time in the world.

I felt her shift a little in my arms as she started to wake up. Since she joined warrior training, she was getting used to her early routine. I pulled her closer to me, planting a soft kiss on the top of her head to get her attention. The sight of her groggy expression as she turned around to look at me was the best image to wake up to. I couldn't resist the urge to touch her immaculate face, sighing in admiration when her big honey-colored eyes landed on me.

"Good morning, my Luna," I whispered in her ear, making her shiver in delight. I closed my eyes to properly enjoy the effect I had on her - after all, I could feel it myself now.

"Good morning, my Alpha," she replied with one of her beautiful smiles. It lit up the entire room, setting my heart on fire.

Calliope brought her hand up to my collar bone, gently using her fingertips to trace the spot where she placed her mark on me the night before. The look of pride and possessiveness on her face as she analyzed her work made me groan. My hands traveled down her curves, grasping her by the waist to bring her closer. Growling lowly, I let my tongue trail the mark on her shoulder, her sweet innocent fragrance fueling my hunger.

"Mine," I hissed, Odin's desires mixing with my own.

"*Mark her again! Cover her in our scent!*" my wolf roared possessively. "*Let the world know she is ours!*" For a moment, I considered listening to him, but I held onto my self-control.

"Yours," she replied in a low voice, looking into my eyes. "I think you made that clear yesterday. For the entire pack," she giggled, referring to the fact that pack members probably heard us in the forest the night before.

"Good. I wouldn't hesitate to take you again and again until they all knew."

"In that case..." Her voice became huskier as she brought her face closer to mine, our lips barely touching. "I'm not sure we were loud enough."

A fierce growl echoed in my throat, my grip on her tightening. Just her words were enough to make me hard. With my lust consuming me, I had to fight the instinct to rip off her clothes. In a moment of clarity, I noticed the sassy smirk on her face, which stunned me. She was teasing me, playing with me, and I fell right into her trap. The innocent Delta... She had grown into a power hungry Luna. And she knew how to tame her Alpha far too well.

"Come on. Or we'll be late for training." Calliope winked at me as she pulled away, leaving me feeling like a fool - but I loved it.

Once we arrived at the gym, I was surprised to notice I had regained my focus. For the past few weeks, my Beta had been able to land a few good blows on me during our sparring sessions, which used to happen a lot less frequently before. I would go as far as to say he could match my strength. However, today I finally seemed to have found my strength and concentration back.

It also made me realize how loyal my ranked members were to me. I had turned into a cold, stubborn leader, yet they never rebelled against me. While I was weaker, troubled by the mess I made, Darrell had the chance to dethrone me if he challenged me. Though Betas were the Alpha's right hand men, it wasn't uncommon for them to use their strength to usurp their leader's throne. The fact that mine not only respected me, but also stayed by my side and protected my mate when I couldn't do so myself, proved just how reliable he was.

It was as if I had been blind for the past decade, and my mate had come to finally open my eyes.

During the second half of training, I noticed I hadn't been the only one to regain my strength. Odin was back to being the powerful Alpha wolf who never let his guard down. Well, except to take a look at our mate from the corner of his blue eyes. She was still training with the Delta, and we were both taken aback by how fast she was growing. Despite being the lowest ranking member and a female, Bellatrix was one of the pack's most skilled warriors. To see Nava pinning her to the ground filled us with pride. Although we shared part of our strength with her by giving her our mark, the desire to fight and improve was still her own.

"Mate is strong. I love it," Odin purred. *"Though I will never allow her anywhere near a battlefield."*

"On that we can agree," I replied adamantly.

Once training was over, we headed back to our room and took our first shower together. It took us a little longer than it should have for us to get to my office afterwards, but I had never been so satisfied with being late before. There were only a few reports to review and papers to sign in the morning. I had previously asked my Beta to cover for me so I could take a half-day for the first time in years. This way, I would have the opportunity to spend more time with my mate and enjoy our completed bond.

When we returned to the Alpha suite for lunch, I ordered a special gourmet meal for us to share on the balcony. The sun was exceptionally warm today, painting my lands golden as if the Goddess herself had been blessing us. After finishing our food, Cal wanted to enjoy the pleasant weather for a little longer, and as we laid in the sun lounger outside, I took the opportunity to enjoy *her.*

"We have the afternoon all to ourselves, my Luna," I reminded her, flickering my tongue under and around her earlobe. Every time she shivered with pleasure, my dick twitched inside my pants. "What would you like to do now?"

"Mhmmm..." she let out a small, thoughtful moan, exposing her neck to me. I didn't hesitate to shower her delicate skin with kisses, giving extra attention to the spot where my mark had been placed. "I think I know what *you* want to do."

"I'll always want you. Your body calls for mine." I slowly lifted her sundress, my fingers tracing and squeezing her thigh, causing her to moan a second time. "If it were up to me, I'd stay in this room and take you until you could no longer stand." The smile on her face said she didn't completely hate the idea. I pulled away momentarily, offering her a few seconds of clarity. "Which is why I'm offering you a chance to choose. You should take it before I change my mind."

"Fine." She laughed. "I really wanted to introduce you to Crystal. She has been growing pretty fast, and I think she will have a better life if she learns to not fear other wolves."

"Whatever you wish, my Luna." I brought her hand up to my lips, kissing it. "I can only hope she will see the good in me, like you did."

"Well, she trusts me. I think that should be enough." She smiled before getting up to lead me to the stables.

As soon as we entered the wooden building, I took a quick look at my four horses. I had raised each of them myself, though I wasn't their caretaker anymore. Alphas rarely had enough free

time on their hands to care for one pet, let alone four. Seeing how strong Calliope's bond with Crystal was, I felt a pinch of guilt for buying the stallions just for status. Maybe I could use the opportunity to give them some extra attention as well.
When we walked into the unicorn's stall, she immediately galloped in my mate's direction. However, she hesitantly stood still when she noticed me. I didn't do a lot of research on her species before I bought her, but I knew they were even more sensitive than horses; not only could they feel someone else's presence without seeing or hearing them, they could also feel their aura. And an Alpha's aura was certainly scary.
"It's okay, Crystal," my Luna whispered, caressing the unicorn's neck. "This is my mate, Levi. He won't hurt you. I promise."
It is known that the creatures were extremely intelligent, but I wasn't quite sure whether they could understand human language. However, seeing how Cal communicated with her, it seemed as if her words were crystal clear.

At first, the filly - if she could even still be called that after she more than doubled in size - was apprehensive. Calliope stayed with her, soothing her with her soft voice while brushing her short pure white mane, until she calmed down. Then, my mate gestured for me to slowly get closer. The task demanded a lot of patience; every time Crystal would show signs of hesitation, I had to go back and start again. At some point, Cal decided to hold my hand, and it seemed to trigger something for the unicorn. In the end, she finally approached me willingly, offering her muzzle to me.

The moment I touched her, right under her magnificent crescent-shaped horn, was magical.

"Levi..." my mate whispered with shock in her tone.

"You're...smiling?"

It took me a few seconds to process what she was saying. It shouldn't be weird for someone to smile, yet for me it was. Ever since my father died, I hadn't been the same. It was hard for me to be happy, and even when I was, I was so concerned about hiding my emotions that the scowl I wore never seemed to fade away. Apparently, my mate had been able to break yet another one of my many walls.

"Well, two pure-hearted creatures accepted me in the last twenty-four hours." I looked into her shiny eyes. "I think that's a good enough reason to smile."

CHAPTER TWENTY-SEVEN

Calliope

I attentively analyzed my opponent as I waited patiently for her to make a move. We both surrounded each other in a careful dance, ignoring the noises around us as we studied our next course of action. I had improved a lot since I left my old pack, but I knew I still wasn't capable of taking down an experienced warrior with a direct hit. The clock was ticking; this would be my final chance to defeat her, and it made me apprehensive.

"Patience is key," Nava reminded me, as focused as I was. I nodded in agreement.

Finally, Trix stepped to the side, ready to land the final blow. After weeks of training with her, I recognized her strategy well; she wanted to confuse me. Her intention was to trick me into defending my left, so she could kick me on the right when my guard was down. I knew exactly what I had to do, but I had never been able to understand the situation beforehand and react on time. However, I was determined not to fall for it this time.

Aware of her plans, I didn't even look at her fist, concentrating solely on the leg she rose into the air. When her foot was inches away from head, I managed to grab it and duck, using the strength of her own movement against her to knock her down. I noticed her eyes widening as she fell, but I didn't wait a second; I threw myself on top of her, quickly pinning her to the ground. She struggled for a while until she realized it was no use.

"Incredible move, Calliope!" Darrell clapped his hands as he approached us. "You mastered that technique very well." He then crouched on the floor, looking into the Delta's yellowish-green eyes with a smirk. "You might have just found yourself some Delta competition, Trix."

I chuckled at his comment before finally letting her go. She rose to her feet in the blink of an eye, using her hands to remove the dust off her clothes.

"She's not a Delta anymore; she's a Luna, and she carries the Alpha's mark." The black-haired woman frowned as she looked at me, but I could see the shadow of a proud smile on her face. It was the closest thing to a compliment Bellatrix would ever offer anyone. "Besides, I taught her everything she knows. It's only natural for a student to go even farther than their teacher."

"Fair enough." The Beta shrugged before turning his attention to the rest of the warriors. "Alright, we're done for the day! See you all tomorrow."

As the crowd started to disperse, I felt firm hands grip my waist from behind. I didn't have to turn around to know it was Levi; aside from easily recognizing his characteristic scent, I had gotten acquainted with his rough touch. His fingers ran up my arm, shoulder, and neck, until they stopped on my chin, pulling me to look at him. When his vivid blue eyes locked on mine they were filled with electricity, like the ocean in a storm.

"My Luna," he cooed, taking a deep breath to inhale my

scent. "Our guests will be arriving soon. Will you be by my side during the meeting?"

"Of course, my Alpha. As promised," I replied as I turned around to face him, resting my hands on his shoulder.

Today, one of Blood Eclipse's oldest allies, Shadow Winds Pack, would be coming over to discuss the terms of a new treaty. I met their Alpha, Jonah Ulrich, at my Luna Ceremony almost a month ago. However, he had since then found his Luna, whom Levi wanted me to meet. During my lessons with Calanthe, I studied a lot about politics, and I knew it was important for our alliance that the female leaders of both packs got along well. I was a little nervous for my first official Alpha meeting, but another thing I had learned was how to hide my emotions - something I had been getting fairly good at.

My mate leaned forward, his hands traveling up my exposed skin. Holding onto my concentration, I remained still. I knew it drove him mad when I didn't let him know what his touch did to me. Frustrated, he pulled me closer, his mouth barely touching mine.

"We must get ready then. Care to join me in the shower?" A few weeks ago, his words would have made me blush. The insinuation was too dirty for the old, innocent me. Now, I just showed him a small smile, holding my head up high as my fingers traced his cheek and chin, leisurely feeling the texture of his light beard. The way he leaned into my hand reminded me of how much control I had over him. Under my touch, the ruthless Alpha was as docile as a puppy.

"I'm afraid I won't be able to accompany you this time." His scowl showed how displeased he was with my answer, but he didn't argue. "I need to check on Crystal first. I'll meet you in the office."

The Alpha nodded, planting a quick kiss on my forehead before he turned around to leave. I did the same, heading towards the stables. It had been a few days since my mate's first interaction with the unicorn, and she was now feeling much safer around him. I was hoping to introduce my pet to the rest of the ranked members sometime during the weekend. Depending on how comfortable she was with their presence, I would evaluate the possibility of letting her roam freely around the pack. The whole territory was secured by tall walls, and I knew she wouldn't go too far because of the bond that tied us together.

After feeding Crystal and making sure she was okay, I returned to the Alpha suite to take a quick shower and get ready for the meeting. Since my reconciliation with Levi, he spontaneously bought a few more elegant dresses to add to my collection. With the amount of options I had in my closet, it took me a long time to pick the perfect one for the occasion. I ended up deciding on a casual but elegant long light blue strap sleeveless dress; I loved the way the color contrasted with my tan skin. The thigh slit offered the plain piece some movement without making it vulgar. Lastly, I styled my long wavy deep brown hair in a dutch braid. One last look in the mirror, and I was off to meet my Alpha at his office.

My mate's attention fell on me the second I walked through the door. His eyes slowly analyzed me from head to toe before he sighed in admiration. Chuckling at his reaction, I made my way over to take my seat beside him, but he quickly grabbed my hand and pulled me onto his lap. He stared at me for a few long seconds, making me lose my breath when he brought his nose to my neck, gently brushing the sensitive area. His lips easily found their way to my mark, and I gasped when I felt his canines graze against my skin.

"You look so beautiful, my Luna," he groaned. "It will be hard to focus on business with the dirty thoughts that are running through my mind."

"I can go change if you'd like," I suggested playfully.

"No need." He lifted me off his lap, taking another good look at my body. "I want to tear you out of that dress myself later. Besides, our guests have just crossed the borders. Darrell will be escorting them to the office soon."

"Is everything ready?"

"Yes. Would you like to take one last look at the issues we'll be discussing today?"

"No, that won't be necessary. I made sure to memorize them over the last few days," I informed him with a smile.

"As expected from my amazing Luna," he whispered, leaning closer.

I could feel the magnetic pull between us, and I closed my eyes to focus on the sensation. However, just as our lips were inches away from each other, there was a knock on the door. Levi pulled away, clearing his throat. In the blink of an eye, he was back to his usual stern form as he rose from his seat. He flashed me one last look before opening the door.

"Welcome, Alpha Jonah. Luna Amelia." My mate nodded respectfully at them.

"Thank you for having us, Alpha Levi," Jonah replied, returning the gesture.

"It's an honor to meet you, Alpha Levi." The ginger

woman offered my Alpha her hand, and he was quick to shake it.

"Please, come in." He opened the door wider, gesturing to me soon after as I rose from my seat. "This is Calliope, my Luna."

"Luna Calliope." They approached me, and Jonah took my hand in both of his. "You look as lovely as you did the day we met."

"Thank you," I replied with a warm smile before turning to the other woman and stretching out my hand. "It's a pleasure to meet you, Luna Amelia."

"Likewise." She smiled softly.

For the first few minutes, the two men chatted about their lives over a glass of whiskey, while Amelia and I got to know each other. Of course, most of our talk was diplomatic, but she seemed like a genuinely pleasant person. Both of them did; they looked like powerful leaders, as well as a loving couple. The next hour was spent discussing the old terms of the treaty between the two packs and what would change. This contract had lasted for five years, so they took their time evaluating each topic. For the most part, they had no trouble coming to an agreement. However, the tension in the room slightly rose as they came to a deadlock on the very last topic.

"I'm sorry, Alpha Jonah, but I cannot agree to lend you half of my warriors in the event of an attack against Shadow Winds." My mate frowned.

"Why not? It seems like a fair price to pay for the territorial expansion you asked for," the other leader retorted. "Besides, it's just a precaution. My pack hasn't been attacked in the past eight years. There's a chance you won't ever have to send me your warriors."

"But in case I do, my pack will be left underprotected. It's too much of a risk, considering Blood Eclipse has quite a few enemies who wouldn't miss the opportunity to come at us while we're weakened."

"I can't give you a portion of my land unless you offer me a good deal."

For long seconds, the two Alphas just glared at each other, while Amelia and I exchanged worried looks. Territory and warriors were the two most valuable goods for a pack; it was hard for a leader to willingly offer either of the two. If they didn't come to a conclusion soon, the contract would be terminated, and we would lose a strong ally. It reminded me of a business discussion I witnessed during my time as a Delta in my old pack, which didn't end well.

I widened my eyes as realization struck me. My past experience taught me exactly what not to do.

When the idea crossed my mind, I immediately spoke. "What if we offer you a fourth of our warriors, as well as half of our trackers and sentinels? During times of war, the last two can be just as useful as the first."

Initially, the two men turned to me with confusion; a Luna wasn't supposed to intervene in pack negotiations. However, they both seemed to find my idea quite intriguing, as neither of them said a word about my unexpected suggestion. At last, Jonah leaned forward in his seat, crossing his hands over the table.

"Sounds good to me." The man shrugged, leaving both my mate and I shocked. "What do you say, Alpha Levi?"

My Alpha hesitated for a while, but eventually replied,

"Works for me."

"We have a deal, then."

After signing a few papers, the two leaders shook hands. Levi and I accompanied them to the door, thanking them for their time. As soon as the couple left the office, my mate unexpectedly pinned me against the wall in a rough movement. He dove his nose into my neck, forcing me to expose it to him. Taken by surprise, I didn't have the chance to fight him back. But honestly, did I even want to?

"I should punish you for speaking during the negotiations," he growled into my neck, his teeth pressing harder against my mark. I might actually have been scared if I couldn't hear his rapid heartbeat and his ragged breathing. The beast inside of him wasn't angry...he was turned on. By my audacity. By my intelligence.

"Really?" I replied confidently, catching his attention. "It seems I have just prevented us from losing a valuable ally. If anything, I should be rewarded."

He smirked. "That you should, my Luna."

The second his canines sunk into my mark, a wave of pleasure hit me. I could feel him tearing off the thin fabric of the dress, and what happened next was bliss.

CHAPTER TWENTY-EIGHT

Calliope

After my performance during the meeting, my mate only stopped rewarding me when his best friend knocked on the door of his office to deliver the week's training reports. By then, I had already reached my climax four times - Levi had the hunger and the energy of a beast, and I wouldn't complain about it. He would have sent his Beta away to take me a fifth time, had I not insisted we went back to business. I had learned how to tame him, but I had to admit he knew how to work my body just as well. He was experienced, and I knew he had had his fair share of women before me, which was understandable; after all, he was eight years older than me. But the thought didn't bother me. In the end, I was the only one who managed to put the Alpha on a leash, and he was all mine.

The next morning, Levi headed straight to his office after training. There were a few things he still needed to take care of, such as signing papers to communicate the renewal of our alliance with Shadow Winds to the Elder Union. Since I wouldn't be of much help, I decided to take a stroll around the main part of our territory to both enjoy the warm weather and talk to other wolves. As Luna, it was important for me to show myself to the other members so I would be more approachable. With the whole conflict between Levi and I, they weren't given a chance to properly meet me, and I wanted to earn their trust.

On my walk, I stumbled upon Darrell. He seemed to be in a bit of a rush, but he immediately stopped to greet me with one of his bright smiles. It felt like ages since the last time we really talked. He was my main company during my first weeks at Blood Eclipse, but once Levi and I decided to work on our relationship, I had been spending most of my time with my mate. The Beta was a fun person to be around; I had to admit I missed our casual talks.

"Good morning, Calliope." He bowed respectfully at me. I had told him many times there was no need for formalities between us, but I guessed it was hard to let go of the habit. At least he didn't address me by my title anymore.

"Hi, Darrell." I smiled at him. "Busy day?"

"Kinda. Just have to check something with Ivar right now. What are you up to?"

"Oh, you know, typical Luna stuff." I shrugged playfully.

His grin grew even bigger. "Levi told me about how you handled the negotiations yesterday. I can't believe the old shy Cal had the guts to intervene in a meeting between Alphas. You've really grown into your Luna title."

I looked away, blushing a little. "I didn't do much. I just wanted to make sure we would keep our few allies. Blood Eclipse is known for having more foes than friends. I'm hoping to change that."

"I'm sure you can do it. We only had a ruthless Alpha, but now we also have a loving Luna. I have no doubts our pack will thrive under your leadership." He squeezed my shoulder reassuringly, and I smiled in return. "Anyway, I should go before I get scolded for slacking off. See you around, Cal."

After parting ways with the Beta, I continued on my stroll along the pack. By lunch time, I had managed to talk to a few pack members, all of which treated me with respect. I decided it was a good time to meet my Alpha at his office so we could eat together. Perhaps I could even assist him with other pack business once we were done eating. However, as I started to make my way back towards the Town Hall, I heard a voice inside my head that made me stop in my tracks.

"Sorry to bother you, Cal, but can you meet me at the south border?" There was distress in the Delta's words, which was uncommon. *"Two pack members are having a quarrel. I usually take care of these situations myself, but they won't listen to me. I could really use some Luna command here."*

I was hesitant, but I didn't show it. *"Sure. I'll head there right now."*

"Thank you." I heard her sigh in relief before our connection was cut.

Honestly, I had no idea what to do. She didn't give me a lot of detail, but judging by her tone, I guessed she was using all of her focus to keep the situation under control until I arrived. As I made my way to the location, it concerned me not to know what to expect. My heart was racing, but I did my best to maintain a neutral semblance; hiding my emotions would prevent the situation from becoming even more stressful.

"You've got this, Cal," my wolf cheered. *"This is exactly what you were looking for: an opportunity to show the pack members they can trust you."*

I took a deep breath. *"You're right. Thank you for reminding me, Nava."*

"We're in this together."

As soon as I arrived at the south border, I was shocked to learn a fight was about to break out. A bunch of pack members had come out of their houses to witness the scene, forming a circle around two angry Omegas. Trix was between them, one step away from using force to keep them apart. It didn't look good at all. What was I supposed to do here? I closed my eyes in an attempt to clear my mind before I finally gathered the courage to step closer.

"What is going on here?" I asked calmly.

Everyone stopped to stare at me. The wolves around us bowed at me, while the Delta flashed me a look of pure relief. The two women stopped fighting for a brief moment to turn their attention to me, nodding curtly. Now that I had a chance to properly analyze them, I realized one of them seemed to be around her fifties, while the other one looked much younger - probably in her early twenties.

"Luna Calliope, I'm sorry to disturb you!" The older one was the first one to speak. "But this little thief stole from me! I caught her red-handed jumping out of my window after she took the last piece of meat from my fridge! I demanded her to either give it back or pay for what she stole, but she refused!"

"You know very well you started this! I saw you taking some of the vegetables from my garden last week! This is merely payback!" the younger one stated.

"Everything grown in the territory belongs to the entire pack! I was just following the law, whereas you broke into my house!"

I couldn't believe there were wolves fighting for food in Blood Eclipse. We were one of the wealthiest packs in the country. Although Omegas were usually the less privileged in the society, they shouldn't have to steal basic goods. However, this wasn't the time to go down that mental rabbit hole. They would jump at each other's throats if I didn't do anything, so I had to act fast. Trix was staring at me with wide eyes, begging me to use my Luna tone on them and command them to stop.

"You shouldn't do it," Nava stated firmly, voicing my same thoughts. *"If you get them to submit by force, you won't solve the real problem. Besides, you will be no different than a tyrant, or a ruthless Alpha."*

"I agree, but will they even listen to me when they're blinded by rage?"

"You're still their Luna. They will respect you."

I decided to follow my wolf's instincts and took yet another step closer.

"Ladies, can I get your attention, please?" I spoke a little louder than usual. They immediately turned to me. "Thank you. What is your name?" I looked at the older one.

"Mirian, Luna."

"What about you?" I turned to the other one.

"I'm Jenna, Luna."

"Good. Mirian and Jenna," I repeated, memorizing their names. "Are you not getting enough food?"

Mirian widened her eyes, shaking. "I am grateful for what Blood Eclipse is able to provide me, Luna." Her reaction showed she was afraid...and she wasn't being completely honest. She probably thought I would banish her if she confessed to being dissatisfied.

"Please, don't be shy. I want to assist you, but I can only do so if you tell me exactly what's going on."

"The Omegas from the South are the last ones to receive

the food aid, Luna." This time, Jenna was the one to speak. "For the past few months, we have been getting less and less... We are hungry."

"This is absurd." When I frowned, she stiffened. Both women were shaking as I approached them, but they stopped as soon as I took their hands. "Thank you for letting me know. I will make sure you get the right amount of food." There was surprise in their eyes as I smiled fondly at them, before turning to the rest of the curious pack members. "If any of you ever need anything, please come directly to me. Blood Eclipse is a wealthy pack, and everyone here shall live with dignity." I lowered my tone, looking back at the Omegas. "Mirian, Jenna, I would like to invite you to have dinner at the packhouse tonight. I'm hoping you two can make amends during a friendly meal."

They exchanged shocked looks before turning back to me. "T-thank you so much, Luna!"

"You are very welcome." I nodded at them, turning my attention to Bellatrix soon after. "Now, if you'll excuse us, the Delta and I should get back to work."

The black-haired woman followed me, not uttering a single word until we had distanced ourselves from the crowd. All along the way, she looked at me with a mix of disbelief and pride.

"What?" I finally asked her.

"That was amazing, Cal. Levi would have never handled the situation like this..." she observed thoughtfully. "Hell, I don't think I could have done it any better, and I'm the Delta!"

"Well, I used to be a Delta, too," I recalled. "I guess I still have some of my old tricks up my sleeve."

"You're a peculiar girl, Luna. But I'm glad to see the shy girl who cried after the marking ceremony is taking the reins of her life, and learning to lead an entire pack."

"I had a good teacher." I winked at her.

CHAPTER TWENTY-NINE

Calliope

Once the situation with the Omegas was under control, I headed back to Levi's office to explain the problem they were facing to him. He was quite surprised - and slightly angry - to find out some of the pack members weren't getting enough food. He usually focused on politics, since the Delta was responsible for being the bridge between the pack and their leader. However, Blood Eclipse was fairly large, which made it hard for a single person to manage. It didn't help that Bellatrix, much like my mate, was quite scary and not very approachable. The fact that the two women resorted to stealing from each other because they were afraid to be punished for their complaints told me how much the pack truly needed their Luna.

Levi immediately stopped what he was doing to assess the problem. With Ivar and Darrell's help, we figured out the price of food had gone up, but no adjustments were made to the budget directed towards feeding the members. In order to simplify the pack's administration, the territory was divided in four districts: North, South, East, and West. The South District was the last to be replenished, which explained why only the wolves who lived there were facing the problem in question. The Alpha promptly ordered the increase in funds, easily solving the issue.

In the evening, I personally welcomed the two Omegas from earlier into the packhouse so we could dine in the private dining hall. The hall was mostly used for formal meetings with high-ranking guests, which was what made Levi hesitant when I told him about my idea. However, he agreed that it was a good opportunity to make the members feel more comfortable about approaching their Luna. Although my mate couldn't be present during the meal, I had a good time with the girls. They were quite shy at first, but as we ate and talked, they started to relax. In the end, they told me about other issues they were facing, and I let them know I would address them as soon as possible.

When I returned to the Alpha suite, I was feeling... accomplished. Like I truly felt helpful for once. I don't think I had ever felt that way in my old pack, especially not after my parents died. It seemed like I had finally found my purpose in life, the one thing that made me happy to be alive. Although it was wonderful to finally be on the right page of my relationship with my mate, loved by my friends and my new family, it was as if I was happy for *me* - not because of everything else.

"That's because you were always meant to be Luna, Cal," Nava chuckled. *"The Goddess planned our destinies before we were even born. It's natural for you to feel good now that we are exactly where we're supposed to be."*

"I had never looked at it that way," I confessed thoughtfully, smiling soon after. *"I guess you're right."* She nodded cheerfully before retreating to the back of my head.

Since Levi hadn't gotten back from the office yet, I decided to go ahead and take a shower before bedtime. The moment I stepped out of the bathroom wearing only a thin towel, I was surprised to find the Alpha sitting in our bed, his fiery blue eyes filled with desire now locked on me. A shiver ran down my spine just from the way he looked at me, and I could feel the familiar heat between my legs. He groaned as soon as he detected the scent of my arousal, standing up in a swift movement to circle me like a shark.

He stopped behind me, making me stiffen. "You've been such a wonderful Luna to our pack lately, Calliope." I closed my eyes, enjoying the feeling of his hot breath against my neck. "I always liked having control of everything, but I must admit I kinda like it when you take control. It turns me and Odin on."

I could feel his smirk even though I wasn't looking at him. A gasp escaped my lips when something hard pressed against my back at the exact time Levi wrapped his arms around me, pulling me closer. I tried to control my breathing as his hands, which were now resting on my waist, moved all the way up to my chest, grabbing the edge of the towel. He kissed my marking spot softly, causing a moan to break free as I let go of the only piece of fabric covering my skin.

I had learned to tame the beast, but he knew how to steal my control just as well.

* * *

The rest of the week went by in the blink of an eye. While the Alpha took care of his usual pack business, I worked on fixing the small issues which had been affecting some of the members for the past few years. Aside from the food problem, there was nothing urgent, but I still wanted to make sure every single wolf had a decent life inside the walls of Blood Eclipse. Levi recognized my efforts, and insisted on refurbishing the old Luna office so I could have my private workspace. Although I didn't mind sharing the office with my mate, it would be nice to have my own space.

When the weekend came along, I decided it would be the perfect occasion to spend some time with our friends while I got Crystal accustomed to other wolves - it would be the final step before I could finally let her roam the territory freely. Sundays were the ranked members' day off, so I knew everyone would be available. My only concern was that Ivar and Hailey might want to go out on a date together, but the Gamma Female freaked out at the opportunity to meet a living, breathing unicorn.

In the stables, everyone stood a good distance away from the back stall where my magical creature was protected by a spell, unable to sense the werewolves. They all had the same mix of apprehension and excitement - except for Ivar's mate, who was beaming like it was the happiest day of her life.

"So... how're we gonna do this?" Darrell was the first one to speak, his eyes never leaving the filly.

"I was thinking it would be best if I took each of you one at a time," I suggested, taking a step forward. "When I first introduced her to Levi, she seemed to feel more comfortable when I was holding his hand. We'll try that and see how it goes." With a deep breath, I eyed each of my friends, smiling. "Who wants to-"

"Me! Me! Pick me!" the Gamma Female cheered excitedly, making me chuckle. Hopefully her level of energy wouldn't scare Crystal.

"Alright, come here."

After intertwining our fingers, we both entered the back stall simultaneously. The white filly twitched her ears in a gesture of happiness when she saw me, but the way she flicked her tail from side to side denoted her anxiety due to a stranger's presence. Much like I did with my mate, I kept talking to her and brushing her neck with my fingers to help her calm down. Once she relaxed a little, Hailey slowly inched closer, until Crystal allowed the girl to touch her. She almost screamed, but I covered her mouth just in time to prevent her from scaring my pet.

"This is amazing!" Hailey whispered, gently brushing the filly's hair. "Ivarrrrrrrr, can I get one toooooo?" She looked at her mate with puppy eyes.

"Oh, my little strawberry, you know I would love to… but I'm afraid I can't afford to buy one with my Gamma salary." The blonde boy pouted at Levi, only making him frown harder than usual.

"If you want more money, you should work more," my mate said blankly. "Perhaps if you stopped goofing around, you would actually find a side job to raise your income."

"With the skills he has, I think Hailey would be better off finding another man," Bellatrix teased.

"Wow, thank you for your advice, Alpha! You two, Trix! *Great* observation." Ivar snapped back sarcastically. "And I thought Deltas were supposed to be the ones who encourage and look after pack members. Maybe that's why the Omegas were starving!" By the glare on the black-haired woman's face, I knew she was about to punch him.

So I acted before they pounced at each other. "Okay, who's next? Maybe you could try, Trix!"

The Delta was thoughtful for a second. "Whatever." She shrugged, heading towards me.

"With her icy heart, I won't be surprised if Crystal-" Ivar didn't even have a chance to finish before he got smacked in the head. "Ouch!"

"You should learn to keep your mouth shut." She smirked.

"I'm still Gamma, you know? I'm above you in the hierarchy!" the boy complained. "Levi, why won't you punish her for her disrespect?"

"What disrespect?" The leader crossed his arms, flashing a small smile at Bellatrix, which only left Ivar even more annoyed. Defeated, he decided to stay quiet.

I took Trix's hand, and she shyly approached the pure creature. It was almost as if she was afraid her strong personality would truly scare it, but I knew she wasn't mean or cruel; unicorns were able to identify a person's heart, and I knew she had a good one. Strangely enough, Crystal didn't seem the least hesitant about Trix's presence. Soon enough, the filly stretched her muzzle in the woman's direction, allowing her to pet her.

"Holy Goddess...the witch is smiling!" Ivar covered his mouth with his palms in disbelief. Trix frowned, causing her smile to fade, and I had to laugh.

"Levi had the same reaction," I revealed, and everyone's eyes widened with shock. It was my mate's turn to furrow his brows, but he didn't say anything.

I repeated the process with the Beta and the Gamma until we were all inside the large stall. After a couple of hours, I finally felt confident enough to guide Crystal out of the stables for the first time. There were a few pack members walking around, which made her a little agitated. However, being surrounded by wolves she trusted, as well as receiving a lot of positive reinforcement from me, she slowly started to calm down. We stayed outside for the entire day with her, just chatting and enjoying the nice weather.

Between jokes and laughter, I ended up realizing something: Blood Eclipse was my home. Here, I had everything I could ever want and more - a loving mate, amazing friends, respect, and a very special, magical pet. As the days went by, it became easier to leave my past of abuse behind. Still, I couldn't forget I had been part of another pack before, even if it never felt much like a home.

I wondered how Kai and the rest of my tormentors were doing back at Moonstone.

CHAPTER THIRTY

Kai

Everything was a fucking mess in my pack!

As I walked through the large hallways of the luxurious packhouse, fuming with anger, the few wolves I crossed paths with instantly fled - although I was still young, they knew better than to stand in the way of their pissed-off Alpha. For the past couple of months since I took over, there had been thousands of problems, and it seemed another one had just been added to the list. I knew my father would scold me for this later, as he did every single time before.

I couldn't understand it. Back when my old man was still Moonstone's leader, everything seemed to work fine. He just sat on the chair in his office all day, occasionally answering calls from friends and allies. Our pack was relatively peaceful; we had very few enemies, and we hadn't seen an attack for more than three decades. For years I had studied with my father, paying minimal attention to his lessons with the certainty I would never have to use any of that. After all, I had never seen him use anything he was teaching me. But of course, as soon as I stepped in as Alpha, the pack started crumbling to the ground.

In my desperate search for answers, I realized the event that marked the beginning of our problems was Calliope's departure from Moonstone. Just a few days after she left with the cocky Alpha, some minor issues came to the surface, and it didn't take long before they turned into an ever growing snowball. Deep down, I believed everything was connected to the new Luna of Blood Eclipse. But how much impact could the absence of a weak Delta have?

To be honest, I didn't even know what her role in the pack was. I never needed to know; she would take care of any problems before they came to my knowledge, or my father's. However, I knew it couldn't be anything important. Every major decision had to be approved by the Alpha first, so whatever she used to do couldn't have been too insignificant. Yet, if that was the case, how did her leaving affect our routine so much?

"Kai! You're finally here." Elliot, my Beta sighed in relief as soon as I arrived at the north border.

"Alpha Kai," I corrected him. I noticed him fighting the urge to roll his eyes, but I decided to ignore it; I had problems bigger than the need to discipline my second-in-command at the moment. "What the hell happened here?"

Frowning, I took a quick look around. The metal door to our storage house was badly damaged, barely hanging by the hinges. There were food packages torn open over the grass, and a few Omegas were trying to save what they could. The sight before me only further enraged me.

"I asked what happened!" I repeated after their long silence.

"Some rogues managed to sneak past our defenses. So far, we know they were able to steal some food, but we couldn't confirm whether they took anything else," my Gamma, Gregor, replied with his head low.

"How?!"

"I...I don't know," he confessed.

"How the fuck do you not know?! The pack's security is your damn responsibility!" I snarled.

"Chill, man! The damage has already been done. We need to focus on how to repair it now." Elliot frowned.

"I'm the Alpha! I tell you what to do, not the other way around!" I reminded him. My tone made him bow his head at me against his will. "I want to figure out the source of the problem before it gets any worse! By the way, where are the warriors you are in charge of training to defend our borders?"

The boy glared at the Gamma. "They're ready, but Gregor hasn't given them any shifts yet."

"Why the hell not?"

"I asked for your permission on one of the security reports weeks ago. Since you never addressed the issue, I thought it had been declined," my third-in-command clarified. The more they spoke, the less sense the whole situation made.

"What reports? I haven't read any reports ever since I took over!"

"What?" There was genuine confusion in Gregor's face. "Were they not sent to you?"

"What do you mean? You're supposed to drop them off at my office, idiot!" I growled, struggling to hold in my anger.

"Really?" He widened his eyes in realization. "I thought the Delta would take them to you. Calliope used to do that."

"That would explain why I haven't heard back on any of the training reports either." My Beta scratched his chin thoughtfully.

I couldn't believe these two.

"Fuck this!" I roared, finally giving up. My ranked members were completely lost. It was no use talking to them now. "Just clean up the mess and meet me in my office when you're done!"

Once I was done with my pathetic Beta and Gamma, I stomped back inside the packhouse, hoping no one would cross paths with me. Moonstone was a relatively small pack, but I was still an Alpha. It was hard to control my powerful wolf, and seeing the mess our territory was in, he was ready to slash some throats. However, as soon as I stormed into my office, I knew I wouldn't get the much needed peace and quiet any time soon. My father was sitting in my chair with arms crossed, wearing the same frown that hadn't seemed to leave his face for the past couple of months.

"First, you couldn't control some rioting members. Now, you let rogues steal from us. What's next? You're gonna let some random Alpha challenge you and take your title?" he spat. He might be my father, and I had immeasurable respect for him, but he caught me on a very bad day.

"I'm doing my part! It's my stupid team that can't get anything right!" I retorted.

"They are your responsibility! If they're not meeting your expectations, you should either assist them or punish them!" he growled, standing up to face me. When I was younger, he would easily tower over me, but now that we were the same height, he didn't scare me anymore. When I didn't shake, he sighed. "Maybe I shouldn't have passed my title on to you yet. You're clearly not prepared to be an Alpha." He shook his head in disapproval before leaving the room.

Finally, some peace.

However, it only lasted a second. I relaxed against my chair, letting my head fall backwards as I closed my eyes to take a deep breath. As much as I wanted to just disappear, I knew I still had a lot to do. If I didn't start fixing our countless problems soon, my father's threat might just become a reality. Although we weren't a prominent pack, it wouldn't take long for other leaders to notice how disorganized we were. If they saw an opportunity to strike while we're weak, they wouldn't hesitate to do so.

"*Clarisse, come to my office. Now!*"

"*Y-yes, A-alpha!*" the young girl replied before I cut our connection.

When Calliope left, we had to find someone else to fill her position - the only problem was, no one had the proper skills to become a Delta, and we didn't have time to train a new one. Lacking a better option, the random eighteen-year-old girl we chose to take the title was making it up as she went. Needless to say, she wasn't nearly as good as Calliope, and not just because she was still new to her job. It was easy to see she would never be as useful. She wasn't smart or quick-thinking, and her wolf was so pathetic she could barely keep up with our weakest warriors. But, she was all we had at the moment.

"Y-you wanted to see me, A-alpha?" she stuttered as she poked her head through the door. I noticed she was already shaking. She couldn't even assume the respectable posture any ranked member should have.

"Yes. Come in already!" I barked. She gasped in fear before stepping closer. "You are in charge of making sure the pack runs smoothly. Does it look like everything's running smoothly to you, Clarisse?"

She hesitated for a while before shaking her head.

"Then what the hell are you waiting for to start doing your job?" I spat, trying to control my ragged breathing. When she jumped in fear at my tone, I sighed in annoyance. "Since neither you, nor my Beta or Gamma know what you're doing wrong, go talk to the pack members. Figure out why they've been fighting so much. Oh, and grab the training and security reports while you're at it."

"Y-yes, Alpha!" She bowed curtly. A second later, she shrieked in surprise when someone else called out her name.

"Clarisse! Clarisse!" I recognized my sister's voice from the other side. It didn't take long for her to open the door, her chocolate brown eyes immediately locked on the Delta. "There you are! Is everything ready for my dinner with Alpha Gedeon?"

"Almost, Chloe," the girl whispered. "I'm still trying to find that pink dress you were looking for."

"Well, go look for it then! Chop chop!" Chloe clapped her hands, flashing Clarisse a menacing look that made her run away as fast as she could.

"Hopefully you won't screw this one up as well," I snorted, causing my sister to frown. "You couldn't even compete with a stupid Delta, and your little show at her Luna Ceremony made us become enemies with the strongest pack of the country!"

"Watch your mouth around me, mutt. I'm still the only hope you have to save this pathetic pack from the mess you made." She scowled at me. "And you're wrong - Blood Eclipse used to be the strongest pack, but new ones are rising. By marrying Alpha Gedeon, Moonstone will have an equally powerful ally," she stated confidently, lifting her head higher. "Don't worry, little bro. I'll fix my mistake tonight."

Her words made me calm down a little, but I was still hesitant. "Are you sure? You know the rumors about how this man killed his fated mate. What do you think he'll do to you?"

"Please. I know how to handle a man." She chuckled, already turning around to leave.

"What if your true mate comes along?"

She stopped dead in her tracks. When she glanced at me over her shoulder, she was dead serious. "So what? I don't care about love. I just want power."

CHAPTER THIRTY-ONE

Calliope

"Thank you so much, Luna Calliope!" A young girl bowed her head respectfully at me as she grabbed one of the baskets from my hand.

Roughly a month after the issue regarding the lack of food for the wolves living in the South District was discussed, I took the initiative to personally accompany the next monthly-delivery. The baskets of free groceries - available to all pack members - were usually separated at the kitchen to be picked up by individuals throughout the first week of every month. However, considering the recent misunderstanding, I decided to organize a truck to bring the supplies myself to ensure they would be correctly distributed.

My visit seemed to be taken as an event by the residents, who made sure to come out of their houses to greet me. Everyone eyed me with a mix of respect and curiosity as they lined up to get their supplies. I was helping unload and distribute the food baskets when a familiar face showed up in front of me.

"I appreciate your kindness, Luna Calliope." The middle-aged woman lowered her head in submission. "I'm sorry for causing you so much trouble. You must be busy with your duties."

"It's no problem at all, Mirian." I smiled warmly at her. "Is this enough for you and your family?"

"It's more than enough, Luna. Thank you. Please tell the Alpha we are thankful for all that he provides us with."

"You're welcome. And I will." I nodded at her, watching as she disappeared into the crowd.

Twenty minutes later, the truck had been emptied and the Omegas' refrigerators were full. It warmed my heart to watch everyone wave me goodbye as I turned around to leave. The driver offered me a ride back to the town square, but I actually enjoyed strolling through the grounds of my home. Blood Eclipse had a beautiful territory I could never get enough of - I loved admiring the gardens, the forest, the villages.

I found my unicorn grazing near the central lake, the morning sun rays bathing her pure white coat, conferring an even more magical look to her. She had been roaming freely for the past couple of weeks, and she was now fully comfortable being around werewolves. A shelter had been built right next to the stables so she could have a nice place to sleep and to hide during storms. She hadn't allowed anyone aside from me and my friends to touch her yet, but she wasn't frightened by others. It also helped that pack members respected her as much as they did me, and they were content to just observe her exquisite beauty.

When I stepped closer, the creature lifted her head up, neighing as she finally noticed my presence. She came trotting in my direction, and demanded I pet her by adamantly pushing me with her muzzle; it always made me laugh. As I brushed her fur with my fingers, I couldn't help but take in how much she had grown in such a short amount of time. She was now taller than Calanthe's mare, although she still had the same playful filly behavior.

After offering her some attention, I let her sunbathe and continued on my way towards the packhouse. All of the members whom I crossed paths with eagerly flashed me warm smiles or nodded at me. Some even approached me to let me know they were doing well, thanking me for helping them with issues they previously had. For the past month, I had been offering the wolves of our pack assistance with whatever they might need. It was hard to fit them in my tight schedule sometimes, but I made sure to hear every single one of their concerns. The hard work definitely paid off, as they were now comfortable with the idea of talking to me. Maybe it was an old Delta habit or a new Luna instinct, but it brought me inexplicable satisfaction being able to take care of them.

A few stops later, I finally made it to Levi's office. He was so focused on the reports he was reading that he didn't even notice me walk in - at least not until my unique scent invaded his senses. His blue eyes had gone slightly darker with lust, and it made me bite my bottom lip. We hadn't gotten into fights or arguments for the past month, which I considered a huge victory. In fact, he had gotten much better in communicating his feelings to me. Especially in bed...

"What have you been up to, my Luna?" he finally asked, his intense gaze drawing me in. "I thought you'd be here sooner."

"I just finished delivering the food to the South District," I informed him, slowly inching closer.

"Always so busy with your duties. I'm lucky you still manage to make some time for me," he chuckled.

Levi put the papers aside when I was close enough for him to touch. Without standing up from his chair, his hands gripped my waist firmly and he sat me up on his desk. I held my breath when his fingers lifted the skirt of my navy blue dress with golden accents. A gasp escaped my lips when he reached my thighs, his head right between my legs. I could read his intentions, and though I was all for it, I had to tease him a little longer. Before he could expose another inch of my skin, I held his hands tightly, restraining his movement. He could easily fight me off if he wanted to, but all he did was look up at me with curiosity.

"I don't wish to disturb your work, Alpha," I whispered, tracing the details in his stern face with my fingertips.

"Of course you don't." He smirked, leaning into my touch. "I'm glad to inform you I am done for today."

"Already? It's not even lunch time yet."

"There wasn't a lot to be done." He shrugged, pulling himself closer to me. "Now, I'm wondering how the two of us could spend our time."

"I'm sure you already have a few ideas." I arched an eyebrow at him accusingly.

"Your body is an incredible source of inspiration."

I finally removed my hand from his, allowing him to keep going. He planted soft kisses along my thigh while continuing to reveal my skin, making my head fall backwards.

"I love this dress," he cooed at the moment his nose reached the spot between my legs.

I had to hold in a moan, unwilling to lose control just yet. "I hope so. You bought it."

"And it suits you perfectly."

"Why are you so eager to remove it then?" I teased.

He chuckled. "Because you look even better when you're not wearing any clothes."

When my mate kissed my most sensitive spot through the thin fabric of my panties, I couldn't fight the feeling any longer; my whole body craved for him. He slid one finger underneath the only piece of cloth standing in his way, ready to tear it off. However, a knock on the door kept him from going any further. He grunted in annoyance, pulling me off the table as he stood up to open the door. One of the Omegas had come to deliver him a package, and as he held it in his hands, he didn't seem as frustrated anymore.

"What is that?" I asked curiously.

"Something I had been waiting for to put our next date into action," he replied playfully, placing the package on the table and encouraging me to open it. When I did, I was surprised to find a complete iridescent horse tack set. Noticing my surprise, he went on, "Since Crystal is fully grown now, I thought we could go horseback riding together. I wanted to get her luxurious equipment to match her majesty."

"It's perfect, Levi." I smiled excitedly at him. "Can we go now?"

"I was hoping you would want to."

"Great! Let me just go get changed." I stood up to leave, but he blocked my way.

"I think you should keep this." He tugged at the satin fabric of my dress, leaning closer to whisper in my ear, "I will make sure to take this off myself later."

✻ ✻ ✻

Once we made it to the stables, all I had to do was whistle for Crystal. In just a few minutes, my unicorn was standing right in front of me, twitching her ears, like she could feel my excitement. Levi quickly saddled up Highlander, his black steed, but I couldn't seem to get Crystal to cooperate with me. Whenever I tried to equip her, she would neigh in protest and avoid me. Her behavior was definitely unusual; she had never been so stubborn, especially not with me.

"Now that you've given her a taste of freedom, she doesn't want to be tamed," my mate joked.

"Could that be it?" I wondered. Well, she was a unicorn. I guess it made sense for her not to want to wear any equipment. I put it aside and approached her, watching her calm down under my touch. "I'm sorry. I don't think she really likes your gift," I said apologetically.

"It's fine," he chuckled. "I'm already honored that you never complain about anything I give you."

"How am I going to mount her then?" She was quite tall, and it didn't help that I was wearing a dress.

Without warning, Levi grabbed me by the waist and helped me climb onto her back. I waited a few seconds to see if she would complain, but she remained still and well-behaved. I guess the problem truly was the tack set. Once my mate mounted his own horse, we set off on a new adventure. Insisting the pack territory wasn't wide enough, he led me past the borders so we could venture through a different land.

It was magical to ride a unicorn as I explored new places. Crystal seemed content with me as her rider, which only brought me more peace. The hours flew by as we crossed lakes, waterfalls, fields of flowers, and woods. On our way back home, we stopped at the top of a hill to watch the sunset together. The romantic atmosphere was accentuated by the hues of orange, purple, and pink on the horizon. Mainly focused on the view, I barely noticed Levi creep closer to me. While both of us were still on our horses, he leaned closer, ready to kiss me. I closed my eyes, longing for his touch.

But it never came.

When I opened my eyes again, he looked utterly distressed.

"Darrell just mindlinked me, the pack is under attack!" he revealed, a mix of fury and concern in his semblance.

CHAPTER THIRTY-TWO

Calliope

My heart was palpitating as Levi and I galloped back to our pack, the peaceful date we had planned disturbed by the unexpected news. Without the proper equipment, it was hard to keep a steady grip on my unicorn's neck when my hands were so sweaty. My concerns seemed to have been noticed by Crystal, who slowed her pace to prevent me from falling off her back. However, in my rush to make it back to Blood Eclipse on time, I wasn't sure if I appreciated it. Highlander was a good few feet away from us as Levi pushed him to his limit, afraid we would be too late.

Thankfully, where we were watching the sunset wasn't far from our territory - a twenty minute trail on horseback, but I was sure we would make it in ten with how fast we were going. My mind was racing a million miles a minute the entire way back as I tried to analyze the situation. We had already been caught off guard, but if I could use the time on my hands to gather more information, we could use it to our advantage.

First off, I wondered who could be striking us. In my first week as Luna, Levi taught me a lot about politics, especially regarding our long list of enemies. After Levi's father was killed, he went on a rampage to both get his anger out, and to turn Blood Eclipse into a powerful, feared pack so any greedy

Alphas would think twice before trying to attack him. There were only a few leaders with numbers similar to ours, but we didn't hold a hostile relationship with any of them. The two most likely scenarios were that either one of our enemies had allied with another leader against us, or we were being attacked by rogues.

Secondly, I tried to understand the circumstances of the event. Legally sanctioned wars had to go through the Elder Council, who would determine a day and time for it to happen with the consent of both packs. Since this was a surprise attack, I quickly dismissed that possibility. The only creatures who didn't follow werewolf law were rogues, but it still made little sense for a small group of feral wolves to try to get inside a highly fortified pack.

In the end, I couldn't come to a conclusion regarding the most recent threat to our home before we crossed the front gates. One of the steed's caretakers immediately came to take Highlander back to the stables, and Crystal followed him. I was concerned about her well-being, but the stables were located right next to the packhouse - if anything were to happen to her, it was likely we would be in much bigger trouble. As my mate and I crossed the territory in a rush, I desperately wanted to know more, but I noticed he was mindlinking someone and I didn't want to interrupt him.

According to Darrell's message, the attack began at the eastern border, which was opposite from the gate we had gone in through. Tension rose as I passed the usually crowded fields that had been completely evacuated. There wasn't a single soul around the town square. I knew it was a good sign though - it meant Bellatrix had done a good job at leading the members to the safety bunker. It also proved our army had so far been able to fight off the enemies; otherwise, they would have already made it to the main part of the territory.

My focus was broken by a dark, negative energy trying to break through me - I immediately knew it was Levi's anger. He had a tight grip on my wrist as he dragged me towards the packhouse. Why hadn't he shifted so we could help the warriors defend our lands? Maybe he was so lost in rage he couldn't think clearly. It was natural for him to be furious during such a situation, but it was also quite scary. I had only seen him in this state twice, and I had grown to learn the outcome was never pretty.

"*We know how to deal with him when he's like this, Cal,*" Nava reminded me with impressive calm considering the situation. "*You can rein in his anger. Just make him listen to you.*"

She was right. Furrowing my brows, I stopped abruptly, standing my ground. He turned to me with confusion.

"What?"

"Where are you taking me?" I demanded to know.

"To safety. The faster we get there, the sooner I can kill the fuckers who dared attack us!" He growled loudly, making the trees and the earth shake, but I held my head high as I looked straight into his eyes.

"This is my home as much as it is yours. I want to defend it too."

"You are not setting foot near the battlegrounds! That's final!" Levi roared, his eyes becoming darker. He was consumed by his violent emotions. "You are the heart of this pack. *You* are *my* heart! And I will not hand you to the enemy on a silver platter!"

"I will not-"

"This is an order, not a request!" He pulled me by my wrist, almost making me crash against his chest. He towered over me, but I wasn't the least intimidated. "Assume the compromise you made to this pack as their Luna and stay safe!"

His anger seemed to be affecting me, because I soon felt the strong desire to yell back and fight him. Old me would have lowered her head and apologized for her behavior, but I now knew I was entitled to my own decisions. Moreso, I was supposed to rule this pack with him, and I didn't appreciate his tone. However, before I could voice my displeasure, the blond boy appeared in my field of vision, leaving me confused.

"Alpha. Luna." Ivar bowed at us. Judging by the way he was slightly shaking, I was sure he could sense Levi's powerful aura.

"Keep a close eye on her," my mate ordered before turning to me. "You better behave until I return." With these last words, he turned around and shifted into the huge wolf with metallic gray fur.

"Hey, Cal." I could feel the Gamma's unease, although I was still scowling at the hard-headed Alpha. "How was the stroll?"

"Shouldn't you be fighting too?" I completely ignored his question when I finally looked at him.

He seemed taken aback by my harshness, but he didn't complain. "Usually, yes. But Levi gave me strict orders to...keep you company, until they fend off the enemies."

"So instead of helping the pack, you have basically been assigned to be my babysitter?"

He was silent for a few seconds, nervous. "Why don't we go talk in the Alpha suite? Maybe we can watch something, or-"

"I'm still your Luna. If I command you to let me go, there will be nothing stopping me from joining the other warriors."

"Please don't do that!" There was true despair in his voice. "Just let me take you back to your room, Cal. I was told to keep you there, and I will be in big trouble if-"

"Fine!" I barked. Though I was overwhelmed with rage, I still didn't want to make Ivar pay the consequences for my stubbornness.

When we got to the Alpha suite, Ivar stood guard by the door while I paced from side to side on the balcony. Blood Eclipse's territory was huge, and it had tall trees that prevented me from seeing very far. However, I could still hear the sounds of battle due to my heightened hearing. Also, being able to feel Levi's anger through our connection wasn't helping me stay calm at all. Although I used to lack the proper training, my Delta lineage made me a born fighter. As Luna, my instinct to protect my people grew even more. How could my mate so blatantly ignore my rights?

"This is a sensitive topic for him. He lost his father because his mother made the mistake of being vulnerable during a battle, when she should have remained hiding." In a second of clarity, it seemed so obvious, but in the rush of the situation, I seemed to have forgotten about his trauma - the very reason why we had had such a rough start. *"Sometimes, the best thing a Luna can do to protect the pack is stay safe. Our real job starts after the battle, when the members are emotionally vulnerable and require our support."*

I had to sigh in defeat. *"I know... But I still don't think Levi has the right to speak to us the way he did."*

"I agree. But it can be hard to think clearly during high stress situations. I mean, you too had an outburst when you threatened the Gamma for simply doing what he was ordered to do." For the first time since this all started, my anger subsided but shame rose in its place. I looked back at the blond boy who never took his eyes at me. He was always so kind and sweet; he didn't deserve my rudeness. *"It's okay to make mistakes, Cal. I'm sure he understands why you behaved that way. About our mate, you should try talking to him again once they get rid of the enemies. It'll be easier to make him listen when he's not so on edge, maybe even flooded with regret rather than rage,"* she stated cleverly before retreating to the back of my mind.

As soon as our conversation ended, I felt Ivar shyly rest his hand on my shoulder. When I turned around, I noticed he was eyeing me with caution. He was wearing his usual smile, and it made me calm down.

"Maybe we can play card games to take your mind off the attack? I'm sure they have everything under control. You don't have to worry," he reassured me.

"I would love that. Thank you." I showed him a small smile, and he nodded in return.

The Gamma headed towards the cabinet, pulling a card deck out of the top drawer. I didn't even know we had one there, which made me wonder if Levi used to organize game nights or something with his friends before we met. We sat down facing each other at the large dining table and started playing Trash. It proved to be a good distraction; as the minutes went by, I slowly calmed down.

"You're really good at this game, Luna!" the boy chanted

after I beat him for the second time.

"It's all about luck." I shrugged.

"Well, you're very lucky."

Both of us laughed. My anger was completely gone, but now I was consumed by guilt. Even after the poor way I treated him, Ivar was doing his best to make me feel comfortable and happy. When it was my turn to shuffle the deck, I pulled the cards away momentarily to look into his eyes.

"I'm sorry for lashing out at you earlier. I hope you can forgive me," I told him sincerely.

"Already forgotten." He winked at me. "I understand why you were mad. I have heard some nasty comments from Hailey for the same reason. She doesn't really want to be a fighter, but she sometimes gets angry for having to stay in the bunker while I fight. Considering how amazing you and Nava are in training, I'm sure it must be even more annoying for you."

"It is." I sighed.

"That being said...I can understand why the Alpha wanted you to stay out of the fight," he went on, looking down. "This pack has improved a lot since your arrival, Luna. We can't afford to lose you."

I couldn't help but smile at him. "Thank you for keeping me company."

"It's my pleasure. Another round?" He pointed at the cards I had been holding during our entire conversation.

Before I could reply, Levi's voice inside my head broke my concentration. *"Calliope. The attack is over. Can you come meet me in my office, please?"*

CHAPTER THIRTY-THREE

Levi

Blood Eclipse wasn't a peaceful pack - at least not since I stepped in as Alpha. Nevertheless, we were usually the ones engaging the attacks, not defending against them. Needless to say, I was quite surprised when my Beta informed me of the urgent situation. My shock, however, only lasted a second before it was overshadowed by my anger. It made me furious to have my precious moment with Calliope interrupted by the audacity of some idiots who dared invade our lands.

And once I made sure my Luna was safe, I was ready to figure out exactly who they were. That is, if Odin didn't tear them all apart first.

The huge gray beast was foaming at the mouth like a ravenous animal by the time we made it to the battlefield. He was seeing red, and I was afraid he wouldn't be able to see the difference between an enemy or a friend if someone tried to stand in our way. Our goal was to make it to Darrell, who was leading the army, but we had a bit of a setback - two wolves trying to sneak past our warriors. Odin didn't hesitate before slashing one's throat out, his movements so quick the creature barely had time to understand what was happening. The other one tried to run, but we knocked him on the ground before he could even take his first step, easily ripping his head off with our sharp teeth. In the blink of an eye, our light spiky fur had been colored crimson.

We reached Banyan, Darrell's wolf, just in time to watch him finish off another enemy. His coat resembled that of a tortoiseshell cat with mixed shades of orange, deep brown, and black. The crocodile tooth piercings my friend wore in his ears were also present in his wolf form; a spell had been cast on them so they wouldn't be damaged or lost during the transformation. He licked his bloody lips before he finally lifted his head up, his intense yellow eyes immediately locking on us.

"*What's our current situation?*" I asked my Beta via the mindlink.

"*Our sentinels have retreated, and I've sent scouts to get more information. So far, we haven't been able to identify the enemy,*" he explained promptly. "*All we know is they are coming in waves, so I instructed the warriors to stay put and wait for them to approach. As long as we are in our territory, we will have the upper hand.*"

As determined as I was to exterminate every single one of the fuckers so I could get back to my Luna soon, I had to agree with him. For all we know, they could be trying to lure us out of our lands into a trap. In my blaze of fury, I would never have managed to think so clearly, which is why the Beta was usually in charge of leading the troops. Aside from being my right hand man, Darrell had studied battle strategy for years and he had enough experience to know what the best course of action was; all I had to do was trust him.

A howl of warning in the distance announced another wave of enemies was coming. Banyan and Odin nodded at each other before marching forward together. There were around two hundred warriors with us, and from what I could notice, we hadn't lost many of our men yet. It was impossible to count the attacking beasts as they lunged towards us, but there surely weren't more than fifty of them.

As my beast slashed every creature who had the misfortune of crossing paths with him, questions arose in my mind. According to my second in command, their motives remained unknown, but why would they even try to strike when they were clearly outnumbered? They weren't rogues - they lacked the characteristic smell of rotten flesh and dirt, which meant these wolves had to belong to another pack. However, legal attacks had to be approved by the Elders, so we should have been informed in advance. And if they were part of a pack, where was their leader?

"*We need reinforcements at the northern borders!*" The Delta's voice echoed inside my head, startling me. Thankfully, Darrell had my back; I turned around to watch him catch a wolf who tried to jump at me, snapping his neck mid-air with a powerful bite.

"*These were probably just a distraction,*" the Beta concluded, letting me know he too had gotten Bellatrix's message. "*Their purpose must have been to weaken us and keep us occupied so they could strike from a different location.*"

"*These fuckers thought they could fool us? The most powerful Alphas in the country?*" Odin scoffed in disdain. "*I hope they're prepared to pay for their mistake!*"

Overcome by our rage again, we charged in the direction the enemies were coming from. My counterpart was swiping his paws and snapping his jaws so fast, it was impossible to understand what was going on. In the blink of an eye, we were standing on top of a pile of corpses, proof that we had successfully destroyed what was left of them. We were panting and sweating, our coat drenched in blood. With a loud growl, I commanded Banyan to follow us. I was done waiting patiently. I would kill every single one of them, and I would do it now!

Blood Eclipse's territory was fairly large, but using our werewolf speed we covered the distance quick as lightning, our paws thundering as they stomped the ground. My Beta's suspicions were confirmed once we arrived at the northern gate - our warriors were having trouble trying to contain around two hundred wolves who had already taken down a good number of our men. The scene only made me more furious; it pained me to see my pack members lose their lives in such a cowardly attack. Odin's desires mixed with my own, and there was only one thought on my mind - kill, kill, kill.

Our cold blue eyes locked on the first enemy who ran in our direction. We didn't hesitate to bear our fangs at him, preparing ourselves for the perfect moment to strike. But then, he did the last thing we would expect - he dodged. Confused, we watched him dart away towards the main part of our lands. We were even more surprised to see him throw himself at a wooden house he found along the way, creating a hole in one of the walls.

"They have been doing this for a while now." Upon hearing Trix's voice again, I turned around to find her black, long-haired wolf. It was hard to distinguish the color of blood in her damp coat, but the red liquid was still dripping from her fur. I expected nothing less from Nyx, one of our best warriors.

"What do you mean?" I finally asked, blocking the path

of another filthy creature. This time, we were aware of his intentions, which allowed us to catch him by his hindleg the second he jumped to the side. He screeched in agony as we mercilessly broke his bones before delivering the final blow.

"The enemies on the front line headed straight to combat, but the ones in the back seemed to avoid fighting. Instead, they've been doing this." Nyx jerked her head toward the wolf that was just killed. *"Running away and trying to damage as many structures as they can before they're caught,"* she clarified.

"Darrell!" I roared.

"I've already sent a unit to stop the runaways." Banyan nodded at me.

Despite their efforts to confuse us, we still had everything under control. I shook my head in an attempt to rid it of the many questions bothering me; I had to focus on the fight. For the first minutes, we tried to concentrate on slowing the attackers down as best as we could. The few who managed to escape our fangs were soon stopped by the reinforcements my Beta had called. As expected, they were losing, and they seemed to realize it too.

Half an hour went by before we heard a loud, powerful howl, which could only belong to an Alpha. Now I knew where their pussy leader was. Unfortunately, I doubted we would have a chance to meet. The sound was a signal, commanding his followers to retreat. The enemies on the frontline suddenly stopped fighting to turn around and leave. Alongside my Beta and Delta, I chased them off to the borders, managing to eliminate a few more of them. It enraged me to realize they thought they could strike and leave so easily. I was ready to continue following them until I made sure not a single one was left, but a man stood in my way. The only one who was foolish enough to defy my ravenous beast.

"Levi, don't!" Darrell screamed, opening his arms in front of me - as if he could stop Odin from advancing. A warning growl left our throat, but he ignored it. "There is no point going after them now. We don't know what could be waiting for us. The best thing we can do is figure out why they were here and discuss the measures we should take." Always the fucking voice of reason.

Against my wolf's will, I forced him to retreat and give me back control. Trix, who was also back to her human form, threw me a towel so I could clean the blood off my skin and cover my body. Once the attack was over, I took a quick glance over the battlegrounds, analyzing the damage the enemy had done; the lives taken, the structures destroyed. The view made the hate grow inside my heart. However, as we made the way back to the packhouse, my anger started to subside. In a moment of clarity, I thought about my Luna and how I wanted her to calm me down.

And as I remembered her, I was reminded of what I had done.

"Levi? Is everything alright?" the Delta asked me. I kept a neutral semblance, but she was probably confused with why I had suddenly stopped walking.

"Yes. The two of you go ahead and get cleaned. There's something else I need to do."

I quickly walked past them, grabbing one of the many spare shorts Omegas were handing out by the entrance of the packhouse. On my way to my office, I linked Cal to let her know to meet me there. I could only hope she wouldn't be too mad to show up. The minutes seemed like hours as I waited for her, but when she did, time seemed to completely stop. She had changed out of the outfit she had worn for our horse-ride, and I momentarily wanted to scold her for not letting me get rid of it myself. But the second I saw her face, all I could do was rush towards her, ignoring her scowl.

Without a second thought, I let my mouth crash against hers, rightly grabbing both sides of her face with my rough hands. She didn't reciprocate the kiss at first, but as I forced my way in, she couldn't resist the temptation to wrestle my tongue for control. I felt her hands on my chest, trying to push me away, but I didn't budge. At least not until she slapped me, my cheek burning as she finally managed to struggle out of my grasp. There was a mix of pride, anger, and desire in my blue eyes as I lifted my gaze up to look at her.

"You don't get to kiss me like that after the way you talked to me," she said sharply, crossing her arms. I knew she wanted me to stay away, but if she only knew how her posture was drawing me in. She looked so hot when she demanded respect.

"I know. I'm sorry." Her eyes widened at my response. She definitely wasn't expecting me to concede so easily, but I knew there was no point arguing with her. After all, she was right; she was my Luna and I shouldn't have raised my voice at her. "In the middle of the chaos, all I could think about was how I needed to protect you."

"I can protect myself," she retorted, taking a step back when I inched closer. She still wasn't convinced.

I sighed. "Yes, and you're a great fighter. But I'd rather not put your skills to test unless extremely necessary."

"You can't keep me locked up in a tower like a princess,

Levi!" she yelled. "I'm the Luna of this pack, and I want to defend it too."

"And you should! Not like this though."

"Why not?"

"Because I can't risk losing you!" It was my turn to yell - not in anger, but in desperation. The day I lost my father played in my mind like a movie. I refused to let history repeat itself.

I approached her again, and this time, she didn't fight me. Instead, she rested her face on my chest as I slowly wrapped my arms around her. I brushed her head with my fingers, placing a soft kiss on the top of her head before lifting her chin up.

"For Blood Eclipse's sake, you need to stay safe. We will crumble without you, my Luna," I whispered, my eyes locked on hers.

"I understand." It was my turn to be surprised. I didn't expect her to agree with me, even though I could tell she wasn't completely satisfied. "But I still don't appreciate the way you talked to me."

"It was a mistake. I promise it won't happen again," I told her sincerely. "It was always hard for me to control my anger, but I will not let it speak louder than my love for you." I rested my forehead on hers, inhaling her calming scent. "I love you, Calliope."

"I love you too."

We remained silent in each other's embrace for a while, but I should have known my moment of peace wouldn't last long.

"*The scouts just got back to me.*" Darrell's voice echoed inside my head. "*Solar Hunt is the pack that attacked us.*"

CHAPTER THIRTY-FOUR

Levi

The information my Beta gave me triggered my wrath to come rushing back at once. I gritted my teeth, trying to hold back the growl reverberating in my throat. My fingers started contracting, pulling inwards towards my palm. However, I couldn't seem to fully clench my fists; there was something soft under my fingertips. I only realized I was still holding Calliope in my arms when she stiffened due to the pressure I was applying to her arms. My muscles immediately relaxed as I pulled away from her, not wanting to hurt her.

The promise I had just made to her echoed in my mind. I couldn't let my rage get the best of me this time. In an attempt to focus, I turned my back to my Luna, facing the back wall of my office. *Stay calm*, I closed my eyes. *Stay calm*, I took a deep breath. *Stay calm*, I tried to rid my mind of the negativity. *Stay calm, stay calm, stay calm*. My eyes snapped open again, blue flames dancing inside of them. *Why can't I stay fucking calm?!*

Consumed by fury, I threw my fist against the wall, burying it deep into the concrete. No matter how hard I tried, all I could think about was murdering the fuckers who attacked my pack and ran off like cowards. Now that I knew who they were, my beast urged me to show them what a mistake they had made. He wanted blood - *I* wanted blood.

But suddenly, in my sea of red rage appeared a single white drop of tranquility - I chose to hold on to it. Calliope's delicate hands were wrapped around my other fist, a look of confusion and concern on her face. Through my madness, she was the only one capable of bringing me back. She was my anchor. I pulled my hand out of the wall, turning around to properly face her. Her pools of warm honey drew me in; the longer I stared into them, the easier it was to leave my anger behind.

"What happened?" she finally asked. Her soft, melodic voice was so soothing.

I took another breath, making sure I wouldn't snap again. "Darrell told me they were able to identify who attacked us. It was Solar Hunt.

She was thoughtful for a moment, probably trying to remember all I had taught her about other packs in our country and our relationship with them.

"They're one of our enemies," she recalled.

"Yes. Our most recent one." I made a brief pause to reach out to my ranked members via the mindlink, summoning them for an urgent meeting. Once the message was sent, my attention fell back onto my mate. "We visited them less than two months ago. Our goal was to establish a peace treaty with them, but I called it off when I learned they had recently made an alliance with Silver Waters." A low growl escaped my lips.

"Oh." Her eyes widened in realization. "*Oh*... That was the day when you came to me to...blow off some steam," she said shyly. I growled again, this time because of my lust. She didn't complain when I roughly pulled her closer by the waist. In fact, the scent of her arousal proved she actually enjoyed it.

"Once we're done here, I will be in desperate need of... release." My voice was husky as I whispered into her ear. The hairs in her neck bristled under my hot breath, further exciting me. "Will you help me, my Luna?"

Instead of hearing my much needed reply, the only sound I could catch was that of knocks on the door, forcing me to pull away from my mate. When I noticed the smirk on her face, I considered ignoring my ranked members for a while longer so I could punish her for teasing me. It took all of my strength to put my responsibilities first and decide against it. Cal leaned against the front edge of the desk while I quickly opened the door, gesturing for my Beta, Gamma, and Delta to take their seats. The faster we were done here, the sooner I would be able to be alone with Calliope.

"What have you got for me?" I looked at Darrell as I leaned back in my chair.

"The scouts I sent earlier managed to get close enough to the wolf who was leading the attack. They recognized him as Alpha Julius of Solar Hunt Pack," he informed me.

"Did we catch any prisoners?"

My Delta snorted. "Would have helped if we did. I'm afraid you and Odin made sure there were no survivors, Alpha."

I could feel my mate's shocked gaze on me, but I chose to ignore it. Once again, my poor anger management skills had made things harder for me.

"In my defense, how was I supposed to know they would call off the attack?" my wolf chimed in. *"If they had stayed and fought us honorably, we would have captured their leader. Cowards don't deserve to be spared!"* Well, he had a point.

"Ivar," I called, catching the young boy's attention. "Any

guesses on why they attacked us out of the blue?" I wondered if Silver Waters was somehow behind all of this. However, I wanted to hear my Gamma's opinion first; he was the pack's analyst and strategist, after all.

"There are a million possibilities, honestly. Blood Eclipse has more enemies than any other pack. They don't lack motivation to strike."

"Could they have done it as retaliation because we declared them as enemies without a reason other than the Silver Waters alliance?" Calliope suggested.

"Perhaps." Ivar shrugged. "The whole situation was too unusual, from what I was told. They came without warning, and left without taking anything. Their plan consisted of placing their strongest warriors in the front line to slow our defenses down, while their fastest wolves charged into our territory - not to steal or kill, but to destroy property."

"It seems a lot like they were just gathering intel, if you ask me," Trix observed.

The longer we discussed the issue, the more I realized we had no concrete information. All we had were doubts and guesses, which wouldn't be useful for the moment. There were more important problems we had to solve, starting by assessing the damage that had been done. Meanwhile, we should try to gain further knowledge regarding our attackers and their motives.

"Darrell, reach out to the Elders and see what information you can find. Any legitimate attacks must go through them, so they should be able to help us," I commanded, watching my Beta nod. "Ivar, check our security and prepare new reports. Make sure to talk to our sentinels as well for their accounts of events." At last, I turned to my Delta. "Bellatrix, assist the pack members who had their houses damaged. Let me know how long it will take to rebuild everything."

The three ranked members nodded at me before standing up from their seats, ready to set off to take care of their newly assigned tasks. As they left, I swiveled my chair around to go through the archive drawers behind my desk in search of a specific folder with detailed information on our current enemy. Maybe I could find something relevant to shine a light on our complicated case.

"What should we do now?" Cal asked from behind me.

"Prepare," I told her promptly without taking my eyes off the papers. "Right now, they are one step ahead of us, and I don't like it at all." As one of the strongest packs in the country, we were rarely threatened by others. For Solar Hunt to attack us so boldly, they had to either be stupid or have a bigger plan in their minds. "If we can't figure out their intentions, it'll be safer to destroy them before they become a bigger threat."

"That's risky," she replied hesitantly. "What if they're already expecting us to come?"

"Even if they are, they're no match for us," I insisted. She didn't seem content with my answer, but she let it go. At least for now.

"Is there anything I can help you with?"

I stopped briefly when I heard her words, an interesting idea crossing my mind. She didn't seem the least surprised when I spun back around with a smirk on my face.

"This situation has stressed me greatly. I'm afraid I won't be able to think clearly in such a condition. Maybe you could help ease away my tension..."

She showed me her sassy smile, which I had learned to love as much as her innocent one. "Of course, Alpha. It is my duty as this pack's Luna to make sure you're in your right mind."

She inched closer, sliding her hand down my chest and stomach, stopping at the waistband of my jeans. She unzipped them, feeling my erection through the thin fabric of my boxers, which she quickly pulled down. When I felt her soft, wet mouth wrap around my cock, I let my head fall backwards with a groan. I closed my eyes to get lost in the amazing sensation as she blew my stress away.

CHAPTER THIRTY-FIVE

Calliope

Once I had properly helped relieve some of my Alpha's tension, I stayed with him in his office to try and put together the pieces of this puzzle. It was mostly a guessing game since we were still waiting for our ranked members to hopefully come back with concrete evidence, but it was a necessary preventive measure. After the mysterious attack, the one thing we couldn't afford to do was to sit back and do nothing.

As stressful as the situation was, it felt good to actually put my analytical skills to use for the first time in a while. Ever since I acquired the Luna title, most of my efforts were concentrated on maintaining a respectable posture, organizing small events, and fixing minor problems. Although no one appreciated my work back when I was still living in my old pack, I was now fully aware of how efficient I was as a Delta. I wanted to feel more useful as a leader as well, which is why I would try to use my abilities at any and every opportunity.

By the end of the day, we had been able to come to a few basic conclusions. It wasn't anything extremely helpful, but it was a starting point for when we gathered more information. At ten o'clock, I managed to convince Levi we wouldn't make any more advances before a good night's sleep. It had been a long, tiring day. Werewolves were more resilient, but we needed to rest too. We had a late dinner in our room before finally going to bed.

The next morning, my Alpha went straight to his office after training, along with his Beta and Gamma. I was impressed at how quickly they managed to write new reports following Levi's orders from the previous day, but it made sense; they were the best at their jobs, which is why Blood Eclipse faced little to no threats. They were capable of solving small issues before they became bigger problems, though the pack had really been lacking someone to look after its members and make sure they were all happy and safe. The ruthless Alpha imposed respect, keeping other over ambitious leaders away. However, only a Luna could ensure the pack wouldn't collapse from the inside.

For that reason, I decided I would be more useful assisting the Delta and the Gamma Female despite how curious I was to know what the men were discussing. The three of us met at the entrance of the packhouse to get the day started. Trix had already helped the pack members who had their homes vandalized during the attack move into temporary housing located in the central part of the territory. She still had to take a closer look at the damages dealt so she could organize and prepare the correct information with Hailey's help. Ivar's mate was a genius much like him, and she was in charge of calculating the costs for the reconstruction of the damaged structures. Meanwhile, I hoped to be able to get a better understanding of the pack members' other immediate problems to help them as best as I could.

As soon as we reached the borders, I was shocked when my eyes landed on all the debris. It was my first time seeing the result of the conflict, and it seemed alarming. Back in Moonstone we were rarely attacked by other packs, so I barely had to deal with similar situations. The only time I saw so much destruction was on the day my parents perished, but then again, Blood Eclipse was a much larger pack with a lot more warriors and resources. How did it come to this?

"This is definitely not normal," Trix observed, as if she was reading my thoughts. "Solar Hunt is a small pack. We're not sure if they had any help yesterday, but they still came in a relatively small number. They barely killed any of our men, yet this destruction looks like it was caused by a gigantic army."

"Because their goal clearly wasn't to lower our numbers, but to damage our structures," Hailey concluded as she wrote everything down in a clipboard she was carrying. "They didn't change their plan after realizing they wouldn't be able to defeat us. This was what they orchestrated from the start. But why would such a small pack risk being destroyed just to take a few houses and storages down?"

"Maybe they were sure they would be able to retreat safely," the Delta continued. "Their Alpha remained hidden during the whole attack. He knew he was the most important piece, so he made sure he wouldn't be vulnerable. As long as he was alive, he would be able to command the attack."

"What do you think, Cal?" The Gamma Female turned to me, probably noticing how concentrated I was.

"Well, Levi and I studied some different possibilities last night..." I started, crouching near the debris in hopes of finding new clues. "One of them was that this attack wasn't random; it was part of something bigger. Forming alliances solely to attack another pack is forbidden by the Elder Council, but if they each strike individually throughout a few days or even months, they could weaken us to the point where one of them could just finish us off."

"Uh, who exactly is 'they'?" Hailey cocked her head to the side.

"A possible alliance under the table between smaller packs to take us down, probably orchestrated by some of our many enemies," I reluctantly revealed.

The girl widened her eyes. "You really think that could be happening?"

"It's improbable, but it wouldn't be the first time it's happened in werewolf history," the Delta answered before I could. "Anyway, let's get to work. A lot needs to be done."

We went around the areas that had been destroyed by the enemies to collect the needed information to fix everything as fast as we could. There were also a few families standing in front of their demolished houses while workers tried to retrieve important belongings that had been lost among the rubble. Both Trix and Hailey made sure to approach the affected pack members to ask if they needed assistance with anything. It was surprising to see how they managed to keep the wolves comfortable during such a delicate situation. Only then, I realized they had been responsible for keeping the pack together.

They were the hearts of Blood Eclipse before I arrived. Now, we were only missing a Beta Female.

"Nina, come back here right now!" An unfamiliar male voice caught my attention.

I turned around just in time to find a father running after his runaway pup. Tears streamed down the little girl's rosy cheeks as she completely ignored her old man, continuing on her way. I immediately scooped her into my arms when she ran by me before she gave the poor Omega a heart attack. She stopped crying as I rocked her in my arms, probably confused after being picked up by a stranger. Although she didn't seem to be older than four, she could run impressively fast.

"Luna Calliope!" The man gasped as he stood in front of me. The next second, he bowed in respect. "I'm so sorry about my daughter's behavior! I turned around for a second and she just ran off!"

"It's no problem, Mr…" In a pack with more than a thousand members, it was hard to remember each of their names.

"Elliot, Luna," he replied, rising back up.

"And you're Nina, right?" I turned to the little pup with a smile. She nodded slowly, still unsure. "Why is a pretty princess like you crying?"

"My…my…wolfie!" she sobbed.

"I'm very sorry, Luna. Her favorite wolf plushie was lost when our house got demolished," the father clarified. "Of course, I wouldn't ask one of the workers to search the debris for a stuffed animal. I was hoping she would forget about it eventually, but she hasn't stopped crying since yesterday."

"I see." An idea crossed my mind. It was my duty to lower the stress of the pack members during this difficult moment, and I really wanted to help. "Is that your house?" I pointed in the direction she had been running to. She quickly confirmed. "Okay. If you promise to stay here with your father, I will try to find your wolfie."

"Luna! There's no need to!" the man assured me.

"Please, I insist. It will only take a minute anyway."

"Wait, Cal," Trix whispered as she pulled me closer by my arm. "Let's get one of the workers here. You could get hurt in the rubble."

"I'll be fine. The workers already have too much in their hands." I waved her off. *"Nava, can you help me out?"*

"Of course. But I can't promise we will be able to find anything."

"I think it's still worth a try."

Pieces of cloth floated in the air as I allowed Nava control. She rushed towards the demolished house, carefully digging through the wreckage. Her pure white fur slowly turned gray as we were covered in dust, but she didn't slow down. It took quite some time, but we eventually found something fluffy and soft among the pile of wood and stone. Nava gently picked it up by the neck with her teeth, as if it were a real pup; if we damaged it, the little girl would be even more devastated.

As soon as I jumped away from the debris, Hailey approached me with a robe she had run off to get after my clothes were destroyed during my transformation. It wasn't uncommon for werewolves to be naked around each other, but considering I was their Luna, I could understand the Gamma Female's concern about not letting others see my body. Once I was back to my human form and dressed, I walked over to the little girl. Her green eyes twinkled when she identified what I was holding.

"Wolfie!" she sang out happily, never taking her gaze off the plushie as I gave it to her father.

"It's a bit dirty, but that can be remedied." I smiled at him.

"Thank you so much, Luna. She will finally let us sleep

now." He sighed in relief. "I'm so sorry for causing you so much trouble."

"It was nothing. I'm glad to-" Before I could finish my sentence, I was caught off guard by the little girl wrapping her tiny arms around my legs in what I suspected to be a hug.

"Thank you, Luna! You saved wolfie!"

My heart fluttered at her sweet gesture. I crouched in front of her, taking her hands in mine. "You're very welcome. Now, be a good girl and take care of it, okay?"

"I promise I will!" She hopped cheerfully before turning around to leave with her father.

"Oh, shit," I heard Trix whisper. I was confused at first, until I saw my mate standing in front of me. She was probably scared he would get mad at them for letting me dig around the rubble.

"Let me see what he wants. You girls go ahead, I'll catch up to you later." They didn't hesitate before walking in the opposite direction.

As soon as they were gone, Levi walked over to me. Although his semblance was impassive as always, I had learned to notice the subtle signals he showed me through his body language. He was growling when he possessively wrapped his arms around me, but I knew he wasn't angry; it was a hungry sound.

"As soon as I saw you with that little girl, I couldn't help but picture you as a mother," he whispered into my ear, his hot breath sending shivers down my spine. "You would look so hot carrying my heir. When will you let me put a pup in your belly?"

I was startled at first. The idea hadn't crossed my mind

yet, but it sounded quite pleasing. "It's probably best if we figure this whole situation..." I gestured around us to the aftermath of the attack, "...before thinking about having a pup."

Once again, he growled, this time obviously mad. There were blue flames in his eyes when he looked at me.

"I will kill whoever stands in our way. No one will ever threaten our family," he promised.

And I had to admit, it made me melt.

CHAPTER THIRTY-SIX

Calliope

Little by little, everything was starting to get back to normal. Blood Eclipse was a wealthy pack, so we had no trouble paying for the reconstruction of the buildings damaged during the attack. It was certainly a setback on our investigation, considering we were mostly focused on making sure our home was fixed, but it didn't slow us down too much. While the Alpha monitored the workers and kept up with his Beta's reports, I stayed in touch with the members, listening to their concerns and personally tending to their every need. In less than a week, we were already back on our feet.

The morning following the last day of construction, I decided to visit the wolves who had been rehomed to check how they were doing. Most of them were doing great, and thanked me for the time I had been dedicating to them. Honestly, I don't think they need to thank me, I was merely doing my job as a Luna, and I loved talking to my people. It was incredible to watch my bond with the pack grow, especially because I could feel they respected me out of love, when they respected their Alpha out of fear. Together, we truly were a powerful couple.

Lastly, I stopped by Nina's new house. Her parents thanked me yet again for rescuing their daughter's plushie, and I was glad to see Wolfie was clean and safe in the pup's arms. She was really excited about playing with Nava, whom she called a superhero. Her father scolded her, saying it was disrespectful to ask the Luna to shift when I was already so busy, but I couldn't resist her cute pouty lip. I gave my white wolf control, chuckling when Nina sighed in admiration.

As I watched my counterpart carefully play with the little girl, I couldn't help but think about my mate's words. I never imagined myself having a pup at such a young age, but then again, my old pack made me believe I was too incompetent to be a mother. Now that Levi had learned to respect me and I had found my inner strength, the idea seemed quite appealing. Maybe it was something we could discuss in the near future, once we made sure none of our enemies would disturb the peace and threaten our heir's health.

After Nava finally managed to tire Nina out, we said our goodbyes and I headed to the stables, where Levi would be meeting me. It was Sunday, and now that the mess had been taken care of, my mate and I were planning on going horseback riding again. Since our last ride had been interrupted by the terrible event, I was really looking forward to trying again - and hoping our day out would be uneventful until the end.

Once I arrived at the wooden structure, I realized my Alpha wasn't there yet. Instead, I found Crystal grazing right outside. Like usual, she lifted her head to search for me as soon as she felt my presence. She neighed before trotting towards me, pushing me with her long muzzle in a clear demand for me to pet her. I couldn't help but laugh. This unicorn was the best gift I could have gotten; she kept me company and always put a smile on my face.

"I've missed you too, girl," I told her as I caressed her pearly white fur.

However, instead of neighing in response, she stiffened.

At first, I was surprised by her reaction, but it didn't take long for me to feel an unusual warmth, heating me up from the inside. It was weird, considering the temperature was cool today, the overcast dulling the intense sun rays. In only a few seconds, it felt like my whole being would catch on fire at any moment. What was happening to me?

The strange sensation was followed by a sudden loss of balance. My legs failed me, causing me to instinctively wrap my arms around my unicorn's neck for support. Crystal uttered a bray in shock, but remained by my side to make sure I was okay. It was all happening too fast, and the inability to understand what was wrong only made me freak out more. The heat became more intense, as if a strong fire had ignited inside of me. When my skin started burning, I could no longer hold in a painful cry.

"Cal!" Just as I was about to fall to the ground, my mate appeared right beside me. I didn't know if he had witnessed the whole scene, or if he felt my pain and rushed to meet me, but it didn't matter. I felt as though I was burning alive; it was the only thing I could concentrate on. "What's wrong?! Someone get the doctor!" He shifted his attention from me to a few scared passersby who immediately obeyed him. "Talk to me, Cal," he pleaded, but he didn't get a response. My discomfort was so intense I couldn't bring myself to utter another word.

As he held me in his arms, Crystal surrounded us, visibly distressed. I didn't really pay much attention to what she was doing, fully concentrated on trying to push the pain away so I could explain my symptoms. Only when she approached my dangling right arm, gently pressing her muzzle against my open hand, I realized her intentions. A glowing crescent appeared in my palm, just like the one that I saw the day she accepted me as her rider, at the same time that her horn shone brightly. Once the light was gone, my pain had died down considerably.

I was in awe. Unicorns could have different magical powers, which could be stronger based on the creature's bond with its rider - I guess this was one of Crystal's. It was my first time witnessing such a mystical scene, and my only reaction was to stare at her in disbelief. However, Levi's voice soon brought me out of my awestruck state.

"What happened? Are you okay?" he asked, desperately rocking me in his arms. His eyes never left mine, full of concern.

After the crazy experience, I had to blink a few times. "I'm better now," I reassured him, and his expression was one of pure relief. "It was...weird. And scary. It felt like I was engulfed in flames. My skin was burning and-"

"I believe you are in heat, Luna." A different voice caught my attention. When I turned around, I was surprised to notice the pack doctor had already arrived.

Levi's semblance darkened. "If that's the case, it'll come back soon." I gasped in horror as I realized he was right.

It was common for she-wolves to go into heat after they found their mates. It would last for three or four days, and during that time, the burning sensation would keep coming back. Unless...

"Thank you, Doctor. I got it from here." My mate nodded

at the doctor, who bowed in respect before taking his leave.

Levi didn't waste another second to carry me into the packhouse. Once we made it to our room on the top floor, there were two Omegas filling the bathtub with water, salts, and some ice cubes. They were done in a minute and bowed at us on their way out.

My mate promptly helped me undress, but it was different than all of the times he had done it in the past. He usually tore my clothes off, so hungry to have me that he acted more animal than human. However, this time he was gentle, delicate; he showed me a side to him I never knew the ruthless Alpha had.

As he unzipped my dress and slid the sleeves off my shoulders, he was careful. He took his time to study my body, his fingertips barely touching my skin as he ran them along my arms. I shivered in delight when his warm lips pressed against my neck, his hands wrapping around my waist to pull me closer. I loved his roughness, but I was also curious about how caring and passionate he could be. It intrigued me.

To my disappointment, he pulled away, making me gasp in surprise due to his sudden absence. Instead of getting rid of his clothes like I expected, he interlaced our fingers and led me towards the bathroom. My entire body craved him. I needed his touch, his hunger, yet he didn't seem ready to give it to me. I couldn't hide the pout on my face, but I didn't protest as he helped me into the tub.

I usually enjoyed hot showers, but I had to admit the icy water truly calmed my nerves down. A moan of relief escaped my lips as I slowly lowered myself in the tub, eager to let the coldness tend to my burning skin. Levi's grip on my hand tightened when he heard the pleasurable sound come out of my mouth, but he hesitantly let go. As I relaxed against the bathtub, he crouched down beside me. For the first time, I noticed the blue flames dancing in his eyes. He was struggling to keep the beast inside of him at bay.

"Wait here while I take care of something. I'll be right back," he reassured me before rushing out of the bathroom.

For long seconds, I just stared at the closed door, hoping he would come back soon. The heat made it unbearable for us females to be away from our mates for longer than a few minutes. It intensified our wolves' need for each other, and it should make my scent even more irresistible for him - if that was the case, he was showing impressive self-control. Eventually, I ended up concentrating on the incredible sensation of the ice cubes brushing against my skin as they floated in the water. It was the most relief I felt even since Crystal took my initial pain away. However, I knew only one thing could truly bring me comfort right now.

And when Levi burst through the door half naked, I realized I would finally get it.

"The plane will be ready to take us to my private island in an hour. We'll stay there until your heat ends," he informed me as he promptly scooped me into his arms, unbothered by the cold water dripping from my body. I was the one experiencing heat, but he seemed even hotter than me.

"You have a private island?" I asked in surprise.

"Yes. It was my father's, but I haven't gone there since I was a pup," he revealed, tossing me onto the bed. "It will give us enough privacy so I can *thoroughly* satisfy your desire." He made quick work of his boxers, and another moan left my mouth as I watched his erection spring free. A wolfish grin lit up his face when he noticed my hunger. "But for the next hour until our flight, my Luna, I can start by fucking your pain away," he growled as he jumped on top of me.

CHAPTER THIRTY-SEVEN

Levi

"Please, Levi! Again!" my mate cried out.

"Yes...my Luna..." I breathed out, barely able to find my voice. I was exhausted, but I would die before I denied one of Calliope's wishes.

For the past three days, we had been enjoying the privacy the island offered us as I tended to her needs. We would spend hours by ourselves at the beach, snacking on the finest delicacies prepared by the chef and only rushing inside once her heat started to come back - at least when there was enough time for us to reach the room. It usually happened four to five times throughout the day, but today, it was more intense than ever. It is known that the symptoms of the cycle are strongest during its final hours, so I had hope that my mate was nearing the end of her heat - I don't think I would be able to go on otherwise.

We hadn't left the bed for the past five hours since we had breakfast. Through the countless orgasms I had given her, I was allowed no breaks. Never in my life had I felt this tired before, not even after my toughest battles. Calliope was definitely testing my limits.

I could literally feel my sore muscles burning. Beads of sweat dripped down my damp hair, yet they failed to cool my feverish temperature. My arms were shaking, struggling to support the weight of my own body. I hoped she wouldn't complain as I closed my eyes, taking a few brief seconds to rest before I had to start all over again. And with a heavy sigh, I pushed myself inside of her another time.

The moan of relief and pleasure that escaped my Luna's mouth made me groan in delight. It was impossible to have enough of the sensual sounds she made, the erotic melody she sang whenever I played her body. Even after draining me countless times, this magnificent woman still made my dick hard. As painful as it was, I loved it. I loved how easily she could tame me when no one else ever could. I was hers, and I would keep going until she was satisfied.

I let my head fall backwards as my sensitive tip explored her swollen walls. She was always so tight, so deliciously warm, and soft. We had mated over a dozen times since we left our territory, but my aching body still craved her. It was insane what she could do to me.

Once I had completely filled her core, I started moving in and out slowly. Judging by her exasperated sighs, I knew it was the opposite of what she wanted, but I needed time to recover my energy. In an attempt to speed up the process, I lowered my nose to her throat, diving my face into her drenched hair to inhale her scent. Her dark coffee and blooming lily scent had intensified due to her heat, becoming more sweet and spicy like chili pepper chocolate. It immediately ignited the fire inside of me.

"I'll give you what you want, my Luna."

A low growl reverberated in my throat as I picked up the pace, causing her groans to echo louder. I could feel her excitement grow each time I rammed my dick into her delicious pussy, ripping out cries of pure pleasure from her as I reached her womb. She seemed to enjoy the times I made love to her, but right now, I knew she wanted - no, *needed* - it rough. Almost as if in confirmation, I felt her nails pierce my skin as she dragged them down my back, drawing blood in her lust. The sharp pain only added to my desire, making me move even faster.

As my mate screamed underneath me, I took a good look at her. My eyes eventually fell on her round breasts, which were bouncing in our passionate dance. Covered in sweat, they glistened like the most precious treasure. I wanted to touch them, but I was afraid I wouldn't be able to hold myself up in only one arm. Instead, I decided to use my mouth. The lack of warning made Calliope gasp as I wrapped my lips around one of her nipples and tried to suck her discomfort away.

"Ah! Levi!"

"Yes, say my name!" I roared, briefly releasing her breast to look into her eyes. "Say my name and I'll make you come!"

A smile played on her lips as she cried out, "Levi! Levi!"

Hearing her repeat my name over and over was driving me crazy. I closed my mouth around her nipple again, switching between sucking and flicking my tongue over it to maximize her pleasure. Her words were becoming less coherent as she ran out of breath, and I knew she was close. I could feel my own climax building up, and with one last deep thrust, her pussy tightened around my cock, forcing me to release what was left of my juices inside of her.

The ecstasy lasted shorter than my previous ones, completely consuming my last bit of energy. I only had a second to roll over before I collapsed beside my mate, my chest quickly heaving up and down in an attempt to find much needed air. Unable to keep my eyes open, I let them shut, dwelling in the darkness for a moment as I focused on the sound of my rapid heartbeat. I never thought I would reach my limit, especially not when it came to sex, but of course Calliope was the one to take me there.

"Levi?" Her faint voice made me freeze. Not again... I couldn't do it again.

"Yes?" I replied hesitantly.

"I think it's gone."

"What?" My eyes burst open at her revelation.

"The heat," she clarified. "I think it's over."

I sighed in relief, dragging my hand over the mattress as I searched for hers. I was still too tired to look at her though.

"That's great. Would you like to take a shower?"

She was thoughtful for a moment. "Actually...can we go to the beach? I think the sea will help me relax."

"Of course, my Luna." I smiled subconsciously. "Just give me a few minutes, then we can go." I heard her chuckling in amusement as I drifted off.

* * *

After a short rest, I finally got up to enjoy the afternoon outside with my mate, just like she requested. We stepped out of our hut right onto the sand, and roamed to the part of the small island where the main buildings were located so I could order us a full course meal. Since we were both starving, it didn't take us long to devour the gourmet dishes that were specially prepared for us.

We laid on sun loungers under the shade of a beach umbrella, allowing the gentle breeze of the ocean to blow away our worries. As tiring as the past few days had been, I was definitely loving spending some private time with Calliope. It had been years since the last time I took a break from my stressful life as an Alpha, and it was different than anything I had ever done before. I was used to having everything happen the way I wanted it to; all I had to do was give orders. However, in my seemingly never-ending pursuit to give my mate what she needed, I let her make the decisions. For the first time, I wasn't in control, but it didn't bother me at all.

The best part - there was no rush. It felt like we had all the time in the world.

When my Luna was ready, I watched her strip down to her turquoise blue bikini. She looked so sexy, it almost made me hard all over again. Thankfully, I don't think she noticed when a painful grunt left my mouth, reminding me I wasn't fully recovered from our earlier non-stop rounds. Pushing my dirty thoughts away, I felt content with just joining her in the water.

Relief washed over me as the tender waves crashed against my feet. I got distracted for a while just watching the water, but my mate's voice soon caught my attention as she invited me in deeper. I didn't hesitate to dive down, allowing the sea to tend to my sore muscles. When I emerged behind Calliope, I instantly wrapped my arms around her. She laughed as I picked her up and spun around with her in my arms.

"Are you enjoying our little vacation, my Luna?" I asked, resting my nose against hers.

"Vey much, my Alpha," she said contentedly, but her smile slowly faded. For a second, I was scared I had done something wrong. "When are we going back?"

By the tone of her question, I realized she just wanted to stay longer. Honestly, the feeling was mutual. "Whenever you're ready. This island is yours as much as it is mine, and we can stay for as long as you want." Her heart skipped a bit, happy with my answer. "I believe we will be able to enjoy it properly if your heat is completely over."

"Weren't we already doing that?" she said playfully. Once again, I felt the deep desire to take her back to the room. Or not. The view was quite romantic where we were, and she looked even more like the Goddess she was as the sun kissed her skin.

After letting our bodies talk for hours on end until our fires were put out, it was nice to take in the peace and quiet. The past few days had been quite hectic with the unexpected attack, which was immediately followed by Calliope's sudden heat. Even at our private refuge, which was inarguably blissful, I barely had time to actually rest.

I had never been a romantic guy. I was surprised by how at ease I felt just standing in the ocean with my Luna in my arms, the water rising up to my chest. We didn't utter a word as the hours rolled by - there was no need to. We just enjoyed each other's company, listening to the sound of the crashing waves, the seagulls squawking as they soared through the dancing colors in the sky, and the wind whispering through the palm trees.

It was heaven.

"You know…I think Nava would enjoy some time with Odin," her sweet voice finally broke the silence as we watched the sunset. She turned away from the mesmerizing view to face me, placing her hands on my bare chest. "It's been all about us since we arrived here, so it's only fair for them to experience this too. She's eager to feel the sand underneath her paws."

"I want to be with her too," Odin promptly chimed in, practically drooling already. *"We don't have this privacy at home. Plus, you haven't let me in days!"*

"We had more urgent matters to take care of," I reminded him playfully before turning back to Calliope. "Like I always say, whatever you want, you shall have."

Taking a deep breath, I plunged into the ocean. By the time I made it back to the surface, Odin had already taken my place. He stood tall, holding his head up high as he tried to maintain his stern Alpha posture, but too excited to prevent his tail from wagging shyly. His façade completely broke the second our mate smiled at us, and he jumped in her direction like a lovesick pup. She disappeared beneath the water before he could reach her. Seconds later, the pure white she-wolf pounced on us.

We let our counterparts play for a while until our stomachs were growling. I would have let Odin hunt our next meal, but there wasn't a lot of prey around, so I took back control. My mate and I went back to the room to shower, and once we were properly dressed, I headed to the kitchen to order food while she chose the best location for our dinner under the stars; she was adamant about enjoying nature in a romantic way, and I was all for it.

But as always, nothing could ever be that simple.

As I was heading back from ordering our food, my eyes

landed on my queen looking so beautiful underneath the moonlight, anxiously waiting for me from where she sat. But our moment was interrupted when my cell phone rang in my pocket. An annoyed growl escaped my throat. I didn't bother looking at the name on the screen as I answered the call.

"This better be urgent."

"It is." My Beta's serious voice on the other side made me stiffen. I'm sure Calliope noticed, as her expression turned worried. "The Elders just got back to us. They confirmed that they hadn't been informed about the attack, which means it was illegal by our laws. They have given you permission to deal with Solar Hunt's Alpha as you please."

I didn't even have time to reply. In a blaze of fury, I crushed the phone in my hands.

That bastard was going to pay!

CHAPTER THIRTY-EIGHT

Calliope

The scowl my Alpha constantly wore had been gone for the past three days, but it reappeared the second he finished the call. I watched his mood change abruptly as he stared silently at the horizon, feeling the anger boil in his chest. He didn't bother telling me what his Beta had told him over the phone - he didn't need to. I heard their brief exchange perfectly,and I immediately lost my appetite.

At first, I thought it was his fury poisoning me through the bond we shared, but it didn't take me long to understand those heavy emotions were my own. Images of my pack destroyed and the looks of horror in my people's faces came to my mind the moment I was reminded of the attack. It wasn't my mate's rage I was feeling - it was mine. There was a fire burning in my heart, an aching desire to punish the one who made my family suffer.

"Would you like to leave now?" I promptly asked, breaking the silence.

Levi shook his head, not turning to look at me. "You should at least eat first. Dinner should be ready shortly."

"We can eat on the plane," I insisted, finally capturing his attention. There was a mix of confusion and admiration in his eyes. "Each second we waste here is another breath that coward takes."

The shadow of a smirk played on his face. "As you wish, my Luna."

We went back to the hut to pack our bags and change into appropriate clothes for the visit we would be making to the Elders' Council. Luckily, I had brought a sophisticated teal blue dress in case we wanted to attend some kind of party or event. While I was getting ready, Levi called the flight crew to have them urgently prepare everything. He also made sure to notify the kitchen to pack our meal to-go.

A little over an hour later, we were ready to board the plane. I couldn't say I was surprised at how efficient the staff was - our team's capability was one of the reasons why Blood Eclipse thrived - but it was still certainly impressive. Our dinner was brought out right after takeoff, and it was delicious. It was easier to enjoy our meal knowing we were already on our way home.

However, I couldn't deny that I was nervous about the situation. In the blink of an eye, I was pulled out from my private paradise with my mate and thrown back into the harsh reality. It didn't help that Nava was restlessly pacing around in my head; wolves enjoyed being in contact with nature and hated being confined in small spaces.

My concentration was broken when I felt Levi grab my hand into his without warning. He brought it up to his lips, causing pleasant shivers to run down my arm when he planted a long kiss on my knuckles, looking straight into my eyes. Sensing my discomfort, he proceeded to rub circles on the back of my hand. To my surprise, he seemed to have Odin under control. They were probably more used to flying than Nava and

I were.

"I'm sorry our little vacation was cut short." His deep voice was full of guilt.

I couldn't help but smile at his concern. "It was wonderful while it lasted, but I also miss our home. Besides, we have more important issues to take care of right now," I assured, causing him to crease his brow. "I would love to come back once the waters are calmer."

That seemed to appease him. "We surely will."

The minutes couldn't go by any slower. After a couple of hours, we finally landed at the small airport built in a secluded area on our territory. It was refreshing to breathe in the air of my home, but unfortunately, I didn't have much time to enjoy our return. As soon as we arrived, we headed to the car that was waiting for us at the border. Darrell opened the door for us before he proceeded to relay what the Elders had told him. They still hadn't figured out any key details, but they had been able to confirm the attack hadn't been approved by any of the Elders in the Council, which was more than enough to take the necessary actions.

It was a two-hour ride to our destination. When the limousine stopped in front of a large golden building resembling a majestic church, I was perplexed. I had only read about the Elders' Council in books during my years training to become Delta, but the pictures I had seen didn't do justice to the monument standing in front of me. It was so stunning that I almost forgot the reason behind our visit.

Two young wolves greeted the three of us by the entrance, bowing their heads before they led us through the tall hallways with white and gold walls. The inside was just as magnificent as the outside. Unfortunately, the room we were headed to didn't share the same grace. The underground prison had dull, cold stone walls, contrasting the warmer shades throughout the rest of the building. Nevertheless, it was much more sophisticated than the classic pack dungeons, looking more like a prison than a torture chamber.

One of the Elders of the Council was waiting for us in front of two very intimidating guards. He immediately nodded at us, and for the first time, I witnessed my Alpha lower his head in respect. Elders were at the top of the werewolf hierarchy, being the wisest and strongest members of our society. They also had more affinity with magic, thus rendering them able to perform various rituals - one of the reasons why every legitimate pack had to have at least one Elder.

"Alpha Levi." The older man held his head high as he addressed my mate. "Thank you for coming so quickly. We were waiting for you to start the interrogation." He glanced at me from the corner of his eyes before turning back to my mate. "I believe it would be best if your Luna waited upstairs. Things might get a bit too...brutal."

I had to resist the urge to arch an eyebrow at the Elder. Surely, it wasn't common for Lunas to fight in battles or witness torturings, but I had once been a fighter. I don't enjoy violence like most wolves do, but I understood it was sometimes necessary. I expected Levi to agree with him and convince me to do as he said; instead, he just looked at me, waiting for me to make my own decision.

"Elder Baldassare, I am Calliope Gaumond, Luna of Blood Eclipse. With all due respect, I would like to stay by my Alpha's side during the interrogation. I don't mind a little bloodshed in order to enforce the laws we abide by." My head was low, but my eyes shone with determination. I noticed Levi smile proudly at me.

"I would like my Luna's wish to be respected."

The Elder hesitated for a moment, but he soon nodded. "Very well."

We followed the Elder inside, Darrell in-tow. Every single one of the ten cells were empty, except for the one at the back, inside of which was a tall man. He was sitting on a stone bench, the glow of his golden locks concealed by the shadows. Strangely enough, it took him some time to notice our presence, but when he did, a mocking smile lit up his face. Although we had never met before, I knew this was Julius, Alpha of the Solar Hunt Pack.

"Levi, my old friend!" the prisoner chanted as the Elder opened the door to his cell.

My mate didn't bother replying before pulling Julius by the neck of his white shirt, throwing him out and onto the cold floor. Even expressionless, Levi was so intimidating, much more than any other Alpha I had ever met. It had been a long time since I last saw this ruthless side of him, but instead of fear, I felt pride - after all, I was the only one who had been capable of taming him.

The blond man winced as he tried to pick himself back up, only to gasp in shock when Levi wrapped his fist around Julius' neck, lifting him into the air as if he weighed nothing. I'm not sure if this scumbag understood the seriousness of the situation he was in as he dared to stare right back into my mate's eyes. Darrell soon stepped in, holding the prisoner's arms around his back tightly. I doubt it was necessary to use such strength to restrain a wolf that had been drugged with wolfsbane, but I suspect our Beta was doing it more out of anger than concern.

"I'm going to ask you a few questions, and you will answer them," Levi started, loud and clear. "Cooperate, and I'll make sure to end your life quickly when you are no longer useful."

There was horror in the former Alpha's eyes as he finally seemed to realize what fate awaited him. He glanced over at the Elder, who stood stone-faced in the corner. Levi was given freedom to deal with the situation as he saw fit, and he would surely take advantage of that privilege.

"What were you hoping to achieve by attacking Blood Eclipse?" The lack of emotion in my mate's voice was jarring. It was impressive how he was able to mask everything he was feeling, especially considering his anger issues.

Julius hesitated for a second - a big mistake. One direct punch to his stomach forced the air out of his lungs, reminding him of his torturer's previous threat. Levi was ready to hit him again, but this time, he made the right decision.

"I wanted to weaken your pack," he breathed out.

"Why?"

A moment of silence went by, and my mate's punch met the prisoner's stomach for the second time. Julius coughed blood, his endurance weakened by the poison in his veins.

"I can't answer your question."

A growl escaped Levi's lips as he prepared to hit the man again.

"I really can't!" Julius insisted. My Alpha flashed him a warning look to let him know he had roughly one second to explain himself, and he didn't dismiss the mercy he had been offered. "I made a dark pact. Even if I want to tell you, the words won't come out of my mouth."

"He is telling the truth," the Elder spoke for the first time, catching our attention. "I can sense the dark magic emanating from him."

"With who?" my mate demanded, turning back to the prisoner. It was evident he was losing his temper.

"I…I can't say."

"It seems you're more useless than I had imagined," Levi scoffed, gesturing for his Beta to let the man go. Darrell took a few steps back, but Julius didn't seem happy about being free - probably because he knew it wouldn't last.

"Wait! I have been cooperative," the blond man tried to argue. "You can't kill me!"

My Alpha didn't bother answering him, anxious to just shut him up. In the blink of an eye, he shifted into his gray beast, towering over the shrinking man. One last scream echoed through the walls before they were painted red, and I felt my heart beating faster. I knew this was going to happen, and I had seen enough violence to not feel sick at the sight of blood, so why was I suddenly shaking? After ripping the man's throat out, Odin turned to me with blood dripping from his sharp teeth, and I could finally understand the reason.

His pale blue eyes were as piercing as they were during the marking ceremony. So icy, it was impossible not to remember the fateful night. I was once again reminded of the cruel monster who forced my wolf into submission, taking advantage of her feelings for him.

"*We don't have to be scared of him anymore, Cal.*" Nava's

voice was calm inside my head, causing some of my tension to subside. "*We know how to tame him now.*"

As if hearing her words, Odin's eye-color turned more vivid; ice melting into pools of blue. The next second, he gave his human back control. The Elder leisurely walked over to Levi to hand him a black robe.

And the first thing he did was rush over to me, wrapping me around his comforting arms.

CHAPTER THIRTY-NINE

Levi

When my wolf took over our body, we were both seeing red. It was hard enough to contain my anger throughout the brief interrogation, but this bastard managed to make me lose the last drop of control. How dare a weakling like him attack me, the Blood Alpha! And be stupid enough to think I would show him mercy! No one messed with my pack and lived to tell the story. If anything, he was lucky I was too blinded by rage to give him the slow, torturous death he deserved.

However, I was also too blind to realize what painful memories my outburst triggered for my most precious treasure.

My blue eyes locked on the honey-colored ones shining across the stone room, forcing me to stop. My wolf dropped the disfigured corpse of the sorry-excuse-of-an-Alpha onto the floor, staring straight at our Luna. She boldly tried to mask her emotions, yet we could still feel her horror through the bond we shared.

"Mate is afraid of us..." Odin stated, still processing the scene. *"Of course, she is! She hasn't forgotten what I did to her."* He held back a low whine, unwilling to show weakness. Aside from being an old Alpha habit, it was also a defense mechanism.

"She knows we would never hurt her again," I retorted. Yet, the sharp pain I felt in my chest couldn't be ignored.

"Yes, but she can't help but remember. The scene is imprinted on her mind," he insisted. Together, we fought back our anger. Odin's raised hackles slowly retreated as we lowered our ears. *"I want to erase that moment from her head. Even at our worst, I want her to know we would never harm her. I want her to feel safe with us, always."*

"So do I," I replied confidently, taking back control.

Once I was back to my human form, I threw on the black robe the Elder handed me and beelined towards her. She tensed when I instantly wrapped my arms around her frame, but it didn't take long for her to melt under my touch. Although I would usually avoid public displays of affection, my priority was letting her know the old me was gone; that scarred child who turned his trauma into hate had grown up. I needed her to see me as the Alpha she tamed and learned to love, not the beast who broke her.

"I love you, mate," Odin whispered into her ear, taking over for a second to make sure she was convinced. By the way she shivered as her breathing steadied, I understood he had done a good job. "Thank you for staying with me."

When she pulled away to look into my eyes, there was no more fear in her semblance. "I'm your Luna. We're supposed to go through everything together."

I couldn't help but smile at her. At such a young age, she already showed so much maturity - certainly more than I had. And I knew she still had a lot to teach me.

* * *

It was past midnight when we arrived back at the territory. My Luna and I headed straight to our room, hopping into bed after a quick invigorating shower. Our days together at our private island had been amazing, but with Calliope in heat, neither of us had much time to rest. It didn't help that we were forced to return from our hidden paradise to deal with a conspiring Alpha. The stress of the situation had certainly worn us both out, but one night with her in my arms was all it took to make me feel better.

Waking up without her wasn't exactly relieving though.

Judging by the intensity of the sun, it should be around eight in the morning. When the glaring light started to bother me, I forced my eyes open with an unhappy murmur. I didn't smell her sweet perfume upon taking my first breath, which made me shift over the mattress. Our bed was large enough for either of us to get lost in it, but she certainly wasn't there next to me. I knew she was safe, so her absence didn't make me worried - just discontent.

Once I rolled out of bed, I put on some fresh clothes and walked out the door ready to find my missing mate. I didn't need to track her scent to find her; I already had a guess where she could be. For that reason, I wasn't surprised when my eyes landed on the woman in a long sundress, majestically standing on the field right next to the stables. The two tall horses surrounding her made her seem so small.

Calliope was so distracted brushing the shiny fur of her unicorn she didn't even notice me. I silently admired her beauty from a distance, watching as she talked and played with the magical creature. The other black horse was also close to her, observing her with curiosity. It was impressive how comfortable the stallion felt in her presence, considering most horses were skittish around wolves they weren't familiar with. I guess it could sense my Luna's pure heart too.

"Do you think her bond with Crystal is stronger than the one we share with her?" Odin carefully asked. I couldn't help but snort.

"Are you jealous of her pet?"

Before he could reply, the sweetest voice broke our concentration. "Oh, good morning!" She smiled brighter than the sun. "I'm sorry I left the room without warning. You looked so tired, I didn't want to wake you up. But I hadn't seen Crystal for days, and I missed her." As soon as she finished her sentence, the black stallion approached her, nibbling on a strand of her hazel hair. With a chuckle, she gently pushed his head away. "And I thought Highlander would enjoy grazing a bit as well. Have you been standing there for long?"

Her question took me by surprise. How long had I been here for, staring at her like a lovesick fool? I shook my head, bewildered by the effect this woman had on me. My feet moved towards her, and I didn't hesitate to snake my arms around her waist, kissing her deeply.

"No, I don't think so," I finally replied. "And don't worry. I'm sure they missed you as well. I can't blame them." I showed her a small smile, making her blush. Seconds later, my semblance turned serious again. "Though, I'm afraid you will have to leave them again soon. We need to head to Solar Hunt and figure out what to do with the pack. It's technically ours now."

She nodded, raising her head. "It's okay. I was able to spend some time with them." She turned to her unicorn, who flashed puppy eyes at her. "I will be back soon, my girl."

Crystal was used to roaming our lands freely, but for Highlander's safety, he was taken back to the stables. Then, Calliope took my hand, and together we walked to the main entrance of the packhouse, where the car was waiting for us. Much like the previous night, Darrell would be accompanying us, while Ivar and Bellatrix would stay behind to take care of the pack.

The first few minutes of our car ride were silent. I couldn't understand why, but I felt slightly tense. I was used to claiming packs - it's all I've been doing ever since my father was killed. So why was I hesitant all of a sudden?

"Shouldn't we let her know what will happen at Solar Hunt?" Odin's quiet question was full of uncertainty. I finally understood he was the one projecting the strange feeling on me.

At first, I was confused by his mood. My counterpart was just as brave and bold as I was. Our ruthlessness was what made everyone else in werewolf society fear us. However, as I observed our beautiful Luna's peaceful expression, watching the landscape through the car window, I was able to make sense of his fears. After the way she felt when we murdered Julius last night, Odin was afraid she would be scared of us again. And much like him, I didn't want to have that happen again.

"Calliope," I called, simultaneously rubbing my thumb on the back of her hand. She turned to me with a quizzical expression. Clearing my throat, I got straight to the point, "I wanted to let you know it is highly likely that more blood will be spilled today."

She remained silent for a moment, but soon forced a smile. “I’m aware of how brutal pack takeovers can be.”

“I will be forced to put down the ones who refuse to accept my leadership,” I insisted, determined to make sure everything was clear as day. “From my experience, most wolves are reluctant to follow an outsider. I’ve had to get rid of as much as two-thirds of entire packs in the past.”

“This is how Blood Eclipse has managed to thrive despite having many enemies. We never miss the chance to eliminate them before they become a real threat,” my Beta added in to support me. We had our disagreements after Cal came along, but the trust we had in each other was another reason why our pack always remained strong.

The truth shocked her, but she hid it well. “Let’s hope that won’t be necessary today.” She shifted underneath my touch, lightly squeezing my rough hand with her delicate ones. Her warm honey eyes locked on mine as she continued, “But if it is, I will stand by you, my Alpha.” I think I momentarily forgot how to breathe.

Although we didn’t have the chance to properly talk about what happened last night, in that moment I realized we wouldn’t have to. There was no need for words when our silent gestures spoke so loudly - her confidence in me, showing in her semblance, and my determination to turn things around. Even after all my terrible mistakes, my Luna had given me another chance to prove I could be the mate she deserved. I wouldn’t let her down.

✻ ✻ ✻

Parking in front of Solar Hunt's packhouse, we all hopped out of the car, and Calliope took a minute to admire the Greek-inspired architecture. I had been here a few times in the past, so I wasn't as impressed. Besides, I could only focus on the sole purpose of my visit. Taking her arm in mine, I guided her towards the town square with my Beta closely following us.

All of the pack members had been gathered at the center. They were whispering to each other, but the second they saw me, you could hear a pin drop. They all avoided looking at me, probably sensing my powerful aura, yet they didn't bow their heads. The pack's Elder, accompanied by one of the Council Elders, soon approached me, giving me the green light to claim what was now mine - the wolves and the land.

"Former members of Solar Hunt Pack," I said loud and clear, holding my head up high. "As you have been informed, I ripped your former Alpha's head off after he was convicted of treason against the laws we abide by. I am Alpha Levi Griffon of Blood Eclipse Pack." I could see most of the shifters before me shudder as I revealed my identity. "Now, I want the ranked members to step forward."

The wolves who held the highest positions in a pack were usually blindly loyal to their roots. They would rarely submit to another Alpha, especially an outsider, but I was willing to give them a chance to prove their loyalty to me. However, when no one showed their faces for the next few seconds, my mercy started wearing thin.

"Don't make me repeat myself!" The earth quaked with my roar, my last warning.

Shaking, one of the pack members took a step forward, his head held low. Judging by his build and stature, I was sure he was only an Omega, but I decided to hear what he had to say.

"T-the r-ranked members le-left after Julius was captured, Alpha Levi," his voice was barely a whisper, but I could hear him crystal clear. And I had a hard time believing his words. "They d-didn't want to submit, but th-they also didn't want to stay and d-die."

My eyes widened with a mixture of shock and disgust. It was extremely uncommon for werewolves to flee their pack because of the loyalty they had for their home. Even when the human's survival instinct begged them to save their lives, their animal side would take control and remain truthful to the vows they made. The fact that the ones who had promised to protect this pack had run away only proved that Solar Hunt was full of cowards. Clenching my fists, I cursed myself for thinking of making a political alliance with these clowns.

"Are there only cowards in this pack?" Low whimpers followed my powerful growl. "This is your last chance to die with honor. Those of you who don't wish to follow me, be braver than your pathetic leaders and take a step forward!" I ordered.

To my surprise, every single one of the two hundred wolves dropped to their knees instead, exposing their necks in a clear sign of submission.

CHAPTER FORTY

Calliope

The moment all of the former members of Solar Hunt kneeled before my mate was unbelievable.

I was so shaken by the scene it was hard to keep a neutral semblance as I eyed every single one of the wolves before me, all of which would soon become part of our family. It was extremely rare for an entire pack to submit to a new leader straight away, without negotiations, without friction. The bond between members of a pack was so strong, even after their leaders died or were forced to step down, some would still refuse to bow their heads to another Alpha.

So why were they all so willing to follow mine?

"Levi and Odin have a reputation." Nava's velvety voice echoed in my head. *"One of the most remarkable traits of a wolf is their loyalty, yes. But we also know strength when we see it. Our mate's aura is undeniably powerful, especially when compared to Julius'."*

"I guess that makes sense. But there has to be more," I insisted before closing our connection so I could focus on the situation.

Through the bond I shared with Levi, I could feel an avalanche of emotions. First, there was anger. Although I didn't always agree with it, I knew he was used to resorting to violence to cope with his rage. He was probably eager to let Odin out so they both could blow off some steam at the cost of the deserters' lives. However, it was his confusion that caused him to freeze in his spot. He had imagined a thousand possible outcomes for how our visit would go, and this certainly wasn't one of them.

I decided to help him, exercising my role as a Luna by stepping forward. "Former Solar Hunt members, I am Calliope Gaumond, Luna of Blood Eclipse. Thank you for offering us your loyalty. Soon enough, you will all be part of Blood Eclipse." I could sense Levi's gaze on me. He was still shocked, but there was now a hint of gratitude and admiration in his eyes. I knew he liked it when I took control of a situation; no one ever dared to challenge him in such a way, and my boldness always enticed his hunger. "You will have today to gather your belongings and say your goodbyes to your old life. Tomorrow morning we will be waiting to welcome you into our family. That will be all."

"Yes, Luna!," they answered in unison, still holding their heads low as they turned to walk away.

When I took my mate's hand, he slowly melted into my touch as his expression softened. "Shall we head home?" He nodded at me before gesturing to his Beta to follow us.

As soon as we hopped into the car, Darrell showed me a bright smile. "Great job back there, Luna!"

I found myself returning the gesture. "I think Blood Eclipse's ruthless reputation is useful to keep enemies away, but our members should be able to see the more welcoming, hospitable side of us." I shrugged. "Besides, I was just glad we were able to avoid unnecessary deaths."

"I still can't figure out why they changed sides so easily," Levi whispered, his gaze focused on the landscape as he dwelled in thought.

Judging by his posture, I imagined he was in such disbelief that he couldn't help but consider if the soon-to-be members of our pack were conspiring against him somehow. It made sense, considering how hostile Blood Eclipse's relationships with other packs were, yet I didn't think that was quite the case here. After digesting the uncommon event for the past few minutes, I had come to a more plausible conclusion.

"It's almost unheard of for an entire pack to accept a new leader so quickly, but I don't think they have ill intentions," I finally spoke my mind, catching both men's attention. Darrell seemed genuinely curious, while Levi had his brows furrowed, skeptical. "In my opinion, the explanation regarding what happened is quite simple - Julius just wasn't a good leader."

"What do you mean?" My mate put his stubbornness aside for a moment to listen to me.

"Think about it. Instead of staying and protecting their Alpha's legacy, Solar Hunt's ranked members simply abandoned their territory, not caring about what would happen to the land or its members. The wolves who stayed seemed lost, but also *relieved* to have a new Alpha."

"You're right. It would explain why no one put up a fight today," the Beta agreed. "Most Alphas train hard to lead a pack, but because the title is passed down from father to son, there is no guarantee that the next-in-line will actually be fit to lead." His eyes were shining with amusement when he turned back to me. "You're brilliant, Cal."

"That you are." Levi flashed a smile at me, squeezing my hand before he was back to his usual serious self. "Still, I would like to dig further into this."

"We can observe and interview the new members during their first days at our territory," Darrell suggested. "Once their bond to Blood Eclipse is established, they won't be able to lie to us."

"Good. In the meantime, we should focus on the preparations for welcoming them tomorrow."

* * *

The rest of the day was spent in the office as we discussed the details for taking in almost two hundred new members. Due to my previous experience as a Delta, I was familiar with the procedures, but Moonstone wasn't nearly as big as Blood Eclipse. We would occasionally accept runaways and refugees, but I'd never dealt with absorbing an entire pack before. It was also different to deal with the issue as a Luna; I now had to give orders instead of simply following them, and my priority was to make sure our new members would feel comfortable in our home.

Later on, my mate ordered room service so we could finally have some private, undisturbed time to unwind. Over dinner, he made sure to point out how amazed he was by my assertiveness earlier at Solar Hunt's territory, and complimenting me for adapting so well to my role as a leader. In his own way, he let me know I had become as much of an essential part of the pack as he was. Since I knew he was a man of few words, who struggled to voice or show his feelings, I was extremely proud of his effort - and proud of myself.

The night seemed shorter than I would have liked, but the excitement to welcome our new members helped me get out of bed in the morning. After a nice hot shower with my mate, I put on one of my favorite dresses - a one-shoulder black dress that faded to a refreshing mint green, adorned with a few well-placed rhinestones. Then, arm-in-arm, we headed outside.

We had sent a group of scouts in vans to gather the newcomers early in the morning, so I wasn't surprised to find the town square packed with foreigners carrying full backpacks. Their curious eyes scoured through the beautiful buildings and majestic lands, whispering as they examined their new home. I could feel Levi's hesitation; bringing in so many wolves usually resulted in trouble. On the other hand, I was rather optimistic about the situation. Aside from representing a breath of fresh air, we could definitely use more working hands to tend to our pack and warriors to help defend it, considering we weren't yet sure about why Julius wanted to weaken us.

"Silence!" My mate's voice boomed, catching everyone's attention. They were probably too absorbed in the new sights and smells to notice our presence, but the Alpha's order made them all go quiet immediately. I squeezed his hand firmly to remind him to be more patient, and though I could feel his urge to roll his eyes, he went on in a much calmer tone. "Welcome to my lands. You will be allowed to live here, share our food and resources as long as you give me your vow of loyalty. If you do not wish to take this vow, this is your last chance to turn around." He waited a few seconds, but when the crowd kept their heads low, he continued. "Good. Together, you will take the oath before the Elders and the Moon Goddess to officially become part of this pack."

A pack oath was a method of accepting large numbers of new members into a pack through a magical spoken vow. The most common procedure for welcoming wolves was a blood oath, which consisted of slicing both the leader and the subject's palms and allowing their blood to mix inside of a silver goblet - the same ritual I had to go through when I joined Blood Eclipse. However, it was hard and time-consuming to perform the ceremony with so many members, which is why the pack oath was more adequate in this case. I had never witnessed one before and I was honestly curious.

"Kneel," Levi commanded, and no one hesitated to do as he said. The Elder approached us both, nodding at my mate in a sign for him to start. "Former members of Solar Hunt, will you swear to break your bonds with your old Alpha and pack, to join Blood Eclipse and follow me?"

"Yes, Alpha Levi!" the crowd roared.

My mate flashed me a quick look and I took a step forward. "Former members of Solar Hunt, do you swear to give your lives, your hearts, and your souls to protect our home? To protect your Luna?"

"Yes, Luna Calliope!"

Levi and I exchanged glances before our voices echoed through the territory, "From this moment on, you are part of our family. You are now members of Blood Eclipse."

We interlaced our fingers as the Elder repeated a few ancient words. Not too long after, I felt a connection being established between each and every one of the wolves before me, like a switch had been flipped inside our minds. And as quickly as it started, it was done.

"Welcome, brothers and sisters!" My Alpha's powerful voice thundered as our new members rose to their feet. "I'm counting on you all to make sure our pack will continue to thrive."

"Yes, Alpha!"

My mate allowed them a moment to celebrate before demanding silence once again. "Your new Beta, Darrell Crawford, will be defining your new roles within our pack, and your Delta, Bellatrix Lenoir, will help you get settled," he finished, ready to turn on his heel to leave. However, I had one last thing to say, and when he pulled my hand I fought to remain still.

"Please, if you have any questions or need any kind of help, don't hesitate to come to us. Alpha Levi and I will be available to make sure your transition to your new lives here go smoothly." My mate's gaze was on me, full of confusion, but I ignored it. "You may go now. I hope to hear from you soon."

As the crowd dispersed, my mate pulled me closer, whispering in my ear. "What was that? We don't have time to tend to each of their specific needs. This is not how we do things here," he complained. I could feel his urge for control, but I stood my ground.

"Then, we will make time for them." Before he could argue, I went on. "Levi, this is the perfect opportunity for you to strengthen your bond with our pack. They have learned to trust me, but they don't see you as someone approachable. While it's good that our enemies fear you, I don't think our members should be scared of their leader," I clarified, and he stood down. "Maybe it's time we start doing things the Luna's way."

I expected him to be angry, or at least frustrated. However, when his lips slowly curled into a smile, I knew he respected my determination. A low, possessive growl reverberated in his throat as he crashed his mouth against mine - his way of accepting defeat.

CHAPTER FORTY-ONE

Calliope

It was fairly hard to convince my grumpy Alpha to join me and personally help our new members get settled, but with the right arguments - as well as some irresistible incentives - he gave in. It's not that he thought himself too highly to waste his precious time with lower-ranking wolves. On the contrary, one of his biggest priorities was to make sure each and every one of our members was well taken care of. Hence why he got really mad when I informed him of the South District food situation. However, he was used to ruling by fear, and he didn't know how to be more approachable. Lucky for him, I was there to teach him.

My two years of working as a Delta offered me enough experience in learning to manage pack member problems. As a Luna, I noticed they all respected me for my kindness and power, rather than the simple fact that I was mated to their Alpha. It was kind of funny, considering how none of the wolves at my old pack respected me despite my title, and here they respected and loved me *in spite* of my title. I guess a little bit of confidence and self-love could go a long way. I was definitely glad I had been able to recognize my own qualities and embrace my flaws.

Now, I just had to show my Alpha that he too could

change for the better.

"I'm still not comfortable about this," Levi mumbled, leaning against one of the walls of our room as he buttoned his silver shirt.

Once I finished getting dressed myself, I slowly walked up to him, closing the distance between us. My hand moved up to his face, caressing his rough stubble beard as I cupped his cheek. Staring at him, I noticed him trying to fight the sparks between us to keep his ruthless Alpha mask. Eventually, my warm honey-colored eyes melted his icy ones and he reluctantly leaned into my touch. He relished the moment for a brief second. A small sigh left his lips before he wrapped his hand around my wrist, gently pushing me away.

I could feel a low growl, similar to a purr, reverberate in his chest underneath my touch. A smile immediately lit up my face as I understood his reaction; he knew exactly what I could say and do to wrap around my finger. "I'm aware, and I want you to know I appreciate your efforts. Thank you for trusting me."

"I promised that you would have whatever you wanted, and I'm a man of my word," he replied, fighting back his smirk. "I wouldn't deny your request without at least trying." He leisurely interlaced our fingers, turning around before adding, "But it doesn't change the fact that I'm not happy about it."

I had to roll my eyes at his grumpiness, but the smile never left my face as we walked out of the Alpha suite. It was still quite early in the day, and we'd just had lunch. I was confident we would have enough time to greet most, if not all, of the new members before the end of the day. As we wandered through our sunlit lands towards the area where the newcomers were now living, we came across our busy ranked members, who quickly bowed their heads before they continued on their ways. They had their hands full with the organization of everything, especially Darrell and Trix.

"We should be helping them instead of wasting our time." There was irritation in my mate's voice. I also didn't miss the way the crease in his forehead deepened.

I took a deep breath, reminding myself to stay calm. "I assure you, this will not be a waste of time. You wanted to know why these wolves were so quick to abandon the vow they made to their previous leader. What better way of getting answers than by strengthening your bond with them?"

"How about by commanding them to tell me," he retorted point-blank.

"Not all issues have to be solved by using force." I sighed, shaking my head in disapproval. "You said you would try. Can we do that before you decide that my method is ineffective?"

He gave me a curt, silent nod, and I knew it was the best answer I would get. It was clear that he wasn't the least convinced yet, but it was better to show than tell - and I was sure our mission would be successful.

It didn't take us long to get to the first house at the village near the main part of the territory. New members were usually sent to live closer to the borders, but a lot of the main buildings located in that area had been destroyed in the recent attack. The workers of our pack hadn't had enough time to rebuild everything, especially not the unoccupied buildings, since the priority was to fix the homes of families who had to move out. For that reason, we had to temporarily allocate the former members of Solar Hunt to the vacant cottages closer to the town square.

Our first few visits didn't yield many fruits. Considering how the families were still adjusting to their new lives, and clearly intimidated by the reputation of my ruthless mate, it was hard to find an opportunity to ask about Julius' reign. However, I knew patience was key, even if Levi didn't. I noticed he was eager to use his Alpha tone to order them to tell him what he wanted to know, but I managed to keep him under control by reminding him through mindlink that our goal was to ensure the pack members felt comfortable in our presence, which seemed to be working. I could see the wolves we visited slowly going from being frightened of their new Alpha and Luna to simply respecting us; they also didn't hesitate to show their gratitude at the attention we were giving them.

Roughly an hour into our walk, we reached the first cottage in the South District. The door was opened by a man who seemed to be in his late twenties. Just like everyone else we had visited, his heart almost stopped when he saw us standing in front of him. As I explained that we only wished to know if he needed any help getting settled, I observed he was visibly more stressed than the others, though I couldn't quite figure out why. Not a minute into our conversation, we heard a high-pitched voice call the man's name, and as the door opened further, we saw a small boy.

"Not now, Ralph. Daddy is busy talking to our new leaders," the father whispered in a shaky voice. The pup observed us both with admiration and curiosity before he gasped, remembering to bow his head at us.

"Don't worry," I told the father before gently touching the boy's shoulder, catching his attention. "You can join us if you want, Ralph." I smiled at him, and he happily returned the gesture.

"Is your mate here as well?" my mate asked demandingly. For some reason, the man started trembling harder.

"N-no, Sir." He lowered his head even more, afraid to look into our eyes. "My m-mate...she was...k-killed. In the attack against your pack, Sir."

A pinch of pain struck my heart at his confession. The pain of losing a mate was so unbearable it usually caused the other one to pass away soon after the first. This single father had lost his destined partner less than a month ago, and yet here he was, fighting back the tears in order not to show compassion towards an enemy to his new pack. It could be considered treason for a wolf to mourn someone who attacked their home, but I would never punish him for mourning his mate; I knew both him and his deceased mate were only victims in this bizarre situation. To my surprise, Levi also seemed touched by the situation. Although he hid his emotions well behind his stern semblance, I noticed the brief moment his eyes glistened with pity as his gaze fell on the pup.

"I'm sorry for your loss," my mate uttered at last, shocking the man. "My condolences to you and your pup."

The man's mouth hung open, but no sound was coming out of it; he was at a complete loss for words. In an attempt to brighten up the mood, I suggested we continue our conversation while taking a stroll across the town square so they could get acquainted with their new home. Ralph seemed very excited about the idea, but his father politely refused, saying he didn't want to cause us any trouble. He only agreed after I insisted, reassuring him it would be our pleasure.

The gesture was even more effective than I had expected, as the man soon brought up the subject we were curious about. He confessed that Blood Eclipse wasn't as terrifying as the rumors made it seem, and that he already felt more at home here than he ever did at Solar Hunt. When my Alpha questioned why that was, he promptly told us Julius didn't really care about his pack or its members. Although he wasn't particularly cruel, he was never transparent about his decisions and barely stepped out of the packhouse, probably refusing to mix with the lower-ranking wolves; it seemed he wasn't really fit to be leader.

I was about to ask him another question when the pup's voice caught us all by surprise. "What's that?!"

As I turned my attention to him, I realized he had his eyes wide open pointing at the pure white creature standing near the lake, only a few feet away from us. I couldn't help but smile as I crouched on the ground beside Ralph to answer his question.

"That is Crystal. She's my unicorn."

"A unicorn?!" he yelled in utter astonishment, unable to take his eyes off the magical horse. Even his father seemed shocked. "I didn't know they were real!"

"Honestly, me neither." I chuckled before standing back up and taking his tiny hand in mine. "Would you like to meet her?"

He started jumping up and down like a bouncy ball, too overjoyed to utter any words as he kept nodding his head in excitement. With another laugh, I called Crystal over. She immediately stopped grazing to turn to me, stretching her neck forward in confusion and curiosity as she noticed the strangers next to me. I encouraged her to come closer, and though she was hesitant at first, she trusted me enough to know she would be safe.

To prevent from scaring her away, I instructed Ralph to calm down. I didn't expect a pup to be so obedient, but it seemed he was determined to do whatever it took to touch Crystal. I gently placed my hand over her muzzle to show him how to approach her, and he slowly brought his tiny hand to her cheek. A gasp of admiration left the boy's mouth as he carefully caressed the unicorn's soft white fur, earning a cheerful neigh in response.

"She's amazing!" Ralph cooed. "Can I play with her again soon?"

"Of course." I smiled at him as Crystal trotted away. "I'm sure you will see her around a lot, and she loves company."

"Thank you, Luna." The father bowed at me.

As I turned to face him, I noticed my mate staring at me with hungry eyes and the shadow of a smile. When I winked at him, he quickly shook his head, regaining his composure. *Oh, my sweet, powerful Alpha.* I loved him so much, and I loved that I made him enjoy the feelings he had fought back for so long.

Ralph's father thanked us for our kindness as we accompanied him and Ralph back home before proceeding with our meet-and-greet. Most of the new members were still quite reserved, but some of them felt so grateful towards us that they spontaneously made comments about how they never received that kind of attention back at their old pack. The more houses we visited, the easier it was to put the pieces together. When we returned to the office by the end of the day, we had pretty much come to the same conclusion.

"The reason for the immediate change of sides from the former members of Solar Hunt seems to be simpler than we imagined," my mate revealed to his ranked members as he sat beside me behind the desk. "Julius wasn't a tyrant, just incompetent."

Since the title of Alpha was usually passed down from father to son, it was fairly common for heirs to not have what it takes to be leaders. While most leaders tried to prepare their sons for the responsibility they would eventually have on their shoulders, it wasn't rare for the pups to become spoiled and too comfortable with the fortune and blind respect they'd inherit. Wolves need a strong ruler who knows how to exercise his power; without correct guidance, they could easily get lost. A pack who doesn't share a strong bond with their leader is prone to be dismantled or taken over by someone more fit to be Alpha, which is exactly what happened to Solar Hunt.

"So we shouldn't expect riots?" Ivar questioned.

Levi shook his head. "It's unlikely they will rebel against us. However, there's another threat from Solar Hunt I would like to be neutralized."

"The ranked runaways," Darrell quickly observed. Honestly, in the middle of this mess, I had even forgotten about them.

"Precisely." My Alpha turned to his Gamma. "I want our best scouts searching the area surrounding the lands of the dismantled pack. They are not to return without the heads of the deserters." Ivar nodded, and Levi turned to his Beta. "Darrell, you'll be in charge of supervising the operation."

"Yes, Alpha."

"Trix," I called, immediately catching her attention. "You

are doing a wonderful job making sure our new members feel at home. Keep at it."

She flashed me a smile. "Of course, Luna."

"That is all for now." Levi stood up from his seat, making a brief pause before muttering, "Good job, team."

The ranked members all bowed their heads before leaving the office. Once we were alone, Levi slowly took my hand, glancing away from me, seeming slightly uncomfortable; it was hard for me to interpret his weird behavior. He nervously rubbed circles on the back of my hand before clearing his throat.

"You were right," he said at last, still avoiding eye contact. "I apologize for being so resistant to your idea."

A gentle smile lit up my face. I couldn't help but find his reaction cute. The fact that he was willing to admit he was wrong showed how much he had grown in the past few months, and I was proud of him. I was proud of us.

"I was just doing my job as a Luna. *Your* Luna," I reminded him, and he finally lifted his head to look at me. There was a hint of confusion in his semblance, almost as if he was expecting me to be mad. "I'm sure I will make mistakes too, and you will correct me. We will keep learning from each other." He gave me a look of realization before chuckling lightly and smiling. It was my turn to be confused. "What is it?"

"When Darrell told me I would never be at full strength without my Luna, I couldn't understand what he meant." He pulled me by my hand, welcoming me to sit on his lap. The ice in his eyes slowly melted into a more serene shade of blue, making my heart beat faster. "But I think I got it now."

CHAPTER FORTY-TWO

Calliope

I had never felt Nava so energetic before. Her vivid yellow eyes shone with excitement as low growls constantly echoed in her throat. Considering she was usually fairly timid and calm, the sudden change definitely surprised me. I wondered if it was her confidence growing as we adjusted to our Luna position - our shared desire to show our growing strength and dominance overshadowing her shy personality. To be fair, it could also be due to the simple fact that I hadn't let her out in a while.

My white wolf had her eyes locked on our target, her mind racing as she planned her next move. She would normally wait for our opponent to attack first and try to counterattack, but as I said before, she seemed to be rather spontaneous today. Still, I was slightly surprised when she took full control of our body, lunging towards the black wolf. Nyx was a fast and experienced warrior who usually had no trouble dodging our attacks, but this time, Nava didn't miss.

With one clean, sharp movement, Nava's jaw locked around our Delta's neck. Nyx gasped in astonishment as Nava's pointy teeth scraped her hide, inches away from piercing her skin. Her bright red eyes locked on us as my wolf finally let go of her, exhibiting a proud wolfish grin.

After blinking a few times, the black beast stood back on her feet, shaking off before her her long shiny fur started retreating through her pores as her majestic frame shrunk. In a matter of seconds, Bellatrix had shapeshifted into her human form, and I followed her lead. We both quickly got dressed in our training clothes, which had been put aside before we let our wolves out.

"Not bad, Luna!" The Delta smiled proudly at me as she ran her fingers through her voluminous wavy hair to fix it. "Nava was quite spunky today, huh?"

"I think she missed our private training lessons as much as I did," I replied with a smile to match hers. Our secret sparring sessions ended once I joined the other warriors for morning training, but with everything going on, I ended up missing a few days. Thankfully, Trix was more than happy to spar on our downtime. "Don't tell Darrell, but I think you're an even better teacher than he is."

Her smile grew more mischievous and bright. "Oh, you bet I'm gonna tell him! I can't miss the opportunity to rub it in his face!" I had to roll my eyes at her, but couldn't help a small giggle from escaping my lips. Trix was so stone-faced when I met her; it was nice to see she had a sense of humor. "Seriously though, you've improved a lot, Cal. It's a shame your potential was wasted back when you were part of Moonstone. From what you told me about their sorry-excuse-of-an-Alpha, I bet he was scared you would challenge him for his pack."

"I'm sure I would have no trouble beating him." I puffed my chest proudly, joining her game. "Either way, I'm fine with being a Luna. I don't think I have what it takes to be an Alpha."

"Are you kidding?" All of a sudden, her playfulness

vanished, being replaced by whole-hearted honesty. "Blood Eclipse is doing a lot better since you came along. We managed to become one of the strongest packs in the country because Levi is strong and stops at nothing. But I don't think we would be able to sustain our status for much longer without you, which is the main reason why Darrell was so adamant about finding this pack's Luna quickly." She made a brief pause, and I couldn't help but think of what my Alpha had told me the night before. "You changed him, Cal. You gave him a heart, and taught him how to control his anger so he could think clearly." Her sincerity stunned me. "He'll always be grumpy and intimidating - I don't think that'll ever change. But you made him a better leader."

My cheeks flushed in response to her remark. "It's not just me. We make a great team, all of us."

"Maybe." She shrugged, winking playfully at me as she walked past me. "I still think you'd make a pretty badass Alpha though."

Since Levi was stuck in his office with his Beta and Gamma, discussing the information they'd received from the scouts and preparing new strategies, I decided to spend the day with the girls. Trix and Hailey were both done with their tasks for the day, which meant we had plenty of time to relax and get our minds off this mess. The idea of spending an entire afternoon without Levi after always having him by my side for weeks was quite odd, but I was also looking forward to catching up with the ladies.

"I think some time away from the boys will be good for all of us," Nava encouraged. *"But do you think Odin would join us for a nighttime stroll?"*

I laughed internally. "*I doubt they would ever turn down the offer.*"

"Hey ladies! Are you ready for our girls day?" Hailey's excited chant pulled me back from my thoughts. I was so distracted I hadn't even realized we had already made it to the entrance hall of the packhouse.

"Can you not call it that?" The Delta frowned. "I'm already regretting having agreed with this."

I covered my mouth with my hand to hold back my snicker. These two were complete opposites, both in looks and in personality. Hailey was like a bright ray of sunshine, while Trix was more like a gloomy shadow. They were unique in their own ways, and aside from loving them as friends, I admired the way they each brought different assets to our pack.

"Whatever." The Gamma Female waved the other woman off. "What would you like to do?"

"I was thinking we could have a picnic by the lake?" I suggested. "It's a beautiful day."

"I love it!" Hailey clapped her hands.

"I have no objections." Trix shrugged.

"What are you girls up to?" A fourth voice caused us all to turn around in surprise. Standing behind us was Luna Calanthe, dressed in a classic gown with the main colors of Blood Eclipse - gold and red.

"We were just discussing what we should do for the rest of the day," I quickly explained, nodding respectfully at her. "The boys are busy today, so we thought it would be nice for us to spend some time together."

"Oh, girl time!" The former Luna smiled brightly. From

the corner of my eye, I noticed our grumpy Delta rolling her eyes. "Would you mind it if this old lady joined you? I might not be young anymore, but I'm still a girl at heart."

"Of course, Luna Calanthe! We would be honored," Hailey promptly replied. "Cal suggested a picnic by the lake."

"Sounds amazing. Would you like to join me for some tea first?"

The three of us exchanged glances before nodding in agreement. The last time Calanthe invited me for tea was quite enjoyable; I was all for repeating the experience with the other ranked girls. We followed Calanthe to her luxurious room, where she gestured for us to take our seats at the round table. She hummed a sweet melody as she happily prepared the hot drink for us. In the meantime, we started catching up.

I told them about my trip with Levi to the private island - leaving out most of the details, of course. Hailey was thrilled about the idea of taking a few days off to travel with Ivar, and she didn't waste time to show me pictures of the only vacation they went on together. To my surprise, Trix didn't seem nauseated by how in love the Gamma couple was; instead, she suggested we all went on a trip together once we figured out the exact reason behind Solar Hunt's attack.

"All done!" Calanthe cooed as she carried the teapot over to the table and quickly began serving us. When she realized the third seat was empty, her eyes darted to the black-haired woman leaning against the wall. "Won't you join us, Trix?" Her tone was demanding, but the Delta didn't seem too intimidated by it.

"I'm not a huge fan of tea, Luna."

My mother-in-law rolled her eyes, but as she took her seat,

she revealed, "There's a bottle of whiskey on the top shelf."

A satisfied smile lit up Trix's face, and she bowed her head at the former Luna before fetching her preferred choice of drink. We chatted for quite a while; I hadn't realized just how much I missed being around them. I didn't have any friends back at Moonstone, and their company here was definitely appreciated.

A couple of hours later, we said our goodbyes to Luna Calanthe and headed to the lake for our picnic. The sun was already setting as we laid the picnic blanket down, and it was impossible not to admire the warm mix of purples, reds, and oranges in the reflection of the water. Even Crystal joined us at some point, probably sensing my presence nearby. The atmosphere was rather calm, until something lunged at Hailey, making her scream.

"Ivar!" She laughed as her mate laid on top of her, tickling her stomach. When I glanced up, I found Darrell and Levi standing behind him, sharing looks of mock disapproval.

"How was your day?" the Gamma asked us all after planting a soft kiss on his mate's lips.

"Wonderful," Hailey quickly replied. "Would you like to join us?"

"Of course!"

I watched as my mate approached me slowly, struggling to not let his stern façade melt. Unwilling to sit down, he offered me his hand to help me up. He wasn't a fan of public displays of affection, so he resisted the urge to kiss my lips, bringing his mouth to my forehead instead as he wrapped his arms around my waist. The loving way he looked at me spoke louder than any words he could utter.

"Aaaaaand it seems like I've been promoted to fifth-wheel. I'm outta here," Trix complained as she jumped to her feet.

The Beta quickly threw one arm around her shoulders. "I would be honored to be your date for the night, Bellatrix," he joked.

"Better alone than in bad company!" She pushed him away, making him roll his eyes as he followed her back inside.

When I turned to glance at Hailey and Ivar again, I realized they too had gone. I felt my mate's index finger under my chin, gently forcing me to look at him. There was a hint of hunger in his blue eyes as he pressed his hand harder against the small of my back, pulling me impossibly closer. Our chests were pressed together, our hearts beating as one as he leaned closer.

"It looks like it's just the two of us now, my Luna." He smirked, and it suddenly dawned on me.

"Did you bring Ivar and Darrell to scare the girls away?" I arched an eyebrow at him, but couldn't hide my smile.

"I may or may not have done that," he replied casually. I enjoyed his lighter mood; it seemed their day of planning had gone well. "What would you like to do now?" His husky voice was barely a whisper.

I closed my eyes, giving in to the sparks of our bond before I recalled Nava's suggestion. "How about a moonlit stroll in the woods?"

"Whatever you want, my Luna."

We walked up to a more reserved area to take off our clothes before offering our counterparts control. For the rest of the night, our wolves mated and cuddled under the stars and light of the moon.

CHAPTER FORTY-THREE

Levi

"The runaways have been caught and killed by our scouts following your orders, Alpha."

Although my expression remained neutral, I allowed myself to enjoy the wave of relief that washed over me at the news. It was just Darrell and I in the office as he broke the news. I was known to be ruthless and impulsive, but I wasn't reckless; I was very careful when it came to eliminating my enemies. The mission had been discussed with my team, of course, but they hadn't heard any updates since Darrell took charge of the operation - both because they were busy with their own jobs, and because the less people who knew about it, the lower the chances of information spreading.

"All of them?" I asked at last, staring right into my Beta's eyes.

"Every last one of them." Unlike me, he didn't bother masking his emotions, a big proud grin lit up his face as he handed me the reports.

According to werewolf law, upon defeating another leader, an Alpha is allowed to take the losing pack - land and people. The stranded wolves then choose whether they accept the new leadership, or reject it. The victorious Alpha has the right to deal with the deserters as he pleases That usually meant sentencing them to death or to live as rogues. However, my case was slightly different, considering the ranked members of Solar Hunt decided to run away before the actual takeover.

After I punished Julius for his stupid decision, the Elders gave me a green light to kill the runaways, but it was up to me to find them. Though I knew I had some of the best trackers in the country by my side, I was still in awe at how fast they managed to complete their mission. It had only been a week since I gave them the order to bring me the heads of the cowards, but the reports Darrell provided didn't lie - there were even pictures confirming that every single one of the wolves we had been looking for had been successfully eliminated.

Taking my eyes off the papers for a brief second to look at my Beta's carefree posture, I allowed myself to lean back against my comfortable chair, relaxing my stiff shoulders. Maybe I too should let loose every once in a while.

"Good job." I nodded at the man who promptly returned the gesture.

Then, my lips curled as an idea crossed my mind. I stood up from my seat, grabbing an old bottle of whiskey from the black wooden liquor cabinet. After studying the fine drink for a moment, I fetched two empty glasses before putting them down on my desk -my second-in-command watching me with an arched brow the entire time.

"Perhaps we should...celebrate the success of the operation." I coughed, answering his unspoken question.

"Levi? Celebrating?" he questioned, obviously amused. Of course he wouldn't miss the opportunity to mess with me. "It's been at least eight years since I've seen you open up a bottle."

"I believe the occasion calls for it." Pouring myself a glass, I gestured for him to do the same as I sat back down. He followed, realizing it was best to do so before I changed my mind. "And make sure to give the scouts the day off tomorrow."

He raised his glass in agreement. "Cheers!"

"Cheers." The shadow of a smile lit up my face as the clink of the glasses echoed through the office.

I was a quiet man, too serious and careful to speak more than I should. However, as my Beta and I shared a drink, I enjoyed our brief conversation. For the first time in years, I was seeing him not only as my Beta, but as my friend - my *best* friend. We used to do this all the time back when we were younger, but things changed. *I* changed.

At last, I was ready to let go of the past, of the walls I had put up out of fear, to remember what true friendship was like.

* * *

I linked my other ranked members to update them on the operation before Darrell and I went our separate ways. He had work to do with the new orders I had given him, and after an entire morning away from my mate, I needed to see her. Odin would often go crazy inside my head, giving me terrible headaches that worsened the longer we were separated from our Luna. Honestly, I couldn't blame him. I had enjoyed my own company for too long, but she made my days...brighter.

And I knew exactly where to find her.

Even for someone grumpy as me, it was impossible not to smile at the woman dressed in a beautiful gown, dancing with the horses on the grassy field. She was as radiant as the sun, her angelic wavy hair flowing in the wind as she spun around like a fairy, the black stallion and white unicorn surrounding her as if she was their goddess - she was certainly mine. I allowed myself to admire my Luna, who was sweet and delicate on the outside, but strong and powerful on the inside. She was simply perfect.

The horses noticed me before she did. They both stopped trotting to look at me with curiosity, standing on each side of her as if they were her bodyguards. Noticing the creatures' distraction, her gaze finally landed on me. She smiled brightly as I walked towards her, wrapping my muscular arms around her delicate frame. Unable to resist my desire to taste her, I pulled her in for a kiss. The expression on her face after she pulled away was definitely not what I was expecting.

"Is something wrong?" My voice was full of concern.

"Are you using some kind of cologne?"

"No?" I cocked my head to the side as she twisted her nose in disgust. Where was this coming from?

"You smell different." She put both hands on my chest, gently pushing me away. As offended as I was, I didn't fight her. "Your scent has always been strong. Fiery like flames burning in a fireplace, deep and earthly like walnut firewood. But today you smell…sweet. Too sweet. It's almost…" She held her tongue before finishing her sentence, but I knew exactly what she was going to say. *Sickening.*

"*Why is she showing aversion to our scent?*" Odin whined, heartbroken. "*A mate's scent is supposed to be special; irresistible to our fated one. Why does she suddenly not like it anymore?*"

"*I have no idea. She didn't complain about it when she woke up next to us this morning,*" I replied in all honesty, instinctively stepping away from her.

"I'm sure it's nothing to be worried about. Maybe you got too close to the flowers in the garden or something." She smiled apologetically in an attempt to make me feel better, but I could still see her holding her breath. "It should go away if you take a shower, right?"

As desperate as I was to have her close to me again, I rushed to our room with her following not too close behind me. I took my time to lather, rub, and wash my skin repeatedly. Never in my life had I taken such a long shower before. When I walked out of the bathroom, I was hoping to see her smile. To my dismay, her nauseated expression let me know if anything, it had gotten even worse.

"I'm sorry, my Luna." The pain must have been noticeable in my tone judging by how she quickly approached me, but I continued before she could protest. "Let's pay the doctor a visit. Maybe he will know what's going on."

Plugging her nose, she just nodded in agreement. *Goddess!* Just when everything was starting to work out for us, she suddenly couldn't stand my scent. My scent of all things?! The scent that the Moon Goddess specifically designed for my mate. For Cal! What changed? Why was this happening? I walked in silence by her side as my mind relentlessly searched for an answer, with no such luck.

Despair must have been written all over my face, because as soon as we set foot in the hospital, the pack doctor widened his eyes. In less than a second, we were surrounded by nurses.

"Alpha, Luna." He bowed his head to us both. "What brings you here?"

I closed my eyes, sighing in frustration. How do I even

begin to explain this? "The Luna claims my scent is, um, making her sick," I hesitantly informed him. Everyone around us gasped in shock. "Have you ever heard of such a thing?"

"Never, Alpha," he confessed apologetically. "But I'm sure we will figure out exactly what is happening."

The doctor led us to one of the many vacant rooms, where he proceeded to ask us a series of questions. Then, he performed a bunch of different exams to eliminate certain possibilities. After taking her blood pressure and temperature, collecting some blood samples, and taking x-rays, he insisted on taking her to a private room to perform a transvaginal ultrasound. As hesitant as I was to leave her, she reassured me it would be okay. Thankfully by then, my ranked members had come to keep me company during this madness.

We were all sitting on small chairs in a random waiting room when the doctor came back. My heart almost stopped when I noticed Cal wasn't with him, but his gentle smile helped me relax a little bit. Just a little, because part of me still wanted to burn down the hospital in search of answers.

"It seems the answer to this uncommon situation is simpler than we thought, Alpha," the man informed me as I jumped up from my seat. My eyes locked on him, silently commanding him to get to the point. He didn't hesitate to continue, "The Luna is pregnant with Blood Eclipse's heir. Although this symptom is rare, her pregnancy explains why she is suddenly more sensitive to your scent."

It felt like the world was spinning around me as I tried to digest this unexpected piece of information. Calliope was pregnant with my pup. Our pup. The heir to our pack. It wasn't much of a surprise considering how sexually active we were, but I certainly wasn't expecting it to happen now. I was overjoyed, and though I tried my best to conceal my emotion, I was certain that my eyes were glistening blissfully.

"Wow. If this isn't karma at its finest!" Darrell laughed. I shot him a death glare. I was still too stunned to do anymore than that. My supposed best friend was insinuating this was the Moon Goddess' way of punishing me for how I had treated my mate when I first met her - wanting to keep my distance from her, both physically and emotionally.

"*Karma...*" My wolf lowered his ears in defeat, but his frustration was evident in his tone. "*I guess we deserve it.*"

Ignoring both of them, I approached the doctor. "How far along is she?"

"Two and a half weeks, Alpha," he promptly replied. I opened my mouth, desperate to know when I could see her, but he was faster. "She is in Room 22. I will give you some privacy to celebrate the news while I prepare a potion to help her deal with her heightened sense of smell." He bowed at me before disappearing through another door.

Without thinking, I took a step forward before glancing over my shoulder to take one last look at my team. They were all holding their tongues, but the silly smiles on their faces showed their excitement at the news. Even the always-so-serious Bellatrix had her lips curled in joy. I couldn't believe my precious mate had been able to bring out the Delta's soft side. I rolled my eyes before leaving the waiting room, now even more desperate to see my mate.

I hesitated when I reached the door to Cal's room, my heart nearly pounding out of my chest. The two nurses keeping guard outside promptly moved to allow me to walk in, and with a deep breath, I finally did. My eyes immediately landed on my woman lying carefree on the white bed, a serene smile on her face. I really tried to keep my distance, but I couldn't. She crinkled her nose when I sat next to her, but didn't complain. In an attempt to ease the discomfort I brought to her, I grabbed her hand to rub circles on the back of it. Thankfully, the sparks of our bond still seemed to work.

"How are you feeling, my Luna?" I whispered as I kissed her knuckles as gently as I could.

"Can't say I'm surprised," she giggled, making my heart melt. "I've never thought about being a mother, but..." She shifted her gaze to her stomach, and I couldn't help but do the same. My pup was growing inside of her... "I'm really happy about it."

"I'm glad. Because you just made me the happiest man alive," I told her sincerely, staring deeply into her eyes.

She smiled sweetly in response, placing her hand on the side of my face to pull me in for a kiss. Hesitantly, I brushed my lips against hers before using my tongue to push them apart. The second I invaded her mouth, I welcomed the fireworks that made electricity explode in my chest. I tried hard to control the beast inside of me, but that was always difficult after tasting her. She was so warm. So delicious.

And she was mine.

A low growl reverberated in my throat when she pushed me lightly, turning her face away from mine. Through our connection, I could tell she was enjoying our kiss, but her aversion towards my scent forced her to pull away. If this was my punishment, the Goddess definitely had a twisted sense of humor.

"Don't worry. The doc said he's working to fix this." Calliope tried to stay positive as she brushed my cheek with her soft thumb.

"Only temporarily," I grumbled. "If this is due to your hormones, it won't go away until our pup is born."

"I'm sure we can-" She stopped mid-sentence when we heard an excited neigh.

Imagine our surprise when we turned around to find the unicorn poking her head through the window.

"Crystal!" My mate chuckled. She was too far to touch the creature, but she seemed content enough just to be in Crystal's presence. "Missed me, girl?" As usual, I found myself smiling at their cute interaction.

However, my calm soon turned into concern when the unicorn's horn started glowing. It seemed to trigger something, as the crescent moon mark in the palm of Calliope's hand shone in an intense white light. Normally, I would know better than to think Crystal would ever hurt her rider, but unaware of the powers she possessed and fearing for my mate and pup's lives, my instinct to protect them kicked in. I stood up abruptly, ready to take action, but as quickly as the event had started, it suddenly ended.

My eyes were just as wide as my Luna's as I tried to understand what just happened. Nothing was different, and it seemed like she was fine. More than fine, actually, judging by the excited grin on her face.

"Levi, your scent!" she yelled happily. "It doesn't bother me anymore! It's gone back to normal!"

Oh, thank the Moon Goddess! Screw it, I'm not hiding my fucking smile any longer.

“I shouldn’t be surprised. Of course Crystal would be just as amazing as you.” I pulled her in for yet another kiss, savoring her properly now that I didn’t make her uncomfortable anymore.

Then, my Luna smiled brighter than ever, glancing at her belly. “I can’t wait to introduce our pup to her.”

“And I can’t wait to meet the little one.” I brushed my nose against hers, placing my lips over hers once again.

CHAPTER FORTY-FOUR

Calliope

As an only child, all I knew about my mother's pregnancy was what she told me. I remember flipping through the pages of an old photo album, pointing at the pictures of her huge belly while she told me stories of what the experience had been like for her. My father would chime in occasionally to tease her about her frequent mood swings. She would usually get mad at him, but they always ended up cuddling on the couch to look at the photographs once I got bored of playing with it.

It was impossible not to think about them after I'd found out that I was expecting three days ago.

I didn't have my mom anymore, but it brought me immeasurable peace to know I had been successful at helping my mate reconcile with his mother before he lost her forever. And now, she was right by my side to assist me with the preparations for her grandchild's birth.

"Oh, yes! Now it looks perfect!" Calanthe chanted with satisfaction, gesturing for the maid to back away after she was done making the adjustments to the gown I was wearing. "It's a shame we didn't have time to prepare something more opulent, but we shouldn't delay the announcement. The pack will be thrilled to know you are carrying the heir!" She clapped her hands over her chest, eyeing me up and down. "Don't worry though, my dear. Your new outfits have been made-to-order to fit you comfortably during your pregnancy."

Deltas are the lowest ranked members, but they are still above most other positions in the pack hierarchy. Moonstone wasn't an extremely wealthy pack, and they never valued me after my parent's death, but my mother did have some luxuries while she was carrying me. Still, what she had didn't come close to the pampering I was receiving.

For the first time, I turned around to take a look at myself in the huge mirror in the Alpha suite. The navy blue dress I had chosen had a lace flower upper half, with long sleeves and a boat neckline. The long skirt had diagonal layers that flowed smoothly like waves. The former Luna was right; it really suited me. My deep brown hair had been styled in a classy braided updo, adorned with a flower branch hairpin made of crystals and pearls, which matched my earrings perfectly.

"Thank you for your efforts, Calanthe." I smiled as I turned back to her. "But I must insist, none of this is necessary. My bump is not even showing yet; there's no need for new clothes."

"Nonsense!" She waved me off immediately. "You are Blood Eclipse's Luna and you shall have only the best. My son wouldn't have it any other way."

As if Levi had been listening to our conversation - honestly, I wouldn't be surprised if he was - he suddenly poked his head through the door. His eyes shyly scoured through the room, widening as they landed on me. Giving in to the magnetic pull between us, his feet paced in my direction. He stopped inches away from me, hesitant; I couldn't tell if it was because he feared ruining my gown by not being able to control himself, or if he was just afraid of being too rough and hurting the pup growing inside my womb.

"You look breathtaking, my Luna," he breathed out as he stared deeply into my eyes. I noticed how he instinctively lifted one of his hands to touch my cheek, but gave up on the idea before we made contact. Instead, he laced his fingers behind his back in a clear attempt to restrain himself.

I had to resist the urge to roll my eyes, but smiled nonetheless. "I could say the same about you, my Alpha."

Levi's outfit matched mine. He was wearing a grayish-blue button up shirt underneath a navy suit jacket and trousers of the same color. His solid silver satin tie stood out against his dark clothes, much like the jewelry I was wearing. Adamant to close the distance between us, I took a step forward too quickly for him to protest, and wrapped my arms around his neck. Without hesitation, I gave him a soft peck in the lips. He stiffened at first, but as expected, it didn't take him long to relax. A genuinely happy smile lit up his face when I pulled away.

"The two of you are the perfect Alpha couple!" Calanthe cooed, catching our attention. For a brief second, I had even forgotten about her presence. "I'm so happy for you. And I'm so happy to see you happy, my son." Her eyes were watery as she turned to my mate. I stepped away from him just slightly to offer them more space. "I never thought you would smile this brightly again." She cupped one side of his face with her delicate hands, and he quickly took it in both of his. After their mother-son moment, she looked at me. "Thank you, Calliope. For bringing back my son, and for gifting me with a grandchild."

I blushed shyly, unsure of what to say. As if reading my thoughts, my Alpha supportively placed his tough hand on the small of my back, carefully kissing my temple.

"Just accept our gratitude, my Luna," he whispered into my ear, giving me goosebumps. "Blood Eclipse has a million reasons to be grateful to you." All I could do was nod in response.

"Well, I'm going downstairs to make sure everything is ready. Don't be late." With that last warning, the former Luna turned around, glancing at us one final time before exiting the room.

Once she was gone, I allowed my hand to travel up my mate's chest, analyzing every detail of his simple, yet sophisticated outfit whilst not missing the chance to feel his muscles underneath the fabric. He closed his eyes, enjoying the sparks of my touch, but it didn't last long. As soon as a low growl escaped his lips, he tensed up, holding both of my wrists as gently as he could. Too gently, not at all like my rough Alpha.

"You're not going to break me, Levi," I reassured him sarcastically. "I'm not a glass doll."

"I know. You're my powerful Luna." He looked into my eyes, finally pulling me closer - still very delicately. "But our pup..."

"They will be fine. They are just as strong as we are. Besides, there's still a good three months and a half before this pup comes out. I don't want you to treat me differently until then."

For a few seconds, he furrowed his brows as he considered whether it was worth it arguing with me, or if he should just let it go. When he sighed in defeat, I knew he had wisely chosen the latter.

"As you wish." He took one last moment to admire me, and soon enough, the serene smile was back on his face. His soft lips pressed against my cheek as he linked our arms. "Shall we go?"

"Of course. They must be waiting for us."

Together, we made our way towards the dining hall. As usual, our Delta didn't disappoint; even on short notice, she had been able to take care of all of the arrangements, decorating the room in gold and red, the traditional colors of Blood Eclipse.

Exactly like on the day of my Luna Ceremony, all of the one thousand plus members were present, now with the addition of the new faces who were once part of Solar Hunt. As we made our way through the dining hall, every wolf we crossed paths with bowed their heads at us. Even though the official announcement hadn't been made yet, I could hear them whispering about the reason why they were here, and their excitement brought a radiant smile to my face. I instinctively rubbed my hand over my stomach; my little prince or princess was already so loved by their pack.

Levi and I joined our ranked members at the larger table at the center, designated specifically for us. We chatted for a little bit as we waited for everyone to take their seats. I noticed how my usually tough and serious Alpha relaxed in the presence of his team, proudly holding my hand at all times. At that moment, I felt more whole than I ever had in my entire life. Surrounded by my mate, my friends, and my pack, I realized I now had the family I'd always dreamt of.

"Attention, everyone!" Levi stood up from his seat,

tugging on my hand to encourage me to do the same. In a fraction of a second, the whole room was dead silent. "Thank you for coming here today. I have requested your presence for a very important announcement." A bright smile lit up his face when his vivid blue eyes met mine, and he didn't bother hiding it this time. He wrapped one arm around my waist, pulling me closer before he turned to face our pack again. "Your Luna is pregnant with the Blood Eclipse heir!" He lifted his champagne glass, and the crowd went wild. "Tonight, we shall celebrate this special occasion! Brothers and sisters, eat and drink as much as you please!"

After the announcement, we went back to our seats and the waiters promptly served us the finest dishes. The rest of the wolves filled their plates at the buffet, taking turns to approach me. It was tradition for the wolves of a pack to offer gifts to their pregnant Luna to celebrate the new life growing inside of her, the leader they would someday follow. The attention I was receiving was overwhelming, but it made me feel so warm and loved. Before long, two very familiar women knelt before me - the Omegas whom I had helped a while ago.

"Luna Calliope!" they said in unison, stretching their arms to show me a giant basket full of various colorful fruits.

"We have gathered these berries from the finest crops growing in our garden. It's not much, but we sincerely hope you enjoy them," Mirian, the older one, went on.

"After you helped us, Luna, I realized it was better to share than to keep everything to myself. With Mirian's assistance, my garden was turned into a community garden." I was in awe at Jenna's revelation; I had no idea my actions would encourage her to do something so great. "It would be an honor if you could come visit our garden someday, Luna."

"I sure will, Jenna. Thank you, Mirian." I smiled at the two as a group of Omegas took the basket to carry it to my room along with the other gifts.

Immediately after, I was surprised to see the single father and his pup, whom I had met not long ago, standing in front of me.

"Congratulations, Luna. Alpha." The man dropped a knee to the floor, his son mimicking his gesture as he showed me a thick book. "This is what my mate used to read on the bad days when she was pregnant. I have flicked through the pages a few times in the past few weeks, and though I can't understand why it calmed her so much, I hope you will find it as entertaining as she did."

My heart ached as I touched the man's shoulder, gesturing for him to stand back up. "Thank you, Lucas, but I can't accept this. You should keep it."

"Please, Luna," he insisted, glancing up to look at me for the first time. "She would want you to have it."

With a sympathetic smile, I took the book in my hands. "Thank you."

"I don't have anything to give you..." Ralph whispered shyly, and I immediately turned to look at him. "But I will promise you something." He put his hand over his heart, probably copying a character from a movie. He was so cute, but the determination in his eyes let me know he was being serious. "I promise I will train hard to become a warrior like my mommy, and I will fight to protect you and your pup."

From the corner of my eye, I noticed his father smiling proudly. "Thank you, Ralph. I have nothing to fear as long as I have you to keep me safe."

The pup saluted me before he and his father left. I could already see more pack members walking towards me, but before the next one came, Levi squeezed my hand.

"You are so wise and kind, my Luna," he whispered against my lips as I got lost in his hypnotizing eyes. "You are the heart I never knew I was missing. And I have no doubts you will be a wonderful mother."

* * *

Bellatrix

Every ranked wolf plays an important role in the organization of a pack. They're like gears of a very complex machine - the whole system can't work properly if any one of them is taken away. As the Alpha's right hand, Betas have to be just as informed as their leaders regarding pack politics since they must be ready to take over when their Alpha is away or killed. The Gammas, also known as the third-in-command, are responsible for security, including the pack's defense system, scouts and trackers.

However, the Deltas are the hardest working of the lower three ranks, although they're not always given the right recognition.

Unlike Betas or Gammas, who focus on learning and taking care of specific topics, we are in charge of managing the entire pack. We must be close to the pack members in order to know their concerns and problems they might be facing, as well as ensure there is peace by solving any conflicts before they escalate. We must be skilled fighters like Betas but also smart and quick-thinking like Gammas, all while remaining approachable. In my opinion, this is why our patriarchal society decided to allow women to occupy the Delta position - a man's brain wasn't capable of multitasking like ours.

And with the pack's heir on the way, I had my hands full preparing everything for their arrival. I didn't mind the workload though; I had worked really hard to earn the position and I truly loved my job. It was the one thing that kept my mind busy, allowing me to stay sane after my mate passed away. Nyx was so weak she hibernated for an entire year after that, leaving me to deal with the unbearable pain completely on my own. It was then that I decided to fully focus on my Delta career and training, so I would always be able to protect the ones I loved.

A lone tear rolled down my cheek as I let my guard down, and I immediately shook my head. This wasn't the moment to grieve - it was time to celebrate! The whole pack was ecstatic about the recent news, and I couldn't be happier for Cal. She was broken when she arrived at Blood Eclipse, but she had grown into a powerful and confident Luna. Levi also deserved to find happiness. He had lost himself somewhere along the way after everything he had been through. He's made a few mistakes, but he never stopped putting his people first. These two were the definition of a power couple, and I was lucky to serve them.

The day after Cal's pregnancy announcement, I was organizing a folder of documents in the Alpha's office when I suddenly heard the door open. I quickly looked over my shoulder to find Darrell walking in with his fair share of papers. He dropped them on the table, greeting me with a nod as he approached me.

"Busy day, huh?"

"Yeah," I casually replied, focusing my attention back on the documents. "Any luck with the search for clues about the weird attack?"

"Not really." It was easy to notice the frustration in his tone. "We haven't been able to advance much. The former members of Solar Hunt only knew what Julius told them, and as we already know from the interviews, he didn't say much." He glanced over at the folder in my hands. "What are those?"

"Bills regarding the pup's Presentation Ceremony, guidelines for the events, guest lists... you know the drill." I shrugged.

"Actually, no, I don't. We've never had to prepare for the arrival of a Blood Eclipse heir." He stared at me as if I had grown a second head. "How do you even know what you're doing?"

I couldn't resist flashing him an arrogant smirk. "Call it Delta instinct."

"You're one mysteriously amazing woman, Trix." Darrell smiled at me before taking his seat, sighing as he let his head fall backwards. There was silence for a moment as he stared at the ceiling, but I had a feeling it wouldn't last long. "This news is a matter for great rejoicing. It's impossible not to notice the smiles on every corner. But...I can't help but feel a pinch of sadness."

"Why?" At first, I wasn't really interested, but I knew he needed a listening ear.

"This is gonna sound selfish. But seeing how happy Cal

is about her pup, I can't help but be reminded of Marisol. She always wanted to be a mother."

"It isn't selfish to wish a lost family member could have lived the life they deserved," I observed. Much like me, Darrell was still grieving. However, I could argue his case was worse than mine in a way, since his sister's murderer was never punished. "Besides, your anguish for Mari doesn't overrule your happiness for Cal."

"I guess you're right." He exhaled deeply before shyly lifting his head to look at me. "Did you...uh...ever think about having pups? When Igor...you know." I immediately stiffened; I hadn't heard that name in so long. Nyx lowered her ears inside my head as she projected distant memories to me. Aware of where this was going, I immediately shut her out. The Beta's voice pulled me back from my thoughts. "You don't have to answer if you don't-"

"He wanted to have pups," I confessed. I would usually avoid discussing the topic, but whether it was the fact that I had been holding my feelings for too long or the comfortable atmosphere, the words simply slid from my lips. "I didn't though. At least not then. I was postponing it because I didn't want to give up my life as a warrior," I continued after a long silence. "Now, I kinda regret it. Had I known he would... Had I known things would turn out the way they did, I wouldn't have thought twice about his request."

"Would you be okay with it? Being a single mother?"

"Yeah. I'd at least still have a piece of him that way."

My hand immediately moved to my eyes to dry the tears that I wasn't able to hold back any longer. Darrell stood up from his seat, wrapping his arms around my frame to offer me some comfort. I didn't like to be seen when I was this vulnerable, but I knew I could trust him. Still, his pity didn't help me feel better. After a few seconds, I gently pushed him away.

"Anyway," I kept going, sniffling for the last time. "If there is one thing I've learned, it's that no matter how hard you wish for it, you can't change the past. There is nothing we can do for Mari and Igor except to move on. They would want us to be happy."

"You're definitely right about that." He showed me a sad smile. "And though we can't change the past, we do have the power to change the future."

"So cliché." I rolled my eyes at him, but smiled nonetheless. "Anyway, we should get back to work."

"We do have a lot to do," he agreed, yet his expression let me know he had a different idea. "But...I'm sure it would be fine if we took a quick break to spar. What do you say?"

"Now you're talking!" I punched his arm playfully, putting away the papers I had finished organizing. "Loser buys a round?"

"Of beer?"

"Whiskey." I winked at him.

"Why do I have a bad feeling about this?"

"Because you know you're already poorer!"

On our way towards the gym, we engaged in a lighter conversation. The sadness from earlier slowly faded away, especially once we set our wolves free. While the pain and grief had been forgotten, I knew our mission would never be.

"*We fight for him,*" Nyx reminded me, her piercing red eyes locked on to her opponent.

"*And we will keep on fighting.*" I nodded at her.

CHAPTER FORTY-FIVE

Calliope

"Are you ready, my love?" Levi calmly asked, stretching his hand out to me.

Before turning to him, I took one last look at my reflection in the mirrored closet doors. I ran my hand over my belly, gently caressing it through the thin fabric of my loose forest green blouse and my comfortable maternity leggings. My small bump had grown considerably over the past month; and during that time, my Alpha made sure to spoil me rotten.

Levi had improved a lot since we decided to start anew, and though I could tell he was trying to be more honest and vocal about his feelings, I knew he still struggled to communicate them to me. So, he continued to show his love and devotion to me by showering me with gifts. However, I was surprised to see him put in the effort to set his stubbornness aside, letting me have my way with everything. According to him, he just wanted to make sure I wouldn't have to deal with unnecessary stress, which could be harmful for our pup. Still, I couldn't help but wonder if it was just me bringing out his softer side.

"Yes, ready! Let's go," I finally replied, smiling at him as he took my hand. He planted a soft kiss on the back of it before leading me out of the Alpha suite and towards the pack hospital.

The second we stepped out of the main building, I was greeted by the sun. It was a wonderful Sunday morning. The town square was full of wolves, most of which would stop what they were doing to greet me and ask about the heir. There were groups of friends chatting and enjoying the nice weather, as well as families watching their pups play. I spotted Ralph among them, but he was too absorbed in a tag game to notice me. Taking a quick look around, I couldn't find his father anywhere, so I just assumed he had chores to do.

Not too long after, my hypothesis was confirmed when I found him tending to the small garden in front of his house.

"Good morning, Lucas!" I waved to him.

He seemed surprised to see us at first, but he soon got up from the ground, brushing the dirt off his jeans and hands. The timid smile that lit up his face afterwards let me know he was already feeling a lot more comfortable at Blood Eclipse than he was when he first arrived.

"Alpha Levi. Luna Calliope." Lucas bowed his head respectfully at us. "I'm sorry about this mess. Had I known you were coming to visit, I would have cleaned the house and prepared some tea."

"Do not worry. We are just on our way to the hospital," my mate promptly replied. Levi was usually stern and serious around the pack members, but he seemed to be warming up to Lucas.

"Oh! To check on the pup," he quickly concluded. "I hope the heir is doing well."

"They've been growing healthily according to the doctor," I assured him before pointing at the recently planted flowers with my head. "Are you into gardening?"

"Not really. But my mate was." Lucas put his hands on his waist, proudly looking at his work. "She loved flowers. I thought growing a garden would help keep her memory alive."

"What a wonderful way to honor her." I smiled at him. "By the way, thank you for the book. It's been helping keep my mind busy."

"I'm glad it's been serving you well, Luna."

"We should get going, my Luna," Levi reminded me sweetly, turning to Lucas soon after. "If you and Ralph ever need anything, don't hesitate to contact us."

"Of course, Alpha. Thank you." He bowed his head again.

After our quick chat with Lucas, we headed straight to the pack hospital. We had an appointment scheduled for eleven, and though we were a few minutes late, I doubt it would be a problem; the medical team rarely had patients, considering werewolves were immune to most diseases and were capable of healing quite fast. The building would usually be crowded during attacks or wars, but in times of peace, it was mostly quiet.

The doctor was waiting for us by the front desk, and he courteously greeted us before leading us towards an exam room. The equipment had already been prepared, so Levi just helped me lie down on the bed. Already familiar with the process, I carefully lifted up my shirt, leaving my small bump exposed.

"We're only doing an ultrasound today, Luna," the man explained, asking for permission before gently rubbing a cold gel over my stomach. He pressed the transducer against my skin, and granulated images started showing on the screen as he moved the wand around. "Everything seems perfectly fine with your pup. Oh, wait… I see something." Both Levi and I stiffened, but the doctor's smile somehow calmed me down. "Would you like to know the gender of your pup, Luna?"

I hesitated for a moment. As trivial as it sounded, I hadn't thought about whether I would like to know our pup's gender in advance. The idea of keeping it as a surprise was kinda interesting. However, as I glanced at my mate, I could easily notice his curiosity. Seeing how excited he was about being a father, I thought it would be fair for him to know.

"Yes, please," I finally replied.

"What were you hoping for?"

"A girl." I smiled.

"What about you, Alpha?"

Levi was reluctant at first, but after clearing his throat, he revealed, "A boy."

The doctor smiled joyfully, seemingly enjoying our tension. "Well, it seems the Goddess has favored your wishes, Alpha. The pup is a male."

For the first time ever, I could actually see hearts in my mate's eyes. Their usual pale blue shade had melted into an electric cyan, and though he was doing his best to keep a straight face, he couldn't completely fight back his radiant smile. It didn't even bother me that our pup didn't turn out to be a girl like I had hoped for, his happiness made everything else seem unimportant.

Once the doctor made sure our little boy was doing fine, he congratulated us one more time, giving me some recommendations before we walked out. Levi hadn't uttered a word, but he was grinning from ear to ear, and the hospital staff seemed just as surprised about his mood as I was. And I was even more stunned when he lifted me in his arms, spinning me around as soon as we left the building.

"Levi! You're squeezing me too hard!" I laughed in a half-scolding tone.

He immediately put me down, letting his mouth crash against mine not a second later. "I'm sorry, my love. I'm just so..."

"Happy?" I helped finish his sentence. Sometimes, his struggle to voice his feelings was cute.

"Exactly." He smiled brighter. "I'm thrilled! Ecstatic! Euphoric!" he exclaimed in between kisses. "You make me so happy, Calliope. Thank you for giving me a pup. Thank you for being patient with me. Thank you for bringing out the best in me. I promise I'll do everything in my power to make sure you and our son will always be happy."

"Oh, Levi..." I smiled close to his lips, pleasant shivers running down my spine as I felt his hot breath against my mouth. "You already do."

* * *

Once we returned to the room, I decided to take a nice relaxing bath while my mate ordered us lunch. The doctor recommended some therapeutic bath salts to help with stress and discomfort, and I had found them to be quite effective. Even with my busy Luna schedule, I still tried to take these special baths at least on alternate days. Sundays were always perfect for some private me time. I had just sat down when I heard the door to the bathroom open, I knew I wouldn't be completely alone.

"Lunch is already being prepared," Levi informed me, taking a few steps closer to the bathtub. Except for my head, my whole body was submerged, yet he still had his eyes on me as if I was the sexiest woman on Earth. It was probably the hormones. "I ordered steak au poivre with vegetables. Is that okay?"

"It's perfect." I leaned back on the tub, sighing and gently closing my eyes. I could feel Levi staring at me for a few moments longer before clearing his throat.

"Would you like some company, my Luna?"

"Sure." I chuckled, opening my eyes again.

My gaze never left him as he started getting rid of his clothes, one by one. First, he lifted his shirt over his head. The sight of his muscular chest and stomach were already enough to make me bite down hard on my bottom lip; from the smirk playing on his lips, I could tell he noticed. Enjoying the effect he had on me, he took his time to leisurely lower his trousers, then his boxers. The moment his erection sprung free, I had to hold back a moan as my whole body lit up in flames.

"I'm hungry for mate too," Nava chimed in. *"We haven't had him in so long."* It had been roughly a week since the last time we had sex, but she was right; considering how active we used to be, it had been a long time.

"He has been so careful around us lately. Do you think he'll want to...?"

"He seems ready to me." She smiled mischievously. *"Besides, the doctor didn't say anything about mating."*

"May I come inside?" Levi's slightly husky voice pulled me back from my conversation with my wolf.

"Oh, yes, you may!" Nava replied, though I'm not sure she was thinking the same thing as he was.

Nodding my head yes, I moved forward a little to allow my mate to sit behind me. He stepped in slowly. Lowering himself into the warm water, he rested his back against the tub before pulling me closer in between his outstretched legs. The moment my ass pressed against his hardened member, I could feel a low growl reverberating in his chest against my back. I closed my eyes when he started planting slow kisses on the top of my head; I didn't even notice his rough hands snaking over my front until they each firmly cupped one of my breasts.

This time, I couldn't prevent a loud moan from escaping my lips.

"Don't hold them in, my love. I want to hear your lust for me," he whispered into my ear, successfully stealing another moan. "My memory has been failing me and it's driving me crazy; it's been so long since the last time I properly touched you. Will you let me remember what that marvelous body of yours feels like?"

"Of course, my Alpha," I obediently replied, not bothering to open my eyes; I wanted to focus on the sensation I had been craving.

Without hesitation, Levi grabbed my right nipple between his thumb and index finger, while his other hand roughly massaged my left breast. My sounds of pleasure echoed through the bathroom as he played my body with expertise. Whether it was the hormones or the fact I hadn't had him in a while, his touch had never felt so good. To my delight, he moved his sharp teeth to my shoulders, intensifying the heat as he grazed them over my mark.

He didn't stop there.

He continued to devour my neck as one of his hands traveled all the way down the bump in my belly, making me gasp when he reached right between my thighs. As his thumb rubbed circles over my clit, I relaxed against his chest, opening my legs wider to offer him easier access. The moment I called his name in a haze, he gladly let one of his fingers slide inside of me, causing my moans to grow louder.

The way my mate leisurely explored my walls was driving me insane. He gently ran his finger up and down inside of me, reaching deeper each time. It didn't take him long to find my G-spot, and as soon as he did, he inserted another finger, forcing me to expand. My breathing was becoming more erratic by the second, my heart pounding inside my chest as the waves of pleasure threatened to consume me.

In a moment of clarity, I wrapped my hand around his wrist to force him to stop; this wasn't how I wanted our bath to end.

"What's wrong? Did I hurt you?" There was a horrified look of concern on his face when I opened my eyes and turned around to look at him.

"No," I breathed out, still trying to regain focus. "I just... I want you to take me there in a different way. I want you to... come inside."

Another growl echoed in his throat. He closed his eyes and took a deep breath before glancing at me again. "As much as I want to take you, my love, I'm not sure it's safe. I don't wanna hurt our pup."

"He won't mind," I reassured him with a playful smile. "At most he will be satisfied that daddy is making mommy happy."

Even with my insistence, he still seemed unsure. It was time to tame my Alpha, command him to submit to me. "Please, Levi. Fuck me."

After that, he didn't try to contain his growls any longer. His fingertips dug deeper into my thighs as he tried to hold on to his last drop of control, not realizing he had already lost it - I was now the one in control.

"Goddess, Calliope! When did you get such a dirty mouth?" The blue in his eyes became more intense, and I instantly knew it was Odin pushing closer to the surface. It turned me on even more. "Fine, my Luna. Do with me as you please."

Smiling triumphantly, I didn't take long to follow his request. I lifted myself up just slightly, positioning his tip right at my entrance before lowering my hips, swallowing him whole in a quick movement. The way his warm cock filled me at once made me arch my back, yet I didn't want to wait until my body adjusted to him. After his teasing foreplay, I was eager to reach my release, so I immediately started moving.

Our moans of pleasure mixed and echoed as I rode him, fast and mercilessly. He wrapped his arms just under my breasts, pulling me impossibly closer to him. As his own climax approached, he thrusted his hips up to meet my movements, causing his cock to press deeper against my womb. The water hit our skin violently before splashing out of the tub. All that mattered was us, our bodies pressing against each other as if they wanted to become one.

At last, he unexpectedly sunk his teeth into my mark, finally taking me there as he too roared, finding his release. I screamed as he exploded inside of me, my pussy tightening around him to milk his dick for every drop of his seed. His grip around me tightened as he continued to pulsate, causing me to shiver in pleasure each time. Every time he made me come was more heavenly than the last.

Our animalistic sounds were slowly replaced by our panting breaths, our chests moving up and down as we tried to recover our oxygen. Once we both came down from our high, he carefully removed himself from me, but never released me from his embrace. He placed soft kisses on the tender spot where his teeth had recently been, making sure I had healed completely.

When we were finally back to reality, we realized the tub was now half-empty and the floor was completely flooded.

"Don't worry. I'll clean it," he reassured me, running his fingers down the length of my wavy strands to untangle them. "You're perfect, Cal."

"You spoil me too much." I laughed as I rested my face between his neck and shoulder.

"You deserve it."

The next second, the doorbell rang, catching our attention.

"I'll go get it while you enjoy the rest of your bath." He smiled at me, kissing my lips before lifting himself up to step out of the tub.

After our rather...interesting bath, I dried myself and put on some new comfortable clothes to join my mate at the table. My appetite had truly grown over the past few weeks, but it did help that our cooks prepared amazing food. Once we were done with our meal, Levi led me outside so we could rest a little.

"Is there anything else you would like to do today? We still have an entire evening," he asked, holding me in his arms as we laid on the sunlounger.

I was about to suggest we go on another horseback ride when I heard Nava's faint voice inside my head.

"The doctor said in a few days it might be harmful for the pup if we shift. It means I won't be able to connect with Odin until our pup is born," she timidly observed, almost as if she was ashamed. *"I was wondering... Would you let me spend the rest of the day with him?"* Her plea didn't sound selfish at all; in fact, I felt a little guilty for not considering the impacts the doctor's recommendations would have on her.

A small grin lit up my face as I turned to my mate. "Actually, Nava has a special request for you."

CHAPTER FORTY-SIX

Nava

"Levi, can you please let Odin come out?" I asked shyly, my eyes focused on my mate as I spoke through my human's body.

Calliope and I had always gotten along well, but I didn't expect her to put her own feelings and desires aside to allow me to spend the entire night with Odin. As soon as I told her about my concerns and wishes, she promptly led our mate outside towards the beautiful lake. Werewolves must have a balance between how much time they spend in each of their forms - staying in animal form for too long could make the human side vanish completely, and vice-versa. Cal was always very understanding, and she tried to let me out as much as possible no matter how busy we were.

Still, I was surprised by how quickly she agreed to let me take over our body right after finding out about our pup's gender. There was a lot she wanted to discuss with our Alpha - I could tell, after all, we share the same mind - yet she didn't mind postponing it to give me this.

"How can I refuse one of your requests when you ask me like this, Nava?" Levi's voice grew deeper as it mixed with Odin's. Hearing it sent pleasant tingles down my spine. Judging by the change in his eye-color and wolfish grin, I knew Levi was already gone, pushed back to the depths of his mind. And not too long after, I could finally see Odin.

The metallic gray wolf sprinted in my direction as soon as he was freed, his blue eyes locked on me. There was possessiveness in them, but they weren't icy cold as they had once been; they were now warmer, reminding me of the ocean shining underneath the sun on a summer morning. My beast's frozen heart had melted entirely for me, and noticing it caused a fire to ignite inside my chest. He stopped a few inches away from me, expectation in his expression as a low encouraging mumble left his lips. Only then did I realize I had gotten so distracted by him that I ended up forgetting to shift myself.

With a deep breath, I endured the brief pain of my breaking bones in order to embrace my true nature. The sensation of the breeze blowing through my soft white fur as it grew from the pores in my delicate human skin was so liberating, and the texture of the earth underneath my paws really put me at ease. However, I would soon remember none of those little pleasures could compare to the best feeling in the world.

Not wasting a second, Odin dove his large muzzle into my neck. He stayed there for a moment, taking in my scent; it was easy to understand how pleased he was by the animalistic sounds of joy constantly leaving his mouth. When he continued to rub himself against me, covering me in his scent, I too couldn't hold back a shy purr. The sparks between us were so strong in our animal form, it was hard for me to not let go of my humanity completely.

"I was dying to spend more time with you in this form, mate." His voice inside my head took me by surprise. Because of our bond, we were able to communicate and feel each other's

emotions even when our humans were in control, but it felt so much more intense this way.

"So was I, my Alpha." With a subtle smile, I licked the spot underneath his pointy ear. He let out a low growl in response before using his weight to pin me against the ground. He had a rough way of showing his love, yet I couldn't help but notice he had grown a lot gentler over the past few weeks.

The huge wolf stood on top of me, our hearts beating in synchrony as his chest pressed against mine. Once again, he started rubbing his muzzle and cheeks over my neck, slowly making his way down until he reached my stomach. Pressing his ear closer against my body, he leaned beside me and closed his eyes. Odin and Levi were usually so troubled, constantly worried or angry about something, but as he calmly listened to the sounds of the little life growing inside of me, there was only peacefulness in his expression.

"How is our pup doing?"

"He's been kicking quite a lot lately. Especially when you're near," I calmly replied.

"Does it hurt?"

"Not really. But it does cause some discomfort."

He lowered his ears shamefully, quickly lifted his heavy head off my belly. *"I'm sorry."*

"Don't be. I love how happy you look when you're listening to him."

I rolled over to face him properly. We lost ourselves in each other's gazes for a moment before he crouched towards me, resting his forehead against mine. Wolves were highly aware of their surroundings, but as we laid there with our eyes closed, the world around us seemed to disappear. It was impossible to tell how much time had gone by when Odin finally decided to stand up, offering me support to do the same.

"What would you like to do during our hours together, my Luna?"

"Honestly, I just wanted to slow down for a little bit."

"Allow me to take you on a nice, relaxing date then. Wolf-style." Lowering his head at shoulder-length, he showed me a sheepish smile, almost as if he was embarrassed of his romantic side. I couldn't help but chuckle at his silliness; this lovesick pup looked nothing like the beast I met during my marking ceremony, and I was happy to see the change.

Although I mostly tried to live in the present, I couldn't help but remember the event. Back then, all of my hopes and dreams of ever being loved were crushed. I used to think Levi was cold on the outside, but considering how wolves are usually crazy about their mates, I thought Odin would convince his human to treat Cal better. But when I learned how cruel my fated partner could be, I realized we couldn't keep waiting for love to save us - we had to toughen up ourselves.

"I was wrong, you know." My gray wolf-mate lowered his ears in shame as he led me towards the lake. *"I made a terrible mistake that night, one I will spend my life trying to fix,"* he revealed as if he could listen to my thoughts. In a way, he truly could; the connection between our animal souls was stronger than our humans', which meant he could understand my thoughts even if I wasn't projecting them to him through our mind link.

When my handsome mate looked at me with his tail between his legs, I didn't need the bond to understand how painfully regretful he was; it was evident in his sad blue eyes.

He really hurt me that night - more mentally than physically - and up until now, I hadn't completely forgotten it. However, he was staying true to his promise. He had been treating me like a queen, frequently going out of his way to fulfill my wishes. While he couldn't change the past, he was trying really hard to suppress that one bad memory with thousands of wonderful new ones.

Maybe it was finally time to put the past behind me.

"*I know. I can literally feel it,*" I replied at last, startling him when I pressed my head against his neck. "*You may have been a shitty mate in the beginning, but…you've changed. And I appreciate it.*" I made a brief pause, distancing myself from him once again to look into his eyes. "*I forgive you, Odin. Just like Cal forgave Levi.*"

He widened his eyes in disbelief, blinking a few times to process my words. Although he might have felt my forgiveness, I don't think he was expecting to hear the words out loud. As soon as he realized I was being completely honest, he lifted his head up to the night sky and howled. The sweet, blissful melody leaving his chest was a song of pure happiness. For the first time, he didn't try to hold back when his tail started wagging; he wasn't afraid to show his joy.

"*Thank you, mate,*" he said when he stopped singing, roughly pushing his body against mine. "*You are the most perfect mate in the world. You are the best part of me, Nava.*"

"*And you are mine, Odin.*" As we sat together by the edge of the lake, I couldn't help but notice our reflections in the water. We looked like two halves of a whole.

"*In a way, we are. We complete each other,*" he said, wrapping his neck around mine. "*Now, sit tight. I'll go fetch some food for you and our pup."*

"Would you like some help?"

"Not tonight." He winked at me as he turned around. *"Tonight, I treat you like the queen you are. My Queen. My Luna."* He lowered his upper half to the ground, kneeling as best as a wolf could. Having this ruthless beast submit to me made me feel so powerful.

I loved it. I loved how strong he made me feel.

"I won't take long," he added before turning around and running into the forest.

Sticking to his promise, he came back to the spot where he left me only a few minutes later, carrying three rabbits in his mouth. He dropped them by my feet, pushing them towards me. Hungry as I was, I didn't refuse the fresh, savory meal. Once our stomachs were filled, we rested for a while before heading to the woods of our territory, where we could have more privacy.

And when morning came, and it was time for us to say goodbye to each other, I couldn't feel more whole.

CHAPTER FORTY-SEVEN

Calliope

The day following Nava's time with Odin, I felt incredibly light. Despite how uncomfortable she'd be until our pup was born, she was extremely grateful for having had a last moment - at least for a while - with her wolf-mate. Honestly, I think it was only fair for both of them, which is why Levi and I agreed to have our consciousness pushed back to the depths of our souls for hours just to allow our counterparts a special night together. Judging by how my grumpy Alpha was smiling more than usual, I could tell his beast was at peace as well - or maybe he was still happy about finding out he would be having a son very soon.

I was, too. A couple of years ago, right after my parents' deaths, I believed I would never feel good about myself again. In fact, just a few months ago, back when I first met my mate, I had lost all hope of ever finding love. I thought the Moon Goddess had completely forgotten about my happy ending, but I was wrong for doubting my faith for even just a minute. It's true that she works in mysterious ways, yet now I could see she had put me on the right track.

The Goddess surrounded me with amazing friends who helped me realize I was strong. She gave me a wonderful mate, who didn't look like my knight in shining armor at first, but became everything I wanted in the end. She made me the Luna of Blood Eclipse, and though I doubted my skills in the beginning, I realized this pack needed me just as much as I needed them. And now, she's blessed me with a pup, the fruit of our love and my most valuable gift. I couldn't be more thankful for everything I had.

"Lunch is here, my love," Levi's gentle voice echoed through the bathroom as he calmly walked inside; it was music to my ears.

My caring Alpha stepped closer to the bathtub, showing me a fond smile as he offered me his hand to help me up. I carefully stepped out of the tub, reaching out for the towel. Once I was dry, Levi insisted on helping me put on a very comfortable forest green dressing gown.

"I can still get dressed on my own, you know." I chuckled, looking into his blue eyes.

"I know. But I have come to realize that I am addicted to pampering you," he said playfully, wrapping his arms around my lower waist to pull me closer and plant a kiss on my forehead. "I hope you don't mind."

"Not one bit, my Alpha."

He wrapped his arm around mine to lead me out of the bathroom and towards our dining table, only letting go to pull out a seat for me. We ate our delicious meal in comfortable silence, simply enjoying each other's company. Once we were done, we headed to the balcony to take it easy for a while before we had to go back to work.

As I rested my hands over the glass railing, Levi stood closely behind me, slightly leaning over me and laying his arms beside mine. Together, we admired the view for long, peaceful minutes. It was another beautiful day - the sun was shining high in the blue sky, not a cloud to be seen. There were pack members working, their joyful whistles joining the other sounds of nature around us. I loved taking in our lands; it always made me feel so serene.

But suddenly, everything went inexplicably quiet. A loud howl cut through the silence, and the birds nesting in the tall trees immediately fled. I tensed up instantly. It wasn't unusual to hear the melodies of wolves, yet this one didn't sound like a song. It was more like...

A warning.

Soon enough, another howl could be heard. And another, even closer to us. I turned around to look at my Alpha, only to realize the smile he had been wearing all day had vanished. His gaze was focused on the direction where the first howl echoed, as if he was searching for answers. Neither of us had to wonder for long though.

"*Alpha, Luna.*" Our Gamma's voice through the mindlink was slightly hesitant. "*One of our sentinels has smelled an army approaching our borders.*"

"*Of rogues?*" I asked.

"*No, another pack. Maybe multiple.*" Levi was clenching his fists so tightly around the metal bar on top of the glass fence that I could see it bending underneath his touch. "*Darrell is already mobilizing the troops. Can we meet in your office so I can inform you of the details I've been able to gather so far?*"

"*Yes. Meet us there now.*" My mate cut the connection between the three of us before looking me dead in the eye, concern evident in his expression. "Stay with me at all times. I cannot lose sight of you right now."

With my stomach turning, all I could do was nod in response. He interlaced our fingers so tightly it was almost painful, but it made me feel safe. As we headed towards his office at the end of the hall, I tried my best to remain calm, at least until I figured out exactly what was going on. If anything, the fact that Ivar had time to talk to us instead of being ordered to join the warriors on the battlefield meant the situation was under control. Although the look of worry on the blond boy's face as soon as we entered the room didn't make me feel relieved at all.

"What's the situation?" my Alpha demanded.

"The enemies should be reaching our borders now. The attack appears to be led by Alpha Gedeon of Crimson Claw Pack."

I had heard that name before somewhere, though I couldn't remember where exactly. It took me a while to search my mind for answers, and when I finally realized who they were, my eyes widened. I had heard of Crimson Claw only once before; they were one of our countless enemies. However, the shocking detail was related to their Alpha - he was the man Darrell's sister was mated to before she was mysteriously killed.

During my time studying the politics of our pack, I learned that an alliance had been established when Marisol found out she was mated to Alpha Gedeon, but the treaty was terminated upon her death. Levi said he made the decision mostly out of respect for his Beta because the man who should have protected his sister didn't put in the effort to catch her killer. They had hints that Gedeon himself murdered Marisol, but not enough proof to press charges.

"Is he alone?" my mate asked after a long silence.

"We can't tell for sure," the Gamma answered promptly. "According to the sentinel's report, he seems to have brought more wolves than he has in his pack, but no other Alphas have been identified thus far."

"Another unsanctioned attack?" I couldn't help but remember the most recent one, when Solar Hunt ignored all of our society's rules to come at us.

To my surprise, the young man shook his head. "I have already spoken to our Elder. He reached out to the Council, and apparently they were aware of the attack and had approved it beforehand. However, the messenger who was supposed to inform us of the date and time set for it to happen disappeared before letting us know."

"Corrupt pieces of shit!" Levi growled, veins already popping out on his forehead. In an attempt to calm him down, I wrapped both of my hands around one of his fists. After closing his eyes momentarily, his anger seemed to be under control again. He looked at me with a mix of love and sadness. "Ivar-"

"It'll be my pleasure to keep Luna Calliope safe until you return, Alpha." The Gamma smiled at me, and despite my nervousness, I managed to return the gesture.

"Good," my mate breathed out, turning to his friend. "I want two of our best warriors guarding the Alpha suite alongside you."

Before he even finished speaking, Ivar's eyes clouded over. "They are already heading upstairs."

Levi nodded at him before focusing solely on me for a moment. He lifted his hand up to my cheek, brushing it gently.

We both knew he had to join the others and defend our pack, and as much as I wanted to join them, my priority was to protect our pup.

"I will come back to you, my Luna," he whispered at last.

"I have no doubts about that." Still, my chest ached at the thought of him leaving.

He placed his rough hands on each side of my head, planting a long kiss on the top of it before finally turning around. With a heavy heart, I watched him go.

"It'll be fine, Cal," Ivar's kind voice caught my attention. I had probably been staring at the door for an awkward amount of time. "The numbers are in our favor, even if it's a surprise attack. Besides, I have yet to meet a wolf stronger than Odin."

"You're right." I sighed in the end, forcing a smile.

"Come on, let's get you to your room. Maybe we can play card games to make time go by faster, like we did last time?"

"I would love that. Thank you."

"Like I said before, it's my pleasure," he insisted.

The guards were already waiting by the door once we made it back to the Alpha suite. They bowed at both of us on our way in, promptly closing the door behind us. While I fetched the card deck, Ivar headed towards the balcony to close the sliding doors in an attempt to muffle the sounds of the battle going on outside. They weren't too loud yet, but I knew they would get quite distracting in no time.

We sat at the dinner table facing each other. This time, I suggested we play Double Solitaire, seeing as I wasn't in the mood for a more fast-paced game. The minutes went by quickly, and before I knew it, I had won. It's not that I was trying hard, but I guess I was so adamant about not thinking about the attack that I instinctively resorted to focusing on our match.

"Nice, Cal!" The young boy beamed. "Another round?"

"Actually, I think I would like to get some rest."

"Do you need help to lay on the bed?"

I ran my hand over my belly. It was quite big, but not enough to the point of bothering me yet. "No, I'll be fine."

"Alright. I'll leave to offer you more privacy. If you need anything, I'll be right outside the door."

"Thank you, Ivar." He bowed to me on his way out, and I stood up from my seat to head to the bed.

I closed my eyes as soon as I laid down. The pregnancy made me feel significantly more tired. I guess the unexpected attack also took a toll on my energy, but thankfully, playing with Ivar offered me the distraction I needed to be able to take a quick nap.

However, before I even fell asleep, my eyes shot open when I heard a loud noise outside the door.

At first, I didn't think anything of it; one of the three men likely let something fall as they stood outside. I called Ivar a few times, but when I got no response, I assumed he was probably busy linking other warriors and ranked members to stay updated on the battle. Still, I didn't think I would be able to rest until I made sure he was safe, so I decided to get up and check it myself.

It was utterly silent outside, but I blamed it on the fact that the room was soundproofed; unless there were exceptionally loud noises, it was hard to hear anything, even with my heightened hearing. Nava was unusually alert inside my head, her ears pointed up, but that was normal considering the danger we were under. I didn't realize how alarming the situation was until I pushed the double doors open and found the three men laying on the floor unconscious.

"Ivar?!" I whispered in horror, but before I could figure out what was going on, a figure jumped out from behind one of the doors.

Allowing me no time to react, they pressed a piece of cloth against my nose and mouth, using their strong arms to hold me in place. At first, I thought they were just trying to silence me, but it wasn't long before I identified the sickening smell - wolfsbane.

My heart started beating faster as the adrenaline kicked in, fear taking over me. I tried to free myself by thrashing my arms and legs around, but it was no use. The poison slowly caused my body to shut down, and soon enough, I had no more strength to struggle away from my captor's grasp. My muscles were forced to relax as my senses died down.

And then, everything went black.

CHAPTER FORTY-EIGHT

Levi

It broke my heart to leave my pregnant mate behind, but what choice did I have?

I needed to protect our territory, our family, our legacy. I was the strongest warrior in Blood Eclipse; Lunas were a pack's treasure and should be protected at all costs, but Alphas belonged on the front line. My followers needed me. Although Darrell knew how to command them well, no one could encourage them like I could. Besides, Odin was a killing machine who would go berserk when disrespected.

However, for the first time in my life, I was marching towards the battlefield not flooded by rage, but by hurt.

Calliope was strong, yet it pained me to see her broken smile as I walked away. I was concerned, too, though not about her safety. She was safe with Ivar; he would give his life to protect her, not just because she was his Luna, but because he genuinely cared for her, much like everyone else in our pack. It was me I was concerned about.

What if I couldn't keep my promise to her? What if I never came back to meet our son? There was always a risk when it came to fighting. Alphas were the most capable of defending themselves against other threats, but we were also the most targeted ones. I used to think I was invincible, so I never considered the possibility of dying in combat. But now that I had something to live for... The thought scared me. As much as I hated to admit it, I was afraid.

But I couldn't be. If I wanted to protect our family and come back to her, I needed to be one hundred percent focused on the fight, which is why I decided it would be best to give my wolf full control. After the night he spent with Nava, I knew he would be careful, but he wouldn't let his feelings get in the way.

"Don't worry. I'll murder them all and still get home in time for us to dine with our mate," he stated confidently, my canines protruding out of my mouth as he pushed closer to the surface. Putting my trust in him, I gave him full control.

Odin bolted as soon as he was freed, closing the distance between us and the battlefield in no time. He tore out throats and crushed hearts as he worked our way towards the front line, where the rest of our ranked members should be. After slaying close to a dozen wolves without hesitation, he finally made it to our Delta.

With her long black fur and ruby eyes, Nyx was a magnificent wolf, but she was also intimidating. I approached her just in time to watch her pin an opponent to the ground. Her sharp teeth pierced the golden wolf's neck, making him whine one final time before she ripped out his jugular, drenching her coat in blood as she silenced him forever. Odin was an enraged beast when it came to destroying attackers, but Nyx fought with so much poise; I always wondered how she did both.

"Alpha. You're here." Her voice inside my head sounded calm and collected, as if she hadn't just brutally ended someone's life.

"Ivar said there are at least two more packs fighting beside Crimson Claw today. Do we already know who they are?"

She shook her head. Before she could go on, her senses caught signs of three other wolves approaching us. Baring our fangs, we stood back to back, covering each other's weak sides. When the enemies lunged at us, Nyx quickly ducked, closing her mouth around his stomach and throwing him against the floor with a fatal blow. Odin sunk his teeth into the second one's scalp, knocking him down to focus on the third one. Two snaps of our jaws, and they were both taken care of.

"According to our scouts, there are no other Alphas among the army," Trix stated as her counterpart licked the recently spilled blood off her fur.

"And what about Gedeon?"

"Hasn't been seen since the start of the attack," she answered annoyedly, then turned around yet again to defend herself against another enemy.

While she was busy, four wolves came at me all at once, probably identifying me as the Alpha. Honestly, that had already taken too long to happen; with his large size and unique metallic gray fur, Odin stood out among the others. Strange...

Odin's cold blue eyes moved fast, trying to keep track of all of them as they surrounded us, but it was a hard task. We were able to kick the first one when he tried to grab our hind leg, pushing his muzzle into the dirt. The second one almost got us, but we managed to dodge and jump at him. However, before we could finish him off, the third and fourth ones attacked us simultaneously, successfully pinning us against the ground. There was no time to think - one wrong move, and it could be our end.

But there was one thing they had forgotten - an Alpha is always protected by their Beta.

Banyan arrived just in time, catching one of the wolves mid-air as they tried to take advantage of my vulnerable position - a foolish mistake, one I wouldn't forgive. Without thinking twice, Odin stood back up, already lunging at the last enemy, who was no match for us on his own. A pool of blood formed underneath our paws as the four bodies laid lifeless around us.

"Sorry I'm late," my Beta said as he approached me.

I shook my head. *"You arrived just in time."*

I was about to ask him about the attacking Alpha, but he was faster, as if he could read my mind. *"I've sent a team of scouts to look for Gedeon, but they still haven't been able to find him. It's likely he's hidden somewhere, just commanding the army."*

"Fucking coward!" I couldn't hold back my frustration any longer. When Odin's aura expanded, I noticed Banyan's legs trembled as he fought the urge to bow before us. *"This is just like what happened with Solar Hunt! If they don't have the balls to fight, why send their people in to die?"*

"I have a theory about that," my Beta replied cautiously, catching my attention. *"I think the two attacks are connected..."*

"So you think they will retreat once they realize they're losing?" I arched an eyebrow at the brown wolf, and he nodded in response. *"In that case, let's not waste our energy fighting to kill. Let's go all out and force them out of our territory!"*

"I will warn our warriors about the change in strategy." Lifting his head up to the sky, Banyan howled before running ahead of us. Not too long after, a group of roughly a hundred

warriors joined us at the front line, and I wasted no time to head the attack.

Once we changed our focus to chasing after the enemies rather than letting them come at us, their courage seemed to vanish. A few minutes later, we heard a howl in the distance, and the wolves started to turn back to leave. Our warriors were ready to go after them, but Banyan barked a few times. As confused as our army was, they stopped. It seemed my Beta was right, but there was one thing I still couldn't figure out - what did they hope to achieve with their mysterious hit-and-run?

"*We will have plenty of time to find answers later,*" my wolf gritted out, squinting his eyes in fury as he watched the last enemies bolt away. "*Right now, we need to get back to our Luna.*"

He was right. Banyan and Odin exchanged nods one last time as we left him in charge of organizing the warriors while we headed back to the town square. Putting my questions and anger aside for a moment, I decided to link Cal to let her know the attack was over. However, no matter how many times I tried to reach her, I simply couldn't. In fact, I couldn't even find our connection; there was only emptiness. It wasn't like a block, it was more like she was out of reach, as if she was too far from me, which was impossible.

A few more unsuccessful attempts later, Odin began to panic, and honestly, I did too. This had never happened before. What could have possibly happened? Was something wrong with my mate? Was she in danger somehow? My heart started beating faster after I tried to link my Gamma only to have the same result. The closer I got to the packhouse, the harder it was to breathe as my fear grew. But, a hopeful thought crossed my mind. Crystal.

This had to be her doing. That sassy unicorn had a weird sense of humor, and I didn't yet know the extension of her powers. Maybe Darrell linked my Gamma to let him know the battle was over, and Calliope wanted to go check on her unicorn to make sure she was okay, considering she had gotten quite stressed after the last attack? Yes, that had to be it! I forced Odin to retreat, grabbing a pair of shorts from one of the Omegas waiting outside and headed to the stables.

To my horror, not only did I not find my Luna there, but I couldn't find her pet either.

In fact, they were nowhere to be seen. My feet instinctively turned to rush back towards the packhouse, while I tried reaching her through the mindlink again. Still no luck, but to my surprise, it seemed my connection to Ivar had been opened again. The news wasn't the least relieving though, as none of my messages were going through; I knew I was able to send them, but it was as if he couldn't hear me.

Then, it hit me - wolfsbane. He had to have been poisoned. And if that was the case... What could have happened to Cal?!

When I finally made it to the top floor, my fear instantly turned into anger as my eyes landed on my Gamma and the two warriors I had left with him getting up from the floor. There was blood dripping from the blonde boy's head, and when he finally noticed me, he froze.

"I'm sorry, Alpha," he whispered in a groggy voice. There was pity in his eyes, but I wanted none of it - I only wanted answers.

"Where is my Luna?!" I growled at him, Odin's voice mixing with my own as I wrapped my fist around his throat to lift him up in the air. Rage. Rage. Rage. In my blaze of fury, I could only see red.

"S-She..." He tried to speak, but no words came out. His face started turning red and he opened his mouth, yet he wasn't able to breathe. He brought his fingers up to my hand, trying to release himself from my grasp, but I didn't budge.

"Where. Is. She?!" I roared.

"Levi! Stop!" A frightened feminine voice begged - maybe Hailey's? It was hard to tell. I couldn't distinguish sounds or faces as my beast pushed closer to the surface. "Please! You're hurting him!"

"Fuck! Stop that shit, Levi! It's not Ivar's fault!" Darrell yelled, though I only registered his voice when someone else stood in my peripheral.

Then suddenly, something hit me in the face. Fuming, I turned to the side to find my Delta fiercely staring at me, disappointment in her expression. I growled at her, but she didn't back down.

"Get your shit together!" Trix ordered. "You causing a scene won't help us find her!"

Her words struck me differently, causing me to finally free my Gamma. Coughing and gasping for air, he would have fallen to the floor if his mate hadn't been there to catch him. I watched as she tried to comfort him, but he was desolate; not because I had just attacked him, but because he knew he had failed. Shaking my head, I could feel my eyes flickering from mine to Odin's, and I immediately pushed him back. I couldn't let him take control; Cal would be so upset if she found out I had hurt our friends in her absence.

But how was I supposed to not lose control? Calliope was

my anchor, and she was gone.

"I'm sorry," I finally addressed Ivar. He was still trying to catch his breath, but he didn't seem bothered by my outburst. I knew I had fucked up though; still, it was so hard to tell wrong from right without her by my side.

"It's fine. It's over. Just calm down, okay?" Trix looked into my eyes, resting both of her hands on my shoulders. "We will find her."

I nodded at her before turning to Ivar. "Go see the pack doctor. Take the other guards with you."

"But-"

"That's an order, Gamma," I insisted. Unable to fight my aura, he bowed his head and led the warriors down the hall. Once they were gone, I turned to my Beta and Delta. "I want the two of you in my office, now! None of us are leaving until we figure out exactly where my Luna is!"

"We will find her," Odin assured me, and once again, I had to hold him back to prevent his rage from taking over me. *"I don't care how many wolves we have to kill to get her back."*

CHAPTER FOURTY-NINE

Calliope

I couldn't tell how much time had gone by before I started to come back to my senses. A small grunt escaped through my slightly parted lips as a dim light irritated my eyes, but I didn't have enough strength to open them yet. My head was pounding like never before, my body numb - probably a lingering effect of the gaseous wolfsbane I had been poisoned with. Remembering the recent chain of events made adrenaline rush through my veins, and my eyes finally shot open.

I scoured through my surroundings as best as I could despite my blurry vision. My muscles still weren't fully awake, so I couldn't move my head to get a proper look of what seemed to be an old stone chamber. Although I didn't recognize the place at first, it was awfully familiar, which only made me feel more hesitant. Taking a deeper breath, I was able to identify something past the foul smell of dried blood and mold. Then it hit me.

I was back at Moonstone - more precisely, in the dungeons of Moonstone.

Fear immediately consumed me. I had terrible memories from when I belonged to this pack, and I had the feeling my stay here would be even more dreadful this time. But how did I end up here? Moonstone wasn't nearly strong enough to launch an attack against Blood Eclipse… Could they be the ones working with Crimson Claw? I shook my head; it wasn't time to try and figure out why I was here, I just had to break free.

Even though I was still far from being at full strength, I forced my arms and legs to move, but something held me in place. The sound of clinking metal made me realize I had been chained, which only added to my despair.

"Oh. I didn't realize you were already up." A familiar voice echoed through the chamber, making my ears twitch. "I thought the wolfsbane would keep you out for a bit longer. You should be thanking Alpha Levi for sharing his power and strength with you through his bite. Enjoy it while you can. You'll go back to being a pathetic, weak Delta soon enough. Maybe less"

I was supposed to be scared, but when my eyes locked on the girl with malicious chocolate brown eyes and shiny black hair, all I could feel was rage.

"Funny…you should say…that." I struggled to spill the first words, but fueled by my anger, I managed to go on. "Why do you seem threatened by a *pathetic weak Delta,* Chloe?" I mocked her.

"You used to be more obedient. With Levi's reputation, I'm surprised he hasn't put you in your place yet." She scrunched her brows before a wicked smile formed on her lips as she stepped forward. "Don't worry, I'll be more than happy to do what he couldn't."

"*Nava?*" I called out to my wolf, but when she didn't reply, I realized she was still too weak to come forth. My heart started beating faster. I realized I would have to get out of here with or without her help. Just as I started to struggle to break free of the silver tightly closed around my wrists, trying my best to ignore the burning sensation,, I heard Chloe's voice again.

"I wouldn't try anything if I were you. You might foolishly think you can beat me, but can you overpower these two?" She pointed to each of my sides with her head. Standing right behind me were two bulky men I recognized as two of the warriors I used to train with. Even if they didn't really respect me back then, their expressions were filled with pity, and it was obvious they were only doing what they were told.

"I knew you and your brother were filthy, but as an Alpha, I didn't think Kai could ever stoop so low," I spat.

"Oh, please!" she laughed maniacally, "Kai would never have such a brilliant idea. This was all me." The proud smile on her face made me nauseous. "Honestly, it wasn't even that hard to convince Alpha Gedeon to take me as his chosen mate. I mean, look at me. I have all the right attributes to be a Luna."

I widened my eyes at her revelation. Suddenly, it all made sense. After becoming Luna of Crimson Claw Pack, she must have convinced Alpha Gedeon to attack us with the help of Moonstone. But how could she have planned everything without her brother's knowledge? And more importantly, what did she hope to achieve? Judging by how eager the girl was to reveal everything to me, I had a feeling I would get the answers to my questions very soon.

"That man is a psychopath. You are *crazy* if you think you will ever be anything to him!"

"He's a beast, and like any beast, all he needed was someone to put him on a leash. I am the one who's really in charge now. He does everything I tell him to do."

I arched an eyebrow at her. Chloe had never been the brightest, but she couldn't possibly be stupid enough to believe that. According to the rumors, Alpha Gedeon had been cruel enough to murder his fated mate. What would stop him from getting rid of the stuck up Alpha's daughter when she was no longer useful to him?

"Anyway, like I was saying, it was too easy," she went on, "An alliance was established between Moonstone and Crimson Claw after my arranged marriage. I didn't need to put in a lot of effort to convince my brother to lend us his army for the upcoming battle. It did help that he was too busy to look into the details. He didn't even ask any questions when I asked him to sign the papers."

"So he doesn't know I'm here." She shook her head, her smile growing even brighter. "How long do you think you can keep this a secret from him?"

"Just long enough for me to get what I want. It won't take too long." She crouched before me. I didn't cower, instead staring straight into her eyes.

"And what exactly do you want?"

"What you stole from me!" she hissed. My heart skipped a bit when I realized what she meant. "Levi was supposed to be *mine*! He was going to choose me on that day, but you had to mess it up! I am meant to be the Luna of the strongest pack of the country, not some weakling like you. The mate bond blinded him, but it doesn't matter now. Whatever feelings he has for you will be gone the second I'm done with you."

"What's keeping you from finishing the job?" I asked cautiously, trying to hide my concern that her threats would come true.

She stood back up. I didn't miss the hint of hesitation in her eyes. "I'm not stupid, Cal. I know Moonstone and Crimson Claw aren't strong enough to win a battle against Blood Eclipse. I'd need help to succeed. And I know just who would be more than willing to help..."

She didn't have to finish her sentence. Deltas were quick thinkers, and Lunas were strategists. I was both. Although my Alpha had many enemies, the only pack who would be this determined to take him down was Silver Waters. They had a decade-long feud with Blood Eclipse; even if their former leader was the one to start the fight by killing Levi's father, his son certainly was after revenge. Considering how our biggest enemy had been growing lately, we were keeping an eye on them, but they still didn't have the numbers to be considered an imminent threat to us. However, an alliance could make up for what they lacked.

"This last strike was only a distraction to get to you. Silver Waters is getting ready to attack your pack as we speak." Her revelation made my stomach turn, but I couldn't show her how it had affected me, for the sake of my mate's safety. "I have been given orders to keep you alive until they get there. It's part of the deal we made. I'm supposed to kill as soon as the war starts."

"To weaken Levi," I concluded, my voice barely a whisper. Even if I was doing my best to keep a straight face despite my horror, my heart was beating loud enough for her to hear it. "You say you want him for yourself, but you're willing to risk his life for it?"

She remained silent for a while, her insecurities showing.

"He's the strongest Alpha there ever was. Even weakened by the death of his fated mate, I have no doubt he will be able to win."

"Even if he does win, why would you think he would be with *you*, the woman who conspired against him?"

"Because I will be on the battlefield when the war happens. I will change sides and help him defeat both Crimson Claw and Silver Waters. And when I do, he will realize I'm the one who's truly fit to rule by his side." She couldn't possibly be hearing what she was saying.

"You're out of your mind!"

She huffed. "I don't expect you to understand how a brilliant mind works. You're just a weak, worthless she-wolf."

"I'm not worthless!" I roared, stunning her. Nava must have finally woken up, because she was lending me her voice. I could feel my eyes glowing a bright shade of yellow as my animal side pushed forward. "I've always been worth something! It's not my fault Moonstone couldn't see it!"

"Aw, you really believe that? That's sweet. Still the same naïve, little Cal." Condescension laced every word, but I could see she was shuddering slightly. As long as I was chained, she felt brave enough to tease me. Coward. "Guys, I think it's time for her next dose." She was talking to the guards, but her eyes never left mine.

Before I could even process what was going on, one of the guards grabbed my jaw firmly, while the other one pulled a vial containing a purple liquid out of his pocket. I tried to struggle away from the man's grasp as a single thought hit me.

My pup.

"No! Please! I'll behave! Please! I'm pregnant!" I broke for the first time. If I had to beg to protect my child, then so be it.

The warrior looked at Chloe for confirmation, and she gestured for him to go on. “What does it matter? Soon enough, the two of you will be dead.”

Hesitantly, the man brought the vial closer to my face. The other one tightened his grasp around my jaw to keep me in place, digging his fingers deep into my cheeks to force me to open my mouth. My breathing was ragged as I tried my best to fight them off, but it was no use.

“No! Please! No!” I kept screaming, in vain, until the liquid was shoved down my throat, burning my body from the inside out. Tears streamed down my face, not because of the pain, but because of the fear I felt for both my pup and my mate. They were all I could think about as my system started to shut down again.

How could it end like this?

CHAPTER FIFTY

Levi

Calliope had been gone for twenty-four hours, and I was on the brink of losing sanity.

Every second that went by without her by my side made it harder for me to control my feral wolf. He was constantly pushing forward, waiting for me to get distracted so he could take control of our body and destroy everything in his path until he found her. I wondered for how much longer I could keep him caged when all he wanted was blood. Hell, I did too, but one of the many lessons my Luna had taught me was that I couldn't solve everything with violence. Now was certainly one of those times.

For that reason, I stayed true to the promise I had made earlier and never left the office, not for one minute. Unwilling to go back to the room we shared, I used the sink of the en suite bathroom to wash my hair and face when it felt like my head was going to explode. I did allow my ranked members to take a break, although they were reluctant to do so. They were just as adamant as I was about finding Cal, but I knew they needed to rest in order to advance in our search - especially considering how my mind was not in the right place.

And my Luna wasn't the only one I was worried about.

She was carrying my unborn son, the one who brought

me so much joy when I learned about his existence, even before he came into the world. I could not stand the thought of losing him before I even met him. However, as the hours went by, I only got more and more concerned. I knew Calliope was still alive because of our bond. Whatever her captors wanted to accomplish by taking her, they were keeping her safe, at least for now. But I couldn't be so certain about our pup. Not being able to feel him was driving me insane.

Aside from them, Crystal had also vanished into thin air. She hadn't been seen anywhere inside our pack, or the surrounding areas since my Luna's kidnapping. Although I hadn't left my office, I had sent a couple of scouts looking for her pet; I knew how important she was to my mate, so I wanted to make sure she was safe. It was fucking beyond me how no one had been able to find a shiny white horse with a huge glowing horn. Odin blamed it on our team's incompetence, and as I gave in to my rage, I was starting to believe him.

My friends were the ones keeping me sane through this nightmare, but while they were away, either resting or gathering intel, I kept myself busy by reading and rereading every report, trying to pull the pieces together. I doubt I would be able to go anywhere with the little information we had, but only death would keep me from doing everything in my power to find her. At this point, I was willing to watch the security footage for the thousandth time just to make sure nothing had gone unnoticed.

It was then that my Delta walked into the room, making me jump up from the chair I had been sitting on for Goddess knows how many hours.

"Tell me you have something. Shit, anything!" It was both

a plea and an order.

Bellatrix had her gaze locked on me for what felt like an eternity. She remained still, though her slightly ragged breath gave her away. "We will find her."

I couldn't take it any longer. With a loud roar, I let out all of my frustration as I knocked everything off the desk in a blaze of rage. Destruction had always been the only way I knew to cope with my anger, but as satisfying as it was to hear glass shattering over the papers with unhelpful leads, it didn't diminish my desire to kill. There was a beast inside of me begging to crawl out, to wreak havoc, and his plans were starting to make more sense than everything I had been doing so far.

"Why can't anybody find my Luna and my pup?! They've been gone for an entire day!"

"Hey! Calm down." Trix's voice was low as she held me by my shoulders, using all of her strength to force me to look at her. She was the only one in my pack who dared look me in the eyes when I was in this state. "Calliope is strong! She might not have known it when she first arrived here, but she is the Blood Luna. She managed to tame you when we all thought you were long gone. She is more than capable of keeping herself *and* her pup alive until help arrives. And when we do find who's behind this, I'll happily join you in making them pay, like we used to do back in the day. Nobody messes with the Blood Alpha and lives to tell the tale."

Somehow, her words settled me and my ravenous beast, keeping him at bay for a while longer. Once my Delta had made sure I was stable, she stepped away to clean the mess I had made, like she usually did. In the middle of this chaos, watching her pick up the pieces of shattered glass off the floor made me realize I wasn't alone. I had never been alone, not even before my mate came along. I had an amazing support unit, and there was nothing we couldn't do together. *We will find her*, I reminded myself.

As if to confirm my thoughts, Ivar burst into the room the next second. "Alpha! I was checking the cameras again, and I was able to find something." My eyes widened with disbelief as he pulled his phone out to show me a recording. Before I could process what was going on, he paused the video. "Right there! Did you see it?" I raised an eyebrow at him, wondering if he had gone mad. Even Trix joined us, curious to know what he was rambling about. "Hold on, let me slow the video down...and zoom in... Here!"

At first, I couldn't understand what he was so ecstatic about. There was no one in the recording he had shown me. No changes in the scenery, except for a harsh breeze blowing through one of the bushes. I was ready to grab him by the throat again for giving me false hope, but remembering how smart my Gamma was, I decided to give him a chance to explain himself.

"What exactly am I looking at?"

"Oh, right." He took a deep breath, only now starting to calm down. "Did you see the way that bush moved? There was no wind at the time of the recording. That sort of movement must have been caused by something, or someone, running really fast."

Slowly, I was starting to see where he was coming from. This boy was a genius. "What camera is this footage from?"

"The one at the north exit." He smiled brightly. "Since the

attack was happening mainly in the South District, there was no reason for anyone to be there. Except maybe…"

"The kidnappers," Trix concluded, her eyes as wide as mine.

Ivar nodded. "It's just a guess, but…I think these might be the ones who took her. Judging by the direction the wind blew that bush when they passed through that area, it's possible to estimate where they were headed. Now, there are quite a few packs in that direction, but the closest one is Moonstone."

I could feel my blood boiling again at the mention of the filthy pack where my Luna had been born. They undermined her. They mistreated her. They tried to shame her during her Luna Ceremony while they were guests in my territory. If they were the ones fighting beside Crimson Claw… If they were the ones behind her kidnapping…

That was it for me.

"Prepare the warriors! We are going there now!" I roared so loudly the walls trembled, and both of my ranked members dropped to their knees in submission.

However, before I could even take a step forward, my Beta rushed into the office, blocking my way out. His look of distress didn't match the determined expressions on my other friends' faces. I would have been worried, but overcome with rage, his reaction only made me madder.

"The Elders have reached out-"

"It can wait!" I growled at him before he could even finish his sentence. "I have a lead on where my Luna is, and nothing will stop me from rescuing her!"

"Wait, Levi!" He stood still as I tried to push him out of my way. I was losing my temper, but I somehow found the patience to grant him two seconds to deliver the message. "The Elders have just contacted us to warn us about another attack."

"When is it happening?"

"Now." The room went dead silent.

"Who?" was all I managed to utter through gritted teeth.

"Silver Waters."

That name alone gave Odin the strength to push forward; I was no longer able to keep him contained. But to be honest, I didn't really want to.

"Let them come! I'll murder them all!" He spoke through my body as he shoved my Beta aside, heading outside ready to spill some blood. "I will tear the fucking world down to get to her!"

CHAPTER FIFTY-ONE

Calliope

As hard as it was to remain calm, I tried my best to take deep breaths and not think about the worst. Sitting around wondering about my baby's health or my people's safety wouldn't change anything. The only way I could try to prevent all of my nightmares from coming true was if I managed to find a way out of these dungeons. So, that's exactly what I did.

The wolfsbane doses were given like clockwork, but they were significantly smaller than the first one I had received. They were just enough to keep Nava asleep without causing my body to shut down. The poison didn't make my thoughts foggy either, which allowed my racing mind to restlessly work on a plan.

Multitasking was an ability I had mastered during my time as an acting Delta, but it had never been as useful before. While I tried to come up with a reliable escape plan, I also counted the seconds in order to keep track of time. It was still an estimate, especially because I couldn't precisely tell how many hours I had been out until I got here, but if my calculations were correct, Silver Waters should be arriving at Blood Eclipse any minute now.

"They are just outside the borders. The battle is about to start," one of the guards observed, confirming my theory. My heart started beating faster as I realized I was running out of time, but I kept on breathing in and out. I wouldn't give up without a fight, even if I was at a clear disadvantage. Breaking my concentration, the man went on, "Stay focused. We will need to...do it. Anytime now." I shivered.

"Are we really going to do this?" The other guy stared at him in disbelief. "She's pregnant," he whispered, but even without my heightened hearing, I could easily hear him.

"I know. But what choice do we have? We were given a clear command. Think about your daughter. She will pay the price if we fail." The first one hesitated, and it finally dawned on me.

Maybe I could use their uncertainty to my advantage.

Yes, that was it! All the while I was here, they hadn't been unnecessarily cruel to me. They were making sure I stayed fed and hydrated, and they were giving me smaller doses of wolfsbane. Their brief conversation also made me believe they weren't doing this out of any sort of loyalty - they had been threatened to follow through with Chloe's orders. If that was truly the case, maybe I could convince them. I could offer them asylum at Blood Eclipse in exchange for their help. It was a long shot, but it was my last resort.

However, just as I opened my mouth to put my plan into action, a sudden light surprised us all. I noticed the door to the dungeons had been opened, and I was overcome with horror when my eyes landed on the familiar face.

Kai.

At that second, all of my hope was gone. My previous Alpha - one of the wolves who made my life a living hell when I was part of Moonstone - would never let me escape. Even if what Chloe said about her doing everything without his knowing, I doubt he would be bothered. He always made sure to remind me of how replaceable and useless I was; there was no way he would favor my safety over his sister's psychotic wishes. But surprisingly, when his mossy-green eyes locked on mine, they weren't as cold as I remembered. Was I not afraid of him anymore? Or was what I was reading on his face genuine shame?

His expression filled with anger, not directed towards me but...

"Bernard! Ryan!" he yelled at the guards, who both held their breaths. "What the hell are you two doing?!" The two men exchanged looks, but just as one of them opened his mouth, Kai went on. "Free her! Now!"

I couldn't believe my ears. Was he really commanding them to release me? And what were his intentions? Chloe never told me who was in charge of executing me. Could it be him?

"Alpha, your sister-"

"Is she your Alpha or am I? You will do as I say, and you will do it now!"

Both of them nodded in agreement. I was in shock as I watched them crouch beside me to quickly unlock the silver cuffs wrapped around my wrists and ankles. They stood back up slowly, but I couldn't bring myself to do the same. My gaze was focused on Kai as I waited to see what he was going to do. He approached me with caution, and I hit my back against the wall as I tried to get away from him. When he was inches away, he pulled something out of his pocket. I readied myself to fight him with all I had, but then I noticed he was holding...a vial?

"Your wolf shouldn't stay dormant for so long. It could have permanent consequences," he said in a rather calm tone. Who was this man? He was nothing like I remembered. "Here, take this. It will help counteract the wolfsbane in your system."

I frowned, still unable to believe him. He sighed heavily in response.

"Of course you don't trust me. Why should you?" He proceeded to open the vial, and I watched as he took a small sip. "See? It's safe." Once again, he handed the small glass to me, and I hesitantly took it in my hands, pondering for a while before I finally drank it. "Goddess, I'm so sorry, Cal! This is all my fault." He ran his hands through his hair in distress.

In fact, now that I noticed it, he did look a lot different. He wasn't wearing his usual malefic smirk. There were dark circles under his eyes, which was fairly uncommon among wolves. He seemed more tired, but also more...humble. As if he had been through hell and realized he wasn't the king he thought he was.

"When you left, I finally noticed the difference you made." Kai turned back to look at me. This time, I didn't feel in danger when he stepped closer. "I had no idea how vital you were to this pack. In fact, it's still beyond me how you were even able to manage so much. It's a shame I didn't realize it until it was too late. This is the reason why Chloe was able to orchestrate an entire war without my knowledge. I was so busy learning and fixing all of the holes that appeared upon your departure that I didn't have time to look into what she was doing. If it weren't for one of the Omegas who told me she had seen my sister and two men carry a she-wolf down here..." He made a brief pause, facepalming himself. "Goddess, I'm such a failure.

All this time, I thought you were the pathetic one, but it turns out that was me."

He glanced at me for another second, waiting for a reaction, but all I could do was remain silent. The sincerity in his voice took me by surprise, but I knew better than to trust him so easily after everything he and his sister put me through. I don't think he was trying to fool me though. Why would he? He could have the world in his hands if he simply killed me right now.

"Anyway, is your wolf responding to you yet?" he asked, and I shook my head. He turned to the guards with a worried expression. "How much wolfsbane have you been giving her?"

A gasp left my mouth as his words triggered me to remember something. "My pup..." I whispered, running my hand over my stomach. Was he okay?

Kai's eyes widened in disbelief. Exhausted and too absorbed in self-pity, he probably hadn't noticed the bump in my belly until now. Again, flames danced in his eyes as he jumped at one of the guard's throats.

"How sick are you? Poisoning a pregnant woman?" he growled.

The other man soon came to his friend's rescue, regret written all over his face. "We had no choice, Alpha! Chloe-"

"Chloe this, Chloe that..." His eyes were turning black as he stared at the warrior, making him shiver. "I'm your Alpha! I'm the only one you should ever answer to! My sister is not even part of this pack anymore. How stupid are you to follow her commands?!" Both men lowered their heads in shame. "Get the hell out of here! I'll deal with you two later!" They didn't hesitate to do as he said. And as soon as they were gone, he turned his attention back to me with the same empathy as before. “Again, I’m so sorry, Cal. I can take you to the pack doctor so she can check on your pup.”

My eyes glistened with hope at his offer. I wanted to make sure my baby was safe more than anything in this world. But the smile soon left my face as I thought clearly. The damage had already been done; if the poison had harmed my pup, I doubt there would be anything the doctors could do to fix it. Besides, I didn’t yet know who was in charge of ending me. As long as I stayed here, I would be in danger, even if Kai was on my side. Of course, none of this diminished my need to find out if my baby was okay after all we had been through, but there was a war going on right now. A war in which they were planning to kill my mate.

That was something I could still change.

“T-thank you, but…” I stuttered, the pain I felt making it harder to breathe. I closed my eyes for a moment, reminding myself to be strong. For my baby. For his father. “I need to get to Blood Eclipse as fast as possible.”

“Shit! The war!” he remembered, stretching his hand out to help me off the floor. “Come on. Let’s get you out of here.” I hesitated for the last time before finally taking his hand and following him out of the dungeons. “Alright, what’s the fastest way to get there? It would take over an hour by car,” he analyzed as he helped me run through the hallways. “What about Nava? Is she back yet? Can you shift?”

I shook my head. “The doctor said shifting could be harmful to the pup now.” *If he was still alive.* The thought alone made my heart sink, and I had to fight back the tears.

“Fuck. Maybe I can shift and you can ride my wolf. My plan

was to stay here and mobilize the rest of the troops, but my priority now is-" He stopped mid sentence.

As soon as we stepped out of the packhouse, we both froze in our spots.

There were roughly a dozen men laying on the grass outside, among whom I was able to identify Elliot, the Beta, and Gregor, the Gamma. I couldn't believe my eyes when I noticed, standing at the center of the circle of unconscious wolves, was the magical white horse.

"What the hell is that?" Kai's eyes were wide, but I paid him zero attention as I rushed towards my pet.

"Crystal! How did you get here?" I smiled brightly, wrapping my arms around her neck to give her a hug. At last, some comfort in the middle of this chaos.

"Is she...yours?" The Alpha approached us reluctantly, but stopped dead in his tracks when my unicorn neighed, moving her head up and down fast as a warning.

"Shh, it's okay, girl," I brushed my hand over her muzzle before glancing over my shoulder to look at Kai. "Yes. She's-"

Before I could continue, I noticed Crystal circling me, occasionally bumping me with her nose as she sniffed me restlessly. What's wrong? Did she not recognize my scent anymore? I was starting to worry until she stopped in front of me, lowering her head close to my stomach. She let out a low, sad squeal, followed by a nicker. Then, her crescent-shaped horn started glowing, and so did I.

"Shit! What's she doing?!" Kai jumped back in shock. I probably would have too if I weren't used to her magic, and I knew she would never use it to hurt me. Although I also didn't know why exactly she was using her powers.

"She's healing us...and our pup." My wolf's voice made me gasp in surprise.

"Nava! Are you okay?" I asked worriedly, but as I calmed down, I finally digested her words. *"Wait, what?"*

"Don't you feel it, Cal?" I was confused at first. Instinctively, I rested my hand over my bump, caressing it slowly and gently. It took some time, but I finally felt it - a tiny kick. It made my heart melt as relief washed over me. *"She saved our pup."*

This time, I couldn't stop the tears from streaming down my cheeks. "Thank you, Crystal," I whispered as I dove my face into her soft white mane. "Thank you so much."

"Calliope." Kai's voice was shy. There was utter confusion in his expression as I turned to look at him; he was probably oblivious to what had just happened. "How fast does that thing run?"

I had to blink a few times before understanding what he meant. "As fast as a wolf." A smile lit up my face.

"Good. Can she take you to Blood Eclipse?"

As if to answer his question, Crystal dropped to the floor. With a long neigh, she encouraged me to sit on her back, and I didn't hesitate to do so. She stood back up slowly, making sure I wouldn't fall. I held onto her mane for balance, and she stood still, waiting for my command.

"I know nothing I say will fix anything, but Cal, I am truly sorry," Kai repeated, his eyes locked on mine. "I will do my best to make sure you don't lose anything else though. I'll gather what's left of my warriors and head to Blood Eclipse for back up." I was in awe at his determination to help me. I had no idea what happened after I left Moonstone, but their Alpha had definitely learned a life-changing lesson. "You go ahead and do what you have to. Would you like me to send a couple of wolves to escort you?"

"No need. We will be fine," I reassured him. I still wasn't sure if I could trust the members of my old pack, and I knew Crystal was more than capable of keeping us safe.

He nodded at me. "Stay safe. I'll see you soon."

Staring into the forest, taking in the distance that separated me from my pack, I finally gave my unicorn the command to run. As we galloped through the trees, all I could do was hope that I wouldn't be too late. I still had no idea how I would save Blood Eclipse, especially because I couldn't shift. It also scared me not knowing how much damage would have been done by the time I arrived there. Thankfully, I could still feel Levi through our bond, and it gave me strength to go on. As long as he was alive, I wouldn't stop fighting.

But nothing could have prepared me for what I would see when I crossed the borders of my territory.

I tugged on Crystal's mane, forcing her to stop. As we both stood there, a safe distance away from the battlefield, part of my hope vanished. My home…it had become a bloodbath - the green grass stained red, houses completely destroyed. Corpses, of both strangers and members of my family, were lying lifeless on the ground, while some wolves, still in their animal form, took their final breaths. I had witnessed the result of a few battles growing up, but I had never seen anything like this. This war was brutal, and for what?

I shook my head, fighting the urge to vomit as the smell of fresh blood hit my nostrils. I was still this pack's Luna. I had sworn to protect my people with my life, and I had every intention of staying true to my promise. The sight before me was awful, sickening, but I had to push through. I clicked my tongue, making a sound my unicorn recognized as an order to move. And together, we ran into the battlefield.

None of the wolves seemed to notice us, either because they were too focused on ending each other's lives, or because Crystal was hiding our presence. Either way, I couldn't help but look through the crowd in search of my mate. It was hard to pick up his tranquilizing fragrance due to the smell of death polluting the air, but I kept trying. Absorbed in my search, I didn't pay attention to where my unicorn was taking me until I saw him.

My Alpha. My mate. He was standing in wolf form right beside the lake.

Tears of happiness rolled down my face until I realized the poor condition Odin was in. His metallic gray coat was covered in red, cuts and bruises all over his body. They didn't seem to slow him down though; he was still standing, baring his teeth and growling like the fierce leader he was. When I looked in the direction his cold blue eyes were locked on, I found another wolf who was just as big as him. It had silver fur with black markings on its face and back, and it wasn't in much better shape. My eyes widened as it dawned on me - the Alpha of Silver Waters.

They were fighting to the death, right before my eyes.

"No!" I cried out, but neither of them noticed me.

As I became overcome with despair, I kicked Crystal in the belly, encouraging her to run faster. I had learned in the past that jumping in the middle of two ravenous wolves seldom ended well, but as I ran out of time, what other options did I have? I needed to do something! Even if it was reckless. Even if I could end up hurt.

"STOP!" I screamed yet again.

Just then, a bright light washed over the battlefield, blinding me.

CHAPTER FIFTY-TWO

Calliope

The clock seemed to have stopped ticking as the intense whiteness took over. Strangely enough, the sounds of battle had also vanished completely. With my eyes still closed, I wondered if this was all some kind of weird dream, until the brightness died down, allowing me to see again.

And I came to the conclusion that reality was much more bizarre.

My lips parted to release a shocked gasp as I stared at my surroundings in disbelief. The wolves around me, both enemies and allies, had suddenly stopped fighting. Actually, *stop* wasn't the right word. They were still in fighting stances, some even had their teeth sunk deep into each other's skins, but… they were all frozen in time. I blinked a few times, trying to make sense of what was going on. Could time have really just stopped?

Upon further investigation, I noticed there was a large aura around me, kind of like a magical barrier. My head was racing as I tried and failed to come up with a logical explanation to all of this, until a possibility crossed my mind. To my right, Crystal was standing peaceful as ever, her eyes curiously studying me. What was going on? Was this her doing?

"Calliope." The voice was low, but my ears would never fail to recognize it.

As soon as I turned around, my eyes landed on the man I had been dying to see again. Levi was back to his human form. His wounds looked even more painful than they did on Odin. Some of them were already healing, but most of them were fairly deep. Blood ran down his arms and chest, staining his shorts. Wait, when did he get dressed? I shook my head, realizing how unimportant that detail was. All that mattered was that I was reunited with my Alpha, and regardless of how injured he was, at least he was still alive.

A relieved smile crossed his face. My confusion and worry seemed to disappear as I waited for him to run up to me, wrap me in his arms and tell me how much he had missed me. However, when he tried to take his first step towards me, he was held back in his place. It was as if a strange force was rooting him to the floor, invisible chains restraining his movements. I glanced at Crystal once again, realizing her horn was still glowing. What was she up to?

"You dirty witch! How dare you interrupt our fight!" Another voice echoed through the barrier, catching my attention. When I turned around, I was even more confused to see an unfamiliar face. The stranger had as many wounds as my Alpha, and a furious expression on his face. This had to be Russell, Alpha of Silver Waters. I thought he was going to charge at me, but much like what happened to Levi, he couldn't leave his place regardless of how hard he tried.

As I switched my gaze from the man, to my mate, to the unicorn, realization finally struck - when I screamed, Crystal probably took it as a command and used her powers to stop time around us. I was the only one who could move freely inside of the safe realm she had created, while the two Alphas could only speak.

Right then, an idea crossed my mind.

"Watch your mouth around my Luna! I'll kill you, you bastard!" Levi countered. He must have already realized that he couldn't move, but that didn't stop him from trying. When his eyes turned to me again, they weren't full of the love they had been a minute ago; they were filled with rage. "Calliope! Tell Crystal to free me, now! I'll end this war right now!"

"Coward! Tell your wicked mate to step away, and fight me like a man!" Russell growled. "I should have known you wouldn't fight fair!"

"Fair?!" my mate retorted, his canines protruding as Odin pushed forward. "You were the one who bribed the Elders so you could attack me without notice! I'm not surprised though. Your father was just as dirty as you are. It'll be a pleasure to rip your head off, much like I did to him a decade ago!"

"Keep my father out of your mouth!"

"Enough!" I demanded, standing between the two men. Around us, our people were suffering, dying. How could they be so blinded by their rage?

"Calliope, get out of here!" Levi commanded, but I didn't back down. "Go back to the packhouse and let me finish this!"

"I don't think so," I stated calmly before looking at Crystal. "I make the rules here, and I won't release you until the two of you settle your feud. In a *civilized* manner."

"You can't possibly be in your right mind!" my mate griped. "I know you don't like violence, but this must be done! Please, Calliope. I would like to keep you out of this."

"This battle is mine, too." I held my head high. "I am the Blood Luna, and I have sworn to protect my family. Especially when their Alpha can't."

"I would, if you just told the unicorn to stop fooling around!" he roared. It would be hard to get him to listen while he was this mad, but I didn't mind waiting. After all, I had all the time in the world - quite literally. "I won't say it again. Leave the battlefield and let me end this war!"

"What are you fighting for anyway? Pride? The thrill of the battle?" I questioned.

"He was the one who attacked us!" Levi turned back to the other man. "I'm just defending my pack!"

"This is payback! You killed my father and sent my pack to its downfall!" Russell barked back. "You killed our leader and weakened us until there were only a few of us left! Children! Women! You killed hundreds of innocent wolves!"

"Your father brought this upon you! He was the one who came after us in the first place. It's a shame he never came back to tell you in person, but I'm sure you heard the rumors of how he used my mother as leverage to weaken my father. He should have thought about the innocent lives back then!"

"Are you even listening to yourselves?" I caught their attention. "The feud between Blood Eclipse and Silver Waters has become a cycle of hate. When will it end?"

"Right now!" the enemy Alpha growled. "As soon as I find a way to get out of here, I'll murder your sorry-excuse-of-an-Alpha and finish what my father started!"

"Really?" I ran my hand over my stomach. Russell's eyes widened; his certainty seemed to briefly disappear. "What do you think my son will feel when he learns the truth about who killed his father? Maybe he will want revenge, like you did." His fury seemed to die down as my words finally sunk in. I turned to my mate soon after. "Or like you did. You know how much misery the thirst for revenge brought you. Do you really want the same for your son?" He looked away silently, a hint of worry in his expression.

"Your pup hasn't even been born yet. He won't be a part of this," Russell argued, desperately trying to justify a reason to keep fighting.

"Oh, but he will grow. And he will learn. A wolf's loyalty knows no bounds. He'll certainly feel the need to avenge his pack and his father," I insisted, stepping closer to him. This time, he didn't show me his teeth. He just watched me with caution. "You know that, don't you? Is that why you were working with Crimson Claw to take me down? Are you going to kill me and my unborn pup, who isn't even part of this, just to get your revenge?"

"I didn't know you were pregnant! I would've never-" the man shook his head before looking straight into my eyes, "I would never hurt a pregnant woman, nor an infant."

I fought back a smile as I realized that my plan was working. "What will it be, then? Look around you!" I gestured towards the battlefield. Blinded by hate, they didn't seem to have noticed the wolves frozen in time outside of the magical barrier until now. "How many more of us will have to die for you two to realize this is too high of a price to pay? How many innocent lives will have to get their hands dirty before this cycle is broken?"

Standing in front of me, the two Alphas exchanged glances. There was no more anger in their faces. Only shame.

I honestly couldn't believe I had done it. Somehow, I had managed to convince two enraged leaders, two sworn enemies, to put their fury aside and think about the consequences of their actions.

"If anyone could do it, it was certainly you, Cal." Nava's voice echoed inside my head. *"Wolves can easily become blinded by rage, but you never let it consume you. Not even after all you were put through. You always fought hate with love. I'm so proud of you, Cal."*

I couldn't help but smile as I realized there was truth in her words. *"Thank you, Nava."* I took a deep breath before turning back to the two men. "All of this can end now. We can put an end to the bloodbath. To the meaningless deaths. All you have to do is declare peace."

Levi sighed. "You're the only one who could ever convince me to give up on a fight."

"I must admit...your Luna has a way with words," Russell agreed.

The two of them stared at each other for a few more seconds. They were both still uncertain, but they seemed willing enough to put an end to the war; if not for their own desires, for the sake of the ones they had sworn to defend. I touched Crystal's neck; no words were needed for her to understand exactly what I wanted. As soon as she neighed, both Alphas were released from whatever force she was exerting over them. They hesitated before stepping closer to each other, and I cautiously watched in case either of them tried something.

As they were mere inches away from each other, Russell opened his mouth. "I still don't trust you."

"I don't trust you either." Levi glanced over at me, flashing me a proud smile. "But I know better than to question my Luna."

A heavy sigh left the leader's mouth as he stretched his hand out to my mate. "For the sake of our people?"

"And to break the cycle." My Alpha nodded at him.

The moment they finally shook hands was more magical than anything Crystal had done up to this point.

"Once the barrier is opened, you have to call off the war," I reminded them. "You're their leaders." I waved my hand towards the warriors once again before looking each of them dead in the eye. "You're the only ones who can stop this."

They exchanged nods before turning to me. As soon as they were ready, I told Crystal to undo her magic. It was impossible not to feel anxious, but I had to trust everything would go well. All I did was blink, and when I opened my eyes again, we were back to the raging war. Fortunately, it wouldn't last much longer.

"Enough!" Both Alphas roared in unison, their auras expanding as they faced their warriors.

It was surprising to watch every single one of the wolves stop fighting to glance at their leaders. There was confusion in their animalistic features, but they couldn't fight an Alpha command.

"Everyone, back off!" Levi continued, his voice loud and clear. "We're calling off the war." The sudden news definitely came as a surprise to the warriors, yet they seemed pleased by it. "We've agreed there are far more important things than tearing each other apart," he added. Wolves would fight to protect their pack, their family, and their honor, but we valued life too. Despite the confusion, it seemed all of them were ready to trust their Alphas and declare a truce.

Or at least, that's what I thought.

"I was promised a war!" A strong voice thundered behind me. My eyes were wide with horror as I recognized Alpha Gedeon. "I'm not leaving until our enemies are destroyed!"

With everything going on, I barely had time to understand his intentions before he shifted into his beast. Without thinking twice, he lunged at me, and all I could do was close my eyes.

CHAPTER FIFTY-THREE

Darrell

I was ripping out the throat of a wolf I had pinned against the ground when I heard the Alpha's voice echo through the battlefield. Banyan turned his head in the direction of the sound, ignoring everything around him. Through his eyes, I was confused to find Levi standing only a few feet away from me, with the Alpha of Silver Waters right by his side. My wolf cocked his head to the side. Weren't they trying to kill each other just a moment ago? When had they shifted back into their human forms? And when did Cal get here?

More questions popped up in my head when I heard his command to stand down. Why? How? What the hell was going on? It was probably the first time in werewolf history that two warring Alphas called a truce in the middle of a raging battle. It was even more bizarre that Levi, who had gone berserk after his Luna's disappearance, suddenly seemed calm again. Staring at the bold woman and the magical creature beside her, I immediately knew they had something to do with this.

As I watched all of the wolves around me back down, obeying their leaders despite their confusion, I found myself doing the same. Putting my questions aside for a moment, I allowed myself to just feel happy about our Luna's safe return. She was the only one who could keep our Alpha under control, and it was definitely relieving to have her back. Judging by her satisfied expression, I assumed the heir was also healthy. I had no idea how she had managed to escape from her kidnappers, but if anyone could do it, it was certainly her. She was fierce!

Eager to welcome her back home, I started jogging towards her when a voice I hadn't heard in a long time made Banyan stop dead in his tracks, only a few feet away from her. It made our skin crawl. My wolf bared his teeth, his hackles raised up as his golden eyes locked on the man we hated more than anything.

Alpha Gedeon.

I could easily recognize him, even in his animal form. I had only seen his wolf once, during Marisol's marking ceremony. The first time I saw his beast's cold gray eyes, I had a feeling something was wrong with him. He didn't look anything like the sweet mate my sister deserved - the sweet mate she *thought* he was. But he was good at hiding his nature, like a true psychopath. Overcome with rage, I didn't pay attention to his words, but when I saw him shift and lunge at my Luna, I didn't think twice.

I would never let him make her one of his victims.

Out of instinct, Banyan jumped in the direction of the bronze-colored beast. He headbutted the enemy mid-air, pushing him away from Calliope a fraction of a second before he could hurt her. Our two wolves rolled over the bloody grass, and somehow, Banyan ended up on top of him. My counterpart didn't miss the opportunity to sink his teeth into the bastard's shoulder, the taste of his blood further fueling our anger.

However, Gedeon was still an Alpha. He easily pushed through the pain and used his hind legs to push us away from him. He didn't waste a second before jumping on top of us, missing our neck by just a few inches. A cry echoed in my wolf's throat when he tore our skin open, the searing pain making our head spin. Before we could regain our senses, he knocked us onto the ground, his heavy paw pressing my skull against the soil.

"Darrell!" From the corner of my eye, I noticed Cal trying to run up to me, but Levi grabbed her in his arms.

At first, I thought he was just trying to protect her, but then I heard him whisper, "This is his fight, my love. He needs to get his justice." And he was right. I might not be as powerful as an Alpha, but I had Marisol's spirit giving me strength. There was no way I would lose this fight.

Gedeon's beast aimed for Banyan's jugular yet again, but he had become overconfident thinking he had the upper hand - but we never let our guard down. At the last second, Banyan moved his head to the side, successfully dodging Gedeon's attack and making him bite a chunk of the earth instead. I knew I needed to act fast, and I didn't hesitate.

Banyan bit the enemy's front paw hard, making him lose balance as we rose to our feet again. Our golden eyes locked onto his weakest spot, and using all of our strength, we managed to land a clean strike. The mighty Alpha howled in pain as we pushed him to the floor, teeth sinking deeper into his jugular.

He was tougher than I had expected though. Unwilling to be defeated, he lifted his paw up to our face and dug his claws into one of our eyes. My vision went black as the worst pain I had ever felt made my head ache. Our legs were shaking, fighting to support our own weight, but we didn't let go. I wanted to rip a chunk of his throat, but I didn't have the strength to do it. All I could do was tighten my grasp around his neck and wait, trying my best to resist the pain caused by his talons tearing my face. Still unable to see, I heard gagging and gasping sounds.

Then, there was silence.

Immediately after, I felt a pair of arms around Banyan's neck. For a second, I thought it was my sister, but Calliope's voice brought me back to my senses. "You did it, Darrell! You saved me!" Was she crying? She sounded happy though. "She would be so proud of you!"

"*Luna,*" I couldn't see her, but I could still reach her through the mindlink, "*are you okay? Is the heir okay?*"

"*Yes, we're both fine.*" Her reply was so relieving, it even eased some of my pain. "*Can you see, Darrell?*"

Her question made me force Banyan's eyes open. It was painful in the beginning, but after blinking a few times, it became more bearable. My vision was blurry at first, but it didn't take long for me to see the sweet, caring woman in front of me. However, something was...different - *felt* different. Judging by Calliope's horrified gasp, I could tell she noticed it too.

"His eye... It'll heal, right?" She turned to her Alpha, worry filling her voice.

"I-I'm sure the doctor will do his best to help him recover." Levi's tone didn't sound the least hopeful. But I didn't care. Losing one of my eyes was a small price to pay to finally bring justice to my sister. My friend crouched in front of Banyan, a proud expression on his face. "You've done a great job at protecting your Luna, and your sister. Now-"

"Alpha Levi!" An annoying voice stood out on the silent battlefield. I couldn't quite remember whose voice it was, but I could have sworn I'd heard it before. With my damaged vision, I managed to see a girl running towards us. "Thank you for ordering your Beta to kill this man! Oh, the awful things he has done to me..." she whimpered. I could sense no honesty in her tone. "My brother forced me to marry him, he traded me for an alliance! But you have freed me of this horrible fate!"

"You were not *forced or traded* for anything!" Another vaguely familiar voice caught my attention. What the hell was Alpha Kai doing here? Judging by how clean and unscathed he looked, I doubt he had been fighting in the battle. Although we did consider the possibility of Silver Waters and Crimson Claw having brought extra warriors from another pack.

"What the hell are you doing, Kai?" The girl frowned.

"I thought you were just a spoiled brat, but turns out you were as sick as him!" he spat, making her gasp. "You must be out of your-"

"Enough!" Levi roared.

When my gaze fell on my Alpha, I noticed that he was seething with rage. I wouldn't expect anything different. We had just undergone a lot of stress, and if our Gamma was right, Moonstone was likely behind our Luna's kidnapping. Honestly, I was surprised Levi hadn't murdered them yet. He was probably holding back, his desire to be with his mate speaking louder than his anger.

"You disrespect my mate in her own territory, and you dare to show your faces again! After everything you've done!" The siblings froze. "I want them taken to the dungeons! Now!"

"What? Wait!" Chloe screamed. In less than a second, the

two of them were surrounded by Blood Moon warriors.

Once the situation was taken care of, the Alpha turned to the leader of Silver Waters, with whom he had apparently made peace. "Alpha Russell, we have agreed to call off the war, but there are many issues we still have to discuss. Now, however, is not the time."

"Of course," the man replied. "We must put our family first. We'll discuss the details of our truce on another occasion."

And just like that, the warriors started retreating, leaving the corpses and the rivers of blood behind. So many lives lost to the greed of a few Alphas. At least it ended before the situation could become even more tragic.

"I've just linked Trix to help us organize the wounded." The Luna's words pulled me from my thoughts.

"Thank you, my love," her mate replied, planting a soft kiss on her forehead before turning back to me. "Now, let's get you taken care of, my friend."

* * *

Not even during my first shift had I experienced such a painful transformation.

Once we arrived at the pack hospital, the doctor instructed Banyan to shift so he could take a closer look at my wounds; apparently, they were as bad as they seemed.

"Werewolf bodies have an impressive regenerative speed, but..." The man hesitated, looking at me with a hint of pity in his eyes. "I'm afraid the damage caused is irreversible."

"No... There must be something we can do!" Cal cried.

"I'm sorry, Luna, but I think this case is beyond medical help. The Beta's left eye has been completely destroyed."

"Maybe... Maybe Crystal can help!" She sobbed as she rushed to the window, from where her unicorn had been curiously watching her. "Please, girl. You helped me more times than I can count. Can you help Darrell heal?" Calliope nervously rubbed the creature's long muzzle, but she only let out a sad nicker, shaking her head as if she could actually understand her rider's words. "Please, Crystal! Please!" Her smile faded as tears streamed down her face.

For a moment, I wished I had gone completely blind. Watching the hope slowly vanish from this incredibly kindhearted woman was an awfully sad sight to see.

The painkillers the doctor had given me had already kicked in, but I was still weak. I almost tripped when I tried to get off the hospital bed, but Levi held onto my arm, helping me regain balance. With a nod, I both thanked him and assured him I could walk on my own. Cal only stopped desperately pleading to her unicorn when I put one hand over her shoulder.

"It's okay, Luna. I would rather lose my life before I let anyone hurt you. All that matters is that you're safe." I smiled at her.

The next second, she threw her arms around me, catching me off guard. "You're an amazing Beta. And you're an even more amazing brother. To both Mari and to me." Her words stunned me. She dried her tears with the back of her hands before grinning at me. "From the day I arrived at Blood Eclipse, you've been the big brother I never had."

I had to hold back my own tears. "Thank you, Cal. You're

like a sister to me, too. I'm glad I was able to keep you safe."

"Thank you, my friend." Levi nodded at me as he stretched his hand out to his Luna, inviting her to come into his arms. "Is there anything else you need?"

I shook my head. "Thank you for accompanying me here, but I don't wish to take any more of your time. I know there's a lot we have to do."

"*We* do," he corrected, gesturing to himself and Cal. "Not you, at least for today. You will be on bed rest. If you're feeling better tomorrow, you can help us figure out this whole mess."

"As you wish, Alpha."

As I watched them leave together, I couldn't help but feel weirdly warm inside. The war had ended, our Luna was back home, and a murderer had paid for his crimes.

And after two years of grieving, I could move forward knowing Mari would finally be at peace.

CHAPTER FIFTY-FOUR

Levi

The cold water fell over our tangled naked bodies, but we kept each other warm.

After the pack doctor tended to my deeper wounds and examined my mate to make sure our pup was okay, we headed back to our room to take a nice, relaxing shower together. The world seemed to disappear as we remained there, unmoving. The white noise created by the streaming water hitting the floor allowed me to focus solely on the sound of our synchronized breathing and beating hearts. As our blood-stained bodies were cleansed, I held her tight, ready to never let go.

I couldn't believe she was right here in my arms again. In fact, I still could hardly believe the events of the past few hours. Calliope had managed to put an end to a decade-long feud using only reason. The way she had managed to convince two violently warring Alphas to set their differences aside for the sake of their people was impressive, and I had no doubts my Blood Luna would go down in history for the many lives she had saved today.

As I took in just how amazing she was, I couldn't help but be reminded of how stupid I had been to deny her at first. It was foolish of me to think she would make me weak. I thought power was strictly related to physical strength, but she showed me that the true meaning of the word "strength" went far beyond that. Without her, I would have never reached my full potential. And to think she was kind enough to trust in me after all I had done...

"Calliope?" I called out, breaking the peaceful silence.

"Hmm?" she answered calmly, her eyes closed as her head serenely rested on my chest.

"Thank you."

She shifted a little in my arms, lifting her head to look at me. When her eyes met mine, she asked sweetly, "What for?"

"For giving me a second chance." I dove my nose into her wet hair to breathe in her alluring scent before planting a kiss on the top of her head. She chuckled in response.

"I believe everyone deserves a second chance, and you made the most of yours." She slowly brought her face closer to mine, standing on her tiptoes to place her lips on mine in a gentle, passionate kiss. The second she pulled away, her expression had subtly changed. She was wearing an apologetic smile I had learned to dread; I immediately knew she was about to make a request I most likely wouldn't like. "Speaking of second chances..." She looked away before staring intently into my eyes. "I was hoping you could show Kai some mercy?"

I instinctively frowned. "The Moonstone bastard? Why in hell should I be merciful towards the one who abused you, my Luna, for years, then kidnapped and threatened to kill you?"

The hairs on the back of my neck bristled as I was consumed by anger. Odin mimicked my reaction, his hackles raised as he bared his teeth. I didn't notice I had tightened my grip around my mate until she brought her hand up to my face, her soothing touch forcing me to relax once again.

"He was a jerk to me back when I was still his Delta, yes, but he is not guilty of any of the other crimes you mentioned. His sister orchestrated everything behind his back. He had nothing to do with it," she clarified.

"He is still the Alpha of his pathetic pack! His incompetence has almost cost two lives, and he will pay for it!" I growled.

"I understand your rage, my Alpha..." Her voice was soft as velvet. It was impossible to remain angry for long when she was near me. "But Kai does not deserve to be punished for his sister's crimes. If it weren't for him, I wouldn't have escaped."

"What do you mean?" I cocked my head to the side, interested.

"He was the one who freed me." I widened my eyes at her revelation. "He even gathered the rest of his troops to help Blood Eclipse in the war, but it had already ended by the time he got here."

I was thoughtful for a moment. Odin was still dead-set on murdering the fucker just to avenge our mate's years of suffering. Honestly, I did too, but I couldn't bring myself to deny one of her requests. Not after I almost lost her.

"Fine. I will interrogate him, and if I decide he's truly innocent, I'll let him go," I replied reluctantly.

A heavy sigh left my chest as I realized I couldn't stay in my private bubble with Calliope for much longer. I was still an Alpha, and I had many urgent matters to take care of, including deciding the fate of the pathetic Moonstone siblings. I turned off the water and turned around, but just as I was about to step out of the shower, my Luna interlaced her delicate fingers with mine, catching my attention.

"I'll go with you."

"Wouldn't you rather stay in the room and rest? You have gone through a lot, my love." I wrapped one of the towels around her beautiful body, helping her dry.

"I'm your Luna. This is just as much my responsibility as it is yours." Goddess, her powerful aura and sense of duty always made me shiver. "Besides, I don't wanna leave your side after everything that's happened."

A warm smile lit up my face. "Fair enough. Let's get dressed, then."

As soon as we walked out of the bathroom, Calliope picked out a light blue off-shoulder maternity dress, while I got dressed in an old T-shirt and a pair of shorts; it was best for me not to use any fancy clothes, since they would likely get stained or shredded very soon. We cuddled for a few more minutes, and once we were both ready, I took her hand and led her downstairs.

It was still fairly chaotic outside, but my Delta was doing a pretty good job at fixing everything. The bodies of the few warriors we had lost had already been retrieved, and workers were roaming around assessing the damage that had been done. Most of the sentinels and healthy warriors were patrolling our borders to make sure we wouldn't be attacked while we were vulnerable, but I also made sure to have some of my best men guarding the dungeons. They bowed their heads at me and their Luna before they let us in.

The underground stone chamber had a sickening smell of rotten flesh and blood. Cal twisted her nose in disgust, but tried her best to keep a straight face. I wish Crystal could help her now, much like she had done when she developed an aversion to my scent, but the magical horse probably needed to recharge after the little trick she had pulled earlier. My eyes landed on the two prisoners being kept in separate cells before I even acknowledged my Gamma's presence.

"Everything's ready for the interrogation, Alpha," Ivar informed me with a nod. It was usually the Beta who was in charge of conducting interrogations, but because of how hurt Darrell was after his duel, I had put him on bed rest for at least twenty-four hours. "Who would you like to start with?"

"Alpha Levi!" The black-haired bitch's desperate voice echoed through the dungeons before I could reply. "Thank the Goddess, you're here! I'm sure this is just a misunderstanding. Please, let me out! I can't stand the stench of this place any longer! If you-"

"Silence!" I roared, and it was enough to make her shut up as her legs trembled, causing her to fall with her knees on the rocky floor. Odin growled in satisfaction as we watched the hope fade from her eyes. When I turned to her brother, I was surprised to see his calm expression. I expected him to be just as scared as his foolish sister. "We will start with the pathetic Alpha," I spat.

The boy stayed still while my Gamma opened his cell, and he didn't struggle when he was taken out. Ivar kicked him behind the knees, making him drop to the ground in front of me. He had his head low in a clear gesture of submission, but I couldn't smell any traces of fear. Either he was sure my mate would convince me to spare him, or he was brave enough to face the consequences of his mistakes.

"My Luna says you had no idea about the war or her

kidnapping. Is this true? Was your sister the only one behind all this?" I started.

"No! I didn't do anything! I-" Chloe dared interrupt me once again, and I finally lost it.

"Silence her! Now!"

Two guards immediately came downstairs, using their werewolf speed to open her cell and immobilize her. She kept trying to scream, but they managed to successfully muffle her sounds.

"Answer me, Kai!" I ordered once the situation was under control.

"It's true, Alpha Levi," he calmly answered.

"Just how weak of a leader are you?" I scoffed. "How could you let a woman who's not even part of your pack control your followers?"

"I guess I'm a failure." He shrugged, sadness in his voice. "I would like to think I will learn from my mistakes and become a better leader for my people, but I will accept whatever punishment you have for me."

His honesty startled me, but I hid it behind my frown. "Before I decide how I'll deal with you, you will apologize to my mate. For the poor way you treated her when she worked for you, and for everything your pack has caused her!"

"I already have, but I'll do it a thousand times." He sighed before his eyes locked on my Luna, who was standing tall beside me. "I am sorry for what you had to go through under my leadership, Luna Calliope. I also apologize on my sister's behalf for the absurdities you had to endure while you were being held prisoner unbeknownst to me."

She simply nodded at him without uttering a word. She

probably didn't want to give him her forgiveness before I gave my verdict, but judging by the way she glanced at me from the corner of her eyes, I already knew what she wanted me to do. Honestly, I was hoping this fucker would confess to any crimes, or to show any kind of hostility. Lucky for him, my Luna didn't seem fond of the idea of punishing him solely for his incompetence.

"Free him," I said to Ivar. He seemed just as surprised as Kai, but he didn't question me. Soon after, he pulled the boy up to his feet and unchained him. "Now, bring me his sister. And keep her mouth covered. I swear I will rip her throat out if I hear her squawking one more time." The two guards didn't hesitate to drag the girl across the floor until she was standing in front of me, tears streaming down her eyes as fear consumed her. "I believe I already have enough proof to deem you guilty. My Luna's testimony is more than enough," I growled before raising my voice. "Chloe Evans, you will now be executed for conspiring against my pack and kidnapping my Luna. Do you have any last words?"

"Alpha Levi." I surely wasn't expecting to hear Kai's voice. Did he want to die that badly? I narrowed my eyes as I turned to him. "I know I am in no position to make any sort of requests, but if you would allow it, I would like to deliver my sister's punishment."

Before I could deny his absurd request, my Luna answered him. "Are you sure you want to do this, Kai?"

He closed his eyes, taking a deep breath before replying, "Yes, Luna Calliope. She has betrayed my pack, and as the Alpha of Moonstone, I would like to exact justice."

Calliope turned to me with pleading eyes. For a second, I

questioned if I was truly the one ruling Blood Eclipse, or if she was. Though I already knew the answer.

"Very well," I uttered at last. "But you will do it here and now, before my eyes. If you try anything, I will have you both killed immediately."

"Of course, Alpha Levi. Thank you." Kai bowed in front of me, but I soon gestured for him to proceed. I wanted nothing more than for this to be over quickly.

As the boy approached his sister, the guard finally took his hand off of her mouth. "Brother! Thank you! I knew you would come to save me!" She smiled, a delusional expression on her face. She had truly lost her mind.

"You have made your bed, Chloe, and now you must lie in it," Kai stated coldly. For once, he had the posture of a true Alpha.

"W-what do you mean?" Her smile faded. "I-I'm your s-sister! You can't do this to me!"

"Before a brother, I am an Alpha. I know that now." His nails elongated, turning into black claws.

The girl screamed louder as he inched closer to her, and she didn't stop until he silenced her with one clean slash to the throat. A pool of blood quickly formed around her before her lifeless body dropped on the floor. Kai's legs gave out, the pain of murdering his own sister visibly taking a toll on him, but soon he was back on his feet. Even if I despised this boy with my whole being, I had to respect him for his boldness.

Once he was done, I gave him ten minutes to leave my territory, and he bowed at me one last time before disappearing from my sight. I instinctively held my mate closer before walking away with her.

Now, I could finally dedicate all of my time to celebrating her presence.

* * *

Trix

One week later

Seven days after the war between Blood Eclipse and Silver Waters, we were almost fully recovered. I had been working 24/7 to make sure our pack would be back on its feet as soon as possible, but I didn't mind it. At least I didn't have any injuries since I didn't fight on the battlefield, instead gathering and protecting the pack members that couldn't fight during the surprise attack.

There was a lot happening aside from the usual arrangements I had to take care of, such as supervising the re-construction of the damaged buildings, organizing the funeral for our lost soldiers, and offering support to those who had lost their families.

First of all, I had to help Darrell with a bunch of paperwork. Since he had been the one to kill the Alpha of Crimson Claw, he had every right to step in as their new leader, but he didn't want to. Said it would be a constant reminder of his sister's death. Instead, the pack was dismantled, and those who had nowhere to go were welcomed into Blood Eclipse.

Secondly, Levi left me in charge of organizing an important dinner for the Elder Council and Alpha Russell of Silver Waters Pack. Upon their truce, an alliance between our two packs had been established, but Alpha Russell would still have to answer for his crimes. Since Cal had been the one to put an end to the conflict, the Elders decided we had the right to witness the trial, therefore allowing it to take place in our territory. The event had been scheduled for tonight, so I was even busier.

I stopped working to go get ready an hour before dinnertime. Since this was an incredibly important event, all of the ranked members were requested to be present and dressed accordingly. I didn't have a lot of formal dresses because Deltas were rarely invited to ceremonies and balls, but I still had the one my late mate had bought me. I couldn't bring myself to throw it away.

Once I finished my make up in the bathroom, I headed back into the room to take a look at my reflection in the full-length mirror. It was weird to see myself in fancy clothes; I almost didn't recognize myself. I had to admit I looked beautiful though. The black dress with off-shoulder long sleeves highlighted my curves pretty well. It also had a few golden details towards the end of the skirt to bring light into the darkness. I couldn't help but smile as I remembered how Igor used to say it fitted my personality perfectly.

After making sure I looked presentable, I headed downstairs towards the entrance of the packhouse. As usual, I was the first to arrive, but it didn't take long for the rest of the ranked members to join me. I wasn't the type to get nervous before big events, but for some reason, I was a little jumpy today. Even Nyx was pacing around in my head, restless. I wondered if the feeling was being caused by the dress reminding us of our mate.

"Alpha Russell has just crossed the borders. The Elders are following right behind him," Darrell informed us. And for some reason, it made me even more anxious.

I didn't quite understand what was wrong with me until a tantalizing scent hit my nostrils. Only one wolf had ever smelled that delicious to me, and I hadn't sensed that fragrance in years. Still, this new scent caused butterflies to dance in my stomach. What the hell was happening?

I watched the limousine pull up a few feet away from me, trying my best to hide my anxiety. However, when the handsome man hopped out of the car, all of the air left my lungs at once. I was sure I had never seen his face before, but he looked so familiar I wondered if he had ever visited me in my dreams. I widened my eyes in disbelief.

Alpha Russell is my second chance...

"Mate." He finished my sentence as if he could hear my thoughts, his husky voice making me melt like a lovesick teenager.

As foolish as it was, I couldn't fight back the urge to reply, "Mate."

EPILOGUE

Levi

One year later

"What a crazy year and a half, huh?"

I was standing at the center of the Event Hall with my second-in-command, right next to the stairway. Dressed in a new red suit I had ordered for tonight, I took a sip of the whiskey in my hands as I carefreely took in my surroundings. The venue, which was already crowded, had been entirely decorated in Blood Eclipse's traditional red and gold colors, from the flower vases filled with roses, to the tablecloths and tableware, to the balloons hanging from the tall ceiling. Every single detail had been carefully planned by my Luna, and noticing what a wonderful job she had done, I couldn't help but smile.

It took me a few seconds to process my Beta's words, but once I did, I turned to him. "Indeed. It was a good one overall though." I shrugged.

"Yeah, if you scratch out the attacks, the kidnappings, the war that almost ended our pack, me losing an eye..." I rolled my eyes at his sarcasm. "Seriously, though, we came out of it stronger, and I think we all got what we wanted in the end. One way or another." I agreed with a silent nod as I immediately understood what he meant.

After years of trying to get justice for his sister, Darrell finally achieved it. Not only did he kill Marisol's suspected murderer with his own paws, he also managed to prove that the bastard was really the one behind it. Gedeon had used his power to corrupt every previous investigation whenever they were close to finding a lead, but with him out of the way, the police were able to collect the evidence they needed to declare him guilty.

Bellatrix also got the happy ending she deserved. As an Alpha, I knew what a loss it would be to let one of our strongest warriors and an irreplaceable Delta go. The fact that she and I also had a good synergy didn't help at all. But as a friend, I couldn't be happier for her. With a strong leader by her side, she could finally reach the full potential she never would have if she stayed here for the rest of her life. Of course, the new couple had a few challenges to face in the aftermath of the war. Alpha Russell was charged with using illicit methods to attack Blood Eclipse. However, with my testimony, he was allowed to both answer for his crimes and serve his sentence in freedom.

And well, I got what I needed, even if it wasn't what I wanted at first.

My train of thought was interrupted the moment a tantalizing fragrance hit my nostrils. I instinctively looked up to watch in awe, from the bottom of the stairway, as the woman of my life, the mother of my child, walked down the steps entering the ballroom with my mother by her side. She had her head held high and her piercing honey-colored eyes locked on me, making my heart throb inside my chest. They looked even brighter highlighted by the natural makeup she was wearing. Her ears, neck and fingers were decorated with expensive gold jewelry, adding to her royal aura.

The satin gown she had ordered specially for the occasion truly fit her frame. It was of a deep shade of red, intimidating and powerful, with tight long sleeves. The long, rounded skirt pooled on the floor around her, flowing with her every movement like a blood waterfall. No matter how many nights I spent with her, or how many parties we attended together, her out-of-this-world beauty would never cease to take my breath away. I still couldn't believe she was mine.

My Blood Luna.

"You look stunning as ever, my love," I whispered, handing my glass to Darrell before stretching my hand out for her.

"You always say that." She chuckled before brushing her nose against mine. I had to fight the urge to kiss her ruby lips in order not to ruin her makeup.

"It's always true."

"Good evening, Luna. Calanthe." The Beta bowed his head at my mate, then at my mother.

"Good evening, Darrell. Are you having fun?" Calliope asked with a smile.

"I guess we were all in need of a night of celebration." He raised his two glasses.

"Are you drinking both of those?" Mom arched an eyebrow at him.

"No, ma'am." He laughed, offering her the glass I had been drinking from. "This was your son's, but I think he's done with it."

"Oh, good. I could really use some whiskey to get this party started!"

"Take it easy, Mother." I frowned at her, and she waved me off.

"Just let her enjoy it, Levi," my mate said, amused. I heaved a sigh of defeat, interlacing our arms before leading her across the ballroom.

The place was so crowded, it was hard to take more than a few steps without having to greet one of the guests. Although we weren't the center of attention, the many Alphas we invited, consisting of old and new allies, all wanted to congratulate us. Just as I thought we had talked to everyone, a familiar voice echoing behind me caught my attention.

"Alpha Levi! Luna Calliope!" We both turned in the direction of the sound as the young boy approached us with a smile. "Thank you for inviting me tonight."

"Thank you for coming, Alpha Kai," my Luna replied promptly. From the respectful way she glanced at the leader of her former pack, it was impossible to remember how terrible their relationship used to be.

Against all odds, Moonstone had started thriving. After taking care of his sister, Kai managed to get his pack back on track. Despite his rough start, he was learning to become a humble ruler with a firm hand to organize his pack and demand the members' respect. It seemed my mate's greatness had helped guide him.

"I heard you successfully defeated the Alpha who attacked your pack a while ago. Congratulations," I uttered.

"It wouldn't have been possible without Blood Eclipse's aid," he instantly pointed out. "I hope our alliance will last for many years to come."

"Likewise." A small smile spread over my lips. "Please,

make yourself at home."

We exchanged nods before I pulled my Luna along so we could continue to venture further into the party. At last, we were able to get some peace, but I didn't miss her nervousness as her honey-colored eyes scoured through the crowd. It was obviously her motherly instincts kicking in.

"Where's Raphael?" she finally muttered, confirming my suspicions.

I opened my mouth to reply, but before I could, my Gamma showed up in front of us. In his arms was the chubby little pup, my son and my proudest creation. He had his mother's shiny light brown hair, and his father's icy blue eyes. Even at only a year old, he already looked like the Alpha he would one day become - dressed in a wine-red suit and sporting a fancy golden bow tie.

"Mama!" He shifted in Ivar's arms with excitement, stretching his little arms out towards his mother.

"Oh, my sweet little boy! Mama was looking for you!" Calliope smiled as she held him close to her chest. "How are you enjoying your first birthday party?" He giggled as she showered him with eskimo kisses.

I couldn't keep my tough Alpha act for long; as I watched the scene, a radiant smile lit up my face. My pup played with his mother for a while longer before his huge blue eyes eventually fell on me.

"Papa!" He almost fell from Cal's arms as he swung himself in my direction.

"Well, it's obvious he has a favorite parent." She rolled her eyes as she handed him over to me. My heart throbbed with joy as I held my little boy close.

"Are you jealous, my Luna?" I asked playfully.

"Well, I'm sure who his favorite uncle is." Darrell joined us again, and my son's eyes glistened with happiness as the man messed up his thin hair.

"It's obviously me!" Ivar frowned.

"Ha! In your dreams!" Darrell patted his shoulder. "Don't you see how Raph's smile grows whenever he sees me?"

"That's just because you have a funny face!" The Gamma pouted.

I was sure the two grown adults would have kept arguing over my son for a lot longer, had my Beta's eye not clouded over. As soon as the mindlink message had been delivered, he turned to me with a huge grin.

"It seems our most prestigious guest has just arrived!" he announced.

"Trix?!" Calliope smiled excitedly.

Darrell nodded. "The guard said she and her mate are waiting for us right outside."

"Outside?" I furrowed my brows in confusion, and he shrugged.

I was about to argue when my cheerful Luna tugged on my arm, urging us to leave the ballroom. I couldn't bring myself to go against her wishes. The moment we stepped outside, my eyes landed on the Alpha couple dressed in matching silver outfits. I barely had time to smile at them before Cal let go of my hand, leaving me with our son in my arms as she rushed over to her dear friend.

"Luna Bellatrix!" Calliope couldn't hold herself back from hugging the former Delta.

"Please don't address me by my title," Trix complained.

"We're family, Cal. That just doesn't sound right." She grimaced, but she hugged my mate back nonetheless.

"Okay, okay. You're right. I'm just so excited to see you again!" My Luna held her at arm's length, taking a good look at her. "Thank you so much for coming!"

"How could we miss the future Alpha's first birthday?" Alpha Russell grinned at me before his eyes fell on the little pup in my arms. "My, you've gotten big since the last time I saw you, little guy!"

"He's growing so fast it scares us sometimes," I joked, smiling proudly at my son.

A muffled, animalistic sound disturbed our short exchange. For the first time, I noticed the other Alpha was holding a medium-sized box, and it was shaking a little. Curiosity got the best of me, but my mate was faster.

"What do you have there?"

"Oh, this?" Russell beamed, glancing at the box. "This is a special gift for our birthday boy." The man slowly lowered the object to the ground, pulling the top off to reveal its contents. My eyes widened as they fell on something I truly wasn't expecting to see.

A very peculiar creature was sitting inside of the box. It had the body of a deer, but its hind paws were more like bird feet. It had tiny wings that were yet to develop, similar to those of a chick, and a short, feathery tail. His body, which was covered in both fur and feathers, was mostly white, except for a few black and red markings. The bizarre animal hybrid poked its head out of the box, his ruby eyes carefully studying each one of us. Not even a second later, my mate's unicorn showed up out of nowhere, swinging her tail and twitching her ears in curiosity as she watched the newcomer from a safe distance.

"What is that?" I asked, eyes wide in shock.

"It's a peryton," Trix revealed, a playful smile on her face. "Don't be fooled by his delicate appearance. They are known for tearing the beating hearts from their victims' chests. They are powerful beings, fit for the heir of the most ruthless pack in the country."

"When my mate told me about Luna Calliope's incredible bond with her unicorn, it seemed like a good idea to present your one-year-old son with a special pet, as well," Russel clarified. "Unlike unicorns, perytons age at the same rate as humans - or wolves, for that matter. I thought it would be interesting for Raphael to have a companion who will grow with him."

"I've never seen one of those. It must have cost a fortune," I muttered.

"Alpha Levi, don't you know it's rude to ask for the price of a gift?" The man chuckled. "Why don't you let Raphael check it out?"

I hesitated for a moment, only lowering my son to the ground when my Luna nodded in agreement. Protective as Crystal was, she stood close to the pup, ready to defend him if need be. Despite my former Delta's remark about the creature's nature, he looked pretty harmless, at least at his current age. When Raph stretched one hand out in the peryton's direction, he immediately shrunk inside the box. However, he slowly seemed to realize the pup would cause him no harm.

The moment Raphael touched his pet's head, right between its two stumps of bones that resembled growing antlers, he smiled brighter than he ever had.

"I think he likes it!" Russell laughed.

"It reminds me of my reaction when I first met Crystal." My Luna caressed her unicorn's mane, and she neighed in response. "Thank you for the amazing gift."

"It's my pleasure, Luna Calliope."

We continued to smile, appreciating the moment in silence, until I cleared my throat. "Now that the whole family is here, shall we celebrate?"

A lot had changed in the past year, but at the same time, being surrounded by the people I loved made me feel like everything was still the same. Wars would come and go; new challenges would always show up at our door. But as long as I had my Luna and my family by my side, I knew there would never be a problem we couldn't solve.

After all, nothing is thicker than blood.

ACKNOWLEDGEMENT

Taming My Alpha was a wild ride from beginning to end. I went through ups and downs during the eight months it took me to finish this book. There were times when I honestly wanted to give up, but some very amazing people kept me motivated through the toughest days.

First, I would like to thank all of my readers. I know I say this all the time, but none of this would be possible without you. You saw my potential as a writer when I struggled to see it myself. Your kind words and positive comments always put a smile on my face, and your criticism helped me grow immensely. I am very lucky to have your support.

A special shoutout to my dear reader, Bianca. Aside from accompanying every single one of my stories and coming up with theories that make my days brighter, you personally took the time to check a few chapters for me when I was having second guesses about them. I am honored to have you as a reader.

Next, of course, is my incredible proofreader, Cailyn. Because English is not my mother tongue, I really mean it when I say none of my books would even exist without you. You literally made it possible for me to follow my dreams by eliminating the language barrier. You have been with me from the start of my journey as a writer, and I hope you'll be here until the end!

My boyfriend, Rennan, who supported me from the moment I decided to try my luck as a writer. Despite not understanding my love for books, you listened to my senseless ramblings, read chapters when I needed a second opinion, and even helped me when I was uninspired. For the seven years during which we have been together, you never once failed to encourage me to do what makes me happy.

My family, especially my father. You can understand me better than anyone else, and you never judged me.

My girls, Priscilla, Luiza, Duda, and Clara. You'll probably never know about the existence of this book (lol), but I would never have gotten this far in life without your friendship. You mean the world to me.

ABOUT THE AUTHOR

Louise Clement was born in 1998 in Rio de Janeiro, Brazil, where she lives with her parents, her sister, and her two dogs. At 23 years old, she has just graduated in Graphic Design. A girl who never knew how to stay still, she has an ever-growing list of hobbies. With an insatiable hunger for acquiring new knowledge and skills, she will often write about her experiences.

Louise's journey as an author began in late 2021, when she published her first English book, a werewolf novel, on a mobile reading app. What started as a hobby and a dream soon turned into reality when her first work quickly became popular, and she decided to continue telling her stories.

Although Louise is mainly a supernatural writer, she has plans to write non-fantasy books in the future. She ventures mostly through the romance genre, but her stories also have a good dose of action, mystery, and a sprinkle of spice. In 2023, she will be releasing her first trilogy, which will be titled "The Peculiar Series."

CONNECT WITH LOUISE CLEMENT ON FACEBOOK

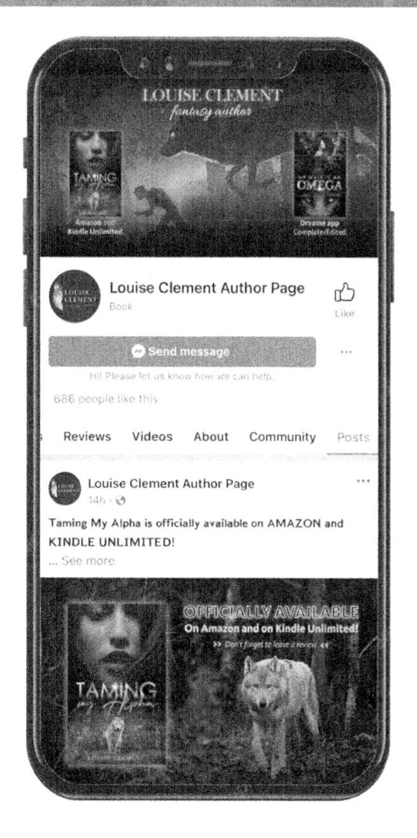

Follow **Louise Clement Author Page** on Facebook to stay up to date with new releases, get access to extra content such as character visuals, and participate in giveaways for a chance to win prizes!

Printed in Great Britain
by Amazon

14000716R10253